SULLIVAN'S LIST

George Barry—The master spy in
mysterious Caribbean retirement

Natalie Benoit—Many men's mistress, but
no man's property

Bernard Castellone—Dealer in drugs,
deception and death, who switched sides as
easily as he crossed borders

Marcel Piri—Homosexual son of a Mafia
prince, with a sense of honor as dangerous
as his gift for deceit.

One of them knew the truth about the
Agency. Sullivan meant to get it. Or kill
trying . . .

THE THIN LINE

*"Intimate, dramatic, exciting . . . as
sharp as a newly honed blade!"*

—DENVER POST

ROY DOLINER

THE THIN LINE

BERKLEY BOOKS, NEW YORK

This Berkley book contains the complete
text of the original hardcover edition.
It has been completely reset in a type face
designed for easy reading, and was printed
from new film.

THE THIN LINE

A Berkley Book / published by arrangement with
Crown Publishers, Inc.

PRINTING HISTORY
Crown edition published 1980
Berkley edition / April 1982

ISBN: 0-425-05289-3
A BERKLEY BOOK ® TM 757,375
Berkley Books are published by Berkley Publishing Corporation,
200 Madison Avenue, New York, New York 10016.
The Name "BERKLEY" and the stylized "B" with design are
trademarks belonging to Berkley Publishing Corporation.
PRINTED IN THE UNITED STATES OF AMERICA

To the Spirit of

DAW THAN MAY,

Her children and grandchildren

THE THIN LINE

PROLOGUE

Extract of testimony by PETER J. OWEN *before the
United States Senate Committee on Intelligence:*
CHAIRMAN, THE HONORABLE THOMAS A. BARNES *(R.
Illinois)*

October 10, 1979

SENATOR BARNES: Mr. Owen, are you presently employed by the Central Intelligence Agency?

MR. OWEN: No, sir.

SENATOR BARNES: By any intelligence organization or agency?

MR. OWEN: No, sir. None.

SENATOR BARNES: What is your present employment?

MR. OWEN: I'm director of the Martindale Institute for Foreign Policy Studies.

SENATOR ARTHUR G. LEWIS (D. Michigan): Where does the Martindale Institute get its money? I mean, does any of it come from CIA?

MR. OWEN: The Institute is privately funded.

SENATOR LEWIS: What does that mean?

MR. OWEN: It was created and maintained by an endowment in the form of a trust by the estate of Stuart Martindale.

SENATOR LEWIS: No CIA money?

MR. OWEN: No, sir.

SENATOR BARNES: Mr. Owen, during the period 1960 to 1963, were you employed by the Central Intelligence Agency?

MR. OWEN: Yes, sir.

SENATOR BARNES: In what capacity?

MR. OWEN: I was case officer in Saigon.

SENATOR BARNES: Who was your Chief of Section?

MR. OWEN: Ralph Kirk.

SENATOR BARNES: Where is Kirk now?

MR. OWEN: Mr. Kirk is dead. He died in 1975, August of 1975.

SENATOR LEWIS: How did he die? Natural causes, or what?

MR. OWEN: Mr. Kirk died near his home in Colorado. He drowned.

SENATOR LEWIS: In Colorado? You fellows are always drowning or getting killed in hunting accidents.

SENATOR BARNES: Getting back to 1962, Mr. Owen. You were case officer in Saigon. Do you remember a covert operation in the northeastern part of Burma, in the Shan States?

MR. OWEN: We had some there, yes. We recruited Nationalist Chinese, deserters from the old KMT. We trained them and sent them back across the border into China. A penetration network, but nothing much came of it. Its code name was Bravo.

SENATOR BARNES: I'm thinking of a different operation. Its code name was Razzia.

SENATOR LEWIS: How do you spell that?

SENATOR BARNES: R-A-Z-Z-I-A.

SENATOR LEWIS: What does it mean?

SENATOR BARNES: It's French. It means a raid, an unexpected one. Do you remember Razzia, Mr. Owen?

MR. OWEN: A lot of what we did in those days was covert.

SENATOR BARNES: Razzia was rather special.

MR. OWEN: Perhaps if you showed me the file.

SENATOR BARNES: There is none. No documents on Razzia at all.

MR. OWEN: There was a lot of talk in those days. Operations that never got off the ground. Some of it pretty far-fetched.

SENATOR BARNES: Razzia got off the ground. It had to do with the opium factories in the Shan States of Burma, and in Laos. The CIA flew the opium out and helped distribute it.

MR. OWEN: I've heard those stories.

SENATOR BARNES: Are they true?

MR. OWEN: No, sir. Not to my knowledge.

SENATOR BARNES: You were case officer. If that was going on, you would know.

MR. OWEN: If it came out of Saigon.

SENATOR BARNES: Then your testimony is that the Saigon office was not involved?

MR. OWEN: That is correct, Senator. Yes.

SENATOR LEWIS: Do you have a pension from the CIA, anything along those lines?

MR. OWEN: Yes. I took early retirement in December of 1975.

SENATOR LEWIS: Right after Kirk drowned. Tell me, Mr. Owens, if you take a pension from the CIA, you're still on the payroll, aren't you?

MR. OWEN: I have no response to that, Senator.

SENATOR LEWIS: It's true, isn't it?

MR. OWEN: No response at all.

SENATOR BARNES: Mr. Owen, did you at that time— I'm talking of the period 1960 to '63—have an agent named John Robert Sullivan?

MR. OWEN: Yes, sir.

SENATOR BARNES: Was Sullivan operating in the Shan States at about that time?

MR. OWEN: Yes, sir.

SENATOR LEWIS: If Sullivan was there, he'd know about this business. Why don't we get him and ask him what he knows.

SENATOR BARNES: We don't know where Sullivan is, or if he's alive.

SENATOR LEWIS: Maybe he had an accident, too.

Maybe he was cleaning his gun, or drowned.

SENATOR BARNES: Mr. Owen, do you know the where-abouts of John Sullivan?

MR. OWEN: No, sir.

SENATOR BARNES: But he was an agent of yours?

MR. OWEN: Yes, he was.

SENATOR BARNES: Had Sullivan anything to do with Razzia?

MR. OWEN: I've already testified that I know nothing about an operation named Razzia. I never heard of it.

SENATOR BARNES: There was no such operation?

MR. OWEN: As far as I know, sir. There never was.

CHAPTER 1

"Hurry, we must hurry." Myat had been after Sullivan since dawn, urging him on through the jungle. "Hurry, before the Chinese General dies."

"They're tough, Chinese Generals," Sullivan said. "And don't die so easily."

"This one will die, I promise you. He has a big hole in him, and a high fever."

But Sullivan wanted a second look at the abandoned airstrip. The battle for it had been over for a week, perhaps two, long enough for the local people to have collected any weapons or equipment left behind. Through his binoculars he saw nothing of metal, nothing that glittered, not even a shell casing. The strip had been picked clean, a desolate spot open to the erratic air currents howling out of the passes through the mountains all around; it was the wrong place for an airstrip, wrong unless one needed above all to keep it hidden.

Sullivan said, "Tell me about the planes that flew in. Were they American?"

"They had no markings."

"Do you know the type of plane?"

5

"The kind with two engines. The Dakota."

"From which direction did they come?"

"East, from Laos," Myat said. "Two planes. They loaded quickly, took off, and flew west. Nobody knows where."

"Only two planes?" Sullivan said. "An airstrip built in the mountains, and for only two planes."

"It's a mystery," Myat said. "Maybe the Chinese General knows. He made his attack too late, and for good measure got himself shot. He has a secret, but only for your ears, Sullivan. He gave me one hundred kyats to find you, and another hundred if I brought you back."

"Then he won't die," Sullivan said. "He won't give up his investment."

Myat untied his pack and took out slices of dried smoked meat and cold rice wrapped in banana leaves. Sullivan ate his slowly, chewing the dried meat until he had all of its flavor and juice.

"Do you smell it?" Myat said. "Tiger. I smell him."

"Tigers don't climb this high," Sullivan said. "We may see a snow leopard, but not a tiger."

Sullivan stood up and swung his pack up on his shoulders. He was taller than the average, broad and strongly built, but thin, dried out, like an athlete who has trained hard. He had been in the mountains of the Shan States for nearly two years and rarely cut his hair or shaved. His beard had grown darker than his hair, which was fair and sun-streaked. He wore fatigue pants tucked into leather boots, a woolen shirt, and a field jacket without markings. Besides the pack and binoculars, he carried an automatic rifle and a pistol in a holster on his belt.

Although the trail was good, it was a steep climb to the main pass through a dense pine forest that covered the face of the mountain. They climbed steadily, sweating under the heavy packs. As they approached the pass, the forest thinned out, and they began their descent on the north face of the mountain, where the soil was dry and loosened by the wind. The descent into the valley was long, but it grew steadily hotter and the vegetation along the trail became lush. After a time they smelled smoke from the teak cooking fires and heard the barking of the village dogs, scampering part of the way up the trail to meet them. They were a large pack and made a great racket, circling and darting in for a closer look before backing off to bark and bluff a warning.

Myat's father waited at the head of the village street. He was a robust old man who wore a short-sleeved khaki shirt, a woven Shan bag in a sling over his shoulder, and an ankle-length *longyi*. He greeted Sullivan formally, pronounced his name—Bon Wat—conducting himself with the modest dignity of a headman welcoming an honored guest.

"It does you credit to have come this great distance to honor the dying wish of an old man," he said.

His English had been learned half a century earlier in missionary schools. It was precise, the sentences fully formed and grammatical, as if prepared in advance, and spoken with the lilting Shan accent.

"The old fellow is still alive, but very sick. I would offer you refreshment, but my belief is that your first desire is to speak to him."

He led the way through his village, which was larger than Sullivan expected to find so deep in the mountains. The villagers were in front of their huts, the women busy at the cooking fires. The men hung back, their faces without expression, neither friendly nor unfriendly. They were Shan, courteous, but thinking first of their dignity. The children were another matter; they swooped in for a better look at Sullivan, scampering back and forth across his path. For them it was a holiday. The women couldn't conceal their fascination with this young white man, and particularly one with a beard and hair nearly to his shoulders. They lowered their brilliant black eyes, glancing up only to catch another glimpse of Sullivan and to wink at each other and make bawdy jokes over the cooking fires. Sullivan knew Shan women were not afraid of their men, or timid before them.

The old Chinese General was kept at the end of the village street, in a one-room hut built of bamboo. He was lying unconscious on a mat, covered with a sheet of homespun cotton, looked after by an old woman from the village, who squatted nearby, bathing his forehead with a rag dipped in a basin of cool water.

Sullivan asked for soap and boiled water and strips of clean cotton. He put the General's age at about seventy, although it was hard to be sure. He was emaciated, bald, without a tooth in his mouth. He was sweating, but his skin was cold and clammy to the touch. His lips were dry and cracked, and he kept trying to moisten them with his tongue, and thrashing his arms and legs and trying to speak, now and then crying out, as if in a nightmare. His pulse was rapid and irregular.

"How long has he been like this?"

"He was feverish when he was brought in," Myat said. "He improved after I took the bullet out and cleaned the wound. But without antibiotics, the infection started up again."

"He was lucid for a time," Bon Wat said.

The wound was in the back, just under the right shoulder blade. The old soldier's luck had held; the bullet had passed below the bone and struck no vital organ. Myat had been neat digging it out, but the area all around was badly inflamed and swollen, and had begun to suppurate.

"It looks bad," Myat said. "Although I did the best I could."

"You saved his life," Sullivan said.

The old woman had set a kettle to boil outside the hut and brought the hot water in a basin along with soap and squares of cotton cloth. Sullivan scrubbed his hands and put two syringes in the kettle of boiling water. He loaded one with a quarter grain of morphine and injected that into the bicep of the General's left arm. The second syringe was for 600,000 units of procaine penicillin. Then he gently washed the wound and dressed it with Aseptol.

"Have you any alcohol?"

"Rice wine," the woman said.

"Bring it, please. And more cotton cloth cut in strips for bandages."

Bon Wat said, "What was it you gave him with the needles?"

"Morphine for the pain. The other was penicillin, which will attack the infection."

"Did you know an Englishman discovered it?" Bon Wat said. "Fleming by name."

"The Queen knighted him for it," Myat said.

"She was correct to have done so," Bon Wat said. "Are you an Englishman?"

"No, American."

"Your country also has great scientists. Edison, the inventor, was one, and those two brothers who built the first airplane. I have one son who is a doctor in Rangoon, and the next year Myat will be going to medical school."

The General was more peaceful now, although his fever was still dangerously high. But he had stopped thrashing his limbs and his breathing was deeper and more regular.

"I know him nearly ten years," Bon Wat said. "He was careful not to cause trouble near my village. I have heard that in China he was a most important General, and when his side lost the war, his army followed him across the border. By now most of the men from that time are dead or married to Shan women."

Sullivan said, "Why did he ask to be brought to your village?"

"It was that or die on the trail," Bon Wat said. "My village was close, and he could expect to be well treated here. He acquired one of his wives from this village, and she used to come to visit her old parents."

Bon Wat clearly knew more than he let on. But Sullivan decided it was useless to question him. He stood silent, his sturdy legs slightly apart and his hands clasped behind his back, chewing on the stem of an English pipe, a venerable Shan headman.

The old woman returned with the bandages and Sullivan bathed the wound and dressed it. Nothing remained but to cover the old General and let him sleep. Bon Wat invited Sullivan to dinner and sent a pair of boys to haul water for his bath and the old woman to set out sandals and a freshly laundered *longyi*. Bon Wat kept a key on a chain around his neck and used it to open the heavy padlock on the steamer trunk beside the bed in his hut. He brought out a bottle of Johnny Walker Red Label Scotch and poured a drink for Sullivan and one for himself. There was a rapid exchange in Shan between the old man and Myat, Sullivan catching only the drift.

"One story about you is that you were born here and speak Shan as well as Burmese," Bon Wat said.

"The stories are exaggerated."

"But your Burmese is quite good, even the accent."

"The Shan less so," Sullivan said. "We lived in Pelair when my father practiced there, and I came with him to the Shan States only on holidays."

"He has a more exciting life now," Myat said.

Bon Wat shook his head, but smiled patiently at his son, and even cuffed him lightly on the arm. "This one wants to hunt tigers," he said, "and dig for gold. Anything but settle down to serious work."

"Did your father want you to be a doctor?" Myat said to Sullivan.

"Yes."

"If he had lived, by now that's what you would be," Bon Wat said.

"Very likely."

"Did your father let you drink whisky?" Myat said.

"It was not permitted in the house."

"Myat claims to be entitled to his own glass of whisky. I told him I'd pour it for him the day he becomes a doctor."

"He did a good job removing the bullet."

"I think you must be taking the son's side against the father." When Bon Wat laughed he covered his mouth with his hand to hide the gap made by a missing front tooth. He had been a handsome man, and was vain still. His hair was neatly parted and brushed for dinner. He laid his heavy hand on Myat's shoulder, and poured whisky into his glass. "My young son was lazy when a boy, and spoiled by the mother. But now he's not so bad."

A girl brought food in china bowls and set them out on a low table in the center of the hut. The men sat on stools, a single kerosine lantern hung from a pole above their heads. Sullivan was ravenously hungry, and the food was delicious; red rice made with tomatoes and served cold with fresh prawns and river fish. There were four or five kinds of vegetables and fresh fruit afterwards.

Bon Wat talked about his youth on the Indian border with the British army, and how he had fought with them in the second war, against the Japanese. Myat had certainly heard all of these stories before, but he enjoyed them and his only concern was that they not bore Sullivan.

The Scotch was followed by rice wine, quite a lot of it,

and only after they had lit their cheroots did Sullivan raise the subject of the landing strip in the mountains.

"The Americans built it," Bon Wat said in Burmese. "They hired some men from my village. Why they built it, what planes came, I don't know. It's not my business. It never was."

"The men in charge, were they American?"

"Nearly all."

"There was one who spoke French," Myat said.

"Did you learn his name?"

"No. We know no names," Bon Wat said.

"What was the French one like?"

"Older than you. Not so tall, and with dark skin. Strong, very strong."

"Was he in charge?"

"Together with another, an American. I think the American was over the other, but I saw little of him."

"The strip was built to fly out opium," Sullivan said. "The Americans, and the French, all were in the opium trade."

"I don't put my nose near that sort of thing," Bon Wat said.

"But you hired out your men to work on the strip," Sullivan said.

The good humor was gone from Bon Wat's face. Opium was a subject never discussed with a foreigner. He moved from the soft glow of the lantern into the shadows, and thrust out his jaw and kept an offended silence.

It was Myat who spoke next. "We know nothing about opium." In crucial matters, he stood with his father. He always would.

"The mule trains from Laos pass a few miles from here," Sullivan said. "They go on to Lashio, to the factories there."

"I've seen no mule trains."

"And no airstrip either?"

"Talk to your own people about that," Bon Wat growled from the shadows. He relit his cheroot, and in a blaze of light from the wooden match his square face looked as if it had been carved from teak. "Take your questions there. Ask them where the opium is collected, and by who."

There was a knock at the door of the hut. It was the old

woman who had been left with the General. She went directly to Bon Wat and whispered in his ear.

"The General has regained consciousness," he said. "He's trying to speak."

Sullivan started for the door. Myat would have gone along, but was held back by Bon Wat. Sullivan ran the length of the village street to the General's hut, his way lighted by the cooking fires. Inside the hut was a single kerosine lamp, which Sullivan set on a table near the General's mat.

His eyes were closed, but they flickered as the lamp was brought near, and he opened them when Sullivan laid his hand on his forehead. He tried to move his lips, which were dry and cracked, and tried to speak. Sullivan laid his hand on his head and held a cup of water to his lips. His fever had broken, his eyes were clear, and he nodded when Sullivan asked if he spoke English.

"You've been given morphine and antibiotics," Sullivan said. "You're going to need more of each, and I want you to drink some water and see if you can swallow a couple of aspirin."

The General's narrow black eyes were steady and still unnaturally bright from the fever. They never left Sullivan's face. It was an uncanny look, mysterious and unsettling; Sullivan had seen the same expression before, in dying men. It belonged to another world. He held the cup of water to the old General's lips, and he again tried to speak. Sullivan lowered his head until his ear was level with the General's mouth.

"What is your name?"

"Jack Sullivan."

"I am known as Han. General Han. But I was born Hso-lin Wo." His breath had the musty odor of a book opened after many years. "Is it true that you are a Christian?" he said.

"Yes."

"Then you believe in heaven and hell?"

"I do, General."

"Very good." He showed his empty gums when he smiled. "I sleep now."

"Not quite yet," Sullivan said. "It looks like you're going to live, General."

"Not too long, Christian. Very short time." He made a pistol with his thumb and first finger, but then he laughed, showing the brown stumps of his teeth. "Same fellows who shot me once, shoot me again. This time maybe aim better."

"Who were they, General?"

"Never mind, Christian. Too many questions. I know you for sure. One of my wives has a cousin, she married a fellow who worked for you. Chow. You know Chow, spoke pretty good English, too?"

"I haven't seen him in months," Sullivan said. "Do you know where he is?"

"More questions. You see what I mean? You lost your spies when everybody ordered to go home. Chow told me. Then you go village to village, asking questions. Where is everybody? What happened to my spies? Listen, Christian, you sleep with a smile on your face because you have a clean soul. No secrets. No double-cross. Keep it up, boy. Stay stupid, is much better for the soul."

Sullivan said, "You'd have died without the penicillin. Without more, you still may. Look at me, do you want to spend tomorrow with your ancestors?"

The General looked annoyed and waved his hand as if shooing a fly. "My advice is to go away from here, back to America. It's nice country, very pretty, although the food is no good. In America I have wind in the belly. Terrible thing wind in the belly. But I don't hate America. I like San Francisco."

Sullivan called the old woman and had her put water to boil for another syringe. The General lay on his side, scratching himself under the covers and watching Sullivan's every move out of the corners of his narrowed eyes.

"You like San Francisco? My brother-in-law has shop on Grant Street. Makes passports for spy-fellows. Very famous."

"Why did you attack the airstrip?" Sullivan said.

"To steal."

"Steal what?"

"I had business with the airstrip men," he said. "My partners, but I stole too much from them. My sin is greed."

He closed his eyes and folded his hands on his chest; they were yellowish white and smooth as ivory. The General lay perfectly still. Sullivan knelt beside him and said, "You need another injection of penicillin."

"Would you let me die, Christian?"

"If you don't tell me what I want to know."

The General opened his eyes, but turned to the wall, away from Sullivan. "I see something when I close my eyes," he said. "A gray thing. A thing with wings. Is it fever?"

"You have a little fever."

"I'm afraid. It's death, the thing with wings." He turned his head and struggled to raise himself, and Sullivan helped, lifting his head and propping a pillow under it. "Are you afraid of death?" the General said. "Is it a thing with wings, from hell?"

"Yes, from hell."

"The man you want is not here."

"Where is he?"

"I don't know. That's true. We became enemies. I suffer from greed." His forehead was warmer, and the rising fever made his eyes glitter. "If I tell you the man's name, will you give more drugs?"

"Give me his name, I'll give you your life."

"There is hell," the General said. "I have seen it."

"His name?"

"George Berry. Big man. George Berry."

"Was he alone?"

"One other. A Frenchman. Castellone."

"Where did they go?"

"Lashio. The men you want went to Lashio."

The General closed his eyes and slipped off. Sullivan prepared a syringe of penicillin and one of morphine and injected the General with both. The old Shan woman brought a bowl of clear soup on a lacquer tray; she kneeled beside the General's mat, lifted his head from the pillow, and tried to feed him, but the morphine had already taken hold.

CHAPTER 2

Before going overland to Lashio, Sullivan decided to
spend the night on Bon Wat's princely British army cot.
For two years he had slept on straw mats or spread his
bedroll on the forest floor. He was used to hard ground,
to a diet of dried meat and rice with a rare treat of fresh
fish hauled from a mountain stream or fruit bought from a
village bazaar on market day. He had gone weeks without
speaking English. He knew no women. He hadn't read a
book, or even seen one, in months. He ate with his fingers
and squatted like a beast at the edge of the forest.

It was a hard and dangerous life, but one he had
chosen. He never thought of himself as odd, although he
knew that others did, and he never asked himself if his
youth might be better spent elsewhere.

He certainly never envied other men of his age, his
classmates and friends, even those who had gone into the
Service and settled into more normal lives. They might
have the pleasures of love, of good times, fine food,
music, and good books, all the rest of it, but he never
envied them or wanted to change places. Yet, he enjoyed
those things. He had normal appetites, a sense of fun. He

15

was remembered as a good friend and pleasant company, although at times a little intense and inclined to be moody. He had been a serious student, a scholarship boy, but not a drudge and certainly not a misfit. He was good at sports, and would go weekends with his friends to Boston and to parties in Washington and New York, where he stood well with parents because his manners were good and with the girls because he was handsome. He had the kind of good looks to make women turn around. It was one of the things both sexes remembered about him, his good looks. Yet he behaved as if it meant nothing. He certainly never used his looks; he was never conspicuously charming, and one had the feeling he disliked and distrusted men who were. His looks were something he took for granted, and when the subject came up, his only reaction was to look embarrassed and talk about something else.

Intelligent women found something else in him. They sensed the way he looked was something they needed to get past; there was about him an air of reserve, of something held back. Nothing dark or ominous, no nasty secret, but his character had an unyielding and resolute core. It was something he seemed to have been born with; he knew precisely what he was and what he believed. Conviction set him apart and made him older than his contemporaries.

Sullivan stood out in his class, and was one of those who are remembered. When his classmates met on the squash court, in the boardroom, or at lunch at the Harvard Club in New York, the name Jack Sullivan would come up, and the talk was of what had become of him. Of course, those who had also gone into the Service—and there were several in the class of 1954—knew he was one of them. One of them, but not quite one of them. Sullivan was in the field, a front liner, one of those in the trenches. He had been to school with them, visited in their homes, and gone out with many of the same girls, all of that; but he was a field agent. He risked his neck out in the open, where cold war strategy came down to opposing agents snarling over the same meaty little intelligence scrap. He served in the sour alley where in the morning an agent is found with his throat cut.

Sullivan was respected by his former classmates, even regarded with a certain awe, but few understood why he had rejected the safety, comfort, and privilege which they took for granted.

Yet it was simple, the most basic of a volunteer's motives: Sullivan served an idea, and the men who represented it. He trusted them and believed in their wisdom. In his hard life, he considered himself the luckiest of men. He was free, because he had chosen to serve. He suffered no confusion between right and wrong. He was in those wild and dangerous mountains on the Chinese border to serve his country. Service was the resolute core of his character.

The Service had recruited him right off the campus and sent him to its language school in Colorado. He was taught Mandarin and enough of the border dialects to get by. Field operations, survival and combat skills were taught in the Sierras, with graduate school in Guatemala and the Bolivian Andes, when the Service's tame generals were still running the show.

Sullivan's job was to contact remnants of Chiang's defeated Kuomintang army, which had fled across the border from southern China, to use these men to put together an intelligence network, starting from scratch, and to train and equip agents and run them back across the border into China.

It was slow, hard, dangerous work, but in time it began to pay off. By the end of the first year, he had half a dozen sound agents operating inside China, with the beginnings of a first-rank communications network. Gossip, news, and eventually one or two harder items came out. This was at a time when Washington knew almost nothing about what was going on inside China. Sullivan's operation took hold. In Langley they said it had begun to show a profit, and gave it a code name with a New Frontier ring: Bravo.

Peter Owen, who was case officer in Saigon, said it sounded like a new model car. "The Kennedy Bravo," he called it.

But after those first heady eighteen months, it began to go downhill. Sullivan stopped hearing from the people he had put across the border, and the ones he was training started to drift away. He was deserted by men whose loyalty and dedication matched his own. Across the border his best agents were blown; they vanished, presumed dead, or were turned around. The network he had built fell to pieces. Saigon got word that Sullivan was to roll up Bravo and come home. The order came in the form of congratulations for a job well done. He had been two years in the field and leave was cited as a cause. There were hints of a bountiful rest and recuperation, accumulated back pay, and promotion to be followed by a lush posting. It was a coded valentine, and it stank to high heaven.

Peter Owen put it on his regular Thursday Flash to Sullivan's fixed receiver, but made no editorial comment, except to omit the code name which he had earlier picked out for himself: Charlie McCarthy. He counted on Sullivan not to miss his meaning.

But Sullivan didn't acknowledge receipt of the Thursday message. Peter called again on Saturday noon, which was their back-up time. By then Sullivan had dismantled the receiver and hidden its components. Under pressure from Washington, Peter sent off a courier, a Sino-Vietnamese with particularly good standing among the KMT in the hills. Word was to be passed to Sullivan: for God's sake, come home.

It was the first order Sullivan ever disobeyed. He had created Bravo, put his life on the line for it, and wasn't going to give up easily. But none of the KMT would talk to him, and it was the same with the Shan, even his oldest friends. Sullivan was frozen out. He was on his own.

He spent six weeks prowling the hills, tracking old comrades from one village to another, questioning headmen and wives whose husbands were off on the opium trails, making a damned nuisance of himself. He was warned about it, he was threatened, even shot at. But he wasn't harmed, which was odd, because of the opportunities in the jungle to kill him in ambush. But he wasn't to be killed. Those who ran the opium trade had made that clear. He was only to be scared off. But Sullivan didn't scare. He was a stubborn man. After another few weeks alone in the wilds, he began to lose track of time. He thought of nothing but Bravo, of why it had been rolled up.

He had been out two months when Myat brought him word that General Han wanted to talk.

Sullivan enjoyed his sleep on Bon Wat's British army cot; it was a great treat to lie two feet above the ground, as if levitating, and there was even a pillow covered with silk for his head. Such honor and luxury enriched his dreams. He was spared ghosts, visited instead by the girl whom, so far, he had come closest to loving. She cradled him in her arms—they were somewhere in the tropics—and gave him sweetened coconut to drink. He slept on. She teased him about his long hair and beard, joking that it tickled her.

But when he awoke, his first thoughts were of George Berry, whom he had known at the Agency language school in Colorado. Berry was an old OSS star, a past master with a reputation for brilliance, known to be difficult, arrogant, and contemptuous. He was Yale and Heidelberg before the war. In the Rockies his mornings were spent gathering specimens for his butterfly collection, and Sullivan recalled him showing up at lectures with the net under his arm, dressed for safari in a broad-brimmed hat with a band of leopard fur, a bush jacket, and a silk scarf knotted around his throat. He had little to say to the other instructors, who wore starched fatigues and concussion-proof Omega watches and spent their mornings jogging; Berry kept to himself, kept busy with his butterflies.

There was also talk of scandal—Sullivan remembered that, although he could recall nothing specific, nothing to nail him to the barn door. But talk. George Berry drank too much, although he was dry for three months at the camp. There were supposed to be too many women, and of the wrong sort. He was erratic, and didn't fit into the Agency mold, particularly during the Eisenhower years. Sullivan suspected he was outside, a freelance, needed for his specific talents and good contacts in Southeast Asia. He was known to be willing to do a nasty job if the money was good.

Sullivan hauled a bucket of water from the well behind the General's hut, stripped, and bathed with the freezing water in the morning sun. He would have liked to dress in clean clothes, but his spare shirt and underwear had been

worn out weeks ago and thrown away. He brushed his
teeth with salt and rinsed his mouth with another bucket
of water drawn from the bottom of the well. It was a
beautiful morning; the sun pouring out of a cloudless sky
warmed his face and dried his hair and beard. He was
hungry and thought about breakfast and tried to give
himself over to the morning, to forget George Berry, to
put aside the evil in the world, and to live simply, for a
time at least to make no demands upon himself.

Myat came up silently, his rifle slung across his shoulder.

"It's a perfect day for hunting," he said. "South of
here, just near the waterfall, is where you find the barking
deer. We can stay overnight in the jungle. Nothing in the
world tastes as good as barking deer cooked over an open
fire."

"I've got to go," Sullivan said.

Myat set his rifle against a tree and drew a bucket of
water for himself. He had a long drink and then said, "I
wanted to spend more time together and become good
friends."

Sullivan filled his canteen and slung that over his
shoulder. "Do you know a man named George Berry?"

"I've heard the name."

"How about Castellone?"

"My father says you're a dangerous man," Myat said.
"He warned me to stay clear of you."

"Did Berry and Castellone fly out together?"

"You're not a real friend," Myat said. "You only
pretended in order to find out what I know. In truth, you
and the General are alike. He wants our gold and you
want to find out what we know."

Myat fetched his rifle and slung it over his shoulder.
"It's greed with the General and pride with you," he said.
"My father told me how nothing matters to you except
punishing the people who took away your spies." He
turned away from Sullivan and marched toward the
jungle. "Go to Lashio," he shouted as he went, not
bothering to turn around. "Find the men you want
there."

CHAPTER 3

George Berry had brought what he was told was the last bottle of champagne in Northern Burma. There was no telling the rigors it had survived, or what it would taste like, but it did come with a fancy label and a limp red streamer tied to the wire cage that secured the cork. Berry had paid through the nose for the wine; he carried it in a bucket of ice and left it in the care of his Shan driver when he entered the terminal to wait for Natalie Benoit's plane.

Bernard Castellone was already at the UBA counter, seeing that his bags were checked through to Hong Kong.

"Since Natalie's plane won't be in for half an hour," he said, "you must have come to see me off."

"I came to apologize," Berry said. "Last night I made an ass of myself."

"You're unhappy because of what happened in the mountains," Castellone said. "You blame yourself, but what the hell, George. Put it down to rotten luck, a bad day. It's nothing to go on about." Castellone wasn't a man to offer words of comfort, or even reassurance. "You've sent for Natalie, let her restore your confidence."

"You think it was a bad idea?"

"Routing a Saigon call through Rangoon, and on an open line?" Castellone made an elaborate shrug, like a Frenchman in a boulevard farce. "Surely it was reckless."

"I needed to see her."

"That's between the two of you."

"Have you never felt like that?"

Castellone responded only with an expression which was surprised and faintly contemptuous. He gave away nothing; he was impenetrable, offering himself as a man who had no existence between episodes.

Berry said, "You were with her nearly four years."

"Was it that long?"

"It's an act with you, Bernard, this indifference. An act I don't believe."

"Believe what you choose," Castellone said. "Only do me a favor, my dear friend. Contact the office in Saigon, remind them that I'm in the open, remind them to be patient, and not to put their noses in. They're to stay clear, tell them that. They'll hear from me only after I've set things up with the Italians."

"What if they need to reach you?"

"They won't."

"But if they do. If I do."

"There's no way, no safe way."

It had become Berry's turn, and he was feeling better. Recklessly, he said, "I can always reach you by way of the Basel drop."

"You walk a thin line, George."

"The bookshop. My dear friend, the bookshop in Basel."

Castellone's plane was called. They shook hands, two friends wishing each other luck, and that was it. Berry watched Castellone's stocky figure walk briskly the length of the terminal and across the tarmac to the portable boarding staircase drawn up to the forward hatch of the UBA Fokker.

"A thin line." Castellone had said it admiringly, and with some assurance. Clever George Berry knows, but won't tell. George wouldn't betray a comrade. Berry wondered if it were so.

After Castellone's plane took off, Berry turned back to the terminal. He counted the people inside. He ticked them off: three generations to see a youngster off on the Rangoon return; a vendor with hot peanuts sold into scrap of newspaper rolled into a cone; four Japanes Business-men and a Burmese army officer. No whites, no Viets, nothing to raise the fine hairs on the back of his neck.

The plane was an old Dakota with UBA markings. Berry watched its broad, lumbering bank and approach, the pilot lining up its nose with the runway.

The plane touched down and taxied until it was opposite the terminal door, accepted a portable staircase, and opened the hatch. First out were a pair of Asians in business suits, a Shan woman who paused at the head of the stairs to adjust a scarf over her head, a man leading a child, a woman with an infant in her arms.

Berry held his breath; an elderly gentleman with a sack of vegetables slung over his shoulder stood aside, and Natalie stepped out of the plane and went quickly down the stairs and across the runway.

She carried a single canvas bag and wore khaki pants tucked into hiking boots, a wide-brimmed safari hat, and a chambray shirt with the sleeves rolled past the elbow.

George Berry stayed back, alert to anyone else who might have come out to meet Natalie, or see him with Castellone. He watched her come into the terminal and look anxiously around, surprised and disappointed at not being met.

He spied no spotters, no one at all. The arriving passengers drifted away, and those departing collected at the boarding gate, the peanut vendor among them.

Natalie straddled her canvas bag, alone in the center of the terminal. Berry hadn't seen her in a month, and had forgotten how lovely she was. Her beauty had often taken him by surprise. As he went on looking at her, it occurred to him that she was probably the last woman in his life. The faces of the others sped by in a blur, too fast to see or remember; all came down to Natalie, and, with her, the tale was told. He recognized a sign of some sort, a portent. He had telephoned through to her in Saigon because he hadn't the nerve to go on without her. He had read the signs; she was the last woman in his life, with him to the end. He went to her across the terminal with his arms open.

He took hold of her bag with one hand. Seen from a distance, she had appeared tall, almost commanding. But beside her, his arm around her waist, he was reminded again that she was barely average height. There was no kiss. She held tight to him and looked closely to see if he was well. It was an anxious glance, a mother summoned to school to fetch a sick child.

"Lord, it's good to see you," he said.

She clung to his arm, in step across the terminal. He sat with her in the rear of the car, the bucket with the champagne on the seat between them. When he pulled the cork, the wine bubbled over.

"I was worried it'd be flat," he said. "Welcome to Lashio."

The driver pulled out of the lot, blasting his horn at a peddler leading a mule with cases of goods wrapped in burlap and lashed to its sides. They turned on to the main street, which was clogged with oxcarts and trucks left over from the Second World War, most of them crammed with livestock and farm goods, and workers from the oil fields on their way to the town.

"Your call scared me," she said. "I didn't expect it, and you sounded up against it. I didn't know quite what to do."

"But you came."

"Sure I came."

"I held back calling you," he said. "I didn't want to drag you in. It won't be a bed of roses."

"The wine isn't bad," she said.

"Did you hear me?"

"You said you needed me," she said. "Listen, old-timer, that's nothing to go on about."

The driver turned off the main street onto the east-west highway. The traffic thinned out and the car picked up speed. Natalie opened the window, turned her face to the wind. "The air in these hills doesn't smell the way it used to," she said. "It must be the oil refineries. The other time I was here, they hadn't started on the oil, and the only smell was pine and hardwood smoke when they made their cooking fires at night." She turned back from the window, her hair tousled and her skin flushed from the wind. She was hungry and began to talk about food.

"What happened to all the food vendors?" she said. "All the time we were here we never sat down and ate in a restaurant. We used to go from one little street-corner shop to the next. I loved the *Kaukswei,* and the fermented fish. What is it called?"

"*Mohinga.*"

"Could we eat that tonight?"

"We'll reek of garlic."

"It's delicious, though."

"Then you'll have it," he said. "We'll have a great feast. Anything you want, anything at all. I'm so glad that you came. I thought you'd be too busy at the shop. I was afraid you wouldn't come. I don't know what I'd have done if you stayed away."

"I never considered staying away," she said. "A call in the middle of the night from my lover, summoning me to Lashio on the Burmese frontier. That's an adventure, eh?" She took hold of his face and planted a kiss on his lips. "Between the midnight flight to Rangoon and my fly-shit of a shop in Saigon, which did you think I'd choose?"

He looked at her with rapture, for a time unable to speak. Finally he said, "I'm going to quit, tie up a couple of loose ends, get out altogether. I want you to come with me. There'll be enough money. Plenty. We'll live well, I promise you'll be taken care of."

"No. That's enough of that now," she said. "We can talk about it later."

"I fell apart the other night," he said. "I didn't know such a thing could happen to me. I started to shake and couldn't stop. I even began to cry, and I couldn't stop that either. I had no control over myself, none at all. The wires had broken. No, they had been torn out, and all of the circuits destroyed." He looked straight ahead, avoiding her eyes, and said, "Has it ever happened to you?"

"Not exactly. Something like it, though."

"What? Tell me."

"What I felt was grief."

"For your father?"

"Yes, when I realized that I'd never see him again, that he was dead, and I was without him, I went to pieces for a time."

"But you knew why," Berry said. "As you said—it was

grief. You had a reason to go to pieces. But I had no reason. That makes it worse, more frightening, because it can happen anytime."

"You ought to get off it," she said. "It's morbid, talking about yourself. And it does no good, not for yourself or others."

Berry acted as if he had heard nothing. His eyes were focused on a spot in the middle distance, and he went on as if she weren't with him in the car. "But it's finished," he said. "An isolated incident, nothing more. One of those mysterious things. At the time, I thought it was over for me. Do you know what I almost did?"

"I don't want to hear," she said. "I told you before to get off it."

"But it's all ancient history," he said. "I'm a different man. It all happened to another person." Then he laughed, loudly, with his head thrown back. "The wires are back in place. Stronger than ever. Stronger than ever."

The driver slowed, blasting his horn and turning out to pass a bullock cart driven by a Shan farmer; a soldier with an M-1 rifle slung on his shoulder rode in the back of the open cart; he smoked a thick cheroot and his feet dangled behind, the laces of his boots untied.

Berry poured the last of the wine; it had gone flat in their glasses and tasted sour. "We do love each other," he said. "It's been a long time coming in my life. I pretended enough, even to myself, but never did a convincing job."

"I don't want you to rely on me," she said. "It's not fair. I can't be responsible for your life."

"I know you love me," he said. "Perhaps not like you did Castellone. But you were a kid then, and in hot water."

He looked away, again with that unfocused stare; and again she felt that he heard only what he wanted.

"Bernard pulled me together," she said. "He got me going."

"You still love him," he said.

"I told you it was over."

"You have a soft spot for him," Berry said.

"A soft spot, sure. And perhaps more than that. You

think I'd kid you? But it's not enough, my soft spot. Not nearly enough anymore."

The road leveled into a long straightaway between a plowed field on the left and a dense forest on the right. The car speeded up. Natalie used both hands to steady her glass as Berry refilled it.

The sound came from the right front of the car, the forest side; a sudden, dead thud. Something had struck the windshield and splattered there. Berry shouted for the driver to move, to speed up; the same instant, he grabbed hold of Natalie and threw her to the floor of the car and drew his pistol.

It was a bird, nothing more than that. A blackbird the size of a crow had been sucked into the airstream made by the speeding car and hurled against the windshield, splattering itself on the glass.

The driver pulled onto the shoulder of the road to peel off the smashed corpse and wipe the windshield with a rag moistened from a canteen carried in the glove compartment. He drove slowly the rest of the way to the hotel, and as soon as they arrived demanded to be paid off. He was through working for George Berry.

"What was all of that about?" Natalie said.

"He's scared," Berry said. "He doesn't want to work for me anymore. He thinks I'm jinxed. What happened on the road was a bad omen."

"Only for the damn bird," she said.

George led her to the suite he had booked, which had a Victorian sitting room, a bedroom with a balcony overlooking the garden and a fourposter bed. Natalie inspected the bathroom, which had an ancient cast-iron tub big enough for two. She was back in good spirits and went about cheering up Berry while she unpacked. She wanted a bath, and as there was no indoor plumbing, a procession of porters brought buckets of steaming water to fill the immense tub. She had a luxurious bath and came out to find Berry brooding over a whisky and water. She didn't want a drink of her own, just a sip of his, and climbed into the fourposter between freshly laundered sheets.

"I'm going to love sleeping here," she said. "It reminds me of the room I had when I was little in the house in

Singapore—the same huge bed, which felt as if it were ten feet off the floor. My old amah slept on a mat in a corner of the room, and in the morning she lifted me down from the bed, so that I wouldn't bruise my little white feet."

"Your little white feet?" he said.

"Yes. And to keep them white, Amah rubbed them every night with milk."

"It sounds as if you had a pleasant childhood."

"It was quite nice," she said.

"Have you little white feet still?"

"Have you never noticed?" she said. "They've held up well, in spite of the occasional bruise and being rubbed with milk only infrequently." She curled like a cat under the sheets and stroked the polished teak of the bed. "My bed was handcarved and inlaid with marble," she said. "Papa told me it had been made for a Chinese princess."

"Did you really live in a palace?"

"Right in the center of Singapore."

"And how many servants did you have?" he said. "Run through the whole marvelous story again for me."

"Come to bed," she said. He nodded, but didn't move. "Come to bed, love."

"I don't want sex," he said. "Not now, anyway. If I did, I would have plucked a bar girl."

"Are they fun to be with?"

"Bar girls? They do what you ask."

"So do I," she said.

"It's not the same thing," he said. "They don't care one way or the other. There's no glint of judgment in the eye. There was a long time I was potent only with bar girls."

"And not with any other? Why, George?"

"I told you. No judgment in the eye."

She got out of bed and helped him undress and made him join her under the covers. She had hold of him, gently scratching with her polished nails, her cool fingers like silk.

"You have to be patient," he said.

"Bernard told me he liked bar girls," she said. "But never less than two at a time."

Berry was contented now, on his back with his belly in the air, smiling with his eyes shut, his hands folded and his fingers laced on his chest. "Bernard told me you were a wonderful lover," he said. "At your best when given presents. He claimed presents made you grateful, particularly if it was jewelry. He said it aroused you sexually. Tell me what you do, you two."

"Bernard and me? We were together for years, don't forget. So we did most things. Neither of us is shy, or particularly reserved. On the other hand, neither are we bizarre."

"He said there was no one like you."

"I'm nothing special," she said. "I was merely good for him."

"And he for you?"

"Oh, yes. He was marvelous that way. We meshed perfectly, it sometimes happens."

"Tell me what you did for him."

"No, it sounds too ridiculous. I don't want you to get the wrong impression. We were tender together, but also absurd." She smiled and said, "Which would you like to hear about, the tender or the absurd?"

"You decide."

"You have no preference?"

"Go on and tell me. What was it you did?"

"I found something he liked, a small thing really, which I discovered by accident. It turns out he liked it so well I had to do it each time, and even in public places, when people were around, but of course done so that it couldn't be seen. If I tell you, you'll think me crazy."

"No, I won't. I promise."

"In public, I used to sneak up behind Bernard and put my finger in his ass."

"Is that all?"

"I told you it wasn't much."

"Your finger in Bernard Castellone's ass?"

"Yes, this one here. He adored it." Her face was quite serious. "One finger, it's little enough to do for one's beloved," she said.

"Would you do it for me?" he said.

"We'll see how it goes." She was able to kneel, bend her legs at the knee, and lower her buttocks onto the back of her heels. She kept her feet arched. She exercised regularly, which kept her body supple. "Bernard once gave me a diamond," she said. "It was the most beautiful thing I'd ever seen. Blue-white, over five carats. I've hidden it, you know, in my vault in France. When I go home I'm going straight to the bank, first thing. I'll get my box and carry it into one of those little rooms where you lock the door. Then I'll open the steel box—the diamond is kept in a little black silk purse. It's beautiful, and I'm going to hold it in my hand."

Berry didn't speak, and was afraid to move, even to stir, although he did part his legs and throw out his arms. She knew just what he wanted and teased him a bit, wet him and brought him along, and slid him inside of her. "Bernard didn't just give me the diamond straight out," she said. "He knew better." She had begun to whisper, her lips pressed to Berry's ear. "He only showed it to me, he let me see how beautiful it was, and then took it away. I had to plead for it, and do all the things he liked—even some he was ashamed of."

But George Berry was past hearing; Natalie put him in a blissful state.

Later on, Natalie went off to sleep, holding tight to Berry. She came awake briefly when he carefully freed himself and slipped away. She reached out for something to hold on to, clutched a pillow, and fell back to sleep, holding tightly to it. She was exhausted from the long night of getting in and out of airplanes and sank into a deep sleep. The fourposter, and the room itself, had indeed stimulated early memories. But with her these were never far below the surface. She smelled Brown's English soap and the beeswax used to polish the furniture. Her father had taught her to use the balance scale which was meant to weigh gold and was kept in a sealed glass case on the counter of his shop. When she woke it was dark, and for a second or two she didn't know where she was. In her palm she still felt the tiny weights used to balance the gold. She called out to Berry, but there was no answer. He had gone, leaving a note pinned to the pillow.

CHAPTER 4

Berry crossed a small bridge, called the Bridge of Hope, into the old section of town and the central market. He wandered around there, a pistol in his coat pocket, sniffing at the stalls and talking Shan to the vendors. He bought some bananas, his favorite tiny golden variety, ate them, and tossed the skins into a refuse pit, where a fire was kept going around the clock.

He made his way to the northern end of the market, at the edge of Thakin Mya Park. The zoological garden was farther along, on an unpaved stretch off the north-south road. Berry walked for a quarter of a mile. He heard the leopards and the deeper rolling growl of the tiger from the zoological garden on the other side of the stone wall. He had forgotten how quickly it got dark, and he was angry at himself for not having brought a flashlight. He hurried along the road as far as the ruin of the old fountain; a car was parked on the road which forked off to the right. The headlights went on, and Berry ran the last fifty yards. He got in next to the driver and turned around to the two men in the back.

"You run well, George." He spoke in French, but with

an Italian accent, the younger of the two, a swarthy man with a pampered mustache, a tattoo on his forearm, and a gold cross on a chain around his neck. "Extremely well, from what I hear." He made a snickering sound and looked around as if his remark were clever, and to see if it were appreciated.

Berry ignored Freddy, and turned instead to the man next to him. "Have you finished, Elie?"

"All here." Elie tapped two suitcases between his legs. "Just twenty kilos. Freddy was with me at the final weighing."

"Number four, pure as new snow," Freddy said. "Enough of it to bury the top of one of those mountains." He was proud of his teeth and liked to show them when he smiled. They went well with the mustache, the tattoo, and the gold cross around his neck.

"It was my most difficult job," Elie said. He wore a jacket, a shirt, and tie, a prim little man with wire glasses and a short beard. The beard was to cover the burns made by the chloric acid used to purify the morphine base. "Do you know what it is to work without proper mixers or dryers?" Elie said. "And only a wood fire to heat the base and the acetone. How do I control the temperature?"

"You want a tough job," Freddy said, "try flying a Beechcraft at night from here to Saigon, and keep it low enough to duck the radar, high enough not to crack up on the side of a mountain."

"The worst part is not the acid burns on my body," Elie said. "Forget it, along with the scar tissue on my lungs, it's nothing. The worst part is sharing a room with this whoremonger. Did you know he cries in his sleep? 'Mama! Papa! I'm sorry. Please forgive me. I'll never do it again.'"

Berry came between them; he needed to be finished with these two before the last of his patience was used up.

"You've been living in each other's pockets too long," he said, and turned to the chemist. "Your work is finished. Well done. Tomorrow you'll be home in Marseilles, asleep in your own bed."

"With his hippopotamus of a wife," Freddy said.

"You've never even seen my wife."

Berry said, "Shut up, both of you." He took an

envelope from the inside pocket of his jacket and gave it
to the chemist. "Banco Suizo-Panameño. Use the branch
in Basel. The number of the account opened for you is
written there. You merely have to sign and show your
passport and the money will be given to you." Berry
turned to Freddy. "Your job is to fly," he said. "To find
Saigon. Can you find Saigon?"

"I can with twenty kilos of number four," Freddy said.
"No need to worry about me. Nobody can accuse me of
losing my guts. By the way, are you still tough, George?"

"I am when I get sore. When I don't like a guy."

"He means you, shithead," the chemist said.

"Both big shots," Freddy said. "A pair of big shots.
But up north, it was me who saved the goods. How many
men did we lose, George? Plenty from what I could see."

"You got off just in time," Berry said.

"It took plenty of nerve to taxi through that ground
fire," Freddy said. "And even in the air, they were using
me for target practice. But once I had altitude, I could see
it all, a front-row seat."

"Chinese bandits," Berry said. "KMT deserters, scum
of one kind or another, out for what they could grab."

"But with automatic weapons, mortars. The works. It
was a hell of a fight. Touch and go. How many died,
George?"

"Six."

"Your whole crew?"

"Very nearly."

"And you without a scratch," Freddy said. "Lucky
George, with a charmed life."

Berry opened the car door, and the interior roof light
went on automatically; they made a perfect target, the
three crowded into the small car.

"The other side took heavy losses, too," Freddy said.
"Even their General got it."

Berry slammed the door and turned around. "You hear
a lot, my friend," he said. "The question is, where do you
go to do your listening?"

Freddy was smiling, having got under Berry's skin at
last. "He's here, you know. Traung is in Lashio. He paid
for the show in the north, and now he's here."

"How do you know that?"

"A girl I know, one of those at the Peacock. Traung stepped in to have his pipes cleaned."

"And the girl recognized him, just like that?"

"She used to work in Bangkok. She knew Traung when he was Vietnamese attaché there."

"Who is it you're talking about?" Elie asked.

"Nothing for you to worry about, darling," Freddy said. "The money is in your account in Switzerland. For the rest of your days, you fart through silk. Except Traung might first decide to cut out your heart."

"Yours as well," Berry said. "And yet you're not worried."

"Traung doesn't want me." Freddy looked from Berry to Elie and then said with emphasis, "Traung doesn't even want our dope. He sent me with a message."

"What does he want, Freddy?"

"You. He wants to talk to you."

"Did you tell him we were to meet here?" Berry said. "And the time, my friend. Did you tell him that, too?"

"Two of his thugs grabbed me at the Peacock. I had no choice," Freddy said. "He could have been laying for us here. He could have tried to make a deal with me. You know, killed you and lifted the stuff. But he didn't. It was intended as a sign of good faith. He said you'd understand."

"Where is he now?"

"Waiting for you at the north end of the market."

Once he was out of the car, rid of Freddy and the chemist, Berry retraced his steps through Thakin Mya Park, again passing close to the zoo. The animals were making a great racket, particularly the big cats. Something had them up and restless.

Berry knew the park to be a dangerous place, particularly after dark, when it was taken over by vagrants and petty thieves. He kept a sharp eye, his hand on the pistol in his coat pocket. He saw two figures, men moving in the shadows, peeking out from behind the cover of bushes and trees. They stalked Berry, but kept their distance, circling around behind, like wolves at a campfire. Berry felt a tingle along his spine, a rush of blood. He needed a fight. Let them come in a pack, so that he might shoot a few before they cut his throat.

The market was shut down, all the stalls locked for the night. The only activity was at the refuse pit, where a great fire blazed, park vagrants huddled around it, roasting discarded scraps of food. Berry came closer to the fire, near enough to feel the heat on his face. There was a shuffling of feet and room was made for him. He belonged among these beggars and thieves. He had come at last to a resting place. The men seemed to come from all over; he saw Chinese, Indians, and one or two whom he took to be white. It was a society in which to vanish, to crawl into a cave during the day and come out at night, to survive on scraps of food, and keep the past to oneself.

Just then something caught Berry's eye, some swift and purposeful movement at the edge of that ragged crowd. His hand closed over the butt of the pistol in his jacket pocket. He knew he was being watched. He never looked around. He gave no sign. He lit a cigarette and decided to give Traung only the time until it was finished. It was a pact, a promise he made himself. He would wait in the light of the fire, a lovely target, only the time it took to smoke a cigarette.

Someone touched his arm. He took care not to start, but turned slowly, a half smile on his face; it was Traung.

He didn't respond to the smile, didn't even see it. He never looked at Berry, but stood quietly beside him, offering nothing in the way of a greeting, although they had known each other for years.

"You have nothing to fear," Traung said, finally.

Berry's smile widened, his finger on the trigger of the pistol in his coat pocket, the muzzle aimed at Traung's heart. "What if I said you do," Berry said.

"How is that?" Traung shook his head. "You come alone. I have you watched, Berry. What can you do alone?"

"I can kill you."

"You'll die too," Traung said. "You don't care about your life?"

"Not all that much."

"Yes, I see." Traung's expression was unchanged, although he glanced quickly at Berry, a fleeting contemptuous look. "You despise the scum you work with, and yourself for working with them. You've lost your way, George. Yet I believe there was a time when you were a virtuous man."

"I can regain my virtue," George Berry said. "I only have to kill you."

Traung glanced at him again, the same contempt in his narrow eyes, and said, finally, "It's not my time to die."

Berry knew Traung to be a man of signs and portents, convinced that he had been chosen to fulfill an illustrious destiny. Traung's youth had been spent reading the signs, discovering the precise nature of that destiny. Berry felt the blind edge of his vanity, his impenetrable arrogance. He was said to be celibate, a vegetarian, given to fasting and the taking of purges, the mortification of the flesh. His followers believed him to be a saint. Certainly he knew how to dramatize sainthood. A saint on horseback, an ambitious saint, no less holy for that. Berry understood Traung, whose saintliness would seize evil and cut its throat.

"I asked to see you for two reasons," Traung said. "First, to inform you that I did not order the attack on the airstrip in the north. My orders were, in fact, that you be left alone."

"Yet someone armed the Chinese General."

"Han."

"Yes, Han. His men had the latest in American small arms. Some were captured after the battle, and they didn't come from us."

"He bought them."

"How was he able to do that?"

"He came here, to Lashio. They were sold him by your friend Joseph."

"Who was it gave Han the money?"

"I gave him some," Traung said. "But it was only payment to keep his eyes open. I wanted to know what you were up to, nothing beyond that."

The Thakin Mya vagrants had vanished, slipping back into the shadows. The fire had run down. Only Traung's ominous hoods remained, three of them, scarecrows in loose coats across the smoldering refuse pit.

"Americans in the dope trade," Traung said. "It puzzled me at first. I thought perhaps the honorable

George Berry had been bent at last, that he had become a smuggler working for himself."

"I can see you whispering in corners." Now it was Berry who was contemptuous. "Sniffing around, asking if George Berry had gone bad. You feed on intrigue, Traung." Berry watched the hoods close in, hats pulled low over their eyes, eager to spring, wanting only a signal from their master. "Cheap gossip," Berry said. "Tawdry bits and pieces come by in public toilets."

"You don't care if you die?" It was said softly. "You really don't care?"

"I'm not afraid, if that's what you mean."

"I could kill you here," Traung said. "Afterwards dump your body in the pit." He lowered his voice and said in English, "You want to die, I think."

"Do you do murder, Traung?"

"Only reluctantly. Life is sacred, all life. I told you, I don't even eat meat. No flesh. Not bird, or even fish."

"What about Ho Chi Minh?"

"I'd eat him." The mood was broken; Traung began to giggle, demurely covering his mouth with his hand. "A tough old bird, Ho. Scrawny. But I'd gobble him up. Ho Chi Minh. You know what, I'd bite off his head." Traung went on giggling. "I want to make war against the Communists, you see. I want to bite off their heads. That's why President Nyo must resign. He won't fight the Communists. He gets you to run dope for him. It's disgusting, isn't it? You are disgusted, George. I saw it in your face, the disgust."

"I don't like that crowd," Berry said. "I never have."

"Are you getting ready to get out?" Traung said. "Is that what the money is for?"

"There is no money."

Traung shrugged. "It's your affair. But I tell you, my friend, this is the wrong time to pick up your chips and move on. The game has only just begun. On your return to Saigon, please tell your Chief of Section, Mr. Kirk. He'll pass it on. The war will be stepped up. Nyo is finished. His time is over."

"And yours is beginning. You're to become the new President?"

"On March fourth," Traung said. "Nyo must be out of the country by then. Please deliver the message to your people, and through them to Nyo. March fourth."

"Less than a month."

"Time enough," Traung said. "Remember, none of us want Nyo dead. He was one of us. To kill him is not our way. Do you understand?"

"What if he doesn't go?" Berry said. "What if he locks the Palace and tells you to come and get him?"

"Then we have no choice," Traung said. "If he makes a fight, he'll be killed." Traung made a motion and the hoods around the fire turned on their heels. A car started up at the end of the market. Traung took Berry's arm. "Let me drop you at your hotel," he said. "At night, this is a most dangerous place."

"He won't go," Berry said. "Nyo is stubborn."

"Then we'll kill him," Traung said.

CHAPTER 5

Natalie was dressed and had had tea sent up, and was waiting for Berry when he returned. "You look shaky," she said. "Let me give you some tea. It's only just come and it's hot."

"I don't like tea."

"I doubt if there's coffee. Perhaps instant, you could ring and ask."

"There's a bottle of Scotch in my bag."

She found the bottle, but not a glass, although she went all over the room looking for one. "Use a teacup," he said. "Stop assing around and give me a damn drink."

She gave him the bottle and an empty cup, and let him pour his own, while she sat across the room doing her makeup, watching in the mirror how his hand holding the tea cup trembled.

"Did you call Joseph?" he said. "The number I left for you."

"I was to call only if I needed him."

"If I didn't come back."

"Well, you're back."

"You're a cool piece of work," he said.

"You fellows go off in the middle of the night, a pistol in your pocket." She shrugged and began to work on her eyes. "I've learned to keep clear of it."

"You don't worry?"

"If I do, I keep it myself."

"Were you scared, waking up alone in a dump like this?"

"No, I wasn't scared."

"I am," he said. "Fear gets you first in the legs. Mine are shot."

"Stay home nights," she said, watching him in the glass, how he gulped the Scotch and poured another. "You ought to get out of the business, George. To do that, you've got to be practical. No high-blown notions, no fancy politics or yammering about duty." She turned around from the mirror, facing him, her dressing gown falling open on her bare legs. "You've got to think about what's real, what counts. Add up your money and see if it's enough to get you through."

"Get down to it?" he said. "Think with one's cunt?"

She put the palms of her hands on each knee and leaned forward, her legs parted. "By all means," she said. "Use whatever you've got."

The liquor had restored him; his color was better and his hand was steady. "From where I sit," he said, "it's apparent you've got all you need."

She crossed her legs and said, "Castellone told me you had plenty put by."

"He's talking about himself."

"He's a clever chap, too."

"After I finish with Kirk in Saigon, we'll go someplace quiet, where I'll let you in on a couple of my dark secrets. We'll stay clear, holed up on a beach for a spell, and I'll tell you where the gold is buried."

She came and sat beside him, and took a tiny sip of his whisky. "Like a pet canary," he said. "I'm going to look after you. See that you get the keys to the vault, simple as that."

"I don't like talk like that."

"You said to be practical. I've got no wife, no family I give a hoot about. There's no will, because all I've got is on the sly. Nobody even knows where or how much. So

I'm going to put your name on the box and give you the keys." He put his arm around her shoulders, cuddled her, and said, "I need to be sure you're set up okay."

The next morning they flew to Rangoon. There was a connecting flight to Saigon, but Berry was in no hurry to report to Kirk, and persuaded Natalie to spend a few days sightseeing in Rangoon. They stayed at the Inya Lake Hotel, which had just been built by the Russians, and was already beginning to fall apart; Berry took her to see the Shwedagon Pagoda, and went on about its glories.

"*Shwedagon* means gold," he said. "The Golden Pagoda. All that gilding covering the stupa. That's real gold, tons of it. Imagine."

"Isn't it lovely," she said. "And all of it lying around doing nothing. Those that look like banana buds, are they gold as well?"

"They're called *Hngetpyawbu,*" Berry said. "Can you remember that?"

"I'll certainly try," she said. "That's not gilt, you know. It's plate."

"Nine thousand plates. I read that. And the *Hti*, the umbrella at the crown, that's covered with diamonds, rubies, and sapphires."

"You don't want to go to Saigon," she said. "You're playing on my greed, my lust for gold and precious stones."

"I don't want to see Kirk," he said.

"Then don't. Go around Saigon," she said. "You can fly out of Bangkok. I'll wind up my business in a day or two and meet you."

"I've got to pay my respects," Berry said. "I was a disgrace up north. Do you understand? I'm not worth a damn, but there's something I've got for Kirk, something I've got to deliver."

Berry began to drink that night, and continued the next morning in the cab to Mingaladon Airport. Natalie had to help him up the steep boarding ramp of the Dakota. She saw he didn't get another drink until they landed in Bangkok. He slept part of the way to Saigon and was sober when they landed.

They went to her apartment on Cong Ly near the A Loi shrine. It was in an older building, a single well-ventilated room with a high ceiling and a balcony which faced east toward the shrine.

Berry checked to see if the phone worked, didn't make a call, and began to drink again, refusing to go out to dinner. Natalie telephoned the manager at Pop's restaurant, who was an old friend of hers and Castellone's and had him send over a couple of hamburgers.

Berry wouldn't eat his, but just kept drinking; Natalie got annoyed and went to bed, leaving him with a bottle of Dewar's. She woke with the first light, and found him asleep in his clothes on the couch, the empty bottle on the floor beside him.

She pulled on a pair of jeans and an old sweater and went to the Ham Nghi market, where she bought fruit, milk, and fresh buns for breakfast. Berry was still sleeping when she got back, snoring heavily, giving off a spongy, faintly rotten odor. Natalie had an urge to undress and bathe him, to scrub his body and shampoo his head. In her fantasy she served and waited on him, tending his most intimate needs, as if he were an invalid. She imagined them together in her house in La Rochelle on the Atlantic Coast. It was always winter and they were isolated. Her life was nothing but service to him and lonely walks on the freezing beach. She was used to fantasies without pleasure, to the hard and gritty denial of pleasure, and to situations which came involuntarily to mind in which occurred those awful things in life she did everything to avoid. Her dreams were full of things she despised.

She made a pot of strong coffee and boiled the milk. After she had showered, she drank a cup of coffee and ate a bun while she dressed.

She cut a papaya for Berry and left the pot of coffee to warm on the pilot light at the back of the stove. She wrote a note explaining about the coffee and for him to look in the fridge for the papaya, and that she would be back that afternoon.

Just before she went out, she had a moment in which she thought staying together was a mistake. She saw it clearly, in one of those pauses, an eternal second or two in which one's fate is revealed; she and George Berry would end badly. Her amah used to say that Natalie had the gift, the third eye, and could see the future. She believed the old amah, but thought the gift natural, a matter of intuition, experience, and judgment, like deciding who could be trusted and who couldn't.

When she looked over at Berry passed out on the couch, she recognized that something serious had gone wrong with him, that he had become erratic and unstable, afflicted by a wicked and irreversible self-loathing. It burrowed under his skin, itching and burning like the fires of hell, a torment. It doomed him.

She started out of the apartment, got as far as the door, came back, and kneeled down near the couch so that her face was close to his; he was snoring softly, sweating, and the sweetish, rotten odor about him was strong. She smoothed his hair; he stirred in his sleep, moaned, drew up his legs, and wrapped himself into a tight ball. Her heart ached for him. She thought of nothing but easing his pain. It was futile, there was nothing really she could do for him, but she wouldn't walk out on him. People thought her clever and avaricious, often greedy, always motivated by self-interest. It was a lie, but she let it stand. There was another side, always the dark and hidden side, the true side. In love, she was the one who stayed on, the one who pleaded, the one who wept.

Natalie earned her living trading gold and precious stones. She had a partner, a Chinese named Chow, who kept a shop in Cholon, on one of the narrow alleys which ran south to the Chinese Pagoda toward the West Quai. It was a tiny place, specializing in porcelain, articles inlaid with ivory, and medium-quality jade. The higher-priced merchandise, rubies and twenty-four-carat gold, which came down from Thailand, were for the most part brought in illegally and had to be kept out of sight. Yet the shop flourished on its own, mainly through the efforts of Madame Chow, a woman a generation younger than her husband. She wore French clothes and had her hair cut and waved in the salon in the Caravelle. She spoke English as well as French, and somewhere had managed to pick up a little Russian, which she liked to bring out to impress Natalie.

She was a bright, chattering, busy woman, quite different from old Chow, who wore scuffed sandals made of water buffalo hide and the black pajamas of the peasant, and when he spoke at all it was in the singsong French of the Cantonese.

He must have paid her father well for Madame—Chow was a rich man in spite of the buffalo hide sandals and the black pajamas—and she had given him lots of children. They were always in and out of the shop, different ones every time Natalie came by. She supposed they were nephews and nieces, or refugee children taken in and raised as one's one. Natalie never knew for sure. No foreigner was ever allowed to fathom the mystery of the Chinese family.

Chow worked above the shop, in a cubicle with a tiny barred window opening onto an alley where several old Chinese sat on wooden crates around a mahjong table. Chow's workbench was pitted and burned by the Eagle brand cigarettes which he chain-smoked. Natalie was at home with the whir of the polishing wheel, the litter of tweezers and pliers, the tiny ball-peen hammers, and the low pop when the gas torch was lit—all the same as in the workroom in back of her father's grand shop.

"You bring back stones?" Chow said.

"No stones."

"Then why you go to Burma?"

"To see a friend."

"Burmese friend?"

"Yes. A pilot in the Burmese air force."

"You like Burmese men?" Chow was a tease, a lecherous old devil, who did photography for a hobby. He was often backstage at the Chinese ballet, snapping pictures of the girls and inviting them to sit for their portraits in a studio he rented by the hour. "Chinese men as good as Burmese. Maybe better," he said. "You like Chinese men?"

"I like you, Uncle."

"I take your picture," he said. "Much respect, much dignity. I even let you keep drawers on."

"Have you polished the stones?"

Chow hunched his shoulders and quickly nodded his head, the long ivory cigarette in the center of his mouth. It amused him that she was eager to see the stones, although it was hard to tell when he actually laughed. He made no sound, his expression didn't change, and his tiny eyes were squeezed shut to keep out the cigarette smoke. He did keep nodding his head, so perhaps he was laughing.

"One stone, one kiss," Chow said. "Four stones, so four kisses."

"I'll call Auntie from the shop," Natalie said. "She can be here when you try to collect for the stones."

Now he surely was laughing. It made him cough and blow his nose in a rumpled handkerchief. But he brought out four exquisite stones wrapped in a square of scarlet silk inside a leather pouch. Natalie had her own loupe, which hung from a key ring at the bottom of her sling bag. She held the stones up to the light, examining each.

"They're beautiful," she said. "You did a fine job."

"Which is best?"

"The small one."

"You bet. Perfect stone. Blue, white. How much you figure?"

She weighed the stone in the palm of her hand. Chow said. "Four point four carats."

"Fifty thousand dollars," she said. "If one knows where to go, and how to bargain."

"No. Fifty thousand? Good stone, but maybe thirty."

"Fifty in Europe."

"Yes, maybe in Europe." Chow wasn't fooling now, no thought of photographing the girls backstage at the ballet. "But who carries steel tube to Europe. You?"

"There are other ways to get them out."

"Big risk," Chow said. "You carry, but I could lose stones."

"I can get the four stones out," she said. "You leave it to me. But I'm going back to Europe for good. You understand, Uncle? I want to sell my half of the airport shop to you."

Chow used a tweezer to move the stones on the square of silk cloth. "Could be done," he said.

"Auntie would be good in the shop."

"She wants that," he said. "All the time pestering me to be in airport shop. Maybe she be good."

"She knows jade."

"Stones, too. Not so much like you," he said. "But I

trust you better. Three years and nothing went in the
pocket with you, at least that's what I think."

"Trust me to sell the stones," Natalie said.

"Sure, I trust. You get ten percent on stones here. In
Europe, I give fifty-fifty. Then I keep shop, all stock,
lease."

"Sixty-forty."

"Fifty-fifty," he said. "Sixty-forty above one hundred
thousand."

"Straight sixty-forty," she said, and then added with a
dimpled smile, "Uncle, all the expenses are mine."

"Expenses? Yes, I see. No steel tube for Countess
Benoit." He squeaked now when he laughed, but had a
wet smoker's cough daintily hawking phelgm into his
handkerchief. "Very fair, very fair." The handkerchief
was open in his palm, so that he might have a close look at
what he had brought up. "Make it fifty-five, forty-five,"
he said.

"Sixty-forty."

"Beautiful woman," he said. "Intelligent, good character. Never stole from old Uncle. Never bullshit. I give you
sixty-forty split, but one time I take your picture, one time
naked. What you say?"

"I'll send you my picture."

"No, I take."

"No, I send."

"With pussy?"

"If you like," Natalie said.

"Okay. Sixty-forty with pussy."

Chow wrapped the diamonds in the square of scarlet
silk and put them in the leather pouch. "Listen, please,"
he said. "I tell you what to do with my forty points. This is
secret. Never tell my wife, you understand? I have niece
in Paris. Good niece, beautiful girl. I give you address and
you give money to niece. She will take care."

"Is she to send a picture as well?" Natalie said.

"No. Not that kind of niece."

CHAPTER 6

George Berry slept on for an hour after Natalie left, and was awakened by a sound outside the door; he imagined someone prowling in the corridor, trying the lock. He reached under the couch, felt with his hand until he found his holster, and drew his pistol. He held his breath, the pistol cool and heavy in his hand, and listened for the sound outside. He heard nothing. His heart stuttered and seemed to stop before starting up with a heavy thump.

Berry got up from the couch and went to the door, the pistol still in his hand. He eased the lock. Nothing moved in the hallway, not a sound. It was empty, a broad old-fashioned gloomy corridor smelling faintly of the chemical used to clean the carpet.

Berry put the pistol in his pocket. His head and stomach ached; he felt a fool.

For some reason the gloomy corridor made Berry think of his father. He remembered a heavy, brooding presence, extended silences, a sober word or two from the shadows at the end of the dinner table. But there were surprises, glimpses of the mystery of his father; wandering through a flea market somewhere near a seashore—

George was a very little boy—his father picked up an old violin, tuned it, tucked it under his chin, and began to play. George was astonished. His father had never mentioned the violin. Strangers turned and looked, caught up by the music, stopped whatever they were doing, and respectfully stayed quiet.

Berry shut and locked the door to the apartment. He was shaky on his way to the bathroom, but otherwise all right. He laid the pistol on the lid of the tank behind the toilet, had a long shower, and brushed his teeth. He blessed Natalie for the coffee she had left. He shaved and even ate a few spoonful of papaya. He smoked a cigarette before calling Kirk's private number.

"We need to have a talk," Berry said. "Something urgent."

"Is there really?" Kirk had a lovely voice, like an actor's, and a courtly manner. He was a Southerner, although educated in the East, in California, and in England. "Really urgent, George?" He was being playful; George Berry was a cherished friend, one he trusted, made excuses for, and chose to tease. "Ten of eleven, and you in Saigon since yesterday evening."

"I've been drunk," Berry said.

"Good for you, George. But you really should have called. We could have tied one on together."

"You drunk? That'll be the day."

"It's been a success," Kirk said. "So far everything is according to plan."

"You're talking shit," Berry said. "With all due respect."

"I agree we need to have a serious talk."

"Absolute shit," Berry said.

"You're not still drinking?"

"It's got to be a private talk," Berry said. "Just the two of us. No tapes, no broadcasts. You and me, okay on the rules?"

"There's company first," Kirk said. "When word came you were back, I set up a meeting. No strain, really. A little fence-mending with the Royal Family."

"Absolute shit," Berry said.

"Please don't be difficult, George. If you'll only oblige me on this, afterwards I promise to be at your service."

"I've got a damn hot potato," Berry said. "There's to be no tape."

"My word as a gentleman spy."

"Send a car," Berry said. "No thugs, and a dummy to drive. You understand? I've a headache. You're not to send a fucking tour guide."

The car arrived in half an hour. It was an American model, too wide for the narrow street, forcing all other traffic to slow down and inch by. An American car was still a curiosity in Saigon, although the Americans had begun to tire of squeezing into Toyotas and Renaults, of hiding their light in a barrel. The neighborhood children admired the great American car, and climbed all over it, stroked its gleaming hide and felt its parts, as if it were a friendly elephant.

Kirk had sent a Vietnamese, who drove with an elbow out the window and one brown hand on the bottom of the steering wheel, a gold PX watch with expansion band on his slender wrist.

Berry's head was heavy; it ached and he began to yearn for a drink, and to take off his shoes and crawl back into bed. He didn't particularly want to see Kirk, to report on Traung and be at Kirk's meeting. He felt numb, a numbness which had spread slowly over the years, numbness earned like a pension.

The driver took the northern route around the Saigon traffic and west on Phan Thanh Gian for fifteen minutes to the Bien Hoa Highway. Since the French collapse the Agency had occupied a villa across the river. Before that an anonymous resident and two case officers ran things from a pair of dreary rooms in the basement of the American Embassy on Thong Nhurt. It was decided that Kirk was to do things on a larger scale, and he was handed a villa that was in the way of being a small palace, complete with tennis court and swimming pool, once the property of a French colon, who had pulled up stakes and moved to South America.

Kirk had taken the colon's library for his office; it was a large and ornate room, with rosewood panels that had been brought over from France, gilt mouldings, and glass doors opening on the tennis court. Most of the period furniture was gone, although a few of the showier and

more bulky pieces were still around. The good things had
been carted off by wives and junior officers with an eye
for these things.

Kirk had no eye. He was the kind of man who never
noticed furniture or surroundings. In the middle of the
day, he worked with the shades drawn and a desk lamp lit.
He had no hobbies and played no games. He had been a
swimmer in college and a middle-weight wrestler. But all
that was long behind him. He had a wife whom he rarely
saw, children in school in America. His life was his work,
the Agency. Little else seemed to interest him. Certainly
not women or money. He was indifferent to luxury and
lived a simple, almost spartan life. He wore only white
shirts with short sleeves, Bass slip-ons with ankle-length
socks, and unpressed trousers cut a size too big, so that
they fell below his belly. He ate cornflakes for breakfast
and hamburger for lunch, and usually for dinner as well.
He drank beer and Scotch and didn't smoke at all.

Kirk was with Peter Owen when Berry arrived, and
both men welcomed him with affectionate but jittery
regard; his hand was pressed, but gently, and Peter
showed him to the most comfortable chair in the room,
just opposite Kirk's desk. George Berry was a valuable
thing, precious china, but with a crack in it.

"You know Mr. Nguyen, don't you?" Kirk said. "The
President's favorite nephew. He'll be joining us."

"Rotten little bastard," Berry said.

"Favorite nephew," Peter Owen said. "The only son of
the President's favorite sister."

"Rotten little fucking bastard."

"He plays good tennis," Peter Owen said. "And his
wife is charming."

"She also plays good tennis." Kirk gestured toward the
French windows. "They promise to be along as soon as
their set is over."

"They're quite the leaders of the Saigon smart set."
Peter Owen was younger than Kirk and Berry, part of the
generation which had come in after the Second World
War. He had risen rapidly in the Service. He was clever
and well connected, a self-assured young man, tidy, cool,
and smart, always in a collar and tie. Berry thought of him
at meetings, seated in front of Kirk's desk with his legs

crossed and a lined yellow pad on his knee, taking notes with a gold Cross pen.

"Who else is to come trooping in?" Berry said.

"Just Nephew and the wife. The three of us."

"What about the Ambassador?" George said. "His Excellency, the Duke of Virginia."

"George doesn't sound in a good mood."

"He really doesn't," Peter Owen said.

"I don't see why," Kirk said. "He's had a difficult job, and he's done it well."

"Pip-pip," George said.

"George is a brave warrior in the clandestine service." Peter Owen was nervy, and sometimes funny, all that in spite of the lined yellow pad and gold pencil. Berry didn't dislike him, at least not usually, and certainly he knew there was a great deal more to him than met the eye.

"The Ambassador is in Bangkok," Kirk said. "There's a SEATO meeting, or maybe a water festival."

"Bangkok is noted for its water festivals," Peter Owen said.

"The Ambassador wants to be President," Kirk said. "He's got a very rich wife, and he wants to be President."

"I want to breed a Derby winner," George Berry said.

"I think George is feeling a little better," Peter said.

"The Ambassador isn't stupid," Kirk said. "An American who rides to the hounds is not necessarily an idiot."

"He knows when to make himself scarce," George said. "Certainly he's managed to stay clear of Razzia."

"I'm not all that sure he knows about it," Kirk said.

"He knows all right," Berry said. "Washington has told him. The White House has been in from the beginning, and now without their Ambassador." He looked straight at Kirk. "You wouldn't have pulled this on your own, without Washington."

Kirk said nothing, and his expression never changed. It was as if the words hadn't been spoken. Deft Peter Owen knew to step in. "We've not heard from Castellone since he left," he said.

"You won't hear until he's in with the wops."

"Castellone is very good," Kirk said. "Don't you think he's good, George?"

"Bernard? He's terrific."

"Clever fellow."

"Terrifically clever," George Berry said.

"Does he double?" Kirk said. "What do you think, George? Is Castellone a double agent?"

"I think he's terrifically clever."

"He's got a lot of money buried," Kirk said. "That's the talk. But of course, it could be just talk."

"He does live well," Berry said.

"Natalie would know about Castellone's money," Kirk said. "She ever let on about it?"

"Natalie isn't interested in money," Berry said. "Never talks about it at all."

Kirk had his foot on the top of the colon's beautiful desk, his sock rolled down, and was thoughtfully scratching his ankle. "If Castellone is a double, the question is, who for?" he said.

"Exactly. That's the real question," Peter Owen said. "Not the Russians, not Bernard Castellone. And not the Chinese."

"The Chinese don't pay."

"Not enough for Bernard."

"What the hell are you scratching?" Berry said.

"My poison ivy," Kirk said. "You ever have it? People make it out to be a joke, but it's not. Particularly if you've got sensitive skin."

"I've had athlete's foot," Peter Owen said. "And it's an absolute torment."

"Poison ivy is far worse than athlete's foot," Kirk said.

"I'd like a drink," Berry said.

Kirk brought out a bottle of Chivas Regal, glasses with the Embassy seal engraved on them, and ice from a bar refrigerator behind his desk.

"To closing down the north," Owen said.

Kirk sipped his drink and said, "Have you heard anything of Jack Sullivan? We called him in—how long ago was it, Peter?"

"Before Christmas."

"And since then not a peep out of him," Kirk said.

"What do you suppose he's up to?" Peter Owen said.

"He's gone into the jungle," Berry said.

"Is he crazy, do you think?" Kirk said.

"He didn't used to be," Peter Owen said.

"I was sorry to lose Sullivan's operation," Kirk said. "It

was showing a profit. I assure you I didn't enjoy rolling Sullivan up."

"I don't think he enjoyed it either," Berry said. "He's the kind to brood on what's been done to him. He might even take it into his head to bite your ass."

"There's not all that much he can do," Peter Owen said. "Razzia left no tracks. No paper, not a memo, nothing. We were very careful."

"It never happened," Kirk said.

"It never happened," Berry said. "And I hated doing it."

Kirk refilled Berry's glass. "You did what had to be done. President Nyo needed money, and we needed President Nyo. The three of us sat just where we are now, in the very same chairs, and decided there was no other way to get it to him."

"We were ordered to get him the money," Owen said. "We just weren't told how."

Berry turned on him. "Washington didn't want to know how," he said. "Nyo needed twenty million to continue his underground war. To line his pockets, buy his goodwill. It was his price, and we were told to pay it. It wasn't to appear on anybody's budget. State wouldn't even talk about it. The President never heard of it. Razzia was ours. It was made here, in this room."

"The truth is, I don't remember whose idea it was," Owen said.

"Neither do I," Kirk said.

"A brilliant scheme, with no one to take the credit," Berry said.

Kirk was again scratching his poison ivy, and Berry told him to stop. "Wash the damn thing," he said. "Put some powder on it. Do something besides scratch it."

Peter Owen took a deep breath and stood up; he appeared small and even frail seated, but was actually a wiry man, solidly made, a fine tennis player who tried to get in a couple of sets every morning before breakfast.

"Perhaps we ought to lay one or two things out," he said. "Level with each other before we sit down with Nyo's nephew."

Berry said, "Get to the point, Peter."

But Peter Owen wasn't to be hurried. He fiddled with his glasses, cleaning them with a folded handkerchief from his back pocket. Owen took risks, but only after a careful look up and down both sides of the street.

Kirk said, "Go on, Peter. Nothing you say will leave this room."

"Razzia disturbs us all," Owen said. "Certainly it does me."

"How does it bother you?" Kirk said.

"In several ways."

"Tell me one."

"Morally."

"What Peter means," Berry said, "is that it stinks to high heaven."

"It always did," Kirk said. "The point is it's done."

"Not quite," Peter Owen said. "We've brought the product only this far. We can kill it here, and only the three of us will know it was an Agency operation."

"You're forgetting Castellone," Berry said.

"Let me be sure I understand," Kirk said. "Are we now talking about aborting the operation? Terminating? Is that the question you're raising, Peter?"

"Yes."

"And terminating Castellone?" Berry said. "Killing him?"

"If we abort the operation, it's to bury it, to keep it within this room. But Castellone is outside. It follows we'd have to do something about him."

"Kill him?"

"I don't know."

"It's trust him or kill him, Peter. Which do you figure?" Berry said.

"It's my decision, finally," Kirk said. "Just as it was mine to bring him in. I thought it necessary at the time. I still do, even with the advantages of hindsight."

Owen said, "We needed him. He was our marketing man. Without him, we didn't know where or how to sell our product."

"There was no one inside the Agency we could use," Kirk said. "We had to go outside, to a contract person. Any time you contract, you open the door a crack. But we've known that from the beginning. We've tried to cut down the risks, but had to take a chance with Castellone."

"We got in this to save Nyo," Berry said. "If we ditch, what happens to him?"

"He doesn't get his twenty million."

"We lose him," Owen said. "He caves in."

"Cave-in or fight?" Berry had caught Kirk's eye, and held it up to the light, testing it for flaws. "What if it has been taken from him?"

Kirk understood; he knew what Berry meant and what he was going to say before he said it. "There's a coup in the air," Kirk said. He came out from behind the old colon's desk and prowled the room, both hands inside the loose waistband of his trousers. "Everyone talks coup," he said. "Of course, it could be just talk."

"More than talk."

"Let's have it, George."

"I saw Traung in Lashio," Berry said. "He's set to come. The date is March fourth. If Nyo isn't gone, they'll boot him out. If he fights, they'll hang him from the Palace gate. Traung will head the new government."

"Nasty son-of-a-bitch, Traung," Kirk said. "Ruthless. One of those holy killers, don't you think, George?"

"Traung? He never cuts a throat that God doesn't tell him afterwards to keep up the good work."

"He's the best of the generals," Owen said. "And he hates Uncle Ho."

"He'd give us a good war," Kirk said.

"Is there to be a good war?" Berry said.

"Washington is losing patience with Nyo."

"That has an ominous ring," Berry said.

Peter Owen glanced at Kirk, and then inched ahead. "Traung can win for us," he said. "Why not put Razzia on hold? Hobble Castellone, but don't let him know. Let's see if Traung comes on March fourth. If he does, we ditch Razzia and go with Traung."

"If he wins?" Berry said.

"He'll win," Kirk said. "Provided we let him."

There was a knock at the office door. Kirk put his finger to his lips and everyone stopped talking. Owen hastily collected the glasses and stowed them out of sight behind the bar. Kirk greeted Madame and Monsieur Nguyen.

They had come directly from the tennis game and were dressed identically: the same shorts and white Lacoste shirts, the same piping on their warm-up jackets, the same smart blue stripe on the instep of their sneakers; even their headbands and sunglasses matched. They were a handsome pair, with raven black hair and flashing teeth. Their photographs didn't do them justice.

Madame Nguyen accepted a Coke, and curled up like a cat on the couch, her bare legs tucked under her.

"We had a terrific game." Nguyen spoke in French, watching carefully as Kirk added Perrier water to his Scotch. It was the only mixer he would drink. Perrier and Chivas Regal, and the proportions just so. He tapped Kirk's wrist with his first finger to stop the flow of Perrier.

"Yes, an absolutely first-rate game," Nguyen said. "Frankly, I had my doubts about your synthetic surface, but I find it really quite acceptable."

"It's a little hard on the feet," Madame said, undoing the laces on her sneakers.

"It's durable and easy to maintain," Kirk said.

"Yes. That's its great advantage," Nguyen said. "And I'm told the young Kahn is installing synthetic courts throughout Sardinia."

"I play better on it than I do on clay," Madame said.

"You play beautifully on both," Nguyen said.

"I'm a determined person," she said. "Three hours of lessons every day. I believe in succeeding at everything one tries, in being the best. Or why try at all?"

Nguyen turned to Kirk. "Did you know she actually beat me a game?" he said.

"Only because you let me." She had a habit of putting out her tongue and running the tip around the cutting edge of her upper teeth. Her father had been a provincial governor under the French, and she had been sent to Paris, where she was supposed to have studied painting, and had become a French citizen. Nguyen had met her there at an embassy party, at which she had scandalized everyone by showing up in boots and black leather, like a member of an American motorcycle gang.

Nguyen said, "You've gotten so good, I'll soon be able to beat you only if I cheat."

"If you cheat, I'll do the same," she said. "Vietnamese women are not even to complain if their husbands cheat. At the same time they are supposed to be virtuous as nuns."

"And are they virtuous?"

"I suppose some are," she said.

"What about you, my darling?"

"I'm myself, emancipated, like an American woman." She glanced at Berry from the corners of her narrow black eyes, and turned her smile on him; it was perfectly done, lacking only spontaneity. She even held a cigarette for him to light, drawing him near for a good sniff of Bal de Versailles and fresh sweat.

Nguyen was talking about America, lecturing on its obligations to contain the Communists in Asia, when she broke in. "I adore America," she said. "It's the only place to get jeans that fit properly."

"My wife is in love with Marlon Brando," Nguyen said.

"Not at all," she said. "For me, Marlon is finished. James Dean is the one I adore. I still haven't recovered from his death."

"These things take time." Kirk had made a steeple of his fingertips, and spoke above it in a grave voice.

"I want to go to America on some kind of tour," she said. "I suggested it to Uncle, and he's very enthusiastic. I want to see all of America, particularly Beverly Hills."

"We'll be going first to France," Nguyen said.

"Uncle has made my husband Ambassador," she said.

Kirk had been doodling on a pad at his desk. He looked up and said, "I hadn't heard about that."

"It was only just decided," Nguyen said. "Uncle and I thought it would help along our plan. You see, if I'm Ambassador, it eliminates any risk of a problem at French customs."

Kirk said, "Have we a problem at French customs?"

"With twenty kilos of heroin?" Nguyen was seated in a Queen Anne side chair in his tennis shorts, his hairless legs crossed and the upper half of his face hidden behind dark glasses, sipping his Scotch and Perrier water. He wore a gold bracelet, which was far too loose for his thin wrist and slid back and forth with each wave of his hand. "My dear friend, one doesn't fit twenty kilos under a cap in a hollow tooth," he said.

"The agreement called for us to bring it in," Kirk said. "Bring it in and sell it. The money is your government's, but the responsibility stays with us."

"This is a better plan."

"That may be," Kirk said. "But it is not the one we agreed to."

"I think we ought to go into details at another time," Owen said. "Don't you agree, Mr. Nguyen?"

"You don't want to talk in front of me, is that it?" Madame had slipped off her canvas shoes and was rubbing her toes in their white wool socks. "You think I'm in the dark?" she said. "An innocent little schoolgirl?" She tugged on her sock and pulled it half off her heel, making a little pout, a charming gesture. "I think I have a blister," she said, before turning back to Peter Owen. "Don't you understand? The twenty kilos is to be carried into France in my personal luggage."

"And customs passes it through straightaway," Nguyen said. "I'm Ambassador, with full diplomatic immunity, which covers my wife as well."

That ended things as far as Nguyen was concerned. He finished his drink, signaled Madame to finish hers and put on her canvas shoes. He had begun to want his bath, his lunch, and perhaps an afternoon nap.

It was Owen who showed them out, walking between them, towering above them and having to stoop to make conversation, he in his gray suit and they in their tennis gear, crossing the formal garden to Nephew's sports car, sparkling in the sun at the bottom of the circular driveway. Kirk watched it all by parting two slats of the blinds of the window behind his desk. All of the lines of his face showed in the direct light. The flesh around his eyes seemed to have grown looser and more wrinkled. He was older, a weary man, needing a rest.

"Do you know anything of Nephew's history?" he said. Kirk turned back from the window and closed the blinds and drew the curtains, turning up the air-conditioner, and lighting the room with table lamps, the bulbs shaded by green glass. The room was cooler at once, quiet, and with a faint greenish glow, like an aquarium. Kirk poured fresh drinks, all made ready for confidences. "Nephew graduated from Saint Cyr," he said. "He was good, too. Top ten his year, Honor Society. During the war, the French decorated him twice. You wonder what changes people."

"You'd like to have the answer to that, would you?" Berry said. "Christ, does it matter? Nephew was ambitious and studied hard at Saint Cyr. He was brave in the war. Later, he became a bugger."

"Yes. But why? There's got to be a reason."

"He had it in him to be a bugger."

"And the wife? Madame Nguyen. That business with the blister on her foot, and her legs curled under her on the couch."

"She does all of that very well," Berry said.

"Watching the two of them causes you to doubt the way you've made your life. Like those kids in California, who do nothing but tool up and down the highways, surf, and screw. You ever look at them, and think you're wrong and they're right? It's odd how one can almost envy Nguyen and his wife. They're like the surfing people. All of them amoral, arrogant, and vain, and having a good time. Look at poor Peter in his collar and tie, his damn laced English shoes. Tell me, George, have you ever owned a sports car?"

"I had a VW once."

"I used to collect jazz records," Kirk said. "I know it's not the same thing, but it was a hobby. It was done for fun. Do you know what I mean?"

"What happened to the records?"

"My wife has them. I had them crated, and she's got them put away in the cellar of the Maryland house." He was thoughtful a moment and then said, "People like Nguyen and his wife do just as they please. They've got enough money, and no ambition because they're already delighted with themselves. Play tennis, swim, eat the most delicious food, but not enough to get fat. Small portions served on beautiful china. They go to bed after lunch, the two of them, and have a lovely screw before dozing off."

They let the image settle between them, sipping their drinks in the air-conditioned room with the curtains drawn against the tropical sun. There wasn't a sound, not a footstep on the gravel outside the window, not the chirp of a bird from the garden. None of the dogs barked, and there wasn't a car horn, nothing to break the spell. "It's not for us," Kirk said.

"What isn't?" Berry's mind had been drifting.

"No, not even the sex. You and I are about the same age, George. We've always gotten on, sort of anyway. We do understand each other. What I mean is, have you ever settled in and screwed like that after lunch?"

"I suppose so."

"I can't remember an afternoon with the shutters drawn."

"Not once?"

"No, I don't think so."

"Not on your honeymoon?"

"We only had a day and a half," Kirk said. "It's not cultural. It's not that Nguyen and his wife are Asian and we're white. Nyo is different from them. He has obligations, the same as us. Poor bastard."

"Poor bastard, indeed."

"For your ears only. Washington wants him out," Kirk said. "That's the straight of it."

"What if he won't go?"

"He must. The army has turned against him," Kirk said. "The air force as well. He's got a couple of die-hards in the palace guard. Our information is that Traung has the rest."

"And you've passed that to Washington?"

"That's our job, isn't it?"

"And Nyo? Have you passed the word to Nyo?"

Kirk would say no more on that subject. Instead, he asked a question of his own. "Nyo or Traung, George? Let me hear an opinion."

"Traung. Traung all the way. Why? Because Traung can whip Hanoi and Nyo can't. And we're here to whip Hanoi."

"Must we whip Hanoi?" Kirk said. "Should we?"

"Excuse me, but isn't that a philosophical question?"

"I suppose it is."

"I don't answer philosophical questions."

"Company man, George? Unregenerate Cold Warrior. Give old George an order and it'll be done."

"I've got a pension to protect."

"Help me out with Castellone," Kirk said. "He's got to be told to slow down, drag his feet."

"You mean wait and see how the coup turns out? If Nyo is alive and safely in exile, we may want to slip him the twenty million. In any case, Nephew gets the heroin."

"It'll be given to him here."

"On whose authority?"

"Washington."

"Washington is a city. A place name. Shit, Ralph, who gave the order?"

"The Director," Kirk said. "But he's nasty about marketing it."

"And you want me to tell Castellone?"

"You're his pal."

"It's too late," Berry said. "For all we know he's already talking to the wops. They catch even a glimpse of us, they're likely to blow his head off."

"You can get word to him," Kirk said. "There are ways, people you both know. He must be told to drag his feet."

"I won't do it," Berry said. "You and I had a deal. I was out, comfy on the beach. Like a sensible man, slowly drinking myself to death. You brought me back to do Razzia. It was business. You paid me. But only for the one operation. I told you I wouldn't go beyond that, and you and I agreed."

"What do you want, George?"

"Nothing. Absolutely nothing." He stood up, swaying slightly, the empty glass in his hand. "I'm finished," he said. "I was a mess in the fighting. Scared stiff. It's over for me."

"Go on then," Kirk said. "Have a nice retirement."

"You're sore."

"No." Kirk touched Berry's arm, and even patted it. "I'm sympathetic," he said.

"It's a rotten deal for you," Berry said.

"I'll see you're left alone," Kirk said. "Take your money and live the best you can."

"I'll need a beach shack," Berry said. "Like those surfers you admire."

CHAPTER 7

Sullivan decided his best way out of the Shan States was west through the mountains as far as the plain which ran to the banks of the Salween River. He followed the river south to the Keng Tung road, where he was able to flag a British Petroleum truck and hitch a ride to the storage depot on the outskirts of Panglong. Union of Burma Airline flew out of Panglong, and he was reasonably sure of catching the afternoon flight to Lashio, where with a little luck he might pick up George Berry's trail.

It was the middle of the night when he arrived at the depot. There was nothing resembling a hotel, but one of the British technicians let him spread his bedroll on the floor of his cabin. The next morning he talked his way on to the company bus, which carried Burmese workers between the depot and the barracks which had been built for them inside the town. From there he paid four kyats for a ride on an oxcart to the airport.

He hunted around until he found the telegraph office and wired ahead to Lashio, where he had one good contact, an Englishman named Joseph, who spent half the year culling the ruby mines between Lashio and Mogok, and the other half squandering the profits on high life in Bangkok and Hong Kong.

Joseph was retired from MI-6, although he kept a hand in, regularly doing favors for his old masters, as well as the Americans. He never took money, because he needed none, accepting Thai passport blanks for his favors, which enabled his couriers to move rubies back and forth across the border.

He kept an apartment and office in the one western hotel in Lashio, called the Sihasana, and Sullivan wired him there with his flight number, asking that he be met.

The plane was a prewar Bristol and arrived in Panglong with its starboard prop feathered. It was on the ground four hours for repairs. Sullivan bought a bag of fried prawns and a paper cone of wild plums sharpened with a pinch of chili pepper. He drank two bottles of Mandalay beer and went to sleep on the grass beside the runway until awakened by the noise of the Bristol's engines.

He flew into Lashio at eight that night, not at all certain if Joseph would be there. He could have been in Mogok, or trading for rubies in any of the wild country in between. It was also uncertain that a wire sent in Burma would get through. But Joseph was there, and Sullivan wasn't surprised. He was the kind who always made it through.

The Bristol was still taxiing when Sullivan looked through his window and saw Joseph's Land Rover parked just beyond the wire fence at the end of the runway. Sullivan knew it by its special fittings, tires and armor plate and bulletproof glass all around the cab. Joseph stood beside it, a tall, gaunt man, wearing a fedora and British battle jacket.

Sullivan was slow off the Bristol, and Joseph was at the bottom of the stair ramp to help with his bedroll and backpack.

"You look fit enough," he said. "I'd heard you'd gone daft in the mountains." He studied Sullivan for a second or two; his eyes were deeply set, triangular, and nearly hidden by bristling eyebrows flecked with gray. His eyes were an odd and startling color—a pale, glacial blue, set off by a darker circle enclosing the iris. He was a shrewd and observant man, fearless and a good companion, and in the gem trade it was known that his word was good. "You look as if you could do with a drink and bit of dinner," he said.

"A bath is what I'd like."

"Praise be, you stink as only a white man can," Joseph said.

As they drove in the Land Rover out of the airport, Joseph pointed out three World War II fighters, P-51s, done over with Burmese markings.

"They fetch an extraordinary price," Joseph said. "And are still available in the States. Fact is, I own three, got them sitting in a hangar in Waco, Texas. You ever been to Texas, Jack?"

"Is there trouble bringing them out?"

"Well, that's it precisely," Joseph said. "Proper export agreements, licenses from your government. It comes down to crossing the right palms, doesn't it? Impact bombs bring a lovely price. Explosives of almost any sort, automatic weapons, well-made pistols, your Browning, your Colt, all worth their weight. Local fellows would rather go about without trousers than a good gun. I tell you, there's more money in arms these days than in gems."

"What about drugs?" Sullivan said.

"Penicillin, that sort of thing?"

"The dope trade," Sullivan said. "Are you in that, too?"

"Me, a doper?" Joseph thought that funny. "What an extraordinary question? Am I a doper? Really, it's like asking if one sleeps with one's sister."

"Remember up to Namhkam on the Burma Road," Sullivan said. "All of us high on golden leaf and rice wine. You told me you *had* slept with your sister."

"Well, I liked Andrea." Joseph patted Sullivan's shoulder. "Such a lovely girl." He was the older by twenty years, and his hand was a trifle condescending, although the affection between them was real enough. "Go slower on the questions, my boy," he said. "Give us both a breathing spell. You look drawn too fine. Hairy, skinny, and stinking to high heaven. Let me get you something to eat and drink and see you properly laid before we get down to business."

"Did you really hear I'd gone crazy in the mountains?"

"That's the talk."

"There's some truth in it," Sullivan said. "Too long apart from the company of civilized thieves."

"Oh, bless you, son, that's just what I am—a civilized thief." Joseph laughed with his mouth wide open and his head tossed back, the sound rolling out like the roar of an antique cannon. "You're precious to me, Jack. You always were. I've got plans for you. Business, Jack. Money. Lots of money. And a girl. A beautiful Shan girl, a prize. Nanidi is her name. Nanidi. Roll those vowels around your tongue, Jack."

"Nanidi, Nanidi."

"She's soft as the inside of a flower," Joseph said. "And with such a sweet scent to her. Just a touch of spice. Cloves, usually, and now and then cinnamon. She's from a fine family and is very well bred, so that her feet are tiny. Beautiful, beautiful feet. Eve tripping about the clover of Eden had feet like our Nanidi."

"I admire good feet," Sullivan said.

"You have gone a little mad, I suppose," Joseph said. "But that's to be expected, two years spooking those hills. Nothing at all to be alarmed over."

Sullivan said, "Tell me about the dope trade."

"Truly, you're either crazy or you've found your life's work." One keen blue eye on Sullivan, Joseph drove with his left hand, the Land Rover bouncing and rattling on the unpaved road. "You're not buying, son, and you're certainly not selling. Not you. It's a matter of character with you. Revenge. It's got to be that. My guess is you're a hunter."

"Two men," Sullivan said. "George Berry is one."

"You reckon yourself on the short end?" Joseph said. "Is that it?"

"That's it."

"So Berry did you dirt, the other chap as well. That's the way you figure it, anyway. And nobody gets away with doing Jack Sullivan dirt. You got to even the score, it's the way you're built, is it? A matter of pride, of justice, and the books balanced."

"Berry is a friend of yours," Sullivan said.

"Of yours, too."

"Have you seen him?"

Joseph waived that aside. "I wish I had a good year left for every fellow that's double-crossed me and got away with it. You don't settle every score, Jack. Life's too short."

"You can't be made a fool of."

"Let it go, son. It won't make a damn bit of difference."

For the time being, Joseph would say no more. They were on a narrow road that came twisting down from the mountain, with a sheer, breathless drop on the right. Joseph concentrated on his driving. A mile and a half farther on, they came on a walled monastery and the lovely Myint Maw Pagoda, its golden stupa fired by the late afternoon sun.

"They've got a Buddha in there that's covered over with pure gold," Joseph said. "The faithful have been laying it on for centuries, and now it's so thick you can't make out the Great Lord's shape."

"You're best staying with the rubies," Sullivan said.

"Two million in gold. Maybe three."

"How would you get it through the mountains and across the border?"

"The gold is Buddha's. I wouldn't steal it."

"You've been too long in these mountains yourself."

"I respected old Buddha," Joseph said. "But you understand that sort of thing well enough."

"Will you help me, Joseph?"

"You'll come back to me one day, won't you?" Joseph said. "You're not a flat-out killer, not you. Old Buddha has you in his eye. So you must promise not to harm George Berry. But there's another fellow, a Frenchie. Castellone. He hasn't our Pagoda side, yours and mine."

"Has Berry a Pagoda side?"

"Oh, yes."

"Where's Castellone?"

"He was here in Lashio, but he's gone. We had a drink, and talked hunting. Snow leopard, and tiger near the Chinese border. You know the kind of talk. I'll have some people sniff around, see if they can turn up a trail. Meantime, you and I let off a little steam."

Nanidi was a lovely girl, as delightful as Joseph promised. She was the daughter of a *Sawbwa,* but by a lesser wife, once younger and more beautiful than the *Mahadiwi,* the prince's main wife. Nanidi's mother, and Nanidi with her, had been driven from the palace and mistreated because of jealousy. That was Nanidi's claim. Sullivan believed her. She was certainly the daughter of a prince, and her mother was at least a queen. She could have been the daughter of the moon and a ghostly spirit, one of those called a *Nat,* which live deep in the Shan forests. He believed anything she said, because of the light touch of her hand and the coolness of her lips. He believed in her virtue, although she took the money which he left each morning under her pillow.

She bathed him, cut his hair, and trimmed his toenails. No one had ever rubbed his back so well. She cooked his red rice and river fish, and was graceful and sweet smelling, making love in every imaginable position. Sullivan got Joseph to sell him a pigeon blood ruby and he gave it to her. She had never had such a present, and her gratitude was unbounded. She caused Sullivan to remember how young he was, and how much pleasure there was to be had in life. He even contemplated putting away his cares, and the need to find the reasons for his betrayal; he dreamed of settling in with Nanidi and getting rich with Joseph in the smuggler's trade.

Joseph's mind was working along similar lines. The afternoon of Sullivan's fourth day in Lashio, he dropped by Sullivan's room. "Are we alone?" he said. "Where's Nanidi?"

"Gone to her mother's village for the day."

"I've got some information for you," Joseph said. "But are you sure you want to know? You're putting on weight and looking better around the eyes and mouth. You could do worse than idling here with Nanidi. I have no doubts you'd make a fine thief, a handy fellow like you. And Nanidi certainly keeps your hair trimmed. She's told her friend, and the friend told me, that you're the best man she's ever known. She's begun to love you, and she swears she'd be faithful to you."

"That's your ruby talking."

"I suppose there's that side of it, all right," Joseph said. "She's a young beauty with a right to expect tokens of

high regard from her brawny white man. She boasts of
your generosity, as well as your strength, virility, and
skill, making all the other girls jealous. She wants to be
your wife, your number one—*Mahadiwi*. That's why she's
gone to her mother—to seek counsel."

"You're making too much of it," Sullivan said.

"Does the notion scare you, then?"

"Settling in? It causes some unease."

"You'll get a handle on that in time," Joseph said.
"That's the ordinary restlessness, sexual in origin. The
grass is always greener over in the other fellow's yard.
New pussy is best, that sort of thing. What drives you,
Jack Sullivan, is something more serious. You can't
tolerate injustice."

"I can," Sullivan said. "Except when it's done to me."

But Joseph was in no mood to be turned aside by a
joke, no matter how serious. "There's neither justice nor
injustice," he said, "because there's no one to keep
score."

"There's Buddha."

"He doesn't give two hoots," Joseph said. "That's why
we get on so well. When your light goes out, dumbhead,
the double-crosses go out with it."

Sullivan was thoughtful. "You're offering me a deal,
aren't you?" he said. "It's your devious way. Joseph de
Sales doesn't talk philosophy unless somewhere there's a
buck in it for him."

"I need a mule train taken through the mountains to
the rebels in Gokteik. One hundred and fifty AKs at two
hundred dollars each, payable here in gold. Get them
through for me, you got half."

"It's a fair offer."

"Only a beginning," Joseph said. "You're the field man
I need."

"Later on," Sullivan said. "But not now."

"But now is when I'm offering it," Joseph said. "Wait
until you're ready, and you'll have missed out. The job
will be gone, and so will your girl. Right there is the sharp
point of life."

Sullivan set himself. "I won't go in with you," he said.

"Suit yourself," Joseph said. "Suit yourself. Berry flew

to Rangoon on the twenty-third. Natalie Benoit was with him."

"And Castellone?"

Joseph shook his head. "He left around the same time for Hong Kong. Then the trail turns cold, I'm afraid."

"He didn't go to Saigon?"

"Probably not."

Sullivan had begun to put together his pack and bedroll. "Give me a couple of minutes," he said. "I can make the Rangoon flight if you'll run me to the airport."

"I don't fathom men like you," Joseph said. "I never have."

"Will you say good-bye to Nanidi for me?"

"Bloody fool."

But Joseph was outside the hotel in the Land Rover when Sullivan came out with his backpack and bedroll. He even had a going-away present, a figure carved out of teak.

"It's a *Nat*," he said. "One of those wood spirits Nanidi is always going on about. They say they're good luck."

"It's rather heavy," Sullivan said.

"That's the pistol inside," Joseph said. "Nine millimeter. I reckon you may need it before you're through."

"I'll be back this way," Sullivan said.

"I'll tell Nanidi."

"Will you get her a present from me?"

"Put your money away," Joseph said. "I'll see to it."

"It was a choice offer." Sullivan held out his hand. "We'd have made a bundle."

"Bloody fool," Joseph said.

CHAPTER 8

Kirk had sent Peter Owen to Bangkok to be sure the Ambassador knew the details of the approaching coup. He had characteristically kept for himself the more difficult job of telling Nyo. It was ticklish and sure to be painful, an assignment he dreaded. Alone in his office, Kirk reflected that it was a crucial moment in his life, one he would certainly look back on and want to do over.

Kirk was fifty-four and tried to imagine what he would be doing in ten years. He owned a piece of land, twenty acres in the Rockies, about thirty miles outside of Denver. A trout stream ran through the property, there was a lake, and a cabin just at the edge of it. An ideal place, which he had bought two hours after first seeing it. He had been in Denver on Agency business, and found himself with an extra day—the fellow he had come to see was sick—and Kirk had rented a car and driven alone into the mountains, wandering without direction along unmarked roads. He just stumbled on the cabin on the lake. It was an accident, a freak. Kirk never took days off in the middle of the week. He shouldn't even have been in Denver. He had been on his way from New York to

California and Denver was an afterthought, a minor bit of business that needed wrapping up. But that bit of land with a trout stream and a cabin on the lake was a place he had been looking for all his life. The oddest part was that he didn't even know he was looking for it. He hadn't a clue. Yet, when he saw it, he knew at once, and had to buy it. He didn't even have it appraised or inspected, ask what the taxes were or quibble over the price. It was the only impulsive thing he could ever remember doing.

Kirk began to think about Berry getting out. They had come into the Service within a year of each other, both by way of the OSS at the beginning of the Second World War. Sometimes it seemed to Kirk that 1940 was yesterday and he had only just begun. It came as a shock to think that most of the men he had come in with were somewhere on the beach or dead or ticking off the days until their pension. Kirk felt no older, but he had watched others in his profession grow odd, cranky, and mean, bristling with tiny angers, leaving the Service to live alone; distrust had made them unfit for most things. These were the men who muttered to themselves in the street, their clothing wasn't quite clean, there was a musty odor to them.

If it was true that each man has his own vision of hell, then this was Kirk's. He wasn't there yet, but he felt it along his spine, he sensed it the way a dog does a prowler.

Then why did he stay on in the Service? It wasn't to further his career, which had probably gone as far as it could. He didn't stay out of patriotism, not anymore. He hated the other side, but knew they were there to stay. He kept on because he wouldn't know what to do if he stopped. His marriage was little comfort, and he barely knew his children. He had his work, the Service. It was a calling, at least it had been once, and he needed to pretend it still was.

Kirk had been given a phone number to call at the Palace, which was supposed to ring through directly to Nyo's living quarters. Kirk had written the number in a small loose-leaf notebook which he kept in the Pohlschroeder safe which the old colon had installed in his library wall. Kirk worked the combination, took out the loose-leaf book, memorized Nyo's number, and then tore out the page on which it was written and burned it. He put back the book and locked the safe before dialing the number.

The phone rang three times before it was picked up. There was a couple of seconds in which it sounded as if the receiver had been dropped, and Kirk heard American music in the background. Finally, a child's voice came on, speaking Vietnamese.

Kirk was startled. His Vietnamese was awkward, and it took him a moment to find the words. The child was very young and spoke with a lisp. Kirk couldn't tell if it were a boy or girl.

"Do you do magic?" the child said.

Kirk wasn't sure he understood. "Is this the Palace?" he said.

"First, tell me if you do magic."

"Magic? No, I'm sorry."

"I can. I can make a coin disappear and pull it out of your ear."

"I know a card trick," Kirk said.

"What is it?"

"You pick a card, don't show it to me, and put it back in the deck. Later I take it out and show it to you."

"The right card?"

"Absolutely."

"Will you do it at my party?"

"Yes. Of course."

"You talk funny," the child said.

Kirk wondered if the phone were tapped, and if it were what would be made of this conversation. "Is the President there?" he said. "I'd like to talk to him."

"You mean my uncle?"

"Yes."

"My big uncle?"

"I suppose I do."

There was a loud clump, again as if the receiver had been dropped. Kirk heard the background music more clearly, the sound of voices away from the phone. Finally, Nyo came on the line.

"This is Ralph Kirk, your Excellency. I'm sorry to disturb you."

"Yes, Mr. Kirk. Quite all right." Kirk had begun in

Vietnamese, but Nyo had answered in French. It was a courtesy, or perhaps he didn't enjoy hearing his language mutilated.

"I need to talk to you, sir."

"We were about to sit down to the afternoon meal." Kirk heard laughter in the background, a woman's voice, the cry of an infant.

"This is urgent."

"In an hour, then," Nyo said.

"I'd rather not be seen entering, sir."

There was a hollow sound, as if Nyo had covered the receiver with the palm of his hand. When he came back on, there was no background noise.

"There's an entrance around by the back, near the guardhouse."

"Yes. I've used it before."

"One o'clock, then," Nyo said.

The phone went dead.

Kirk had a light lunch at his desk: cottage cheese, canned peaches, and a glass of skimmed milk. He had ordered his usual hamburger, but there had been a mix-up. He suspected the lunch belonged to Owen, whom he had seen eat this sort of thing. Kirk didn't complain or send it back, although he hated cottage cheese and the peaches were too sweet. He drank the skimmed milk, which was tepid. He had once eaten with the Director in his office, and they had been served grilled filet of beef and skimmed milk which had been decanted and served in a bucket of ice, like white wine.

Kirk left his office by a private door, without a word to any of his staff or making an entry in his personal log. He used the back entrance to the building, where there was no daytime guard, only a door with an Electra lock, the combination to which was known only to him and Peter Owen.

It was hot, the paths around the villa shimmering under a dazzling sun, and Kirk, who habitually kept track of the temperature, as he checked the number of miles to the gallon he got on his car, stopped at the outdoor thermometer, which he had installed in the garden. It was eighty-eight in the shade, ten degrees hotter in the sun. The inside of Kirk's car was stifling, and he ran it with the air-conditioner on full, driving slowly across the river, reflexively checking the rear-view mirrors to see if he were followed. He turned on to Nguyen Binh Khiem and parked near the museum grounds in an illegal space, protected by his diplomatic plates. He hailed a taxi from the rank at the southern end of the museum and had the driver take him to the Basilica. From there, he walked, doubling back on Thong Nhut as far as the Palace.

There was a faint odor of rot in the air, of overripe vegetables and fish trucked in from the coast and let stand too long in the open market. The air was heavy, humid; the city needed to be freshened by rain, swept by a cool breeze. Kirk slipped on dark glasses, waited for the traffic light to change, and hurried across the double thoroughfare. He turned off Thong Nhut and ducked across the narrow street just behind the Palace.

He presented himself at the back gate, giving his name to one of the two guards on duty. While one checked by phone in the guard box—Kirk noted that he consulted no roster of names, and kept no written log of visitors—the other raised his automatic rifle, which hung from a strap around his shoulder, and took a bead on Kirk, his glance one of passionless menace, the yellowish whites of his eyes showing under a deadly black gaze. The Palace guard were an elite group, all spit and polish in starched khaki and waxed webbing, armed to the teeth. They were presumed to be loyal to Nyo, perhaps the last troops who were. But Kirk doubted their will to make a fight of it, or if there were enough of them to matter.

He was admitted and escorted across the quadrangle and shown into the Palace. Once inside, he was patted down for weapons, and pointed in the direction of a staircase; Nyo himself waited at the top, a short square figure in a dark business suit, neat white shirt, and gray tie. Kirk had never seen him dressed any other way. He doubted if any Westerner had. These were appropriate clothes, they were proper; Nyo was a student, a man who learned a lesson and stuck to it. He had been told that in the West heads of state wore dark suits and white shirts.

Nyo shook hands awkwardly—unlike the dark suit, it was a lesson he hadn't mastered. He found the act distasteful, and he dreaded touching Kirk, merely brushing his fingertips before snatching his hand away. Kirk was despised; he was a Westerner, an American, too big, too clumsy, his accent vulgar and his voice too loud.

Yet, Nyo was polite, even courteous, and showed Kirk to his study, standing aside to let him enter first. He smelled faintly of cologne and the powder with which he dusted his neck after he shaved, and which settled like pollen, discoloring his shirt collar; he was a fastidious man, and compulsively clean. Gossip had it he bathed three times a day and used a small lavatory back of his study to scrub his hands after each meeting.

His study was a simple room, with a large bare writing table and few chairs. There was no phone, no television or dictating equipment, none of the electronics of high office. The walls were lined with books in French and Vietnamese, and a few in English as well. Nyo had been a scholar, and talked of being a scholar again, when his service to the state was ended. He showed Kirk to a chair and offered him tea.

Now that they were together, Kirk didn't know how to begin. He had never known a man so difficult to talk to as Nyo. Nyo was patient, a patience born of shyness and the dread of saying the wrong thing, of putting his foot in it.

Kirk complimented Nyo on the tea. He went so far as to say he preferred it to coffee. Nyo said that he never drank coffee. It was said gravely; coffee upset the stomach of President Nyo. Kirk held his chin in the palm of his hand and listened intently. Coffee gave the President of Vietnam gas. Kirk said he was sorry to hear it.

The conversation ran down, and stopped altogether, Nyo watching from behind his bifocals, his eyes like those of a fish in a tank.

Kirk said, "Have you had the opportunity to speak to your nephew, sir?"

"Yes. I'm kept informed."

"Then you know that he asked that the product be turned over to him," Kirk said. "That those were your wishes."

"I was told you refused."

"I was surprised," Kirk said. "My understanding of the arrangements was somewhat different. We were to trans-

port and make the sale. Only the money was to be given
to your nephew."

"He is my sole agent in the matter."

"But giving him the product . . ."

"My sole agent," Nyo said. "Absolutely. Give him the
money, or the opium. What does it matter? My sole
agent, you see?"

Nyo spoke so softly Kirk had to lean forward in order to
hear. He had a sense of the President's attention being
elsewhere, of his being distracted. Kirk had been with the
Secretary of Defense when the Secret Service was around,
each agent with a transceiver button in his ear and a voice
crackling directions. Kirk couldn't hear the voice, but the
agent could. Nyo was like that.

"My concern is not with the details," he said. "I care
only that I have the means to deal with the insurgents. Do
you understand?"

"To provide the means was the purpose of the operation."

Nyo's eyes came back to Kirk. "Is it still the purpose?"
he said. "Has there been a change in policy?"

"In policy? Not to my knowledge. If you want the
product given to Nephew to transport, then I'll see to it."

Nyo folded his hands, and his expression was again
preoccupied. Kirk wondered if it were deliberate, a tactic
to avoid being pinned down.

"What has changed, Mr. Kirk?" he said. "You asked
for a meeting. Important, you said. Urgent." His voice
rose. "What is so urgent? What have you come to discuss?
Please, may I be informed."

"I want to talk about Traung."

Nyo struck the desk with the flat of his hand. "Traung is
a criminal. I don't talk about criminals."

Kirk waited a second or two, his eyes directly on Nyo
and said with no change of voice, "There's to be a coup,
sir."

"I said I don't discuss criminals." Nyo was shouting.
"Traung is a traitor, a worm to be ground under my heel.
I tell you this—Traung is powerless. He may even be
dead. Very likely, he's dead by now. Yes, Traung is
dead."

"I'm afraid that's not so, sir."

"I'm not obliged to discuss dead criminals," Nyo said. "I have a duty to my country, and a great task to perform. My time cannot be spent discussing this dead criminal. I was summoned from exile, summoned out of the wilderness, to lead my country. There was nothing but confusion, confusion and despair, and everyone turned to me. So I came. I took power, but not for glory, not for power itself, and not for wealth. I prefer the simple life. My character was formed that way by my parents. Both were teachers, you know. Strict people, but virtuous. What is a virtuous person? A person who demands more from himself than from others. That is Nyo in a nutshell. One who makes greater demands on himself than on others. If that were not so, I would retire. I would return to the wilderness. I can be celibate, you know. I can live simply. A simple retirement, that's all I wish for."

"Then go now, sir." Nyo hadn't heard, and Kirk repeated the words. "Go now, sir."

"Resign?" Nyo smiled and shook his head. He heard only his own voice, whispering in his ear, and God. Nyo heard God. But God had left off whispering. God thundered.

"Traung is dead," Nyo said. "There is no coup."

"Where was he killed?"

"In Hong Kong. He goes there for the whores."

"When did he die?"

"Today is Friday. I had him shot. One week ago."

"He was in Lashio only four days ago."

"It's not so," Nyo said. "Traung is dead in Hong Kong, his body thrown into the Pearl River. Perhaps, it has washed up in Canton by now. Let's hope the tides are right, and his body is carried up the Pearl River to Canton. That's a good joke, isn't it? Traung's body in China." Nyo liked the idea and came out from behind his desk, offering Kirk a mint from a carved teak box. "Tell Washington that I'm firmly in power," he said. "Assure them that I'm ready to lead a campaign to crush the insurgents. Tell them in Washington I have endured enemies all my life, at every stage of my career. There have always been people who wish to betray me. But none has succeeded in bringing me down. I am Head of State. Isn't that so, that I am Head of State?"

"Yes, sir."

"Head of State." All of Nyo's vehemence passed as quickly as it had come. He repeated the words "Head of State," seeking to reassure himself. But it seemed to be ineffective. He slumped wearily in his chair, staring off into space. "I've done my duty," he said.

"No one questions it, sir. We all admire that and your courage."

"My courage? I don't know . . . . I'm not afraid for myself. I don't fear death. I never have. It's nothing, death in this life."

"You've done your share," Kirk said. "You've served your country."

"My Generals?" Nyo said. "Are none loyal to me?"

"None."

"But why?" He slowly shook his head, and his eyes reddened. "Don't they know I've done my best?"

"Send your family away," Kirk said. "Pack up what you need. Go quickly."

"My family is loyal."

"There will be enough money," Kirk said. "We'll see to it."

"The coup? Has a date been set?"

Kirk met his glance. "None that I know of."

Nyo sipped cold tea and made a faint nod. Otherwise he was motionless, the mask back in place. Kirk thought of the child who had answered the phone and wanted to know if he would do magic for a party. There was another side to Nyo, but no one outside his closed circle, certainly no Westerner, ever saw it.

"Shall I make arrangements?" Kirk said.

"Not at all." Nyo stood up, ending the meeting. "I will continue in my post." He turned back at the door. "I'm Head of State," he said, and went out. "Head of State."

Kirk returned to his office the way he had come, using all the same precautions. He ignored his messages, two cables, and half a dozen phone calls including one from the Director, all accumulated in the hour and a quarter he had been gone.

Kirk took off his jacket and tie and stretched out on the couch. He rarely napped in the middle of the day, but he had slept poorly the last few nights; his eyes burned with fatigue, and his body ached as if it had been beaten. Even so, he wasn't able to go right off to sleep. His mind ran over the events of the last few days, the meeting with Nguyen and George Berry. His failure to persuade Nyo to leave, his anxiety about Castellone. What was to be done to hold him off? Kirk turned his face to the wall, his arms crossed on his chest and his fingertips stretching as far as his back. "A wrapped parcel," his wife had called him. "Sealed and ready to be mailed." He dozed off thinking of her, but dreamed of Nyo; Nyo dead. The Director entered the dream, demanding Kirk identify the body. But there were only parts of it available—a toe, and a hand that was cold and smooth as ivory. Nyo's hand, which Kirk had touched earlier in the day, when the President was alive. "Such an odd way of shaking hands, brushing the fingertips and snatching his hand away," Kirk was explaining it to the Director.

The dream woke Kirk. But he didn't know where he was. The dream lingered, and the touch of Nyo's cold fingers. The inter-office phone rang. It was Peter Owen, back from Bangkok.

Kirk took a few minutes to wash and put himself together before he let Peter in.

"I'm afraid I went a long way for very little," Peter said. "My audience with the Ambassador lasted three minutes. How long were you with Nyo?"

"Ten, perhaps fifteen."

"You see? Your man listens to God. But when mine talks, God listens."

"I'm very glad to see you, Peter."

"Can I have a drink?" Peter said. "I had two on the plane, but they only made me thirsty." He waited until Kirk had opened the bar and made the drinks, and each had one securely in hand. "It was hell even getting a word with his Excellency," he said. "He did all he could to avoid me. Aides everywhere, running interference, hurling their devoted bodies in my way." Peter opened his collar and lowered his tie, the first time Kirk had seen him do that. "I just kept after him," he went on. "The cool, smooth, hypocritical son-of-a-bitch. I made an unholy pest of myself. I even acted rudely."

"I know how hard that must have been for you."

"You can laugh, but in fact it's terribly hard," Peter said. "But it worked, and I finally got his Excellency to see me alone—three minutes at the airport in the Pan Am VIP lounge."

"Three minutes?"

"Yes. I timed it," Peter said. "I told him that Traung was coming. I told him the March fourth date, and I assured him it was hard stuff. I also let him know that Nyo was finished."

"Did he know any of it before you told him?"

"I don't know."

"What did he say?"

"Nothing. He didn't say a word. He didn't nod or shake his head. He didn't fucking blink."

"Do you want another drink?"

"Yes, very much," Peter Owen said. "You've got to see how it was. The Ambassador and I were side by side on an imitation leather couch. Blue. Pan Am blue. And he's looking straight ahead, so that all I see is his profile, his movie star profile. I told him the whole tale, and he went on, without a word, drinking his diet soda."

"He's our best-conditioned Ambassador," Kirk said. "And his eyes are Pan Am blue."

"We're the enemy, you know," Peter said. "He gave off waves of hatred. He doesn't want to hear what we have to say. He doesn't want to know what we do. He doesn't want to think about us in the opium trade."

"Nyo won't leave," Kirk said. "He expects our support. He's been promised it, and he expects the promise to be kept."

"Then he's a dead man," Peter said.

"That's what the Ambassador doesn't want to hear," Kirk said. "They want a good war, so they'll let Traung come. We don't make policy, so there's nothing we can do about it. All we can do is cable the Director, advising that a coup is imminent. At the same time, we'll enter George's report of his meeting with Traung in the secure file. But we won't send it."

"We won't?"

"No. Instead, we'll amend it slightly. In George's report, which we file, we'll say that Traung told him that Washington had already been informed of the March fourth date. And we hold that file in case anything goes wrong. You see how it shapes up? Washington does in fact know of the March fourth date, but hasn't told its own intelligence people. Why?"

"So we can play stooge if it goes sour."

"But they can't if we have George's doctored report in the file."

"We'll need George to go along with it."

"George will. He needs his favors, and we need ours."

Peter reflected a moment and then said, "What about the opium? Do we abort? Call in Castellone?"

"Not yet. When Nyo sees Washington has sold him out, he may still decide to pack up. But he'll want the twenty million. Then everyone turns to us, and we're empty."

"We can put a drag on it," Peter said. "Slow Castellone down. We don't break him off, but we don't help him. If we have to burn Castellone, it can be done later on."

"Where's your friend Jack Sullivan?"

"He's been seen in Lashio. Our people say he was asking questions about George Berry and Castellone."

"Talk to Sullivan when he gets here," Kirk said. "Send him on to George. George will play him, and Sullivan will let him. They're old friends."

"And have George send him on to Castellone?"

Kirk smiled and said, "Sullivan and Castellone, now there's a match-up."

CHAPTER 9

February 1963

Bernard Castellone turned his back to the German and faced the window which overlooked the prison yard. It was early morning and bitter cold. The office was heated by a small coal fire in a black iron stove. Castellone used his gloved hand to clear the moisture which had condensed on the cold windowpane and looked into the yard. It was deserted, a place of gray brick and broken cobblestones, with four thick posts set in a row at the western end and a wall of sodden sandbags behind.

"It's taking too long," Castellone said. "The prisoner was to be ready when I arrived."

His German was fluent and he was able to affect the kind of lisp which suggested the years between the wars had been spent cloistered in Heidelberg.

"It's the processing, I'm afraid," Commandant Lot said, "medical and administrative." Castellone turned back from the window and Lot added, "The famous German thoroughness, Herr Decru."

"Much overrated in my view."

"In mine, too," Lot said, although his large ears had reddened.

He had a second look at the French diplomatic passport Castellone had placed on his desk, and the extradition order signed in the Office of the Ministry of Justice in Bonn. Lot's smile was meant to be gracious, showing all of his square, brown teeth; Castellone thought of a sideshow he had seen as a child, a Czechoslovakian troupe with a strongman who had ended his act by biting through a twopenny nail.

"The charges against the prisoner, Marcel Piri, are not that grave," Commandant Lot said. The diplomatic passport was open to the photograph page and Lot's eyes flicked from it to Castellone. "Yet there seems to be considerable interest in him. The Americans want to get their hands on him, you know."

"Do they?"

"My government is unusually eager to oblige the Americans."

"Mine somewhat less so," Castellone said. "But our friend has a tale to tell in Paris."

Lot was slowly turning the pages of the diplomatic passport, making a show of it. "Is that why you are going to so much trouble?"

"The tale promises to be good. Piri is very well connected."

"Do you like your work, Herr Decru?"

"I've been a cop all my life."

"I would have guessed otherwise."

Lot's eyes were still on the passport; when he raised them it was with a glint of mockery, and the beginnings of a clever little smile at the corners of his mouth.

"Myself, I've never been anything else but a cop," he said. "Even in the army I was with the military police. My father, too. Lousy job, don't you think."

"We get to see a little of the world in my section," Castellone said. "Some of us take on airs, but it's a cop's life just the same."

He took out a tin of Brazilian cigars, gave one to Lot, and lit it for him. The German drew on the cigar with a faint sucking noise and pinched it between the tip of his thumb and first finger, as if he were squeezing a pimple.

"It was an American Piri knifed," Lot said. "One of

their soldiers on pass. There was a fight in a bar and Piri carved him nicely."

"You have the signed extradition," Castellone said. "You did your job, and you have the pleasure of telling the American to shove it."

Lot liked the idea. He liked Castellone, liked his cop's conversation and Brazilian cigars. "Once I smoked a Havana," Lot said. "The real stuff, but only once in my life. Can you imagine, one Havana cigar in my whole life? But that's a cop's life, a cop's pay." He took Piri's passport from a desk drawer and laid it in the center of the desk, exactly halfway between them. "Antonio and Cleopatra. Isn't that a lovely name for a cigar?" Lot pushed Piri's passport an inch closer to Castellone, moving it like a chesspiece. "There's something about this passport," he said. "Have a look yourself, while I tend to a call of nature." He went out, fiddling with the buttons of his fly.

Alone in the office, Castellone knew just what had to be done; he drew three one-hundred-dollar bills from his wallet and folded them inside Piri's passport. Then he took a moment to reflect, glancing at the office door. The toilet flushed in the lavatory down the hall. Castellone took back a hundred-dollar bill and returned it to his wallet.

When Lot returned, Piri's passport was just where he had left it, and Castellone was at the window, finishing his cigar.

"I had a look at the passport," he said. "I think you'll find it in perfect order."

Lot used the phone on his desk, and Castellone went back to examining the prison yard, the location of the arc lights, and the solitary guard stationed in the observation tower. Castellone saw him plainly, a black watchcap pulled low over his ears under a plastic helmet liner, carrying an American M-1 rifle in a shoulder sling. A second guard entered the quadrangle with a black shepherd dog barking and tearing demonically at his lead. The guard released the dog, which bounded straight to one of the four posts, sniffing and raising his leg.

Lot hung up the phone. "The paperwork is finished. You merely have to sign for the prisoner."

He took a printed form from his desk, typed in Piri's name, and Castellone signed it. They left the building and started across the quadrangle. Lot had hold of Piri's passport, and the two hundred dollars inside had put him in a more agreeable mood. He even began to talk of coffee and sandwiches for the long drive.

"I can send a man with you," he said. "A driver, at least as far as the border. What do you say?"

"There's no need."

The wind howled across the open quadrangle and both men huddled against it. There were already snow flurries whipped by the wind, and the smell of more to come. At the center of the quadrangle, Castellone stopped and took his time looking around, his hands deep in the pockets of his coat. He studied the stone walls, the arc lights, and the armed guard in the tower. Lot led the way to the detention cells.

A guard had brought Marcel Piri to one of the tiny cells which was furnished with a wooden table and two chairs. Marcel sat with an old gray Wehrmacht blanket over his shoulders, shivering in the unheated room. He hadn't been allowed to shave or been given a change of clothes since his arrest. His face had a sickly pallor, one eye was bruised and swollen shut. Castellone remembered him with a rosy complexion and dandy's mustache, a lovely man of fashion, the only son and heartbreak of the legendary Achille Piri.

"I've come to see you safely back to France," Castellone said in French.

"Quite nice of you to come personally, Inspector," Marcel said. "And have you brought anything for my diarrhea?"

"Only my best wishes."

"Let's get moving," the old guard said.

"Not without my coat," Marcel said in German. "What in hell have you done with my coat?" And then in French to Castellone, "A coat made up for me in Rome. The lining is genuine fox, and it came from Alphonso on Via Condotti."

"You can have the blanket for six marks," the guard said.

"A nice blanket. You can use it to wipe your ass."

"I did that before I gave it to you."

"They've stolen my coat," Marcel said to Castellone.

"He never had a coat," the guard said. "Probably it was left in the bar where he had the fight."

"*Salop*," Marcel called the guard.

"I know what that means," the guard said. "I heard it enough in 1940."

Lot gave Marcel's passport to Castellone without a word. His good-bye was businesslike but cordial, a handshake for Castellone and a pat on the shoulder for Marcel, who shuffled across the freezing quadrangle with the Wehrmacht blanket thrown over his head like an old woman with a shawl. The guard went along as far as the gate, grumbling about being called a *salop* and the six marks due him for the blanket.

The prison was just south of Ludwigshafen on the Saarbrucken road. Castellone drove a Citroen DS19, which he had hired in France with Paris plates. Even with the heater on, Marcel complained of the cold. He also complained of his stomach and the loss of his coat, which made him very unhappy.

"Four of my best English shirts are still at the hotel," he said. "And my Lob shoes. I can't tell you how worried I am about the Lob shoes."

"I had them packed and put away."

"Did you remember the trees?" Marcel said. "They were made specially for the shoes."

Marcel had a look at himself in the mirror behind the sun visor on his side of the windshield. "Awful brawl, I could have used you, Bernard."

"Tell me about the fight," Castellone said. "How did it start?"

"No fault of mine. I cut the guy, but only after he and his pals went after me. Honestly, have you ever known me to start a fight?"

"Tell me why they went at you," Castellone said.

"Lover's spat," Marcel said. "I fancied his pal. The boy fancied me back, and he was alone in the bar. It was a crime of passion. An opera really, although I don't know that Germany is the right place. And you should have found me in my cell dying of consumption, not diarrhea."

"Let's get it straight," Castellone said. "You picked up

a boy in a bar. You left with him, and outside a couple of his pals jumped you?"

"I had the feeling they were waiting for me," Marcel said. "I was set up, Bernard. I think I knew it right off, before I went outside with the boy."

"He must have been a damn pretty boy."

"He had a naughty look to him," Marcel said. "That little sulky expression around the mouth. A bit of the rebel. Adorable, really."

"One day you'll get your throat cut."

"What can one do when the boy is so pretty?" Marcel said. "Have you ever been tempted that way yourself? Just an innocent question between pals. They say everybody has a little of it in him." He peeped coyly out from under the Wehrmacht blanket. "I don't fancy you, not in that way, Bernard. Although I don't suppose it would do me any good if I did."

"Send me roses, you'll find out," Castellone said.

"Have you never been tempted?"

"It's like eating cabbage as far as I'm concerned."

"You mean you'd try it only if you were starving?"

"I might."

"What about when the Algerians had you in jail?"

"It crossed my mind once or twice," Castellone said. "But only if the fellow had a particularly nice bun on him, and made an effort to keep himself clean."

"You're a good pal, Bernard. Working one of your scams to get me out of jail, and looking after my Lob shoes. Now trying to lift my spirits." Marcel fiddled with the radio dial. "It occurs to me, you may be after something in return."

"There'll be a bill, of course," Castellone said.

Marcel switched off the radio. "I'm getting the cramps again."

"We'll get you a nice lunch."

"Toast and a boiled egg," Marcel said. "My stomach couldn't handle more than that."

"Tell me what you were doing in Germany."

"I had business."

"Try to be a little more specific," Castellone said.

"I don't rat on my friends, you know. I must retain my self-respect. A man is nothing without his self-respect."

"I wonder what brought you to Germany," Castellone said. "You've told me you dislike it so."

"It was to meet a fellow," Marcel said.

"Currency running, something to do with that?" Castellone said. "When you called Zola and said you were stuck and needed help, he naturally checked. The fellow you were to meet is American. But we never did find out his name."

"My business isn't with the Americans," Marcel said.

"Not with the Americans? Are you certain?" Castellone continued in a mild way. He could appear dim when he chose, unsure, and only groping in the dark. "Yet Zola learned you had gone to the Florida to meet an agent of theirs."

"Is he really named Zola?"

"No. It's his operational name."

"I see, a sort of code. Do I have an operational name?"

"No. You're called Marcel."

"I suppose only big shots get operational names."

"Tell me about the American agent you were supposed to meet in the Florida bar."

"He called me in Paris and said his name was Brown, and I was to meet him," Marcel said. "But he never showed. Only the naughty little boy did. Him and his pals outside in the alley."

"Have you told anyone about coming to work?"

"Not a soul."

"Still, you were set up," Castellone said. "The Americans coaxed you to their sector. My guess is, it has to do with General Pershing."

"Who the devil is that?"

"Your father."

"Not even an agent, and he's got a code name."

"The Americans don't know you and your father are on the outs," Castellone said. "They figured that if they got hold of you and squeezed, it would be a handle on your father."

"They're wrong," Marcel said. "They don't understand how our families are. The last scrape I got in, the old man bailed me out, but swore it was the last time. He went down to the cemetery and took an oath on my mother's grave. He did an opera, my father, the way the old wops do."

"You're still his son," Castellone said.

"He wants no part of me," Marcel said. "He called me a faggot and threw me out. That's not right, Bernard. I can't help my inclinations, can I?"

"Did you know he was sick?"

"I heard something. I even tried calling him when I heard, but he wouldn't come to the phone. I don't think it's bad, not him. He's strong as a bull."

"He's got cancer," Castellone said.

They approached the signs for the Karlsrhue exit. Castellone tipped the signal indicator, glanced into the rear-view mirror, and slid into the right-hand lane and onto the exit ramp. The access road crossed a dense pine forest, opening on a small lake set with picnic tables and benches, iron grills and trash baskets painted orange and black, the colors of the Federal Republic. Castellone drove through town to Marcel's hotel and waited in a café while he bathed and changed his clothes and collected his bags. He eventually joined him in the café, shaved and smelling faintly of lime cologne, looking very much as good as new, his discolored eye hidden behind dark glasses.

"I need two soft-boiled eggs with a piece of toast broken up and put in with them," he said. "That and a big mug of coffee."

"You're sounding more confident," Castellone said. "More like your old self."

"I've got on the Lob shoes."

"They're lovely." Castellone waited until Marcel had given his order to the waiter and said, "We'll cross the border at Seltz. You can get the Strasbourg train and connect with Paris."

"Aren't you driving through?"

"Not directly."

Marcel said, "You've gone out of your way to help me out of a scrape."

He touched Castellone's arm, and smiled in an unpracticed way. The gesture was not provocative and the smile not worked out in advance before a mirror. Marcel had a dizzy side to him, and got into foolish scrapes. He lived a tabloid life, and one expected to find his picture in *Paris-Soir,* with a story that his throat had been cut. But Castellone liked him. He had been spoiled as a boy, brought up badly. Yet some light came through. There was goodness in him.

"It's no bargain being the son of Achille Piri," Bernard said.

"You think that's why I'm a fag, because Achille is my father?"

"Perhaps it's a kind of rebellion."

"What, being a fag?"

"Why not?"

"Because that's a lot of shit, that's why not."

"I must have read it someplace," Castellone said. "I was only trying to put a good face on it."

"I like women, at least sometimes. But boys more. That probably makes me queer, although I don't try to make it out something it's not," Marcel said. "We're friends, right? There's no small-time shit between us. The truth, Bernard—do you respect me?"

"Yes. You know how to be a comrade."

"Well, we're friends," Marcel said. "How does it work, friendship? There's no sex to carry it along, and no hatred. I can hate my lovers, but not my friends. Never my friends. Yet hatred holds people together better than anything else."

"You're thinking of your father."

"Sure, I do hate him. Of course, I also love him." Marcel interrupted himself, and looked into the distance, as if he had lost his train of thought.

"He's dying," Castellone said. "Time you made it up with him."

"I want to," Marcel said. "You go talk to him, tell him I want to be forgiven. Tell him I want his blessing. He'll see you, and perhaps listen to what you say. He thinks highly of you."

"You'll have to do it properly," Castellone said. "You'll have to go on your knees."

"Then I'll go on my knees," Marcel said. "Perhaps it's where I belong. On my knees before my father, before General Pershing. He's a brute, and I was expected to be

like him. But I wouldn't do it." Marcel again offered that
ingenuous smile. Castellone was disarmed; he understood
the appeal Marcel had for men, and for women as well.
He suffered what others only dreaded. "I refused to be a
brute," Marcel said. "But perhaps carried it a bit too far
the other way."

"I'll try to set it up with your father," Castellone said.

"When?"

"It'll take a few days," Castellone said. "You know
how it is. One doesn't just knock on Achille Piri's door."

CHAPTER 10

Castellone turned south after he left Marcel Piri at the
station in Seltz, wound in and out of half a dozen country
roads until he was satisfied there was no one on his tail,
and then crossed back into Germany at Lahr. He picked
up the north-south highway at the circle just outside of
town, where he had the gas tank filled and the car
serviced. He had a long drive ahead; his destination was
Basel.

Traffic was light, and alone in the comfortable car, he
settled in for the long drive, glad to be free of Marcel, to
be alone with his own thoughts. Castellone was a private
man, and sometimes craved solitude as one does the sun
after a long winter. Yet he never organized his time alone
or put it to any purpose. He seldom read beyond the
newspaper. He didn't do crossword puzzles; he never
gambled. He did like to eat well, and would go to a fine
restaurant and order carefully, eating slowly and savoring
the food and wine alone at a table. He liked women, and
was attractive to them. He could be romantic and courtly,
and he was always generous and easy to be with. Most
women came away saying he was a fine lover, and whores
valued him for a straightforward client.

He would have liked to have lit one of his Brazilian cigars and let his mind wander as he drove. But he was trained to be watchful, never to let his attention drift, and when a dark green Mercedes lingered too long in his rear-view mirror, he pulled off the road until it passed, his hand on the grip of the automatic pistol in his coat pocket.

When the Benz roared by with no one in back or seated beside the driver, Castellone returned cautiously to the road. His reputation called for at least a two-man tail, one to work communications, to keep an eye out, and for cover in case Castellone turned. This reputation was earned, he was proud of it and did all he could to keep it, like the proprietor of a restaurant awarded stars in a travel guide.

Castellone didn't expect to be followed. The small organization he had put together was airtight. At least it was so far. Castellone had a good nose for leaks, and as yet he hadn't smelled a thing. He also knew that by the time he did, it might be too late. The essential rule of his business was that one works only with men one trusts, and then never trusts them.

Only Zola knew he was in Germany, but even he hadn't been told where or for what purpose. The passport Castellone had shown Commandant Lot was a cold one, a French diplomatic blank without number or history, made out in a name plucked from the air, Castellone's photo under a seal above the signature. He hadn't gone to the Bureau for the blank, but bought it in the street, as a thief might, paying street prices out of his own pocket. He left no marks in the sand, certainly none that would find their way to the Bureau.

Castellone lay back of the Mercedes for twenty minutes, until it slowed approaching the Riezel turnoff and its amber directional light began to blink. He watched it climb the exit ramp, brake at the intersection, and cross the highway by way of the overpass. No other vehicle got on at Riezel, none came into his rear-view mirror and locked in. Castellone had been in the field most of his life, and the precautions were reflexive. Some of it was good sense, more of it the vanity of the clandestine, egotistical enough to think that someone cared enough to send a car and driver. Not that Castellone believed in the impor-

tance of what he did. He cared for the art, and respected
it, but without fervor. There was no fanatic in Castellone,
and very little faith. He was an agent because the way
suited him, because the risks of ordinary life were
insufficient. He put himself in the line of fire and then was
careful to duck, to stay alive. But it wasn't a game,
nothing foolish or frivolous about it. He needed life's
volume turned up. If he feared anything it was the despair
which comes when one cares for nothing.

Castellone needed to remind himself that he did care
for some things. He had been a patriot, although that was
long in the past. He had friends—Zola was one—and
there were women he had loved. Natalie Benoit's face
bloomed on the freezing German road. Pain made him
tighten his grip on the wheel. Pain was proof he loved her
still, would love her always. He felt a rush of the same
sexual feelings as when he had gallantly courted her, the
same eagerness and flutter in the stomach.

Castellone booked a room in the Euler, a hotel near the
station in Basel. It was one of the older hotels in town, built
in the last century, and while it had its share of dusty potted
plants, of flaking paint and worn spots on the carpet, the
original box elevator was made of mahogany and brass, and
the rooms were on the grand scale with plaster carvings
along the ceiling molding, and bathrooms with the kind of
deep claw-legged tub in which Castellone could stretch his
legs. He had a double cognac sent up and soaked in a hot
bath after his long drive, half dozing for nearly an hour.

Hotels of this sort gave Castellone a sense of well-
being. He liked to have his food sent up and eat in his
pajamas and robe. He liked to smoke his cigar sitting up
in bed, newspapers in three languages scattered around.
He had never owned a house, never lived in one for more
than a week or two and always as someone's guest. He
had never signed his name to an apartment lease.

"Bernard Castellone is a man who lives in hotels."
Natalie had said it as if it were a definition—"Brussels
sprouts are vegetables like tiny cabbages which sprout in
clusters from a stalk." She said it so often it got to be a
joke with them, eventually rather a bitter one. She was
going to have it carved on an obelisk to be erected in the
garden of the Ritz in Paris after he had passed on.

"Life can offer nothing better than residence in a fine hotel," Castellone said. "My father taught me that. Those were his very words, uttered while on his daily rounds as a messenger boy."

"Your father wasn't a messenger boy," Natalie said.

"What was he, then?"

"He was a bonded courier."

"Fancy name for the same damn thing."

"You loved your father, Bernard."

"No. You've got it wrong. It was you who loved yours."

"I sure did. I loved mine right out in the open, with no strings attached. Bless Max, I had my good times with him," she said. "He would have liked you, too. Whenever I meet a man, and it looks like we may get down to it, I ask myself if Max would like him. I put the chap to the test, you see."

"And what if he fails?"

"Then he's flat out of luck," she said. "The truth is you and Max are two of a kind, and it's possible you wouldn't have gotten along. He was a crook, you know, the same as you."

"Not like my old man," he said. "A bonded courier, straight as a string."

"You did love him," she said. "I never saw a man grieve so for his father. I know because I've wound myself around your heart, and I know how you suffer, although you never say a word, and there's never a flicker in your eyes, let alone a tear. You should let yourself go, cry if you feel like it."

"Shall I start now?" he said. "Break down and go totally to pieces?"

"It would be a good start," she said. "And I'd never tell a soul. I would mother you, press you to my breasts. They're small, but you've always treated them with tender regard."

Natalie was always after him, digging into his life, trying to learn all there was about him. She wanted to know the name of every girl he had ever slept with, and what they were like. Did he love any still? Did he daydream about any? And what about his mother? She was always curious about his mother.

"There's a blank spot there," he said. "Such a dim

memory I have of her. Smallish woman, with not much to
say, but went about her business. She baked good bread,
and it was said she was handy with a needle and thread."

"Is that all?"

"She was patient. A patient woman, and she liked to
garden."

"You had a garden then?"

"No, a window box."

"There's got to be more to her than that." Natalie's
eyes had filled with tears. "You must have loved her. She
must have petted and fondled you, her little boy. Someone adored you when you were little. I can tell. I can,
because of the way you are now."

"I never think of my mother," Castellone said. "She's
dead twenty years or so."

Castellone swished the last of his cognac in the bottom
of his glass and breathed the fumes rising with the steam
from his bath. He closed his eyes and imagined Natalie
was with him in the tub, for bathing together was a
favorite pastime. They drank white wine, Burgundy when
they could get it. Castellone remembered the wine and he
remembered everything that was said. Natalie had a
favorite dressing gown made of yellow Thai silk, and
Castellone was able to visualize her in it as vividly as if she
were with him. She had to reach around to open the clasp
at the back of her neck and undo the buttons fastened in
tiny loops made of white silk thread. There were six of
them, all the way down her back, and it took time to
do. He had to be patient. It was her way of teasing
him, of exciting him. Finally, she'd tug on the sleeves
and wiggle out of the gown and step gracefully into the
tub and lower herself between his legs, proudly taking
hold of him. The tub was her place of submission, of her
service to his pleasure. Elsewhere he might serve her. Sex
between them was something that never failed. Yet rarely
was it tender or languid. It stood on its hind legs. It was
wicked, dark, and dangerous like that between a brother
and sister. The intimacies came afterwards, in conversation, with Natalie pouring wine into him to loosen
his tongue.

"It's to get me to tell you where the bodies are buried,"
he said. "Where I've stashed my gold."

"You can keep your gold," she said. "I want to know about the women in your life."

"There are none."

"Well, there were. And I hate them. Oh, how I hate the thought of any woman putting her hands on you."

"Then why do you want to hear about them?"

"I don't. I don't want to hear about them or you. Not a word, nothing."

"Now you're sore at me."

"I'm not sore. I'm just going to pack and get out."

"There's no other woman but you. None before that mattered, and none now at all. Besides, wouldn't you rather hear about my gold?"

"You haven't any," she said. "It's not in my character to be with a poor man, yet here I am. Love out of character is the most dangerous kind. That's why our love is sexual. There are times it lacks depth. And because of that the sex is uncluttered, unsentimental. If we loved more we'd fuck less."

"It's the sentiment that arouses me," he said. "Particularly when you tell me how it was when you were a kid."

"You like to hear about Max," she said. "About Daddy."

"Yes, Daddy. Just the way you say it gives me a hard-on. But with Max it had a halo around it."

"It was that he loved me, and I had to do nothing. Do you understand? I was loved because I existed. I existed in order to be loved. If we go on about Daddy, I'll begin to cry. And those tears soften me so, once again I'll be at your mercy."

"At my mercy?" He rolled his eyes and even licked his lips, but it was done comically, to make her laugh. He had always been good at making her laugh. It was one of the sources of their love. "A perfect childhood," he said. "A paradise that lasted thirteen years."

"It wasn't perfect."

"What was wrong with it?"

"I can't put my finger on it, not exactly. There were dark places, scary, shapeless things like storm clouds. I don't know which is worse—to be happy as a child or unhappy."

If she went on too long about childhood and her father, even Castellone couldn't help her. Nothing cheered her up. She had to sing in Russian, the songs learned from her father. These were their best times together. It seemed that only they existed, Natalie and Bernard, and time went on without a stop. The past was with them. There would be no end, no parting.

There was plenty of wine, and if they were in a hotel room with no refrigerator, the bottles would be kept in the bidet filled with ice cubes. Whenever possible they stayed in big American hotels, with an ice machine on every floor, and plenty of hot water for the bath.

She encouraged Castellone to talk about himself, about his mother and father.

"They'd speak Russian to each other, when I wasn't to understand," he said. "I don't know where he learned his. He was always hazy about his early days, hinting at political activity of an illegal sort. He couldn't have been a bomb thrower, there wasn't a radical bone in his body. Bless him, he was a bootlicker, carrying jewels for Cartier to the hotel suites of the aristocratic few who didn't deign to set foot in the shop on the Place Vendôme. It must have cost him."

"It cost you more," she said. "He wasn't the first man to bend his knee in order to get by in life. There's no disgrace. But why drag along one's son to see it?"

"So I'd learn my place early." Castellone sighed as he spoke, but there was no bitterness in his voice. "My father had had his share of hard times, which had made him a fearful man. Now he'd found a safe place. He valued that, and he wanted the same for me."

Natalie said, "Didn't he once buy you a gun?"

"Yes."

"And teach you to shoot?"

"He was handy with a gun, although I'd forgotten that. And one time he pulled a fellow off a streetcar because he was rude to my mother."

"And the Russian," Natalie said. "If he was Italian, where did he learn it? And your mother, where did she?"

"I don't know."

"Did you ask?"

"To their dying day, they refused to say. It was a secret of some kind."

"You see, it's what I've always told you. There's always more to one's parents than one knows."

"And between us as well," Castellone said, beginning again to tease her.

Castellone had driven to Basel to see Zola, and should have used a safe number to call him and let him know that he had freed Marcel Piri and was on his way with tales to tell. He should have been in contact with Zola at that moment instead of wallowing in a hot tub, swilling cognac and thinking about Natalie Benoit. But it wasn't laziness that kept him, or that he had grown indifferent. He was sure the Americans had set up Marcel, and he wanted to let the dust settle, and then confront Zola face to face.

He didn't call at all that night, but instead ate a good dinner and went to a pleasant bar where he drank with a young woman who claimed to be with a troupe of stranded Rumanian acrobats. He spoke to her in Italian, and she insisted that he feel her bicep. She claimed to be able to support her weight by her teeth, and even chin herself. She thought Castellone was German or American, although she had to admit that his Italian sounded like certain rich Milanese who had paid one hundred marks to see her walk on her hands and hang by her teeth naked.

She took Castellone for an educated man—she thought a lawyer or an architect, something of the sort—and certainly he was rich. She knew he was rich because of his shoes. She always noticed a man's shoes, and his were of the finest quality.

"I had them made at Lob," Castellone said.

He wore no marriage band, and she guessed his age at about forty-five, but that was because of his grave features and gray hair. She noticed his movements were heavy and deliberate, but not in the least sluggish. She concluded it was because he had many people working for him who had to listen carefully to every word he said, and so he took his time and spoke slowly. She could hear him breathe and see his thick chest rise and fall inside his shirt. She noticed his hands and neck, and thought he must be very strong. He looked as if he were made of brick.

She was disappointed when he didn't take her back with him to his room, although he made it up by pressing a bill into her palm when they said good-night. It was for one hundred American dollars, the same bill he had taken back from Commandant Lot. She had never seen one before, and it took her several seconds to work out how much it was in francs. When she realized, she ran out of the bar into the street to thank him. But he was gone.

It was the middle of the next morning when Castellone arrived at the French-English bookstore which Zola ran as a cover in Basel. Castellone hadn't been in Basel in over a year and was surprised to find the bookstore modernized and enlarged; there was now a counter with magazines and newspapers from a dozen countries, a line of English and American paperback books had been added, and the dowdy prewar radio had been replaced by the latest in high-fidelity equipment.

Castellone remembered Zola's bookstore as a cozy roost for winded agents, a listening post and relay station for information bound for Paris. A quiet place, the radio tuned always to Zurich for the Mozart. Zola even served tea and little snacks, which made his bookstore a favorite with agents of a prewar, Middle European culture.

All that changed when the new crowd took over in Paris, beginning a ruthless system of modernization based on American methods. Zola was made to acquire a safe house and look after its housekeeping. He was given a car, which he never learned to drive, and was sent two clerks for the bookstore, one an electronics expert to keep the Paris line free and regularly sweep the premises for listening devices; the second was a weary ex-colon and failed pornographer, brought in for his Asian languages and experience in the book trade. Zola didn't trust either, although he played two-handed pinochle with the old colon, who knew his business well enough to put the bookstore in the black. In all of the history of French intelligence, it was the only commercial cover actually to show a profit. There was even some talk of letting Zola and the colon share in that, with a few crumbs falling to the electronic expert, but the new crowd in Paris soon put an end to such talk.

Castellone found Zola alone in the shop with three

Japanese shopping for guidebooks. One spoke a kind of French and wanted to know if there existed a *Guide Michelin* for Japan. Zola told him they hadn't gotten around to that and the Japanese wound up with a stack of *Michelin Vert,* and the current guide to France. After they left, Castellone said, "Have you a copy of *L'Assommoir* by Victor Hugo?"

"L'Assommoir is by Emile Zola."

"Is that why it isn't on the shelves under Z?"

"What a lot of shit," Zola said. "You're Victor Hugo and I'm Emile Zola. We sound like lunatics in an asylum."

"We're members of an ultra-secret illegal organization." Castellone made himself sound as if he were delivering a lecture. "We can't call each other by our real names or people would know who we are."

"Who would care?"

"Our enemies."

"I haven't an enemy in the world."

"Of course you do."

"Name one."

"Ferrer."

"He's an imbecile, that Ferrer."

"That may be, but he despises you."

"He accused me of having an affair with his wife. Do you remember Alyce?"

"Of course. She was very attractive."

"Yes, and a fine pianist. Technically quite sound, and with an understanding of the music that was of the first rank. Particularly the Chopin."

"She had a beautiful ass," Castellone said.

Zola made a deep sigh, solemnly bowing his head. "The most beautiful I ever saw." Zola went on in his solemn way. "I'm not an unhappy man," he said. "I have my cello, my family. Those new bastards in Paris have tried to screw me out of my pension, but working with you has prolonged my miserable career. I've even been able to buy that bit land in Spain, and build a house. Once this deal is finished, I can retire and live as I choose. Hugo, I'm not an unhappy man."

"But unfulfilled."

"Yes, exactly."

"Because of Alyce's ass?"

"Yes, but not exactly. At least not concretely. I've made of it an abstraction, an ideal which represents all that I've missed in life."

"Listen, Zola, I agree that it was beautiful, that ass of Alyce's. It should be seen first in moonlight, like the Taj Mahal. But really, you're making too much of it."

Zola brought out a canister filled with tea and set a pot of water to boil on an ancient electric ring, the kind Castellone remembered from before the war. It was out of place in the modern bookshop, but Zola was more comfortable with old things; he wore carpet slippers in the shop and carried the same Waterman fountain pen he had been given as a schoolboy.

He brought out a little tray of pastries, offered one to Castellone, and took one himself. "Do you think she has a warm feeling toward me?" he said.

"She made a comment about your hands," Castellone said. "I remember now. She told me they fascinated her, particularly when you were playing the cello."

"Tell me her exact words?" Zola peered over his glasses, and Castellone noticed his eyes, which were an intense blue, the lashes around them long and curling upward. Castellone had never noticed them before, and found them startling in Zola's familiar and rather homely face. "It's imperative that you remember Alyce's exact words," Zola said.

"About your hands?"

"Damn it, anything she said about me."

"She liked your eyes," Castellone said. "She said they were a lovely shade of blue."

"They're gray actually," Zola said. "Although in some light they look blue."

Castellone finished a linzer torte and helped himself to an almond horn. "She said you had romantic eyes," he said.

"But she was fascinated by my hands," Zola said. "God help me, and she thought my eyes were a lovely shade of blue. Why was I such an idiot?"

"Perhaps because of Beatrice."

"My wife? What has she to do with it? If anyone is to blame, it's that damn Ferrer. We were friends, and Alyce was his wife, so that was that."

"Did you ever tell her how you felt?" Castellone said.

"Of course not. All I ever gave her were a few stupid pecks on the cheek. Hello, good-bye. And a handshake for Ferrer."

"And never a real kiss?"

"Never."

"What about a pat? You must have done that, if only in a friendly fashion."

"Yes. On two occasions. Both during that summer we were in Arles."

"The pastry is excellent," Castellone said. "If you're not going to eat the eclair, please let me have it."

"I always save a little bit for a snack later in the afternoon." Zola looked thoughtful. "That summer in Arles was just after the war."

"It was later than that," Castellone said. "Fifty or fifty-one. I was with my dancer, Christiane. The one from Martinique."

"Yes. A lovely girl. And very clever. She taught me how to make a snare to catch pheasants. Whatever happened to her?"

"I don't know."

"How is it you lose track of people?" Zola said. "Christiane de Monverde. Such a beautiful name. It would be a shame if she ever married and had to change it."

"You remember her name because it was beautiful, and that she taught you to trap birds with a snare."

"What's so odd? A lovely girl, and you don't have the slightest idea where she is or what became of her. One day someone will ask, 'What happened to your old pal Zola?' And all you will do is shrug and look stupid."

"No. I'd say you went off with Alyce Ferrer," Castellone said. "Together at last in the moonlight."

"From your lips to God's ear," Zola said, and gave over his afternoon eclair.

Several people came into the shop at once: an American couple and a party of English businessmen, whom Zola ignored as long as he was able. Castellone was unable to watch him without amusement. He had been to school with Zola, escaped to England with him during the war, and both returned to France on Normandy Beach

with the Lorraine Division under Leclerc. Between them
was all the affection and easy bantering of old comrades,
of men with very different tastes, who had shared a
harrowing time. Zola was married and a doting father; his
son and daughter studied the violin and accompanied
Zola on weekends when they performed for friends. In
spite of his passion for the legendary Alyce, his family and
his cello were all Zola cared about. He grumbled and
made fun of everything else.

He was well over six feet tall, bony and stooped, with a
drooping mustache and a battered beret, which he wore
everywhere to hide his baldness. He looked and acted like
a music hall Frenchman. In the service, he was considered
ridiculous, particularly by the younger generation, which
had just taken over. But Castellone had fought at his side
all through France and knew that under fire he was brave
as a lion. He and Zola were together with de Gaulle at the
liberation of Paris, arm in arm, young men on the
victorious march down the Champs-Elysées.

When the English and Americans had left the shop,
Zola locked the door, drew the shade, and although it was
just past eleven o'clock, hung up a notice that he had gone
to lunch. His manner had become quite businesslike. He
knew of Castellone's visit to the Ludwigshafen prison and
Piri's release.

"One of my trained fleas in Bonn," he said. "He
dutifully called with the news that you and Piri drove off
together. I hope you've chained him safely to a post, the
Swiss can be harsh when it comes to making a nuisance of
oneself in a public toilet."

"He should be in Paris by now," Castellone said.

"And you've been dawdling ever since?" Zola was
unable to maintain his businesslike attitude; his comic
gifts included double-jointedness, and when he wagged
his bony finger from side to side, it was to emulate a
windshield wiper in a heavy rain. "You've begun to take
your work too casually. I'll have to fudge my report so
that Balzac doesn't hear of this."

"Who is Balzac?"

"That's the name Friedmann has taken for himself. He
gives me Zola, and takes Balzac for himself."

"That's just like him," Castellone said. "If anyone
deserves to be Balzac, it's you."

"Try telling that to Friedmann," Zola said. "You remember how he gave himself airs during the war. Now that you've brought him into our organization, and made him administrator, he thinks he's back in the Resistance, giving everyone code names. He's only done it so that he could take Balzac for himself."

"I can let you have Victor Hugo," Castellone said.

"That's very kind of you," Zola said. "But it's too late. Everyone in the organization would be confused. Like it or not, I'm stuck with Emile Zola."

A client rattled the door handle, tried to peep under the shade, and rapped angrily on the window before going off.

Castellone said, "Piri had the feeling he was set up by the Americans. It did sound that way."

"My Bonn flea came to the same conclusion," Zola said. "The Americans wanted him cooled."

"An American operation," Castellone said. "Why should they cool it down?"

Zola shrugged. "Maybe cold feet, second thoughts about being in the dope trade. I think about it sometimes, don't you? What if something goes wrong? We could look guilty as hell."

"It's a waste of time to think about it."

"Either do it or get out?"

"Exactly."

"I'm not so simple, and neither are you. Neither are the Americans for that matter. I want a comfortable retirement, and I worry too much about money, about not having enough. I walk instead of taking a bus, and I carry my lunch. I'm fearful, and I've become a penny-pincher. I don't buy new clothes, although the ones I've got have become shabby."

"They always were," Castellone said, kindly.

"I walk around in a state of perpetual indignation," Zola said. "Everything annoys me. But only the petty things, the small day-to-day matters. The older one gets, the smaller life becomes. Soon I'll be living in a chicken coop. When I was twenty I would gladly have given my life to bring justice into the world. Now I spend half my time trying to decide if my acre in Spain is big enough for two houses, so that I can rent one for the income. It's not that half the world is dying of gluttony and the other half of starvation that drives me nuts, it's the rudeness of clerks in stores, the litter on the street, and the dog shit."

Castellone had waited calmly for him to finish. He was used to Zola's outbursts and took them in stride.

"I want to know why the Americans have put the lid on," he said.

"It doesn't matter why," Zola said. "Without the Americans, it's closed down. We're out of business."

"They don't own it," Castellone said. "Not the business, not you or me. We can take it over, we can still pull it off. But without the Americans, we won't know when the stuff is coming, we won't know anything."

"Balzac will know," Zola said. "He's got his lines to Saigon, to Washington, too."

"And I've got Marcel Piri."

"It's the father you need. Old Achille."

"With Marcel, I've got the means to get him," Castellone said. "Get hold of Balzac. Tell him I want to know the American stance: for, against, or just indifferent? And when the stuff is coming. When and how. We pull this off, you go out in a blaze of glory. Have a film made of your adventures and resume your former life as a playboy."

Castellone had Zola smiling again.

"I could, I suppose, get myself a lovely young girl, although I fret about my powers of concentration."

"You do it from memory," Castellone said. "Close your eyes and think of Alyce. If not that dear old bottom, at least one as good."

"Alas, for me there will never be one as good," Zola said.

CHAPTER 11

Sullivan flew out of Mingaladon airport in Rangoon on Union of Burma Airlines. He spent two days in Bangkok, having his hair trimmed and being fitted for a presentable suit of clothes, before flying to Saigon. He had a warm number to call in Bangkok as well as Rangoon, but never bothered. He knew where the Chief of Station hung his hat, but stayed clear. It was a breach of etiquette, rather a serious one. Sullivan was on edge, not at all sure who his friends were. Instinct told him to look both ways before crossing the street.

The passport he used was his own, and with his backpack and the shaggy look he brought as far as Bangkok, he easily passed as a youthful American vaga-bond-scholar on an Asian field trip to support a doctoral thesis; Sullivan's subject was the Sanskrit roots of the Indo-Burmese languages, with emphasis on the vital linguistic link supplied by the ancient Pali manuscripts preserved by the monks in the great pagodas. It was a subject obscure enough to turn away inquiry. Yet it suited Sullivan, who dreamed of the cloistered life of a scholar; he sat in a bar on the Sukhumvit Road in Bangkok, the pistol Joseph had given him in a new leather holster under his armpit, and remembered George Berry's admonition to put his mind on a long lead when inventing a cover story, and how he learned so much that surprised him about himself from what turned up and worked best.

Berry claimed there was a lot of actor in every good agent, a lot of ham. Bits and pieces of their conversations came back to Sullivan, who remembered Berry as the best of companions. He respected George Berry, liked him, felt a certain sympathy for him.

On the third day in Bangkok, Sullivan took the morning flight to Saigon, and arrived just before noon. He had a window seat, and taxiing across the tarmac at Quo Son Hut, he counted twenty-nine American fighters parked wing to wing in neat rows. There were at least as many transports, and a general bustle of trucks and military buses coming and going. There was a drum roll of dollars; the Americans had arrived in force.

The Bangkok plane was filled with them, the Special Forces vanguard, hung over as they trooped on board, but refreshed and made boisterous by the hair of the dog at arrival time in Saigon. Most had the well-conditioned, vigorous look of athletes a little past their prime, and all were fitted with a stainless-steel chronometer flattening the blond hairs on an eight-inch wrist, and all carried a Samsonite attaché case.

Sullivan had drunk with them on the flight over, swapped stories of Bangkok night life, but drifted off as soon as he was through customs, trotting off under his bulky backpack. His intention was to make his way downtown, check his bag in a locker in the Central Post Office, and sweep the journalists' bars until he turned up a lead on George Berry.

But just as he stepped through the electronic beam that sprung the sliding glass door at the terminal exit, a green Chevrolet swept up to the curb, its rear door flung open. Sullivan stepped back, his right hand reaching instinctively for the pistol in the holster strapped to his left side under his jacket. A figure moved deep in the shadows of the car. Sullivan had a closer look; it was Peter Owen.

"You ought to have let me know you were coming." Peter Owen had learned to warm his upperclassman's smile, and to go about without a tie and to stuff a square of yellow silk into the breast pocket of his blazer. He was taller than Sullivan remembered, altogether more impressive physically. He had eliminated his stoop, and with it all traces of the diffident bookworm manner.

"No real pals to drink with in Saigon," he said. "No metaphysical chitchat at all."

"Nice of you to come out and meet me, Peter. The question is how you knew I was coming."

Owen's new smile never faltered; Sullivan marveled at how well he had learned to oil his parts. "We do run an intelligence network," he said, and took hold of Sullivan's arm, pinching his bicep. It was an old habit of Owen's, one that stuck, and Sullivan remembered a football coach who had done the same thing. But Owen wasn't testing, not measuring potential. He pinched and held tight to Sullivan as a small boy might clutch his father's hand.

"Lucky thing I was going through the Burma cables or I wouldn't have known at all," he said.

"Lucky thing."

"Given time I would have laid on a motorcade." He moved Sullivan smoothly into the back of the Chevrolet. "We have a six-car senatorial special with outriders that might suit."

"Do I get to ride in the hearse?"

"It's been suggested," Owen said. "Not by me. I'm your one true friend."

The driver started up and drove off without being told where to go. He was an Asian, too chunky for a Vietnamese, and with a bashed-in ear like a wrestler. He never took his eyes from the road or paid the slightest attention when Owen drew the plexiglass partition, which had been rigged for privacy.

"Am I in hot water?" Sullivan said. "Have I done wrong?"

"The word is out you're a difficult case," Owen said. "How exactly shall I put it? Rebel, loner. Ralph Kirk says you've got a wild hair up your ass."

"How is Kirk?"

"Traveling at the moment."

"And George Berry? I'd like a word with George. Could you arrange that?"

Owen gave no sign that he heard; his eyelids fluttered, but that was all. He took a pair of dark glasses from his breast pocket, careful not to disturb the square of yellow silk.

"George Berry," Sullivan said. "Is he in Saigon?"

"George has retired. I'm not sure where he is, but I'll ask around."

"There's a girl. Natalie Benoit. I hear George is with her."

"You've only just come into town," Owen said. "And yet you already know all the gossip."

"I haven't heard anything about you, Peter," Sullivan said. "Peter Clean. Do they still call you that?"

"I hope not."

"We were good friends, Peter."

"We still are."

"I think I make you uneasy," Sullivan said. "I'm sorry if that's so."

"You do have a wild hair," Peter Owen said. "You're bitter. You made your operation from scratch, you created it, and it's been yanked out from under you. You're indignant. You want to know who and why?"

"Yes. Who and why, Peter?"

"Oh Lord. I don't remember you being stupid. Do you suppose the planning council is going to sit down and write you a letter of explanation? You've been cancelled. Finished. You've got accumulated leave. Go see your uncle in Florida, the one who married money. Have him take you bonefishing. February is the perfect time, the tides are right, or so I'm told. With a bonefish on the line, I promise you'll never again think of life as meaningless."

Sullivan liked that. "I'm happy for you, Peter. I can see that you're enjoying yourself."

"I'm moving ahead." Owen spoke slowly, with a little curl to his lips, on guard against being teased. "I'm doing well enough, I suppose."

"And you look well. Filled out, more solid. It suits you, Peter. Each of us has a time of life that suits us best, and I think you're only just coming into yours."

Peter Owen studied Sullivan, his eyes hidden behind the convex lenses of his aviator glasses, which made it difficult to guess what he was thinking. But the tension in his lips relaxed, and his voice lost its hard, self-protective edge. "You're talking about yourself," he said. "You're thinking how rosy things looked when you were at school, how fine you were. Scholar, athlete. You were a hero of mine, you know."

"But not anymore." They were quite alone in the back of the car, the soundproof partition closed and the windows sealed to conserve the air-conditioning. "You have different heroes now," Sullivan said. "What's the word they use in Washington? Pragmatic. Your heroes have become more pragmatic men."

"Not quite. Not altogether," Owen said. "I still admire you. Two years in the Shan hills of Burma risking your neck for your country. You're still a bit of a hero."

"The shine is off," Sullivan said. "What you see is just another threadbare spook, a field man looking for something to hang on to. Not like you, you've got your ambition, your career, faith in success. You want to make something out of your life, isn't that it?"

"I want to make good," Peter Owen said. "You want to be good."

Sullivan looked out at the streets, feeling for a moment bewildered and disoriented by the traffic passing soundlessly on the other side of the glass. He needed air. The window was operated electrically, and he had to hunt around to find the button and then figure out how it worked. When he finally lowered the window, it let in a blast of hot air, dirt, and traffic noise. Saigon was totally changed, another city altogether. He remembered the broad streets filled with bicyclists, waves of them, like flocks of birds. Now there were only American and European cars, and trucks, military hardware, buildings going up, trailers hauling steel fittings and lumber.

"It's a boom town, isn't it?"

"We're going to make a real war," Owen said.

"What is it we used to call the President here?"

"The Little Saint," Owen said. "I'd forgotten that. His Holiness. It seems we doubted his declaration of virtue even then."

"I hear his ass has had it," Sullivan said. "The Generals want him gone. Your office, too. At least that's what we hear up north."

"Do you really? I mean hear that up north?"

"Come off it, Peter. We're Yanks, the two of us. Both on the same side, honest Injun."

"The President is loyal, and he's a patriot," Peter Owen said. "On the other hand, he's not a military man, and he doesn't have the confidence of the military."

"So you want him gone?"

"A lot of us think it would be best if he left."

"Is that why we're in the dope trade," Sullivan said, "to help ease him out?"

"I know nothing about the dope trade." Peter Owen reached across Sullivan and worked the button which raised the window, sealing them in again. "I've got you a room at the Majestic," he said. "You remember it, the old Grande Dame. You stayed there with that little Chinese girl."

"Her name was Gloria Woo."

"She worked for Air France," Owen said. "Let me call around and see if I can run her down. Gloria Woo. If I can't, I know one or two others. Lovely girls. Let me arrange it. Dinner, and someplace we can dance."

"Are we still friends, Peter? And are we still on the same side?"

Owen took his time. Sullivan never doubted that they were in fact friends, and that loyalty flowed freely between them. Owen wouldn't patronize him with a glib answer. He probably wouldn't lie, and he certainly wouldn't tell all the truth. All of that flashed through Sullivan's mind.

"We're on the same side," Owen said. "With similar notions of virtue and service."

He had chosen his words carefully, and Sullivan said, softly, "What do you know about the dope trade?"

"Bits and pieces, gossip. Probably the same kind of thing you've heard. Some of our people are supposed to be involved. You were there, on the spot. A good guess is you know more than I do."

"Then why haven't you asked me what I know?"

Owen didn't hesitate. "I don't want to know what you know." His patience seemed finally to be strained. "It's best for me not to know, best for the Service as well."

Sullivan started to answer, but checked himself. Truth

sometimes oozed bit by bit, and sometimes, even between the best of friends, not a single drop came. These were Sullivan's thoughts; he said nothing.

The driver swung the Chevrolet onto To Du Street and turned right past the National Assembly, inching through the thick traffic and finally joining a line of taxis backed up at the circular entrance of the Majestic. Owen said he would make all the arrangements for that night. "Wine and pretty girls," he said. "No shoptalk, just a good time. I'll call for you at seven."

Sullivan checked in and was shown to a room, where he deposited his bag, and almost immediately went out. He glanced in the bar, saw no one he knew, and strolled through the lobby to see if he drew a tail. He walked as far as Ham-Ngi and wandered in and out of the side streets which ran between it and the docks. It was an area of bars and tiny restaurants, each with a drum of boiling oil to fry the *cha-gio,* and open stalls peddling everything from dried fish to Malay pearls. Closer to the waterfront, the streets narrowed. Sullivan had picked up a tail, spotted him lingering at one of the food stalls, where he bought a *cha-gio,* and continued after Sullivan, licking the fish sauce from his fingers. He hadn't the look of Owen's thugs, more that of a local with a hefty pistol jammed in the waist of his pants, its butt making a comic bulge under his flowing shirt.

Sullivan thought of ducking around a corner and into a doorway, dropping behind him, putting a lock on his neck, and taking away his big pistol. He was mean enough. He could feel and hear the snap of the little gunman's neck under his armlock. But he had to keep hold of himself. He didn't want a run-in with the locals. He dare not be reckless or stupid. In the end he ducked into an open doorway, sprinted through a courtyard hung with drying wash, and jumped a low gate at the back leading to another alley. He found a cab stand at the French Line pier, where the cruise ships once docked, and took it across town. He strolled in and out of the Basilica until he was certain that he had shaken the gunman. He found another cab and took it to a bar called the Express in the Gia Dinh; it was owned by a German named Willi Wolfe, a broker in the Saigon rackets, who had been

brought into the intelligence trade during the war, when
the British dropped him into Holland in 1943 to rebuild a
network swept clean by the Abwehr the preceding year.
The British called him "The Dandy," and the name suited
him. He had been an actor in German films and on the
London stage before the war. Although his father had
been a waiter in a Berlin café, Willi's English sounded as
if he had been born in the West End. He was a dancer and
a gymnast, whom Sullivan had seen win one hundred
dollars by drinking a bottle of champagne and then
walking on his hands from one end of the Metropole bar
to the other.

He lived in an apartment above the Express, and
greeted Sullivan wearing his dressing gown, although it
was midafternoon. There was a boy with him, Australian
by accent, small and fair, who had been exercising in
cotton briefs and sunning himself on Willi's tiny balcony.
His name was Freddie and he had the pinched, pale, sour
look of those who lived by self-denial, a jockey or an
underwear model, skinny but with the upper arms and
shoulders of a body-builder, slabs of muscle laid on as an
afterthought.

Willi sent him down to the kitchen for a snack and
watched Sullivan's eyes following him out the door.

"I liked boys before the war," Willi said. "And I
thought I'd take it up again."

"Has it worked out?"

"No. I've lost my taste." For some reason that struck
Willi as funny. Sullivan knew his habit, despite his
flawless English, of mentally translating into German,
where perhaps the remark had a double meaning.

"I'll bet you're in the money," Sullivan said. "When
you laughed just then, I noticed your teeth. They're
new."

"D'you like them?"

"I liked the old ones. You were very proud of them. I
remember how you bragged to the East German Ambassador that they were prewar teeth, made for you in Berlin
when the Germans still did things well."

"Did I really say such a thing? I must have been drunk.
What did the Ambassador say?"

"He was a very serious man," Sullivan said. "He told

you that in socialist countries nobody has rotted teeth in the first place, because the dental care is all free."

"Oh, Lord," Willi said. "I really do despise them. I have from the beginning."

Sullivan said, "Are you in business now?"

"Oh, yes. I've got the bar downstairs. Dice and poker and a couple of clean girls."

"No drugs?"

Willi showed his teeth again, but it was no smile. "I heard you had a tough time in the Triangle, that they ran you off. Your own did, that's the story anyway. People say you went crackers. Let your hair and fingernails grow and ate roots. I never believed it. I said, 'Jack Sullivan doesn't go crazy.' But now I do wonder. Do I run drugs? I mean that is a doozy of a question."

"Do you?"

"Sure. But in such a small way. Not like your old pal George Berry. It's him you're looking for, ain't it?" Willi said. "If anybody could finger George Berry, it'd be me."

"That's what I hoped."

"I don't know where he is, darling. I haven't the first clue. I swear it."

"You hear things and so do I," Sullivan said. "He's in Saigon."

"No more, he's not. He was here, staying at the Majestic. One day he packed up and left. Owed me for a few things, but I wasn't nervous. I know my George Berry. Man of Honor. One day the money came in the mail."

"A check?"

"You mean a bank draft?" The smile was genuine this time. "From an old hide-and-seek artist like George? American dollars, he sent, washed clean as a fresh nappy."

"Anything else?"

"Nothing at all."

"Where did he get his mail?"

"God knows. One or another dead drop. He could have his choice."

"There's a girl. Natalie Benoit."

"She dropped out the same time he did," Willi said. "The talk around is that she went with him. She used to

work at the duty-free in the airport. She's no artist, she
might have left a trail. Natalie is your best bet."

"Who do you know that worked with her?"

"I know the top, darling. The Chinaman who owned
the franchise. He and I did a little business out of Hong
Kong. Not a bad sort as chinks go."

"Call him for me?"

"I'll do better than that," Willi said. "I'll have Freddie
run you over in my new Jaguar."

"You're sure it's no trouble?"

"None at all," Willi said. "The Jag is new, the twelve-
cylinder, and Freddie is mad to drive it. He takes any
opportunity."

"Where's Freddie now?"

"Didn't he go for coffee?"

"That was half an hour ago and the kitchen is downstairs. He had no reason to put on a jacket." Sullivan
drew his pistol and held it on Willi. "Tell me where
Freddie went," he said.

"You're not going to get sore?"

"Not if you tell me."

"There's a flyer out on you," Willi said. "Tender
regards from the powers that be. You're not to worry,
Jack, at the moment they want no harm to come to you.
They're fond of you and only want to know where you are
every minute."

"Who does?"

"You know the answer to that," Willi said. "Your old
pal, Peter Owen. He's very clever, Peter is. He got down
inside your mind, Jack, and because he knew what you
were looking for, he was able to guess where you'd go for
help."

"And he came up with you."

"I work a tiny corner," Willi said. "And keep it only by
their sufferance. Were I to displease them, their Excellen-
cies could do me like a mop does a puppy's piddle. One
swipe and poor Willi is gone, and not even a damp spot to
mark his time on this planet." He opened his hands and
closed them in a gesture of prayer. "Anytime at all, they
do the same to you, Jack."

"Where's Peter now?"

Willi shook his head. "A bit of piss on the carpet, that's

all we are," he said, glancing at his watch. "You've been here fifteen minutes. I reckon he's in the neighborhood by now."

Sullivan put away his pistol and left Willi, passing through the bar on his way to the street. Freddie was wiping glasses and stacking them, and never looked up, but did cause the muscles along his bare right arm to twitch, either by way of greeting or threat. Three European seamen were drinking German beer, a specialty of the Express, and with them were a pair of bar girls, as alike as sisters, a teenage pair picking at the change on the bar and doing a titless dance to the early American rock on the jukebox.

The green Chevrolet was at the curb, Owen's thug with the mashed ear leaning against it, his arms folded. Sullivan opened the door himself and joined Peter on the back seat.

"Shopping with Willi Wolfe? What's got into you?" Peter said. "Come to me with your questions. Or Kirk, if you must. We're all on the same side."

"And yet we seem to be opponents."

"I swear that's not true." Owen passed his hand over his face; he looked older than he had only a few hours ago, the lines of his face deeper.

"You look wrung out," Sullivan said.

"Part of it is this lousy climate," Peter said.

"You weren't made for the shady life, Peter."

"Yet here I am."

"You can quit."

"Is that what you've done?"

"No. Not yet," Sullivan said. "The Service is all I know, all I've got."

"I hope you don't quit," Peter Owen said. "If you do, I'll know it's because we're rotten. And I can't quit. I can't quit, and I can't go against you."

"I need to get things straight," Sullivan said. "It's become an obsession. I need to find out why I was double-crossed, and by whom."

"You want revenge?"

"I don't know," Sullivan said. "I won't know that until I get there."

"We're decent men," Peter Owen said. "I believe that,

and I swear I place it above everything else. Not saints,
perhaps not even terribly good. But decent." He swallowed hard and set his mouth. His face was white and
strained, as if it were about to crack. He struggled to hold
tight to himself, to keep from coming apart.

"What is it, Peter?"

"Things are out of control," he said. "I thought we
could handle it, but we can't. Webber is in Saigon. Do
you know him?"

"The Director's hatchet?"

"He still thinks it can be handled," Peter said. "Nyo
has been kissed off. He's got to go, if need be belly up.
And you nosing around, asking embarrassing questions
about the opium, will make someone decide you're best
dead. Do you understand, Jack? One of our own will kill
you. I won't hold still for that—if I have the courage—and
they'll have to kill me as well."

"So you want me out of Saigon?"

"I'll put you on to George Berry," Peter said. "He's in
Jamaica, Hotel Bellevue in Ocho Rios. A very nice place,
and you can find out more there than here."

"Will he know to expect me?"

Peter Owen nodded. "And to hold still until you get
there," he said.

Peter Owen dropped Sullivan at the Majestic and drove
off. He had been summoned to a meeting at the American
Embassy and was already late. Webber had called the
meeting, giving it a sense of urgency. But in his dry and
low-key manner he managed to suggest the same urgency
in all his activities. He was by nature a secretive man,
suited to his profession; he had no family, few friends,
certainly none outside the Service, and his only pastime
was sailing. But he even did that alone, in a small,
beautifully fitted skiff, which he kept in Chesapeake Bay.

He had flown into Saigon under a false passport, fitted
out in a disguise, and had himself driven directly from the
airport to the Embassy, where he stayed, hidden away in
a tiny room on the third floor, until a meeting could be
arranged at the Palace between him and Nyo. He took his
meals in the third-floor room, and even had a cot brought
in. He ate alone, cold sandwiches and Campbell's soup on

a tray on a beat-up steel desk, and slept on the canvas cot. He was a tall man, and Peter Owen imagined his feet dangling over the end of the cot. He understood Webber, the solitary meals eaten at a steel desk, the miserable nights in an airless room, tossing on a steel cot. He thought of him sailing alone on Chesapeake Bay. Peter Owen understood. Webber spoke so softly, and without moving his lips, that even seated next to him in the tiny room, one had to strain to hear his words. Webber had a terror of being overheard, perhaps of being heard at all.

Owen was afraid of Webber, but not for any harm he might cause him. It was a more primitive fear, deeper and more phobic, impossible to explain.

"I've just come from Nyo's office," Webber said. "He's a very stubborn man. Irrationally so, I thought. I wonder, did that occur to you?"

"That Nyo was crazy?" Kirk sat on the cot, sharing it with Peter Owen, and Webber was on the swivel chair at the steel desk, the remains of his lunch tray pushed to one side. There were no other chairs in the room, no furniture of any kind. "He's holding the line," Kirk said. "That's it with Nyo." He kept his elbows on his knees with his fingers laced and his chin on his thumbs. He was tightly wound; Webber was his superior, the Director's right hand, but Kirk was determined to fight for every inch, yield no more than he had to. "Nyo is tough," he said. "He's also straight. He's no thief. Nyo is a patriot."

"And a fanatic, as well as an incompetent," Webber said.

"You got all of that from one meeting?"

Peter Owen took a deep breath and held it. There wasn't a sound but the squeak of Webber's swivel chair. Insurrection was in the air, Owen smelled it, like a whiff of gunpowder.

Webber didn't react, his mild brown eyes steady. "It was a longish meeting," he said, "and I did think that Nyo was unnecessarily dogmatic, and not accessible to reasoned argument. Certainly, he wasn't thinking clearly."

"He doesn't trust us," Kirk said.

"Why is that?"

"Because we've lied to him."

Peter said, "We lied about Traung." He hadn't planned

to come down on Kirk's side or even thought about it one way or the other. It was done spontaneously, flat out, an act of loyalty which surprised and then exhilarated Peter Owen. "We've been in touch with Traung, negotiated with him, and then denied to Nyo that it ever happened."

Webber said, "That's not altogether accurate."

"You have met with Traung."

"And Nyo was told of it."

"Only of the meeting last November," Kirk said. "There was a second meeting—you and the Ambassador and Traung, last week in Bangkok."

Webber's eyes didn't waver, and not a muscle quivered in his long, pale face. "How did you find out about that?" he said.

"From Nyo, actually," Kirk said. "His people in Bangkok are pretty good."

"They must be," Webber said.

"Then it's true?"

"There were four of us at the meeting," Webber said. "State sent Packard. Did Nyo know about him?"

"He didn't say."

"It was the Secretary who sent him." Webber's voice was so low that both men were drawn closer to him. Their faces were only inches apart, Kirk and Owen together on the cot, and Webber on a swivel chair. "Packard spoke for the Secretary, and gave his word."

"His word?"

Now in whisper, "That our government was prepared to back Traung."

"In a coup?"

"We discussed only a change of government. Nothing was said of a coup." Webber had begun as an academic, and would end as one. The Director would see to it; a word to one of his friends, one of those whose money kept the universities solvent, and it would be done. "Our talks with Traung covered a wide range of subjects, and the possibility of change in government was only one of several issues touched upon. We expressed our confidence in him as a responsible leader and assured him of our support were he to become President."

"Traung makes a coup," Kirk said. "If he wins, we back him. It comes down to that."

"Not at all." Webber at last showed some emotion. "No one spoke of a coup. The word was never mentioned. I've told you that twice."

"Sure, but how else are you going to get Nyo's ass out of Saigon?" Kirk was deliberately vulgar, hectoring Webber. "That's one stubborn little son-of-a-bitch."

"Idealistic," Peter Owen said. "And yearning for martyrdom."

"Traung will help him there," Kirk said. "Traung will stick his little head on a pole right outside the Palace."

"There will be no coup," Webber said. "Nyo will resign and leave the country, creating a power vacuum. Traung simply moves to fill it."

"Nyo won't resign."

"That's what he says, but I don't believe him."

"I do."

"The army is with Traung, the air force as well. Nyo hasn't a prayer."

"He's been told that."

"Then he must leave."

"He won't."

"But it makes no sense."

"It never has." Peter Owen had been thinking of Sullivan. "Nyo isn't one to act simply in his own best interests. He'll do only what he feels compelled to do. He'll listen to his own conscience."

"Yes. Nyo and his rather overworked conscience," Webber said. "Fortunately, Traung isn't similarly burdened. He'll simply get on with the damned war, and we'll support him because that's best for us. You do see that our choice isn't between Traung and Nyo. It's between Traung and going home, giving up. So to stay with Nyo would be irresponsible. You are professionals, you do see that?" Webber let his words hang in the air, their sarcasm quivering like a knife in the wall above Kirk's head. "We are obliged to make the kind of choice which comes about in the real world. We must either do what is unpleasant or lose what is essential." The meeting was over.

Webber stood and started for the door of the cubicle. "Please see that Nyo is flown out, and his twenty million deposited in the Swiss account." His hand came to rest on the doorknob. "Turn the merchandise over to Nephew,

and see that your man in France brokers the sale. There
have been complaints from that end. People dragging
their feet."

Kirk remained seated on the cot, his elbows on his
knees, not quite ready to leave. "Just so I understand,"
he said. "Are you ordering me to turn the merchandise
over to Nephew?"

"I am."

Kirk glanced at Peter Owen. "You heard that?"

Owen nodded, and Webber managed a thin smile.
"Just try to get the lead out, you two," he said.

CHAPTER 12

Sullivan didn't fly directly to Jamaica. He entered the United States by way of San Francisco, checked into a hotel on Powell Street, and spent a week tending to business.

He rented a post office box, using that as a mailing address for an account he opened in the Bank of California. He next wired the Florida Bank, in which the Agency had been depositing his semimonthly checks, and had them send out a statement and a draft for $10,000. The draft went directly into his new account at the Bank of California, and the statement arrived two days later at his post office box. It showed a balance of just over $28,000 after the $10,000 debit.

He made out a check to cash for $5,000, and drew it against his California account. Then he went to Grant Street in search of General Han's brother-in-law, Loo Sim. The entrance to number 193 was actually off Grant, a six-story tenement at the head of a narrow alley. The street floor was given over to a shop peddling a better grade of tourist items, bolts of silk from mainland China, spices and herbs and jars of beauty preparations. The shop was run by a young woman, who was startled enough by Sullivan's slow but correct Mandarin to break down and tell him where Loo Sim lived: two flights up in the rear.

Loo Sim was as old as General Han, perhaps older, but sturdier and in far better condition. He was alert and moved quickly and was as scrappy as a city sparrow. His skin was dark for a Chinese, his rheumy eyes flat and watchful, and in the loose skin under them there grew nests of harmless little tumors, tiny, hairy things, like mold on stale bread. Sullivan knew to be polite, and to speak to him first in Mandarin. But he spoke it better than Loo Sim, and so Sullivan, who had a sure feel for matters of face, switched to English.

"Your brother-in-law sends his greeting," Sullivan said. "And his best wishes for your good health."

"Best wishes is easy," Loo Sim said. "Han send money?"

"Nothing was said of money."

"He owe me plenty."

"He said you were a very skillful man," Sullivan said. "That if I needed help, I should go to you."

"You need help?"

"I need a cold kit," Sullivan said. "Passport, driver's licence, social security card if the passport is American."

"You pay cash?"

"I'm not your brother-in-law."

"Either is Han," Loo Sim said. "That guy big blowhard. Call himself General, call himself my brother-in-law. One time I married his cousin. Very pretty girl until she lost her leg."

"How did she do that?"

Loo Sim closed his eyes, and when he opened them, the question was gone. "How much you pay for cold kit, passport American?" he said.

"A thousand dollars."

"For thousand dollars you get maybe Thai passport," Loo Sim said. "For that you need Thai face to put on it. American passport in San Francisco is mostly stolen. Stolen passport for dumb kid maybe."

"Then tell me how much."

"In China it is very serious when a woman loses her

leg," Loo Sim said. "That is because Chinese men are very sensitive."

"And wooden legs are expensive."

"These days very expensive."

"How much for the cold kit?"

"Three thousand."

"I'll pay two thousand five hundred," Sullivan said. "The passport has to be blank, straight from the printing office. Date of issue is to be put nine months back, and the serial numbers checked so that it matches the issue date. The name on it is Rainer, Alan Drew. Date of birth September 12, 1931, in Cleveland, Ohio."

Loo Sim had written it all down. "Entrance and exit stamps?"

"Rainer has been twice to Europe," Sullivan said. "France, Italy, England. He last re-entered the United States two months ago."

Loo Sim brought out a thirty-five millimeter camera and a strobe light. "Same face for Rainer?" he said. "No beard, nothing, Mr. twenty-five-hundred-dollar hot shit?"

"No beard. Take it as it is."

Loo Sim ran a roll of film. Sullivan gave him $1,250 and was promised the finished kit the next day.

He left Loo Sim and walked to North Beach. He was tense and eager to be on his way after Berry, but he knew not to go unprepared; he dare not go unarmed or without money, and the means to disappear. He wouldn't move without Loo Sim's untraceable passport. Alan Rainer had never existed, he was a name plucked from the air, given an identity by Sullivan. Rainer liked North Beach bars, where he drank beer and listened to the music. He smoked marijuana when it was offered. He was the right age. He had been to school. He looked like a Christian.

In one of the bars, he met a girl who told him a story about something that had happened to her in the street.

"These kids were playing baseball," she said, "and this little red-haired *momser*, he's like maybe a big eight, and wearing a baseball cap with a letter C on the front. You know what I'm talking about?"

"C, as in Chicago Cubs."

"Wait. That's right. Because I'm a nice lady, and a mother myself, I asked him if the letter C is for Cleveland or Chicago. And you know what he says? He says, 'No, it's for San Francisco.'"

"It's a good story."

"I notice you didn't fall down laughing. I suppose it's a better story than it is a funny story. Do you know what I'm talking about?"

She was tall, easily Sullivan's height, with fair hair in tight curls cropped close to her head, and small ears without lobes and a nose that turned up at the end. She wasn't pretty but there was something about her that made him lift his head. She knew it, and it made her lean toward Sullivan; she liked him, he was the kind of man for whom she came out at night. Her name was Terry.

"Short for Teresa," she said. "My family is Catholic, Italian on my mother's side, Polish on my father's."

She supplied details, an autobiography, so as not to be a girl in a bar. Sullivan helped her. "That's why you're blond," he said. "The Polish father."

He had made her happy. "I never saw you in here," she said. "I know just about everybody. Lord, I'm sorry to say it, but true is true. Do you trade, anything like that?"

"Nothing like that at all."

"I don't use drugs," she said. "I swear to God, not even aspirin. What about you?"

"Maybe once in a while a little grass."

"You said that as if you'd learned it by heart," she said. "I think you drink milk before you go to bed, and maybe eat a cupcake. What's your name?"

"Alan Rainer."

"You're not a cop, are you, Alan? A clean-cut cop?"

"Nothing like that."

"I wouldn't care," she said.

"I work on the oil rigs," he said. "The money is good and I get to travel."

"You could be a cop," she said. "I wouldn't care."

She took him to another place where they ate hamburgers and listened to a girl with shoulder-length black hair who played the guitar and sang ballads from the 1930s, songs of social protest, and others which were new, or at least new to him. He preferred the new ones, and was certain they were better, more truthful, and closer to the experience of the lovely girl who sang them.

But Sullivan knew very little about music, or any of the arts, although he did remember reading books of poetry and fiction when he was a boy. He remembered not only the books, but the act of reading itself, lying on his stomach on a Chinese rug in a corner of his mother's bedroom.

"You do like the music," Terry had been watching him. "Except you look like you've never heard any of it before."

"What's the girl's name?"

"Joan Baez."

"She's very good."

"How old are you?"

"Thirty-one."

"Across the great divide," Terry said. "I know there's something just a little off about you, but I can't put my finger on it. Baez and all the rest of it is your scene, but it's new to you. You should have been there from the beginning, if you know what I mean."

"I missed out," he said.

"Have you been in jail, like that?"

"First a cop, now a jailbird."

"Then how is it you missed out?"

"I was out of the country," he said. "Working on the oil rigs."

"Where was that?"

"Indochina."

"I thought Americans couldn't go to China."

"Indochina is different than China. It's made up of countries like Vietnam and Laos."

"Is it nice?"

"Parts of it are."

"I'd like to go sometime. I really would. My family were all seamen, at least on my mother's side they were. Wayback as far as the Romans, probably. That's why I've got travel in my blood. Itchy feet, Dave used to call it."

"Who's Dave?"

"Dave? Dave is this guy I used to be married to. He went back east to Detroit to get a job. Detroit or Cleveland, one of them. It's not a bad job, though. I heard from him Christmas, when he sent a check for the Little Bastard. He's his father, you see."

"How old is your son?"

"Two in April," she said. "I call him the Little Bastard, but it's all in fun, really it is. It's a term of endearment."

"Does he live with you?"

"Absolutely. He's got a room of his own, toy cars, stuffed animals, the whole bit. I love him, and I'm a good mother. Maybe not Mother of the Year, but good as possible under the circumstances."

They went to another club and had more to drink. He switched from beer to Scotch, but drank too slowly for it to have much effect. Sometime after midnight, she invited him to her place, out on Geary Boulevard near Golden Gate Park. Her car was a few years old, and not in the best of shape, but it was a car, and she lived on a handsome street in one of a row of attached houses, each with a porch and a little garden. She didn't seem concerned about getting up and going to work in the morning, and she hadn't married money, and there was no reason to think she had been born to any. Sullivan drank, fooled, listened to music, but never forgot to wonder where the money came from.

He waited in the kitchen, while in the parlor Terry added up the hours the babysitter had stayed and calculated how much she owed her. Sullivan was thinking again of George Berry, who called distrust the disease of spies, and faith the miraculous cure. Looking through the kitchen window at the backyard with a sandbox and a jungle gym Sullivan remembered thinking at the time that the disease would never infect him. He was too clever, too sure of being able to hold his soul in his hands, to warm it with his breath, and shape it as he chose. He had been wrong—arrogant and wrong. He had become a spy, a solitary, set incurably in the ways of distrust.

When the babysitter was paid and the door locked behind her, Terry took Sullivan on a tour of the apartment. She was quite proud of it; she had painted it and built the bookshelves and some of the furniture. She showed him her spotless kitchen and put on a kettle of water for tea. She had three kinds of cookies, each in its own airtight jar. She showed him the parlor, a long Victorian room with ceiling moldings and a fireplace, and a couch that opened into a bed. They had tea and listened to records. They kissed and, without any talk at all, she began to get the room ready for the night, pulling shades and drawing curtains, even seeing that the clock was wound and turning down the lights.

The last thing she did was to take a baby bottle from the refrigerator and set it to warm in a saucepan of water.

"The Little Bastard gets hungry just about this time," she said. "And then he's got to be changed."

The one bedroom had been made into a nursery. There was a playpen, a blackboard· on an easel, and toys scattered all around. The baby was sleeping on his side in his crib, his legs drawn up and the covers twisted around his ankles. He was restless and fussing in his sleep. Terry patted him to see if he was dry, and when he wasn't, she quickly and expertly changed him, so that he never fully woke up. When he was dry she rocked him in her arms and fed him from the warmed bottle until he was sound asleep, and ready to be laid on his stomach in the crib.

"What's his name?"

"Mark."

"Call him that, then," Sullivan said.

She wanted to shower before they made love, and he hung away his clothes and wore a terrycloth robe she gave him. He browsed in her books and examined her framed photographs. He even glanced inside her closets and bureau drawers. He needed to know more about her. He wasn't prepared for the loneliness that had come on him so unexpectedly. He stood in the doorway of the darkened nursery and took a deep breath, inhaling the smells of warm milk and Johnson's baby powder. He listened to the sound of Terry's shower and imagined her under it. Alan Rainer's passport would be ready tomorrow; he'd be leaving for Jamaica tomorrow.

He rapped on the bathroom door and called out to Terry above the shower spray. She opened the door, drew the shower curtain, and let him in. They soaped and fondled each other, carrying that playfulness to her daybed in the parlor. Their lovemaking became serious only much later in the night, after they had gone off to sleep and he woke locked in her arms, one heavy leg of hers flung over his back. It was a deep and slow love they

had, a love of silence, of faces and places dredged from
the bottom of the mind.

She woke when the baby cried, but he slept on, and
woke dreaming of the forest, of the pine cones and needles that covered the ground, of their fragrance, and of
waking to the first light filtering through the tops of the
trees. He saw the mountains in the Shan, and the snow at
their summits, and leopard tracks in the snow.

Terry had left a toothbrush and razor on the table next
to the bed, and when Sullivan joined her and Mark in the
kitchen, he was already shaved and dressed.

He played with Mark, while she fried eggs and bacon.

"Is there a number I can call for a cab?" he said.

"I'll drive you downtown," she said. "No cab will come
out this far."

"There's a Geary bus. I can take that."

She served his breakfast and took the baby, sitting him
on her lap. Sullivan broke off a piece of bacon and asked
if he could give it to him.

"Have you kids of your own?" she said. "I only wonder
because you knew to ask before you gave Mark the
bacon."

"No kids. No wife."

"You could one day," she said. "You're temperamen-
tally suited."

"Does Dave ever visit?"

"No. Only the check Christmas."

"How do you get by? Have you a job?"

"I'm an RN. Registered nurse. I make out nicely, and
work pretty much my own hours."

"I'm relieved to hear it."

"Why is that?"

"I just am. I want to know you and Mark are in good
shape."

She didn't keep coffee and had brewed tea, fine
Darjeeling tea, as good as any he had ever tasted.

"Will you be back?" she said.

"If only for the tea."

"You're a very charming man when you want to be,"
she said. "And with a talent for making difficult situations
just a little easier. But the truth is you're on your way
someplace else, and you won't be back."

"No, I won't."

"Are you going far?"

"Yes."

"Would it do any good to ask where?"

"I've got errands to do." He remembered old Loo Sim closing his eyes to a question and opening them after it had gone.

"I just hope you don't get hurt," she said. "I won't know, because I probably won't see you again. And that's a pity because you're very sweet."

He said good-bye after breakfast. The morning was cold, blustery, and wet, and he hadn't a coat or hat. He waited half an hour on Geary Boulevard for the bus, his only shelter under the branches of a tree, a solitary man shivering with his hands in his pockets on a windy suburban street.

He warmed up a bit in the bus, but the loneliness that had come so suddenly the night before came again. His face reflected in the bus window was older. Life had narrowed, taken on a single direction, and he wondered why that was so. He searched the other faces in the bus. They had no need to set things right. Why had he? What hand had wound him up and set him running?

He left the bus at Van Ness and walked north to California, where he caught the cable car near Loo Sim's shop on Grant. But the old Chinese had gone out. The girl who minded the shop invited Sullivan to wait there. It was a quiet day, the rain kept down the tourists, but a few did come in to browse and Chinese dropped in to visit with the girl. Sullivan gathered she was a niece of Loo Sim, possibly a goddaughter.

Sullivan was content in the shop. He took a local Chinese paper and read it slowly. He bought a small cigar and smoked it with a cup of tea the girl gave him. He thought of Terry and the child, and how simple life could be, and how pleasant in ordinary ways.

He was there almost an hour when Loo Sim looked in, glanced at Sullivan, who followed him up the stairs to his studio.

The passport was perfect, the numbers, the seal, everything just so. Loo Sim was an artist.

"Twelve hundred and fifty dollars." Sullivan counted it

out, and took back the negatives from the roll of film Loo
Sim had shot earlier. "The girl told me that every morning
around this time you go to the horse parlor to make your
bets."

"You play ponies?"

"I invest in the stock market."

"Electronics, sure thing," Loo Sim said. "Buy RCA,
buy Zenith."

Sullivan walked back to his hotel. He emptied his safe
deposit box, packed his bag, and paid his bill. In the cab
to the airport, he had another look at Alan Rainer's
passport.

He had enough cash for a start. That and the passport
were all he needed. He thought of the breakfast in Terry's
kitchen, of the ordinary people coming in and out of Loo
Sim's shop while he smoked a cigar and read the Chinese
papers.

In the end he put Alan Rainer's passport in a safe place
and bought a one-way coach ticket to Miami. It was his
best connection to Jamaica, to George Berry.

CHAPTER 13

Marcel had insisted on meeting in a restaurant in Les Halles, which turned out to be crowded and uncomfortable. Then he came late, which annoyed Castellone, who had made it a point to be on time.

"Why did you pick this damn place anyway?" he said.

"The hamburgers are like New York," Marcel said. "Like Clarke's. And all the movie crowd come here."

"Is that why you showed up with a comic entourage?" Castellone said. "Today you reconcile with your father, a great scene to go before the cameras. We have to discuss how you are to play it, and that's best not done before witnesses."

"Antoine is my assistant."

Castellone glanced further along the crowded bar, where Antoine, who was a head taller than everyone else and dressed all in leather with little fringes dangling from him like an American Indian, was talking to a faded blond woman in a luxurious mink coat, the second member of Marcel's entourage.

Castellone said, "Since you have no business or work of any kind, and are in hock to everyone, what does your assistant do?"

133

"Antoine talks to Marilyn," Marcel said. "So that you and I are left alone."

"She's rich, eh?"

Marcel gasped and shook his hand as if he had just touched a red-hot stove. "The father is Appollo," he said. "You know Appollo, the spark plug? It is sold all over the world, particularly in South America. My dear friend, we are speaking of perhaps two hundred million in dollars."

Marilyn looked over, perhaps sensing that she was being talked about. Marcel wiggled his fingers at her, and showed that charming smile in which his mouth curled up at the ends, the same smile which had kept him clothed and fed for so long. Antoine continued to glance at his own reflection in the gilt mirror behind the bar.

"She's crazy about you," Castellone said.

"Yes, apparently."

"You don't seem happy about it," Castellone said. "She's not bad, you know."

"For two hundred million, she is gorgeous."

"She's prettier than Aurora."

"Aurora was a fiend," Marcel said. "She tried to run me down in her husband's car."

"Does Marilyn have a husband?"

"Not at the moment. She has had two. The last was a bum she picked up in a Rome bar. Like all Calabrese, his dream was to immigrate to America. So Papa Appollo bought them a mansion in Beverly Hills for a million. All day this miserable Calabrese sat around the swimming pool with his tattooed arms, and at night went out looking for starlets. He was finally bought off with the house and a hamburger franchise."

Marilyn was again looking in their direction; she did not grow angry at being neglected, only more watchful. Marcel appeased her by going over, patting and kissing her, and lighting her cigarette with a lingering and soulful look, finally rejoining Castellone farther along the bar.

"She's a good skate," Castellone said. "Patient and probably quite loyal. Behind the varnish, it's possible to see the poor little rich girl."

"But too eager, and with the natural arrogance of the rich, a genetic defect, like being unable to clot one's blood." Marcel spoke only to Castellone and without moving his lips, looking straight at Marilyn along the bar, his charming smile always in place. "The heiress to two hundred million," he said. "And with her I can't get a decent hard-on." He winked and wiggled his fingers in Marilyn's direction, but continued in an undertone to Castellone. "When my father kicked me out, I decided to go into this line of work only after taking careful stock of my assets. I was objective. I concluded that I was not bad looking, perhaps not of movie star caliber, but certainly attractive."

"You're reasonably intelligent," Castellone said.

"But when I'm with her and I feel a little stirring, and I think that everything will be fine, she turns those sad, pleading eyes on me," Marcel said. "What follows is pure fiasco. Tell me, Bernard, you're a man whose views I respect. Has it ever happened to you?"

"Certainly."

"And what did you do?"

"I made a joke of it. Once I even turned it into a kind of game."

"Game? What sort of game?"

"I told the girl to sing a little song, a cheerful one. Another girl I told to pray. So she warmed the poor little fellow in her hands and recited the Lord's Prayer."

"Did it work?"

"Not exactly. But for a time, it distracted us both."

The headwaiter at last appeared with the welcome news that their table was ready. Castellone was famished, and all during the conversation had been thinking mostly about his lunch. Now Marcel insisted he order hamburger.

"The hamburger is delicious," Marilyn said. "Exactly like Clarke's in New York. And all the movie crowd is here."

Marcel patted and smoothed her hair.

"I don't like hamburger," Antoine said.

"Even so, it's possible to like New York," Marilyn said.

Marcel turned halfway around in his chair, facing away from Marilyn, and whispered to Castellone, "How much money do you think my father is worth?"

"Achille Piri? Ten million without the slightest doubt."

"It could be more," Marcel said. "He was always

careful with his money. In fact, a cheapskate. Every place he went, he made sure there were people to pick up the check. While he had old Rocco to drive the car, he dressed himself like a fruit seller on his day off. His only indulgence was silk underwear—wealth was a secret to be guarded from one's enemies, and one took down one's pants only in the dark. Of course my poor mother was obliged to scrub floors, and I went around with holes in my socks."

"Remember that he's your father, and you're the only son," Castellone said. "Think of the ten million, and not the holes in your socks."

"Is he really sick?"

"He's dying."

"You know, I can't believe it. I can't imagine a world without him. He fills the world, the old bastard. I say that, but I don't want to see him weak and old." Marcel's eyes suddenly filled with tears. "I don't know how it'll be when I finally see him."

"You only have to ask him to forgive you. Kiss his hand in the old style. That's the way to get around him."

"I'm scared stiff," Marcel said. "I couldn't sleep a wink. My nerves are shot, but I don't know why. He's an old man, dying, and with no power over me. None at all, and yet just the thought of him puts butterflies in my stomach."

"Remember only that you're his son, his only son. Remember that he loves you, in spite of everything. Do as I say, kiss his hand, and above all don't act like snot."

Marilyn said, "What are you two whispering about?"

"Nothing at all, my darling." Marcel hugged her and kissed her cheek. "See how she is, always worried about me," he said. "But nothing is wrong. My dear friend Bernard reminded me of a poem I wrote as a boy. A scrap of a thing, but I was touched that my dear friend should have remembered it." He slapped Castellone's cheek affectionately. "Ah, the vain dreams of our youth."

The lunch went well after that. Marcel was in such good spirits, he ordered champagne, at the same time confiding in Castellone that he hadn't the cash to pay his rent. When the bill came, he nudged Marilyn under the table, and laid his open palm in her lap. She ignored that, smiling across the table with her eyes sparkling, flirting with Castellone while polishing off her champagne. The daughter of Appollo Spark Plugs did not pay for un-delivered merchandise. Castellone raised his glass in her honor, and was rewarded with a conspiratorial wink and the bill for lunch. Before leaving with Antoine, Marilyn pressed his hand and slipped into it a note with her phone number.

Of course none of this was lost on Marcel. "I could see that you made an impression," he said. "It's the rugged look, she wants to try that. If you're any good at all, you can be assured of at least a steel Rolex with gold trim." Marcel smiled wickedly. "It's the model considered ap-propriate reward for ski instructors."

On the way out, he borrowed ten francs from Cas-tellone, folded it into his handshake with the *capitaine*, and continued through the door in excellent spirits.

Castellone had returned the Citroen and hired another car, a Peugeot 504. He changed cars every few days, so none became too familiar.

He drove with Marcel along the Champs-Elysées and around the Etoile onto avenue de la Grande-Armeé in the direction of Neuilly, where old Achille Piri lived.

"When I was a kid there was no villa in Neuilly," Marcel said. "A cockroach palace on the rue de Poitou was good enough."

"Put the bitterness aside," Castellone said. "You've got to put yourself in the right frame of mind."

"But I hate him. At times it simply swells up inside of me, and I can't control it."

"You were in such a good mood in the bar," Castellone said. "Try to be as you were then—charming and insin-cere. You need that kind of nerve to carry it off with your father."

"I don't want to see him," Marcel said. "Without him, I'm my own man. I have my self-respect, even playing the gigolo. It may sound absurd to you, but only free of that old bastard am I able to breathe."

"Do you want me to turn the car around?"

"You went to a lot of trouble. I know what this deal means to you."

"Turn around or not?" Castellone said. "Tell me what you want to do."

Marcel was silent, sliding low in the seat, making himself small, with his arms folded across his chest, a far cry from the debonair figure in the bar. "It scares me to see him again," he said. "I know he'll try to humiliate me. When he threw me out, he told me it was the end of us. He said I disgusted him. I was a faggot, his own son."

"Yes, but now he's dying, and you're still his son. He wants to take you back."

"You want me to be the Marcel of the bar, the Marcel who borrows ten francs to tip the headwaiter. But don't you see that none of that matters, none of it is real. Me and the old man, that's real. Do you know what I mean, Bernard?"

"I had a father, too."

"What happened to you when he died?"

"To me? Nothing. He died, that was all."

"Did you grieve? What about guilt? Or maybe you were relieved. He was your father—you once loved him—so when he died, what did you feel?"

"I don't remember. But I sent him money regularly," Castellone said. "A check every month, arranged through a bank in Geneva."

"A good son."

"You don't think so?" Castellone said. "I did what was right. What the hell is all this about anyway?"

"Tell me what it's like to give money to your father?" Marcel said.

"Now I see what you're driving at," Castellone said. "From the son to the father, instead of in the other direction. You're not a simple guy, are you Marcel? And surely not such a buffoon."

"I'll be a buffoon again." Marcel spoke in an even voice, without a trace of self-pity. "You'll see me perform at Neuilly, at my father's bedside. And when he finally dies, you'll see a performance then."

Achille Piri lived at the end of a cul-de-sac, in a house set back from the street and hidden behind trees and bushes. There was a locked iron gate, opened for them by Rocco, long Achille's chauffeur and bodyguard.

He stared for several seconds at Marcel, as if trying to

make up his mind about something, and then he howled
and shouted out something, and ran at him as if he were
going to tear him apart. But it wasn't anger. Not at all. He
was nearsighted or had only just recognized him, and
wanted to hug Marcel and kiss him on the mouth.

"This little bastard," he said. "I used to change his
diapers."

"Rocco is my father's trusted friend."

"And yours, too," Rocco said. "Although there were
times I wanted to kick your ass." He turned to Castellone.
"He was a sickly child, and with skin dark as an Arab.
Rest her soul, his mother used to rub milk over his body
to bleach it."

"Goat's milk."

"And who had to carry the milk from the market?
Rocco. Rocco, the donkey."

As he led them toward the house, a pair of Great Danes
came bounding up, sniffing the strangers and leaping all
over Rocco, who threw a stick for them to fetch.

"You remember old Tarzan?"

"Yes, the first dog we had."

"These are his grandchildren," Rocco said. "A re-
markable dog, Tarzan. At twelve years, which is eighty-
four in the life of a man, he was able to make it stand up
like an iron pole."

"The same will be said of you, Uncle."

"It is in God's hands," he said, thumping his chest with
the flat of his hand. "I'm the same age as your father."
Rocco was short and broad, with a wide neck and thick
shoulders. He never wore an overcoat, even on the
coldest day, and now he was in a cotton shirt, the sleeves
rolled over his brawny arms. "Your father and I come
from the same village. He always looked after me, and
now I look after him."

"How is he feeling?"

Rocco shook his head. "He's not like he was," he said.
"The doctors say he's finished, but they could be wrong.
He was always careful with his health, and he comes from
a long-lived family."

"What exactly do the doctors say?"

"That he'll be dead by the summer."

The house was smaller than Castellone thought, judging by the grounds. It was modestly done, with old-fashioned furniture and solid things made by hand. There were several excellent carpets and some silver pieces, but nothing ornate, and nothing in any way pretentious. As Marcel had said, Achille Piri was never one to flaunt his wealth or draw attention to himself.

Rocco led Marcel upstairs to his father's bedroom, and Castellone was left alone in the sitting room, which also served as a library. The books were in Italian as well as French, all bound, and of the kind which nobody reads. The television set was the very latest and best, fitted with remote control, and set before a well-worn armchair next to a table with a humidor of Cuban cigars that smelled heavenly. Castellone would have liked to smoke one, but restrained himself.

"The old man was happy to see him." In spite of his bulk and age, Rocco had entered the room without making a sound. Thirty years ago he must have been formidable, and even now one would not like to tangle with him. "He loves the boy, no matter what. It's the blood, eh?"

"You and Don Achille have been together since the beginning?"

"Sure, I told you we were kids together from the same village," Rocco said. "The funny thing is we started as enemies. We always fought. Like two young bulls, we tested ourselves."

"Who was best?"

"In those days, I was." Rocco said it without pride, but with a certain heaviness in his voice. He glanced at the armchair opposite the television, but sat elsewhere. That chair belonged to old Piri, to his master. "I was the stronger," he said. "He had the brains and I had the muscle."

"He was known as a very clever man."

"A fox. Even now, old and sick, he's the same—wily as a fox." He was silent a moment, and then said, "Castellone, were your people from the south?"

"Just above Naples."

"Do you speak the language?" He had switched to Italian.

"Yes, of course."

"Tell me, do you think my Don will die?"

"I'm afraid so. At least I've been told that by people who have spoken to his doctors."

"I hear the same." He took a deep breath, and in the silent room, Castellone heard it rattle around in Rocco's broad chest, like the plumbing in an old house. "At this moment I'm dying for a cigarette," he said.

"I don't have one," Castellone said.

"No, I gave them up," Rocco said. "It's a sacrifice. You understand. I put it alongside my prayers for him, to show that I was serious."

"Whose cigars are those?"

"His. You can have one if you wish."

Castellone shook his head. "Perhaps there'll be a miracle," he said.

"Do you believe in miracles?"

"No. They always turn out to be something else." Then he said, "Has the Don seen to your old age?"

"I told you we've been friends since boyhood. He knows I'm loyal always."

"And what will you do?"

"Go home. I have a house. My sister is a widow. I let her live in it and she looks after it for me. I'll be well looked after."

For the next half hour Rocco entertained Castellone in the cellar, where he stored the vegetables and fruit which he grew on the grounds, and the wines, which were in oak barrels. They tasted the wine, a pure grappa made from grapes from the Abruzzi.

"They're taking a long time upstairs," Castellone said.

"The Don has his secrets." Rocco tapped the side of his nose and tried to look crafty, although his face was flushed from the wine. "He's telling the son where the money is buried. Gold coins. That's all he cared about. Solid gold coins that he buried like a squirrel."

"I got a hunch you know where they're hidden."

"Maybe I do."

"You're an old fox yourself, Rocco."

"Not such a fox, like the Don."

"Would he put it in a bank vault?"

"The Don? Never."

"Then around the house," Castellone said. "Maybe

right under where we're standing."

"You think I should get shovel?" Rocco said. "What do you say we have ourselves a nice look."

"We got to wait for him to die."

"He don't die so easy."

"Then we have to be patient."

"You think the fairy son will be patient?"

"I think you'll keep your eye on him."

"How about another glass of the grappa?" Rocco refilled their glasses. "You're okay, Castellone. The Don told me you were a real tough guy. Smooth, but a good hand. How many people have you killed?"

"Thirty-one."

"How old are you?"

"Forty-two."

Rocco patted his back. "A good start. Thirty-one. You still got your best years ahead of you."

"Like your hard-on, it's in God's hands," Castellone said.

Marcel's leather heels made a racket on the uncovered wooden steps to the cellar.

"He looks terrible," Marcel said. "He must have lost fifty pounds, and he's yellow. His skin, the whites of his eyes."

"It's in his liver."

"I think I cheered him up, though," Marcel said. "At least he said he was happy to see me."

"He was happy all right," Rocco said.

"He wants to talk to you," Marcel said to Castellone. "He wants to thank you for arranging it."

Castellone had never dealt directly with Achille Piri, never even set eyes on him, contacting him indirectly, through intermediaries. Piri insisted on that. It was one of the ways he protected himself from the law as well as assassination.

Castellone couldn't imagine the man he must have been. Propped up on pillows in the center of an immense four-poster bed, there was only a head, fleshless as a skull, with dry yellow skin drawn over the protruding bones. Only the eyes were alive, and they were huge and luminous, a shade lighter than Marcel's, and calm, oddly so. Death had hold of old Piri, and he knew it; it was there in those watchful black eyes. But he seemed to look at it squarely, without terror. Death was another enemy, another betrayer, but one against which he would have no chance to take his revenge.

Marcel introduced Castellone to his father, who weakly gestured that he was to come closer.

"I can only whisper," he said and took Castellone's hand. "I want to thank you for bringing me and my son together."

His hand was hard, and smooth as wax, although ice cold, as if he were already dead. But there was still strength in his bony fingers. He clutched Castellone's hand and held tight. "What you did was a good thing," he said. "It doesn't matter that you did it in order to earn a favor in return. There's no fault to be found with that. It's how the world is."

"You did a favor for both of us," Marcel said. "For the family."

"I have this one son." Achille Piri was able to smile, but with a certain malice. Marcel was conciliatory, as he had promised, even kissing the old man's ass, perhaps with sincerity. Yet, Piri, with that wicked toothless smile, could whisper, "One son only. Not much, but all God gave to me."

"You'd better hold your tongue," Marcel said. "God can hear even your whisper. He's close now."

"Along with the Angel of Death?"

"You're an old man. Old and sick."

"He wants me dead," Piri said. "The Angel of Death. You heard it."

"I want you to be peaceful. A kind of bliss, if you know what I mean," Marcel said. "If I knew how, I'd prove it to you. All of my sympathy is with you. Even my love. In spite of everything, my love, too."

"He wants my money," Piri said. "You heard him—in spite of everything. He said it. All he wants is my money."

"I'm Catholic," Marcel said. "The same as you, and as my mother. So I believe your soul is immortal, the same as mine. Don't you see? I have to love you and make peace, because we'll meet again."

Castellone said, "Don Achille, your time is short."

Marcel pulled his chair closer to his father's bed and took his hand. "We've got to make it up," he said.

Achille Piri turned his eyes on his son. Distrust was ingrained in him. He had prowled in the dark all his life, suspicious and on guard. This distrust was in his black eyes, and something else, a hint of mockery. Marcel was a faker, not to be trusted, but he was no threat, not so much a menace as a clown. The old man looked at his son with contempt. He liked to tease him, to dangle money in front of Marcel, who was always in desperate need of it. It was a secret this teasing, and a vice, which caused a delicious little spasm whenever old Piri thought of it. Castellone saw through the dying man, straight to the malice in his soul.

"Castellone, you be the judge. Is my son here for my money?" Piri's voice was stronger, and his spirits better. Baiting Marcel had temporarily restored his strength. "Well, Castellone, what about it?"

"He's your son and you're rich," Castellone said. "It's natural enough for him to have his eye on your money."

"You say that's natural?"

"As natural as for you to want to keep it."

Piri found that funny; his thin laugh made a dry rustling sound. "And he'll get it, Castellone. He'll get it all right. But because of you. You see, he also owes you a favor, see if you can make him pay."

"It's you who'll pay."

"Will I? Why is that?"

"Because I've done you a favor as well," Castellone said. "And you're the kind who must honor his debts."

"Don't be so sure. I could easily change my mind, or just say thank you, shake hands, and let it go at that." He was laughing again, the same thin rustling sound. He liked to tease others, to make them squirm. Even if he intended to pay, he first made one dance. He liked his money's worth.

"It's the opium, isn't it?" he said. "A large shipment from Indochina. You see, I know. I lie here, never moving, but I know what's going on."

"I want you to distribute it."

"Do you? And how much is being brought in?"

"Twenty kilos. All of it number four, direct from the Triangle."

"Then you are taking about fifteen million in dollars."

"More like twenty."

"I'm not big enough for such a shipment," Piri said. "I say it modestly, my syndicate is the biggest, but not big enough to buy twenty kilos of number four."

"It will require the cooperation of the syndicates."

"The syndicates work together? That's your problem right there. The syndicates look to cut each other's throat, not work together and make a profit."

"But you have the respect of all the bosses," Castellone said. "That's why I come to you."

"It could be done," Piri said. "Sometimes they listen, if the pie is big enough."

"Twenty million," Castellone said.

"A nice fat pie it makes," Piri said. "You know what? In my life only money has kept all its promises." He raised himself up, and Marcel was quick to stuff an extra pillow under his head. "Tell me about your twenty kilos, Castellone," Piri said.

"It will be put down in France."

"You can do that?"

"Delivery will be made in Paris."

"And how much of an advance do you want?"

"Nothing. Not a franc."

"Twenty kilos of number four delivered in Paris," Piri said. "That's a good trick." He motioned for Marcel to give him a cigarette and waited until he had lit it for him. "I know who built your factory in the Triangle, who flew the chemists in and out. The Americans. Not American Mafiosi. Not at all." Old Piri was proud of his few words of English. "Real Americans, not lousy wops like you and me." He laughed so hard he almost choked, and Marcel had to take away the cigarette and run for a glass of water.

"Papa doesn't like the Americans," Marcel said.

"They stink on ice, the Americans."

"How about the Germans, Papa? You like Germans?"

"They're worse than Americans."

It was a game, something that went back to Marcel's

childhood. "Papa, what do you think of the English?"

Old Piri held his nose.

"Papa doesn't like the French either."

"The French? That's the worst of the lot."

"Who do you trust, Don Achille?"

"My money." He patted the mattress. "I trust my money, because only my money has kept all of its promises."

He was laughing so hard he had to go to the toilet. Marcel helped him out of bed and half carried him to the bathroom, but the old man couldn't stand at the bowl by himself or open the buttons on his pajama pants, so Marcel had to do that for him, and hold him up while he struggled to pass his water.

"Now you got to wait a minute while I shake it," old Piri said. "I don't like the last few drops to wet my leg. It feels cold."

Marcel looked over his shoulder at Castellone. "It feels cold," he said.

"Hey, big shot," old Piri said to his son. "Maybe you shake it for me."

"You can shake it yourself."

"You think so? If you love me, you can shake it."

"What if I don't shake it?"

"Then you don't love me."

Marcel shrugged and said, "In for a nickel, in for a dime." He took his father's penis between his thumb and index finger, shook it daintily, and then tapped the head as if flicking an ash from a cigarette. He even buttoned his pajama pants, and led him back to bed and tucked him in.

"It takes all my strength just to pee." Piri motioned Castellone to sit next to him on the bed. "I want to tell you a big secret about life." He took hold of Castellone's hand, held tight with his cold bony fingers. "Marcel, what if I adopt this one? You want a brother, an older brother, when you get out of line he kicks your ass."

Castellone managed to free his hand from the old man's cold grip. "All I need, Don Achille, is permission to call the other syndicates together in your name."

"I got it!" Piri said. "Now I remember the big secret, it's about how to live your life. Listen carefully. You have to be fair. That means distrust everybody the same.

Distrust everybody, you get along with everybody, and you make money with everybody. But that don't go for Americans. Americans you got to distrust more than everybody. You know why? Because with Americans, it's not always money. Sometimes it's politics. The wind blows this way, it's yes. It blows that way, it's no. You see what I mean, Castellone? The Americans bring you so close, they let you get a good whiff. Money is like pussy, you want to get down on your knees and give it a nice kiss, but at the last second the Americans always yank it away."

"The American part is finished," Castellone said. "They have no more to do with it."

"Don't be so sure," Piri said. "They got a long arm, the Americans."

Marcel said, "We need to call the other syndicates in your name."

"You're in, too?" Piri said. "Castellone, you put my son in a good spot?"

"He can be rich."

"When I die, he'll be rich."

"May you live forever, Don Achille."

"I'm tired now." He closed his eyes. "I used to have a lot of fun," he said.

"Many more years, Papa."

"The hell with it."

"You'll live a long time yet."

"Sure, the same to you." He was falling asleep. "My sincere blessing. Call the syndicates in my name and the same blessing from me to you."

CHAPTER 14

The Americans have a long arm. Castellone thought of old Piri as he had said it: the warning finger, like the claw of a chicken, and the crafty and malevolent squint. The Americans did have a long arm; the old gangster might be half cracked, but he certainly wasn't stupid.

Castellone sensed a shift in the American mood. It was nothing he could put his finger on, nothing he could document. He had simply stopped trusting them. But it was not directed at any one man, not at George Berry, at Peter Owen, or Kirk, or even at those powerful figures above them in the shadows. It wasn't just the Americans he distrusted, or the British or the French. It was all of them. It was the nature of the work they did. The nature of the work he did.

He needed to find out what was going on, and the best way to do that was through Balzac. But no one in the field ever contacted Balzac at headquarters directly. It simply wasn't done, a matter of etiquette as much as secrecy.

He got to Balzac by way of Albert, the concierge at the Florida Hotel on the rue de Berri, just off the Champs-Elysées. Castellone kept a room at the Florida, although he seldom slept in it, but used the hotel safe, which was probably the best of any in Paris, a custom five-tumbler system made in England by Chubb.

In 1936, Albert had been champion of France in the épée, but went on to lose a leg blowing a German railroad switching station in Norway with the OAS. He had a decent pension, a comfortable nest egg acquired by skimming the rich profits of the shady currency traders who, in the decade following the war, needed ready access to the Chubb safe. He continued to work as night concierge at the Florida because he claimed to have been an insomniac for so long that he had lost the habit of sleep, although when Castellone appeared with a suitcase three nights after his meeting with Piri, he found Albert with his feet up, sound asleep at his desk; the truth was that Albert was the sort who needed at least a sense of adventure, and even more he needed intrigue, he needed the secrets and dark exchanges of the Florida, and he needed to play at the hushed second life of a spy.

"Traveling again, eh Castellone?" he said, taking Castellone's key from its hook. "You're looking tired, my friend. And certainly old enough to settle down."

"Marvelous trip. Rome was never lovelier."

"The weather was pleasant?"

"Perfect every day. Sunshine, clear skies, and just a little nip in the air."

"I saw in the *Tribune* where it rained for three days."

"Did it?"

It was a game they played; Albert to pry, and Castellone to lay down false trails. But Castellone wasn't much interested; he yawned and rubbed the stubble on his chin, and mumbled something about wanting a bath, a shave, and a few hours' sleep.

"I have a Yugoslav in 311," Albert said. "And on the fifth floor, a fancy Hungarian bugger. Leapfrog with the lift boy, and custom shoes outside the door. Sound like anybody we know?"

"Search me."

"Marcel Piri."

"Marcel's not Hungarian," Castellone said.

"He's in Paris to be with his dying father. I hear you three had a nice chat."

"Bless you," Castellone said. "You're a good spy."

"I get the job done," Albert said in English.

Castellone leaned across the concierge's desk and lowered his voice, although there was no one else in the darkened lobby. "It's low-grade stuff," he said. "My friend, I need a favor."

"A snooping favor? Discretion called for. Bureaucrats outwitted by one-legged currency smuggler?"

"I need a sitdown with Balzac. Get me the old darling, Albert. Do Cupid's work."

Castellone took the lift to his room, slept a few hours, had a long bath, and was shaving when Albert knocked.

"Our friend was feeling cranky," he said. "Or at least Mademoiselle Joyce was. Do you know Mademoiselle Joyce? She does his appointments."

"You did get through?"

"Eventually. Did you know Balzac has put in his papers?" Albert said. "The retirement house in Spain, he's been planning it all these years."

"I thought he was for Greece."

"Fat lot of difference." Albert had just eaten breakfast, and was using his tongue to work the last of it from under his gums. "Greece, Spain, a few years in the sun and they all die or go balmy."

Castellone had finished shaving and was buttoning his shirt. "Not for you, Albert?"

"Not for you either. Old warhorses, the two of us."

"Where am I to meet Balzac?"

"He fancies a safe house out on rue Dupleix, just off the Caserne. Do you know it?"

"What time?"

"Eleven."

Castellone completed the business of dressing, his wallet in one pocket, pen, reading glasses, cash, finally buckling the leather harness which wound under his armpit and around his waist and secured the holster for his pistol. His eye caught Albert's, reflected in a mirror; he stood off to one side with his arms folded, his face gray and aged in the morning light. His glance was shrewd, but at the same time sympathetic, although it contained a final judgment on Castellone.

"You ever go out without your gun in that contraption?" he said.

"Never."

"I suppose you take it off when you sleep," he said. "The same way I stand my stump against the wall. Exactly like that. A hell of a thing, eh Castellone?"

Castellone could manage nothing beyond a foolish and rather guilty smile. Certain truths were startling, and rude, a rock thrown through a library window.

"There's no cure for peg leg," Albert said. "Even retired and living in Spain, I would still wear my harness."

Castellone knotted his tie and put on his coat. Albert hung on, and eventually said, "I should have the sense to keep my nose out of other people's business."

"You never have." It was said kindly, with Castellone's hand on Albert's shoulder.

"It's due to my frustrations," Albert said. "Particularly, having to give up fencing after I lost my leg. And then it makes me shy with women. My doctor had psychological training, and has explained it all to me."

"I didn't know you were shy with women, Albert."

"Yes. Because of my having one leg. It puts some women off, you see."

"I don't see why it should," Castellone said. "In fact I remember one girl who didn't seem to mind at all."

"Blossom, the little Vietnamese," Albert said. "I was giving serious thought to Blossom, despite the obvious differences in our background. But she had a family. Mother, father, brother, God knows what else. And all Vietnamese. All gobbling rice out of little bowls with sticks."

"She loved the stump, though."

"She did. She really did," Albert said. "And you're a good pal, Bernard. You know how to build a fellow's confidence."

"What is it you wanted to tell me?"

"I want to warn you," Albert said. "I know you're into something. You, Balzac, one or two others. A secret service within the Service sort of thing. I don't know what you're up to exactly. I don't care. None of my business, is it?"

"No. It's not."

"But I do want to warn you," Albert said. "People have been nosing around. The last couple of days, people monkeying with the phones, your mail."

"Whose people? If you've something to say, let's have it."

"Our people, Bernard. Our very own."

"You mean Frenchmen?"

"I'll give them credit, they sent the best in snoops. They're in like smoke curling under the door. But I did collar one in the hall coming out of your room. He had been in for a look around."

"Did you two have a talk?"

"No. He ran over me and kept going."

"And the Americans?"

"Their thugs are all over the place," Albert said. "Not that it matters. They have their business, we have ours. Pals in the war, allies, right enough. But they're Americans, easier to live with than Russians, but Americans. What tics me off is our people. What are they buzzing around you for? What have you done?"

"Stay clear of it, Albert. That's a friend's advice."

"You haven't crossed them, have you? No, not you." Albert had flashes of cunning, veins of it, like ore glittering in rock. "They would be the ones to do the crossing. The snoops. They've got the dirty hands, and you're going to blow the whistle."

Castellone left the Florida and walked along the Champs-Elysées for several blocks, his eyes sweeping the doorways and parked cars. Small trucks were suspicious, spotters used them, and workmen planted in the street, fellows behind newspapers; his attention went at once to anyone or anything designed not to attract attention. All of his tension was controlled, none came near the surface. He was without tics, without odd mannerisms. He did nothing out of the ordinary, absolutely nothing, while part of him glared narrowly at the dangers in the street; part of him was cold and cunning; part of him was mad. He saw that and it made him smile, it broke the tension, making him think of the gun under his arm and Albert's wooden leg.

He noticed a pretty girl with a yellow scarf at her

throat. She was young, too young for him, and passed him without a glance. He counted the years. How much of his life was left? He had heard it said that man is the only animal that knows he must die, the only creature to live with that certainty. In the same way Castellone lived with the certainty, the inevitability of his actions. He was a spy, a spook, a man who lived in hotels. Inevitable acts, taken freely. Castellone nudged the contradiction into place; it locked, he heard the satisfying click.

But even as he told himself that he was free, something nagged. He saw Natalie's face, not settled in a particular time or place, but only her features floating miraculously in space, ravishing, and just out of reach, as the moon in the sky must appear to a young child or a savage.

Near the Rond-Point, he ducked into a cab and had the driver take him to the Place des Invalides. Castellone paid the driver and went for a stroll on the esplanade, stopped for a coffee and brioche on the rue d'Estrées. He saw no French spotters, no American.

He turned north along boulevard des Invalides toward the Seine and caught the number four bus as far as the Pont Alexandre III, where it turned east on to the Quai d'Orsay. From there it was a short stroll to the house on the rue Dupleix. Castellone knew it well, had used it several times, and the concierge was a familiar face, the widow of a noncom who had served under Balzac in the 18th Paras. Balzac was the kind to repay old debts down to the last penny. He had once told Castellone that he had not made a new friend after the age of thirty-five, and lost those he had only through death. He was a constant man, perhaps a rigid one, fussy and irritable, but fair; it was always said of Balzac that he was fair.

He was also punctual, as Castellone was habitually tardy. Castellone found him reading in the tiny attic room that he favored; he read whenever he was left alone, as an old dog will sleep. The book was in German. Balzac had served in Germany before the war and written a history of the rise of National Socialism. He was tall and stooped, and wore half-glasses with gold frames even when not reading. His shirt collars stood away from his neck, and his clothes hung on him as if he had recently lost a lot of weight. He was always taking things out of his pockets—

diaries and ballpoint pens and a little steel tool like a spade to ream his pipe. He liked to fuss with these things and move them from place to place on his desk. He kept crossing and uncrossing his long skinny legs, and wore short socks with the elastic on the top unraveling, so that they drooped, exposing his skinny white shanks.

"You're looking well," he said. "Very fit. Your color is good. You have a boat, don't you? It's the fresh air. I wish I had more opportunities to get out. I've been thinking of buying a boat myself. Something small. Secondhand, of course. Do you advise it, as a pastime I mean?"

"If you live near a body of water."

"Oh, I see. You're quite as witty as ever, Hugo."

Castellone had asked for the meeting, and Balzac settled back to listen, peering over his half-glasses, his chin in the palm of his hand, his first finger upright alongside his temple with his index finger at right angles, extending the length of his upper lip.

Castellone said, "Tell me why I'm being covered."

"Covered? Who by?"

"Our own people. Albert has seen them."

"Albert has? Yes, of course, Albert. Tell me, Hugo, have you seen them?"

"No, but I know they're around."

"But you've not actually seen them."

"I don't have to."

"I did forget about your sixth sense, your mystical side."

Balzac didn't smile, although he did put a curl in his voice. The doorkeeper at the old headquarters building had been to primary school with Balzac, and he swore that as a boy he smiled regularly.

"At least once a day," Castellone said.

"I beg your pardon."

"I was thinking of the doorkeeper at the old headquarters building."

"You mean Pinard?"

"He claims to have seen you smile."

"He's mistaken."

The contempt in Balzac's voice was faint, but not so faint that Castellone hadn't heard. He didn't care for it, or for Balzac's blandly supercilious gaze above the gold half-glasses.

"We made a solid plan," Castellone said. "But there could be absolutely no leaks. We agreed to trust no one outside our circle." Castellone fixed his eyes on Balzac. "Who have you brought in?" he said.

"Brought in?"

"It's getting on my damn nerves," Castellone said. "You repeating what I say. Stop the chess game. Stop your evasions, and being clever. I've gone to Achille Piri, and through him to the other syndicate chiefs. You've turned in your retirement papers and are thinking of buying a boat. You've built a fucking house in Spain. You're secure, you're doing the last of your time, Balzac, but it's my life on the line."

"No one has been brought in."

"I was thinking of the Minister."

"Now that is funny. Very funny. Call Pinard, the doorkeeper. Tell him I'm on the verge of a good smile."

"I appreciate why you would want the Minister brought in," Castellone said. "It's the politics. In your place I might do the same. We've created our own unit inside French intelligence. Secrecy. Bring together all the syndicate chiefs and once and for all break the back of the opium trade in France."

"Once and for all," Balzac said.

"But the plan is risky," Castellone said. "Twenty kilos of number four heroin brought into the country, and a neat double-cross of the Americans."

"Blast the Americans," Balzac said.

"Bring in all that heroin, double-cross the Americans, *and* exclude our Minister," Castellone said. "If we fail, he is to get all the blame. Worse for a politician, if we succeed, he gets none of the praise."

"A bold stroke, I thought."

"Too bold," Castellone said. "The Minister will see you in hell. Hell is retirement with no pension. You see what I mean, Balzac?"

"We both have taken risks," Balzac said. "You with the syndicate chiefs. Me by never telling the Minister."

Balzac began to fiddle with the gadgets from his pockets, and took his time stuffing his pipe, lighting it.

Castellone waited, barely breathing, giving Balzac all the time he needed.

"Are you tired, Hugo?"

"I'm fine."

"What about money? Have you enough put aside?"

"I can put my hands on a little."

"You're right about it being risky. There's talk old Piri sent someone on ahead to talk to the chiefs. He's suspicious of you."

"I expected he would be."

"You were with the chiefs. What were they like?"

"They were suspicious. They're always suspicious."

"Things have heated up on the other side. That's what I hear. The Americans again. They've given the product to Nephew."

"When does Nephew arrive?"

"He's here, the product with him. We had a look inside his and his wife's baggage. Twenty kilos, all number four."

"The stakes are big, my friend."

"The odd part is that he's not at the Embassy," Balzac said. "He went straight to the house in Montbazon. Do you know the place?"

"I've been there."

"He has the product, now he wants his money. Simple as that."

"Tell him he must wait. It doesn't do to move too quickly with the chiefs. They get edgy. And they particularly don't like SPDEC thugs nosing around."

"There'll be none."

"The bets are all down," Castellone said.

"I'll see you're left alone," Balzac said.

Balzac intended to be as good as his word. He called the Minister's appointments secretary, a man named Roger Braun, and asked if he could be slipped in for a precious ten minutes with the Minister. Braun said it was a very bad day, but would do what he could and get right back.

Braun was an obliging man, particularly to Balzac, or anyone else in the intelligence service. He was a bachelor, living with a widowed sister. Balzac thought he was probably homosexual, although of the inactive sort. It occurred to him—not for the first time—that he ought to pull Braun's file for a closer look, and even put him in the light for a month or so. But just then his phone rang and Braun came back on the line.

"The Minister will be having   ch at his desk," he said. "One o'clock, if that suits yo ."

"It's fine, thank you. We will be alone?"

"I'll see to it," Braun said. "Will you have lunch as well?" Balzac hadn't imagined lunch with the Minister at his desk. "I've ordered cold chicken and salad from the commissary," Braun said, "and they can do two just as easily."

"Thank you, I'll have eaten."

"They really do a good lunch," Braun said.

Balzac eventually persuaded Braun that he didn't want lunch with the Minister in his office; he cleared his own desk, and presente 1 himself at the Quai d'Orsay at two minutes of one. T' Minister was on a call and he spent a couple of minute: th Braun in his outer office.

Balzac rarely   uced how people looked   essed. His memory for faces was poor, although quite   d for names and dates; as a schoolboy he had been   le to repeat twelve digits spoken slowly by an instructor, but failed to recognize his older sister when, after a separation of two years, he was sent to pick her up at the Gare de 1'Est.

When he had a closer look at Braun he was surprised to see that he was above average height and broad through the shoulders. He had always thought of him as a small man, a drab and shadowy figure dressed always in gray.

"That's a nice tie," Balzac said.

"How nice of you to say so."

"What color would you call it?"

"Mauve."

"Really? Mauve."

The Minister was at his desk, which was a grand affair with an inlaid top and gilt at the corners and elaborately carved legs. There were knickknacks and mementos from his days in the Resistance, from the Far East, about which he had written extensively, and from the archaeological digs he had worked in Egypt. There was the Cluzot drawing—a caricature really—of the Minister with a pen in one hand, while brandishing a sword in the other.

While he was known to be proudest of the literary aspect of his varied career—his works had been translated into most languages and were considered classics—yet not one copy appeared anywhere on his shelves. Only the books of friends were displayed, nearly all of the great names of contemporary European and American litera-ture, and all of them inscribed.

Balzac noted that there were no photographs of famous men; the Minister collected only their books, their ideas.

But there were other photographs, one of the President of the Republic, taken in Paris on the day of liberation; there was the Eisenstaedt portrait of the Minister's wife, snapshots of children and grandchildren, and a portrait of his grandfather, who had been chief Rabbi of Riga.

There was also a dog in the office, a handsome gray animal with yellow eyes, who came and sniffed Balzac and tried to work his muzzle into his crotch.

"Do you like dogs?" the Minister said.

"Not so much that I care to own one," Balzac said.

Balzac wasn't intimidated by the Minister and was able to make his little jokes with him. They had been to school together, and while the Minister had stood high in his class, Balzac had stood higher. They had fought together in the Resistance. Balzac's wife was a cousin of the President of the Republic. The daughter of another cousin was engaged to the Minister's son.

"I bring the dog on Friday because I go directly from here to the country house," the Minister said.

"That house of yours. Have you repaired the roof?"

"Yes. And it cost a bloody fortune."

"Don't complain, it's only a roof. Wait until you have to build a house from scratch."

"You'd have done better to buy that old place down the road from me." The Minister lifted the cover on his lunch tray and poked at a quarter chicken with the tip of his knife, severed the wing, and began to nibble at it. "You could have bought it for two hundred thousand. Today you couldn't go near it for less than four."

"It's a nuisance rebuilding an old house."

"Much of life is a nuisance. In fact, nearly all."

"How is Marie-Elizabeth?"

"The same."

"And the children?"

"Arrogant, argumentative, and uninformed."

"And the chicken," Balzac said. "How does it taste?"

"Decent."

Balzac said, "I've just come from a talk with Victor Hugo." The Minister stopped eating and looked puzzled. "Hugo, Zola, you remember?"

"Yes, I see. Castellone. What did he want?"

"He asked if you had been brought in."

"I expect your denial was convincing."

"Hugo is no fool," Balzac said. "I can deny bringing you in until I'm blue in the face. He doesn't believe it. Not for a minute. He recognizes that the responsibilities are too great for me to have assumed them on my own."

"Why has he waited until now to bring it up?"

"Because now he's in danger. Someone has sent in snoops. That's either stupid or a double-cross. You do see? These snoops know where to look, from which Hugo deduces an intelligence source. A leak. The question is who and from where to where?"

Balzac was patient, but with an edge to his voice. The Minister's cleverness was indisputable, yet he tended to be easily distracted and think too much in the abstract. He was a theoretician; in day-to-day matters he sometimes needed to be led by the nose. Balzac's position in the inner cycle was secure enough for him to do the job.

"Hugo has gone to the syndicates," he said. "Which puts his neck in a noose. They must think he's one of them, not one of us. But snoops mean someone sent them. Someone outside our little network."

"And that has your man worried?"

"Very much. We don't know who the leak is, or to whom he reports. Information could be finding its way to the Americans, or even to the syndicate chiefs."

The Minister was slowly shaking his head. Balzac had the clear impression he hadn't heard a word.

"I've never been happy with your scheme," the Minister said. He was sipping an American soft drink, one of those which used a sugar substitute. "Too risky by half," he said. "Too complicated, too many ways to go sour."

"Not really," Balzac said. "Not if we all keep to the rules." Balzac's reputation was as a hard man, outspoken, one who rubbed too many delicate pelts the wrong way. "The Americans set out to help Nyo bring opium out of the Triangle. Hugo had been set up to them as renegade agent turned importer with appropriate connections in both the Triangle and Europe. The Americans bought Hugo. The syndicates have now bought Hugo. You do see that? We are now in a position to seize both the opium and the chiefs."

"No doubt we have considerable to gain," the Minister said. "We wouldn't have gone this far otherwise. But we have more to lose. Playing fast and loose with the Americans is bad enough. All right, we can survive that. Nothing does more for French self-esteem than to make asses of the Americans. It's the heroin that has me worried. Twenty kilos distributed inside France would be a social and political disaster. No, I would do nothing to risk that. No snoops. Nothing. I assure you, the scheme has never gone beyond this office, and I've ordered no snoops."

"Then who has?"

"My guess is the Americans," the Minister said. "They may have soured on the deal, or grown wary of it. Second thoughts, left hand not knowing what the right is doing. I don't have to instruct you in the failings of bureaucracy, particularly of the American sort."

"But what of Hugo?" Balzac said. "Where does that leave him?"

The Minister sat slumped in his chair, deep in thought while scratching the head of his dog and sipping his sugarless drink.

Balzac repeated the question, this time by way of an accusation. "Where does this leave Hugo?"

"Out in the open," the Minister said. "I'm afraid there's no way to avoid that."

CHAPTER 15

The Minister had taken no notes during his meeting with Balzac, but as soon as it was over and his memory still fresh, he recorded all his impressions. He did this after every important meeting. His purpose was to keep an intimate record of his years in service, with an eye to retirement to his villa, which was in the Loire, and where he contemplated writing his memoirs.

The tape was given to Roger Braun for transcription. The Minister would trust no one else with it, and Braun was instructed to do the actual typing himself. He followed orders, but kept a carbon, which he carried with him from the office in the inside pocket of his jacket.

He closed and locked the office just after six, and walked across the Seine on the Pont Royal. It was a chilly night, but he strolled through the Tuileries, which he did most nights, and bought the evening papers from a kiosk in front of the Automobile Club. He continued on to rue Boissy, which ran beside the American Embassy, crossed the Faubourg, and stopped further along at a café in the shadow of the Madeleine.

The café was called the Churchill, and the waiter who

served Braun recognized him, and greeted him as a
familiar patron, although without knowing his name.
Braun drank a bottle of English ale, and read the *Herald
Tribune*. When he had finished, he left the newspaper
behind, neatly folded on his seat. The waiter quickly
picked it up and took it to the washroom, where he found
the copy of the transcript of the Minister's notes of his
meeting with Balzac.

The waiter put the envelope back in the *Tribune,* called
a number at the American Embassy, and a man was sent
to pick it up. By midnight the transcript was on its way by
pouch to Washington. The next morning was the second
of March. By the late afternoon of the fourth, a coded
one-page summary arrived in Saigon on a military jet and
was delivered to Peter Owen.

He and Kirk had been in their offices since Nyo's first
call, which had come early that morning. Kirk had
recorded the conversation, and played it for Owen.

"I need to get hold of the Ambassador," Nyo had said.
"I have called the Embassy. Several times now I have
called. But I'm informed he is in Washington. He is in a
hospital there. That is what I am told."

The telephone lines weren't working well, and the
recording tape was imperfect; there was a distracting burr
of static, and Kirk's voice came through unnaturally high-
pitched and metallic, like that of a character in an
animated cartoon.

"The Ambassador is in Washington. I can assure you of
that, sir. And there is a medical problem."

"What sort of problem?"

"Medical. Talk of a hernia. An inguinal hernia, I
believe."

"My concern is with the political situation," Nyo said.
"Certain parties have organized demonstrations. Army
units are involved, and certain of my general officers have
been making mischief."

Kirk said, "We have received reports of troop movements in Saigon. I am informed that the airport has been
closed and the power station has been taken over."

None of this surprised Nyo; he certainly wasn't hearing
it for the first time. "What is the U.S. position in all this?"
he said. "I want to know that. The U.S. position."

"I am not able to tell you that, sir. It's not within my authority."

"The Ambassador is the one to tell me. The Ambassador is the official charged with that responsibility. But he is in Washington. Well, then, someone else in Washington."

"It's too early in Washington, four o'clock in the morning. We can't get hold of anyone."

"I am Head of State. Remember that, please. And also what I told you at our last meeting. I have done my duty, and I will continue to do so. What is your opinion? Is it a full rebellion? Well, tell me. What does good sense require at such a time?"

A second or two passed in which neither man spoke; the static stopped, there was a faint sputtering sound before Kirk's voice came back on, sounding more like himself. "I can only express a personal view, sir. I cannot speak officially. I am not speaking for the U.S. Government."

"Yes, yes, your personal view. Your advice. As a friend, what do you advise?"

Kirk didn't hesitate; his voice was clear and steady. "You must resign," he said. "Accept safe conduct for you and your immediate family."

"Who is it that guarantees that safe conduct?"

"I think it can be done. It can be arranged. I will try to make contact with the Generals. But I must have your authorization. If I am to speak for you, you must give me that authority."

"To speak in my behalf to Traung?"

"To whoever is in charge."

"I'm trying to re-establish order."

"I will wait here for you to telephone."

But Nyo didn't call a second time. Kirk's agents reported roadblocks on all the main streets leading to the Palace, and armored troop carriers and even tanks brought in to man these. The radio station and bus terminal on Petrus Ky Street were seized, and there was a report of shooting between Traung's forces and the Palace guard. Just after seven o'clock, the phone went dead. The rattle of small arms fire carried across the river from the city. The lights in Kirk's office flickered, went out briefly, and then came on.

Peter Owen said, "It's time we went over to the Palace and had a look."

"No sense waiting here for a dead phone to ring." Kirk was on his feet, buttoning his shirt collar and pulling up his tie, not giving a thought to what he was doing. "No weapons, no guards, not even a driver. We give no cause for alarm. We drive to the revolution in your Chevrolet." He had put on his seersucker jacket, and was patting the pockets for his glasses and billfold. He had become eager and enthusiastic, making no effort to conceal his gaiety. He locked his desk and the office door, humming the "Battle Hymn of the Republic." "Get us a flag, Peter," he said. "Old Glory, the Stars and Stripes. We're going to show the colors, we're going to fly it from the Chevrolet."

But Peter had trouble finding a flag. While Kirk waited in the Chevrolet, impatiently sounding the horn, Peter hunted around for one in the cellar. He finally came up with something taken from USIS educational kits stored in cartons and long forgotten. It was a tiny thing on a short wooden stick, the kind of flag distributed to school children to wave at motorcades, and Peter used rubber bands to lash it to the radio antenna.

The highway was empty in the direction of Saigon, but a short time out Kirk picked up headlights in the rear-view mirror. He lightened his foot on the accelerator, slowing to thirty-five, and the two headlights came up suddenly, springing out at them out of the darkness. It was a military transport, which pulled out with an ear-shattering blast from the horn and roared past, a squad of Vietnamese airborne in battle dress riding steel benches rigged in the rear.

Kirk drove to the eastern end of the highway, where a roadblock had been set up at the Nguyen-bin-Khiem road. There were a pair of jeeps fitted out with police lights, and a dozen or so ARVN smoking beside them, or squatting nearby with rifles between their legs.

A non-com ordered Owen and Kirk out of the Chevrolet, raising the muzzle of his M-16 to the level of Kirk's chest. Three other soldiers made a tight semicircle, each with a finger on the trigger of his weapon. Kirk was made to produce his passport and diplomatic ID; one of the ARVN pointed to the tiny American flag on the radio antenna, and a laugh went around the little band.

The non-com wanted to know where they were going and for what reason. Kirk handled it smoothly, careful to pluck the right word and tone of address from his limited Vietnamese vocabulary. The non-com had only a few words of French, and no English at all. Kirk explained they were on their way to Presidential Palace, summoned there for a meeting of the greatest urgency. The non-com listened intently, his face expressionless, his narrow and suspicious black eyes never leaving Kirk's face.

Owen concentrated on the other soldiers. They did nothing to threaten or intimidate him, their faces expressing a mute and enduring patience. They looked at him without interest, as if he were a picture on a wall, a sign written in a foreign language. He didn't matter to them, and it was that quality he found most chilling. He knew how dangerous they were. He saw the indifference in their eyes, their unfeeling cruelty.

Kirk went on with his explanations to the non-com, his voice slow and steady. If he was afraid, there was no sign of it. Standing beside him, Owen stopped being afraid. He trusted Kirk. Neither of them would die there. Kirk would explain to the non-com. He would convince him.

Kirk said, "It's getting late. We must go now. Please return our documents."

The non-com hesitated. He was thinking only if letting them go would cause him to lose face. Kirk smiled and held out his hand for the passports. The non-com laid them gently in his open palm.

As they drove away, Kirk said, "Did you think they'd shoot?"

"No. It went on too long," Owen said. "I never thought my life would end there. I was thinking of the money spent on my education." It came out as a joke, although he had never been more serious. "I even thought of the fortune it cost my father to have my teeth straightened," he said, "and I knew all of that money couldn't go to waste."

Kirk took care to drive slowly through the streets. There were no bicyclists, no pedestrians, and the only other traffic was military. Steel curtains were down in front of all the shops. But the shooting had stopped. The city was quiet, unnaturally so, except for the occasional wail of a siren.

There were more roadblocks and soldiers and military hardware, but no sign of fighting, and they drove straight through in the Chevrolet until they came to the Palace gates, which were ringed with tanks. Anti-aircraft guns had been brought in and a pair of huge searchlights, but there was none of that random bustling about, and no confusion. There was plenty of coming and going, but all of it orderly and controlled, well planned, as if those in charge knew just what they were doing.

Kirk found the officer in charge, a Colonel with Eleventh Corps insignia and an American airborne badge over his ARVN decorations. Kirk asked the Colonel if Nyo were inside the Palace.

"Nyo has resigned." The Colonel spoke flawless French. "About two hours ago."

"There was no announcement."

"That is being prepared."

"Then I need to speak to General Traung. If he is in the Palace, please arrange for me to be taken to him."

"For what reason?"

"I represent the United States Government. I need to know who is now Head of State."

"I can tell you, sir. I can assure you it is General Traung. He is now Head of State."

"Please call him. My name is Ralph Kirk. My associate is Peter Owen. I need to know the whereabouts of President Nyo."

"He is not President."

"My concern is his safety," Kirk said. "I want to arrange safe conduct. If it is needed, my government is prepared to provide transportation for him and his party."

The Colonel used his radio transceiver to call inside the Palace and deliver the message. There was a wait of several minutes. A black Citroen preceded by an armed personnel carrier pulled up to the Palace gate. A line of other vehicles followed; there were armed jeeps, some fitted out with police lights and mounted guns. The Colonel had a look inside the Citroen, came to attention, and saluted. Kirk strained to make out the face deep in the shadows at the back of the car. It was Traung. The Colonel signaled for the gate to be opened, and the motorcade passed into the Palace grounds.

A little later, the Colonel's call was returned with instructions to admit Kirk and Owen and to escort them to a small reception room on the first floor of the Palace. The gate was opened again and an officer was assigned to lead them across the Palace grounds, which were lit by batteries of strobe lights. For the first time there were signs of fighting. Kirk had heard that the Palace guard had stayed loyal to Nyo, that they had resisted the insurgents, and now he and Owen passed their corpses on the cobblestones of the Palace Square, laid out side by side, all in a neat row, like fish sold in an open market.

Soldiers passed without a glance at the corpses. Only Peter Owen was affected and stopped to look. The bodies were vivid under the brilliant strobe lights, their wounds and gaping mouths more ghastly than he was prepared for. He had seen few dead men, and none shot down at close range by automatic fire.

Kirk and the officer hurried off, but Owen turned back for a second look. He was horrified, yet couldn't tear himself away. He felt that nothing he had ever seen before was real. He began to shake, his legs trembled, and he had to clench his teeth to keep them from rattling. It wasn't fear; it was something more. He had looked for the first time under the placid surface of life and had a glimpse of the terrors that coiled and twisted there. He stood trembling before the row of dead men. Then Kirk called out to him, and he followed him and the officer into the Palace.

They were taken to a small conference room and turned over to a second ARVN officer. Others were present, but they paid no attention to the two Americans.

"Have you come to see Nyo?"

"Yes. I must see him," Kirk said.

"Of course." The officer was small and slight, even for a Vietnamese, with a black patch over one eye and poor teeth.

He led them down a long curving staircase through a large ballroom, which was used for formal receptions and

was hung with tapestries and an immense gilt mirror.
Someone had thought to roll back the elegant rug and
spare it the soldiers' muddy boots.

They continued through a long, gloomy corridor which
led to a service kitchen and butler's pantry. Two Vietnamese women and a fat little boy were eating noodles
around a table; only the child looked up as the two
Americans and the officer entered, but he showed no
particular interest, and went back to eating the noodles
with his fingers.

They left the kitchen by a door at the rear, descending a
flight of wooden steps, through a crawl space with a dirt
floor, coming out in a covered passageway leading to a
large wooden shed at the back of the Palace grounds. A
car was parked in the shed.

It was an American model; a Cadillac, Kirk thought, a
gift from the American President to Nyo. He had been
present when it had been given to him in Hawaii.

The officer with the eye patch pointed to the rear door
of the car, showing his bad teeth in a smile.

Kirk opened the door, certain of what he would find.
He and Owen exchanged glances. There was no doubt of
it. Nyo's body was sprawled on the floor of the car, a
bullet hole in the back of his head.

Kirk demanded to see Traung, but with no effect. He
was shunted from officer to officer, and finally spoke to an
air force general, who told him Traung was not in the
Palace, or even in Saigon. Kirk looked the general in the
eye and told him of seeing Traung being driven into the
Palace.

The general shrugged it off, not bothering to carry the
lie further. Kirk was free to believe whatever he wanted.
It was no concern of the general. He was a famous combat
pilot, an ace, trained in the United States, and known for
his flamboyance. The younger pilots idolized him, imitat-
ing his swaggering walk and pearl-handled pistol which
rode his hip like a cowboy's.

He probably knew who Kirk was but didn't give a
damn. He simply turned his back and swaggered away,
two of his private gunmen closing ranks behind him.

Kirk gave up on seeing Traung, and he and Owen

started back to the residency to compose a cable and send it in code to Virginia.

Word of the success of the coup had spread through the city. People had begun to show themselves in the streets and were mingling happily with the soldiers, and driving around sounding their car horns. Photographs and posters of Nyo were torn down and burned. Kirk was reminded of a post-game rally on a football weekend, and was relieved to cross the river and return to the quiet of the residency. He went straight to work composing the cables, which Owen coded, using the scrambler whose only complement was in Virginia.

It was past three o'clock when they finished. Kirk was exhausted and stretched out on the cot in his office. Owen brought out a bottle of Scotch.

"We've still not settled the business with Castellone," he said.

"Let it ride."

"Did you know he was a French narc?"

"No, I didn't know. I should have guessed, though. We thought he had come in for the money. That's what he said. But it doesn't fit, does it?"

"What do we do? Do we stop his show?"

Kirk didn't answer; he was drinking with his eyes closed and his head propped up by a cushion. "I'm not sure he's a narc," he said. "With a bird like Castellone, there's nothing sure. He's wily, with him the truth takes years, it peels off him, like layers of paint."

"What do we do?"

"We pass the word to the chiefs," Kirk said. "Hold our noses and pass the word." He sighed, and his words came slowly, as if he were drifting off to sleep. "Let the chiefs do Castellone for us."

"And Nephew?"

"Later on. Later on we draw lots. Winner gets to do Nephew."

Owen went back to his own office, but he was in no mood to work, and far too keyed up to sleep. He carried his glass and the bottle of Scotch into the garden, where he sat on a bench near a lemon tree and drank from the bottle. It was a clear night, and there was a moon. It was the first time he had noticed that. The air was soft and fragrant, there was even a faint breeze, and he could smell the lemon tree.

Just then he heard sounds coming from the direction of the swimming pool. Someone was swimming, but he couldn't imagine who. He carried the whisky bottle by its neck and went to have a look.

A girl was in the pool, swimming laps. Owen hung back in the shadows, and watched her move effortlessly through the water. She was a superb swimmer. He supposed she worked at the residency; several new people had just come from other assignments. But even with the moon on the water, he couldn't make out her face. He wondered what kind of girl it was who went swimming alone in the middle of the night. He wondered if she had done it before, if she did it regularly.

Then he wondered if she were beautiful. He certainly hoped she was. Beautiful and naked. He even prayed she was. It wasn't so much lust, at least not simply that. It was reverence, and the magic of the moment, and his enchantment with it.

It wasn't a large pool, and she swam so well, he had the feeling she could swim back and forth, on and on, forever. And he could watch her forever. He couldn't take his eyes off her, this mysterious girl swimming in the moonlight.

He finally stepped out of the shadows. But then he held back. She might stop if she saw him, and the spell would be broken. He took off his jacket and waited. She would be cold when she came out of the pool, and he would need his jacket to wrap her in.

CHAPTER 16

Sullivan took the morning flight from Miami to Montego Bay, and went on from there by cab, another two hours along the coast road, east to Ocho Rios. It was nearly noon when he checked into the Bellevue, which had been built before the Second World War, when the island still belonged to England. While now the property of a Lebanese family with interests all over the island, the English colonial style was carefully maintained. Tea was served every afternoon on white wicker tables in the shade of royal palms planted on the broad and beautifully kept lawn. There were at least a dozen black gardeners to care for the flowering plants and trim and water the lawn. There was a swimming pool, a white sand beach, tennis, croquet, overhead fans in the lobby, and even a small library with a pair of writing tables. The inkwells were full; Sullivan checked them.

The place reminded him of the old Strand in Rangoon, or Raffles in Singapore, but of course smaller and just a little seedy. There was the same wide, shaded veranda with white rockers, Malay chairs, and rattan tables, and even the same aging and genteel British, the men in white and the women wearing stockings and print dresses, writing letters home and reading novels, and passing the time until lunch with iced drinks made of gin and lime juice.

It was an unlikely place to find a man like George Berry. But he was there, as Peter Owen had said, seated in a canvas chair at the edge of the surf, drinking a planter's punch, a pair of prewar Zeiss binoculars around his neck.

"I had my glasses on you from the moment you came on the veranda," he said to Sullivan. "I could tell you didn't know, even though you take in everything. Your eyes already have the nervous darting habit that all of us get eventually." He sipped his planter's punch and dug in the sand with his long white toes.

"Did you cock your fingers and aim at me?" Sullivan asked. "Tell me true, George. Did you go bang-bang?"

Berry looked up from the chair into the sun, shading his eyes. He gave the question a second or two serious thought, and then slowly shook his head. "I'm one of those who's glad you're alive," he said.

"And glad to see me?"

"I'm not quite sure of that." Then he smiled and said, "Yes, I'm glad, with you around, at least I won't be bored."

"But you're not surprised I'm here," Sullivan said. "Were you told to expect me?"

"I didn't know you were coming," Berry said. "Which doesn't mean I'm surprised you're here."

"I've come a long way to talk to you, George."

"Go home. I've nothing to say. I'm an aging boozer, happily retired from the intelligence services." Berry had been a man of great charm; Sullivan saw its shadow, saw it flicker in the light blue eyes. "You've come for help, isn't that so?"

"You're getting a bad burn," Sullivan said. "Better put something on, or get out of the sun." He sat on the footrest at the end of Berry's old-fashioned canvas chair. "What's gone wrong?" he said.

"Nothing. Everything is dandy."

"Not with me," Sullivan said. "I'm ass over tea kettle. Confused, George. I'm terribly confused."

"You're confused and I'm an old drunk," Berry said.

"I believed in shared ideals," Sullivan said. "In probity. The brotherhood of men of good will."

"It has a nice ring to it." Berry slowly nodded his head. "Men of goodwill. They're the ones sure to put a knife in your back."

"I need you to put me back together," Sullivan said. "I need to get straight."

"I'm not traveling alone, you know. There's a woman. Natalie Benoit. I need to provide for her. Maybe you can help there." Berry sighed and stood up. "Let's get out of the sun and have something cold to drink. You and me and Natalie. She's gone to town to shop, but should be back before lunch."

He had started across the beach and abruptly stopped, a look of pain crossing his face. He seemed to sway and even staggered, and dropped his hand heavily on Sullivan's shoulder. Sullivan helped him sit on the footrest of the beach chair.

"I'm afraid I've had too much to drink. I'll be fine in a minute."

Berry was shaken and gray under his suntan. Sullivan carried a towel to the edge of the sea and wet it. By the time he had wrung it out and returned, Berry's color had improved and he was smiling.

Sullivan said, "You are feeling better?"

"Yes, much."

"Tell me, George, are we on opposite sides?"

Berry waved the question aside. "Fair-haired boy, tops in his class at spook school. The Director took note, even began to think of you paternally. D'you suppose one little beer would do me any harm?"

"Scotch would do better for us both."

"Good for you, Jack," Berry said, taking his arm. "Fairhaired boy. I know a little something of the burdens imposed by that role. In 1935, I was at Heidelberg when FDR sent Uncle Tim to sit me down and explain what was what. Uncle Tim was married to my mother's half-sister, and was also FDR's cousin. He was a lawyer, but worked on The Street as they used to call the securities business in those days. He had made a lot of money in the 'twenties and held on to it after the crash. I don't know just how. Uncle Tim wasn't just another clever man, though. There

was more to him than that. He used to correspond with
Alfred North Whitehead and Gilbert Murray, and he
owned a Rubens. Imagine that, he actually owned a
Rubens."

"Was it hung in his house?"

"Oh, yes. I remember it very well. Beautiful thing."

"What happened to it?"

"It passed to his son," Berry said. "My cousin Craig.
He gave it away to a museum in Texas. It became a tax
write-off, the Rubens did."

"Tell me about Heidelberg?"

"I was there before the war."

"Yes I know. Heidelberg is how we got started on
Uncle Tim. FDR sent him to have a talk with you."

"I suppose I'm getting dotty," Berry said. "Funny thing
is I don't really mind. Senility turns out to be an immense
relief, like undoing one's shoes at the end of an exhaust-
ing day."

"Uncle Tim."

"He took me to lunch, and we talked about duty and
responsibility, and I gave up the German philosophers
and went to work for my country," Berry said. "America
was so much smaller then, or that's how it seemed. First
of all, it was all in the East. And the OSS was certainly
special. It was an adventure. I never dreamed it would be
for life."

"No need to regret the choice. You've done a good
job."

"Yes, of course. I've done my duty. I only wish Uncle
Tim were here to help me draw the moral line with more
precision. You *always* do this and you *never* do that. He
lived to be eighty-eight, you know, and died peacefully in
his sleep. His mind was clear right up until the end, and of
course he was always a great but discreet fucker." Berry
slapped Sullivan's knee and said. "I wonder what the old
fellow would think of some of my dark deeds."

"You've done your duty, George."

Berry took a breath and went on. "Uncle Tim didn't
have to persuade me to give up the German philosophers.
Heidelberg bored me to death. I craved excitement. Not
that I didn't have my ideals, the same as you. And formal
training as a philosopher. I understood that moral con-

sequence was inseparable from an act, and that it followed it, wiggling behind like the tail of a spermatozoon."

Sullivan said, "And the act was to leave Heidelberg. To say yes to Uncle Tim, and to FDR. And the moral consequence followed that."

"One dark deed led to another," Berry said. "And finally there's the business in the north of Burma. You do know about it, it's why you're here, isn't it?"

"I don't know the details," Sullivan said. "Not all of it."

"You know enough. You know you were double-crossed, and that's got your blood up." Berry had a long, careful look at Sullivan. "I suspect you have changed," he said. "And for the better. Things are not quite so black and white. You're more generous in your judgments, less the fair-haired boy," Berry said. "The fast start slowing down. I know what that's like. I've forgotten if I've told you I was at school with the Roosevelt boys and spent a summer with the family at Campobello. FDR wasn't happy with the way his sons were turning out, and he took a shine to me. My own father was dead by then." Berry held back, a dark look settling on his face, and then said, "My father killed himself. I don't know if you knew that. He lost all his money, then he developed diabetes and they cut off his leg. When he got out of the hospital, he went to live in a YMCA in Brooklyn. He kept me in school, he managed that. I really had no idea how bad it was for him, not until after he was dead and I went to his room to collect his things. Such an awful little room, and of course he had been such a great sport. I suspect he'd had a fast start, too. He still had a suit of clothes left from the old days, made in England for him, a beautiful thing left behind on a wire hanger in that awful room in the Y in Brooklyn." Berry slowly shook his head and was thoughtful, looking out at the empty horizon. When he turned to Sullivan, his eyes were misty, but he had control of himself, and even smiled and said, "I've lost my thread again. Where the hell was I?"

"Roosevelt had taken a shine to you."

"He really did, you know," Berry said. "My father had been a couple of years ahead of him at Groton, and when they got to Harvard I think he bullied him a bit. Back then there was still a little of the bully in my father. But FDR was a very complicated man, and it gave him considerable satisfaction to take up the son of a man he had detested."

Sullivan said, "Why have you quit, George?"

"I no longer enjoy my work."

"Just like that?"

"The pay is poor. I don't want to risk my neck."

"It was always poor," Sullivan said. "And always risky. Tell me why you've quit."

Berry didn't bother to answer. "Do you plan to stay on here?" he asked.

"I don't know."

"I wish you would." He gripped Sullivan's wrist. "Just a short while. It's a lovely place, and I want you to get to know Natalie." He looked past Sullivan at the sea, at a small boat which had come up and seemed motionless on the shimmering curve of the horizon. "I've always liked boats," Berry said. "My friend Bob has a boat. We can hire it, and he'll take us out. You and me and Natalie." He squeezed Sullivan's arm and said, "I've rented a shack down the beach. It was falling down, and I've had it fixed up. But I don't know what I'm going to do. It's day to day."

"Were you forced to quit, George?"

"No."

"Have you gone over?"

"I'd never do that."

"But it's something like that, isn't it?" Sullivan said. "You need to confess. That's why you want me to stay."

Berry slowly shook his head. He lifted himself from the canvas chair with great effort, and he seemed to totter, as if his legs were too weak to hold him.

His long fingers dug into Sullivan's arm. "You must stay for your own good," he said. "I need to warn you."

"Of what?"

But Sullivan had lost him; his gaze shifted from one end of the beach to the other, to the sea, anywhere but at Sullivan. He seemed not to have heard the question, or pretended he hadn't. He was being crafty now, and Sullivan wondered if the preoccupied stare of a moment ago was a good act. Berry was a damned good actor, and always one to take his own sweet time.

Berry stuffed his things into a flight bag, and they walked along the beach to the steps leading to the veranda. Berry stopped to brush the sand from his feet and slip on sandals. He had to balance on one foot and lean heavily on Sullivan for support.

"I swore off the booze when I first came here," he said. "Got myself a trainer, and ran on the beach."

"Why did you quit?"

"I haven't the discipline. I haven't the will."

"What is it you want to warn me of?"

Berry smiled and took his arm, teasing him now.

Sullivan pulled free. "It may be a game to you, it's not to me," he said.

Berry started to answer when a girl opened the door from the lobby and stepped onto the open veranda. She called to Berry, who returned the wave, touched Sullivan lightly on the shoulder, and said, "We'll talk later. Come and meet Natalie."

CHAPTER 17

Sullivan had met Natalie before, at a large party in the British Embassy in Bangkok. It was before he left for the field, nearly three years had passed and they had talked no more than fifteen or twenty minutes, but now on the veranda he recognized her at once. He even remembered that at the Embassy party she had sipped only orange juice, and that her thumb was bandaged. He had asked her about it, and she said she had cut it that morning opening a can of coffee. A number of beautiful women, Asian as well as European, had been at that party; Bangkok is noted for its beautiful women. He had met several that night, but she was the one he remembered.

She was not the most beautiful, certainly not the most striking; he would not even have said that she was his type. But of all the women there, she was the one he wanted to know better. His desire for her caught him by surprise, and he passed over an exquisite Thai woman, moist and scented as a flower, in order to talk to Natalie Benoit. She wore no jewelry or perfume, no makeup at all. He remembered that. Her dark brown hair was cut short, like a boy's. She was smaller than average, slender and tanned, as if she spent a lot of time outdoors. He had the impression she was good at sports. Her eyes were large, set far apart, and clear blue. Before they had spoken ten words, he knew that she was intelligent. Perhaps it was the expression in her eyes, their clarity and focus, and the way she weighed what he said and ran it through her mind. There was no getting by Natalie with charm or good looks, no rogue's smile or gleam in the eye, nor flash of white teeth against tanned skin. If he was to hold her interest, he had better know what he was talking about.

Berry knew nothing of that meeting and introduced them on the veranda as if they had never met before. Nothing Natalie did suggested that she remembered Sullivan at all. He searched her face for a hint of recognition; there was none, not a flicker. She coolly held out her hand and smiled and it was left to Sullivan to wonder if she remembered him at all.

"My two favorite people," Berry said. "Meeting at last." His eyes had that sly and excited glitter which comes from having glimpsed another's hole card.

"George said you had been shopping," Sullivan said. "Did you find anything pretty?"

"Yes. Some lovely fabrics. Batiks, and raw silk in the Indian shops."

"You look happy," Berry said.

"I am," she said. "Happy and hungry."

Lunch was served at a table near the pool, under a wide trellis with a roof woven of palm leaves. There was a breeze, and it was cool out of the glare of the sun. There were lots of birds, little black ones with yellow breasts, and crows which drove them off and perched on the backs of empty chairs and stole bits of food. Service was slow, as it always was on the island, the waiters roosting in corners, fooling and turning dance steps and beating time with their thumbs on the sides of steel serving trays. Now and then one sauntered by with a plate of food or a cold drink. Berry fussed with them, anxious for another planter's punch.

Sullivan tipped back his chair; at the boundaries of the lawn, where banana trees had been planted, a circular water sprinkler threw a rainbow haze into the air. Berry was finally served his planter's punch. Natalie drank orange juice, as she had in Bangkok.

"Natalie doesn't drink," Berry said. "I've tried to find out why, but all she'll say is that she doesn't like alcohol."

"It's really that simple," she said.

"I don't believe it," Berry said. "The reasons for never drinking are as sinister as the reasons for always drinking."

"Maybe it has to do with my father," she said. "If you insist on a reason, my father didn't approve of alcohol."

"Natalie had a very strict father," Berry said.

"He was a marvelous man," she said.

"And he taught you not to drink?"

"Yes. And not to smoke."

"What else?" Berry said.

"Not to make noise with my soup."

Berry said, "Natalie and her father adored each other."

"That makes it hard for the men who follow him in your life," Sullivan said.

"He stands alone," Berry said. "Max the Merchant Prince."

Berry polished off his drink and waved his empty glass to catch the waiter's eye. "Papa walked out of Russia alone," Berry said. "He wasn't Max the Merchant Prince then. He was thirteen years old. It's a pip of a story. Tell it, will you, Natalie."

Natalie folded her arms across her chest; she was patient, determined to be patient. "You've heard the story so many times," she said.

"Jack hasn't."

"My father was the oldest son," she said. "The family had been prosperous, but then conditions changed, their property was seized, my grandfather beaten up in the street. So my father was given the family fortune—half a dozen diamonds—and he walked with them from Russia to India, where he could sell them at a decent price."

Berry said, "But tell Jack how he carried them."

She turned on him. "In a hollow steel tube in his rectum," she said.

"For a solid year," Berry said.

"Why don't you eat something," Sullivan said.

"I'm not hungry."

"Have the hamburger," Sullivan said. "Have the cold chicken."

"Try the fruit salad," Natalie said.

"I think George would like an avocado."

"I only wish I had one to give him," Natalie said.

Berry took it all in good humor. He even put down his drink and nibbled at a roll and butter and then at Natalie's salad. She had slipped off her sandals and under the table her bare feet brushed Sullivan's. He felt the same rush of blood he had when they met in Bangkok. He wondered if she knew what he was thinking. He caught her eye and held it until he was sure he had gotten his message across. He felt her stir. She shifted her weight in her chair—she had a way of sitting upright and on the very edge, like a young lady who has been properly brought up—and finally she dabbed her lips with a napkin and flexed her bare toes.

Sullivan put away his club sandwich and asked if she had been born in India.

"Yes, but I was raised in Singapore."

"Papa Max prospered in the gem business. M. S. Benoit, Limited," Berry said. "There's a little of the hebe in Natalie."

"More than a little, actually," she said.

"Benoit Limited is well known in Asia," Sullivan said. "I remember a branch in Rangoon on Dalhousie Street." He leaned forward on the table and brought his face closer to hers. "My father bought my mother a stone there and had it made into a ring."

"What sort of stone?"

"A ruby."

"Do you know the kind?"

"I've forgotten."

"If I mentioned it, would you know? Mogok. Was it a Mogok ruby?"

"Yes. From Mogok in the north."

"That's the best kind," she said. "The very best in the world. Does your mother still have it?"

"She's dead, and I don't know what's become of it."

"That's a pity. They're rare, or at least the good ones are. And the price has gone through the roof. Buy good stones and never sell them."

"There's another of Max the Merchant Prince's Rules to Live By," Berry said. "Put your money in precious stones. The price is sure to go up."

"And you can hide them easily," she said sweetly, "and carry them with you if you've got to leave the country in a hurry."

"Particularly if you're a woman," Berry said.

Natalie lifted her water glass and Sullivan thought she might throw it at Berry. He knew he had gotten under her skin and watched her with a self-satisfied, somewhat drunken smirk, pleased to have goaded her this far, and trying to decide if he should take it a step further.

Sullivan said, "Isn't the island lovely? I think this is the nicest part of it. If you get bored looking at the sea, there are the mountains."

Natalie laughed and put down the glass. "And if you don't care for the mountains, there's the waterfall."

"I hear it's a marvelous waterfall," Sullivan said.

"The best for miles around," she said. "George has promised to take me. Haven't you, darling?"

"Would you really have thrown a glass at me?" Berry said.

"I still might," she said.

"It's been a lovely lunch," Sullivan said.

"It still is," Berry said. "And after this lovely lunch, there'll be a lovely nap. I nap every day after lunch. Have I told you that, Jack? I also read the English newspapers, and sometimes I work on my radio. I bought the parts in Kingston. Did I tell you I was building a radio?"

"What do you listen to on it?"

"He can't get it to work," Natalie said.

"There's the woman's view," Berry said.

"And what does that mean?" she said. "Is something less true if said by a woman?"

"Usually more true," Sullivan said.

He had a way with him, but Natalie wasn't taken in. "It's neither more nor less," she said. "Truth is truth. And if you are a fool, you'll want to go back to intrigues and risking your neck. But if there's a woman who knows how to make a good life for you, if she builds you up by tickling you here and there, you won't be so fast to leave. Let a man feel like a hero in bed, cook him a good dinner, and even the worst jackass will know to stay put."

"Is that what you did with Castellone," Berry said. "Cook his dinner and make him a hero in bed?"

"Only partially." She smiled prettily. "In Bangkok one eats mostly in restaurants."

"She's cute, eh?" Berry said.

"It's you always bringing up Castellone," she said.

"Do you think of him often?"

"Why don't you get off it."

"Do you or don't you?"

"Sure," she said. "Particularly, his cock."

Berry looked very pleased, while Natalie's face flushed a deep red. She was steaming at Berry, and at herself for letting him get under her skin. Berry rose unsteadily, nearly knocking over his chair and grinning foolishly. "Got to piss," he said, and tottered in search of the gents.

Alone with Sullivan, Natalie apologized. "I'm not like that really," she said. "At least, I try not to be. George brings it out in me. He does all he can to provoke me, so that I'll hurt him. He's begun to hate himself and wants to be punished."

"The booze makes him mean," Sullivan said. "What about you? Why are you here?"

She dropped her hand on Sullivan's arm; they both ignored it, her light touch on his bare arm. "I'm just here," she said.

"Was George good to you? Are you being loyal?"

"Why I'm with him doesn't matter." She took her hand away. "You want things clearly laid out, you want to know where you stand?"

"We've met before," he said.

"In Bangkok, the British Embassy. I was still with Castellone. I didn't want to go into all of that in front of George. You see how he is."

"Yes, how is he?" Berry had returned without either of them noticing. "How is old George?" He had splashed water on his face and run a comb through his hair. "The two of you huddled together puts shivers up my spine," he said. "Are you planning to do me in?"

"Yes. But first we're going to take you fishing," Natalie said.

"If it's to be a death at sea, be sure to wrap my body in

the flag," Berry said. "And be sure also that I'm dead first. I don't fancy drowning, never have."

"You do talk a lot of shit, George."

"You won't have to kill me," Berry said. "I'll save you the trouble. But it won't be by drowning. I'll use a gun. I have a Walther, little Frau Walther." His was the only laugh, its ring turning heads at the next table. "Mauzer is a male gun, so is Colt. Smith and Wesson is a comedy act."

"He's showing off," Natalie said. "Although he might do it if we dared him."

"I'm more interested in the fishing," Sullivan said. "There's supposed to be barracuda and small tuna this side of the reef."

"Then we'll go after them tomorrow," Berry said.

He promised to make the arrangements, and that night at dinner announced that he had been to see Bob and arranged to go out the next morning at eight.

"The boat isn't much," Berry said. "But it's service-able. There's a flying bridge, and an ice chest for beer."

Sullivan turned in early that night, and was up and running on the beach before dawn. He ran for about a mile along an empty stretch as far as the ruins of an old fort which had been built by the Spanish before the English came. It had a haunted look in the gray first light. As the sky lightened, Sullivan ran closer to the water's edge, past the tiny shore birds, which darted ahead of the rollers and followed them out, picking at the wet sand for crabs.

He ran on, lengthening his stride, running effortlessly. He imagined that he was free of his body, that he was floating. It was a feeling of rapture. But it lasted only a few seconds, and soon he began to tire. He saw a shack set on a high dune about a quarter of a mile off. He set that as his goal, and dug into the wet packed sand to reach it.

It looked to be abandoned, although in good repair. There was a broad deck on the ocean side, which had partially collapsed, and a few windowpanes were broken, but it was otherwise sound. Sullivan peeped inside and saw the place was neat and compact, with a small gallery and a pair of bunk beds with a sea chest and a folded U.S. Navy blanket at the foot of each.

The door was locked, and because he didn't want to force it, he worked a shard of broken glass from a window frame, reached in and released the latch and lifted the window. He climbed in and had a look around.

The place had the damp, musty smell of boarded-up beach houses, but it was clean, and whoever had occupied it last had left it in good shape.

Sullivan nosed around the shack, had a look in the sea chest, which was empty, and the kitchen drawers. The house tempted him. He had heard the story of Kirk coming by accident on a cabin in the Rockies and buying it the same day. Sullivan had always wanted a shack on the beach; he wondered if, like Kirk, he bought it on impulse, he would never go near it again.

Sullivan left the shack as he had entered, by way of the window, which he closed behind him. As he trotted back to the hotel he tried to imagine living in such a place day by day. He had had too many stretches of empty time, and he wondered now how he would fill it. He would learn Russian, he would fish and fiddle with a small boat and run on the beach. But he no longer wanted to do it alone. The only person he could think of being with was Natalie. He liked the idea of having her alone in an isolated place. He wanted her to himself. He needed to concentrate on her, to bear down. It was a sexual feeling. He wondered if they would eventually get restless or bored with each other. He couldn't imagine it at the moment, but he was experienced enough to realize that was because they had never slept together, hardly knew each other. In time, they would get on each other's nerves, they would make each other suffer. Sullivan felt it in his bones.

He cooled off after his run with a swim, had a shower, shaved, and dressed in fresh white ducks and was at the dock at seven-thirty. Bob was already there. Sullivan introduced himself and helped take on fresh water, bait, ice, and a case of local beer.

"That's for Mr. Berry." Bob said.

"We ought to just leave it on the dock."

"We ought to right enough," Bob said. "I got him away from the drink for a time, and had him running and sparring with me. He's a strong man, you know." Bob rubbed the side of his jaw. "Punch on him like a mule's kick."

Bob was about five seven or eight and lightly built, although wiry and strong enough, without an ounce of excess flesh. He was very dark and his eyes had a narrow upward slant, with old scar tissue on both brows.

Sullivan asked if he had been a boxer.

"That was a long time in the past," Bob said. He could have been thirty or fifty, it was impossible to tell. "I did pretty okay on the island, and even in Trinidad, and some in Venezuela. But up in the States . . . ."

He slowly shook his head, amused to remember the beatings he had taken. "I fought very good people. I know you heard of Lou Walker, went on to be lightweight champion. I fought him in the Madison Square Garden. I didn't win, nothing like that, but I give Lou Walker a fight. Yes, sir, I give him a hell of a good fight." He laughed again and shook his head. "That Lou Walker had a punch on him, you know. But I kept all of my brains, what little God gave me, and even kept a few of them American dollars."

"Is that how you got the money for the boat?"

"This boat?" Bob found that hilarious. "This boat is my inheritance from my father. He was an angel, that man. He made up his own songs and sang them. And he played cricket for Jamaica the year Trinidad beat hell out of us. The singing got him three beautiful wives, my mother and two others. He was a lovable man, but not one for commerce."

They finished loading the boat, and Bob passed the time tying baitfish to the trolling lines and telling Sullivan about his girl, Eloise, who worked as a waitress in the hotel.

Sullivan questioned Bob about the beach shack he had seen.

"That would be the one used to be owned by a fellow from Kingston. A doctor, he was. I took him out for wahoo and sometimes bonito. He sewed up my hand one time I went and cut it, and wouldn't take no money for it. I heard he left the island."

"Is the place for sale?"

Bob got busy with the bait, avoiding Sullivan's eyes. "It's a nice place, if you put a little work into it," he said. "There's even an old pier runs out from the west end of the cove. The bottom is flat there, no rocks at all. You like boats, I expect."

Natalie came out of the hotel, George Berry trailing just behind. She bounced along in shorts and sneakers and oversized sunglasses; he looked as if he had been dragged from bed, his face shielded from the sun by a wide-brimmed planter's hat, shuffling unsteadily behind like an old man. From the end of the pier, Sullivan could feel the tension between them.

Bob started the engine idling. Sullivan untied the bowline and helped Natalie on board. As soon as they were under way, Berry went below and had a nap.

It was half an hour before they reached the reef and put the lines out, and another hour trolling without a strike.

Natalie was good company, making jokes about her beginner's luck not holding, not complaining about the sun or the choppy water on the open side of the reef. Neither of them bothered with food or water, or much in the way of small talk. Natalie was serious about the fishing, or at least behaved as if she were; Sullivan kept his eyes on her baitfish skimming the wake, hoping to spot her fish a second or two before it struck, giving her the lead time she would need to set the hook. After a time, Berry came up on deck; he drank beer and brooded in a deck chair under the wide brim of his straw hat, tossing the empty cans wide over the side, cocking his arm and passing them in a tight spiral, like a quarterback.

Just after three o'clock, Natalie had her first strike. Sullivan saw the fish clearly, saw it flash silver in the white water. The next instant it hit, bending the pole double. It was stronger than a barracuda; a wahoo, and a big one, by the feel of it.

But Natalie was a shade slow; the fish took the bait and was gone, leaving the empty line trailing in the water.

"I've lost him," she said. "Damn it, I didn't know what to do."

"At least we know they're around," Sullivan said. "There'll be another."

"But that was a big one."

"You see him hit?" Bob said from the bridge. "Man, he was cutting in, big as a house." He loved fishing and never lost his enthusiasm. "You hit the boss wahoo."

"I was too slow," she said.

"We'll find you another, Miss."

"Does one eat wahoo?" Berry asked.

"You got to grind the meat into a hash," Bob said.

"Sounds bloody disgusting." Berry threw another beer can into the water. "Have you a gun on board?"

"No firearms on board, sir."

"I like to pop beer cans," Berry said. "Next time I'll bring one."

A few minutes later Natalie had a second strike, nearly as big as the first, and this time she was ready. It turned out to be another wahoo, which put up a terrific fight. Natalie brought it alongside. Sullivan took the wheel, and Bob gaffed the fish and hauled it in. It was her first real sport fish, and everyone was thrilled but Berry, who didn't get up from his deck chair.

It was late in the afternoon, but neither Natalie nor Sullivan had had anything to eat or drink. Sullivan always fasted until the first fish was caught—he said it was a way of paying for his luck—and she had gone along with him. But Bob had brought along a thermos of sweetened ice tea and lemon, and Sullivan poured three glasses; and they drank to her first fish.

"I didn't know how thirsty I was." She was sweating and flushed from the sun and battling the fish. "And hungry, too. But I forgot all that once the fish was hooked. God, it's exciting. He is big, isn't he? Do you think he's as big as the first, the one that got away?"

"He's damn big, Miss," Bob said from the bridge.

"And mean looking," she said. "And fast. I've read wahoo is the fastest fish there is."

It was a long sleek fish, pale blue above the lateral line and silver below, armed with a single row of spiky murderous teeth set in a long narrow head which came to a point, like a spear.

"Now that I've caught him, I want to throw him back," she said. "Can that be done?"

"Bob had to gaff him to bring him in," Sullivan said. "He'll bleed to death in the water, or probably draw sharks."

She looked with pity at the great fish oozing blood and flopping hopelessly, glassy-eyed in the catch box built into the stern.

"Do you still want to go after marlin?" Sullivan asked.

"Sure."

Berry said, "Natalie is a great sportswoman. She hunts as well as fishes, the bigger and more ferocious the game the better. Once she even shot a tiger."

"That's not true," she said.

"She had him in her sights," Berry said. "She was looking down the barrel, but didn't pull the trigger."

"I didn't want to kill him," Natalie said. "May I have another iced tea?"

"Have a Scotch," Berry said.

"I'll stay with the iced tea, please. It's so good in the sun, particularly with sugar and lemon."

"So good in the sun. Particularly with lemon and sugar." Berry was a ruthless mimic. "There's a duchess for you. Our little Natalie. Sensible shoes and flawless English. Virginity into one's late teens. Natalie could fool the Queen herself. Not a whiff of the kike there at all."

"All that because of a little tea, George?" She was a miracle of good humor. "My father always kept a samovar going in his study. So did all my uncles and aunts. Jews love tea, George. I thought you knew that about us."

"And Jews aren't sots," he said.

"Some are." Her good humor held; Sullivan guessed that sometime last night she had resolved never again to let Berry get under her skin. "I'm having such a good time," she said. "Catching that huge fish was so exciting." She squeezed George's forearm and said with great sincerity, "Please don't spoil it for me."

"Sugar and lemon," Berry said. "Particularly with sugar and lemon."

"There's a bottle of Scotch in my bag," Sullivan said. "Drink it, George, drink it all, but for Christ's sake shut up."

Berry turned on him. He had been drunkenly slurring his words, but combat, like a whiff of pure oxygen, cleared his head. "I notice that you neither eat nor drink when you fish. Not a sip of water, not a crust of bread. Why is that?"

"It's a habit."

"Is it the same when you hunt?"

"I don't hunt."

"But you kill," Berry said. "Do you fast before you kill?"

"Where's your bag?" Natalie said. "I need the bottle. I want to give George a drink."

"Is it mystical?" Berry said. "You go without food and you see visions. Is it something like that? You're not a simple gunman, not one of those stone figures made up of bravery and revenge. You're a more complicated man. It's got to be ritualized, the killing does. Part of a larger religious experience."

"You're raving, George." Sullivan's voice was deliberately calm. He was smiling and trying to soothe Berry. He even reached out and took hold of his arm.

"Raving? Natalie, do you think I'm raving?"

"Yes, but it's perfectly all right."

Sullivan took the bottle from his bag and passed it around.

Natalie drank first, and then each of the men, Sullivan passing the bottle to Bob on the bridge before drinking himself.

Berry's mood changed almost at once. He began to relax and take on a benevolent glow. He told some funny stories and even sang a Cantonese love song about a girl pining away for her lover lost at sea. But then he climbed back on Natalie and started to tease her again, insisting she tell about the time she had been hunting tiger in Burma.

"You've heard it half a dozen times," she said.

"But Jack hasn't," Berry said. "An epic tale." He had

:ilted his deck chair, put his bare feet up, and was swilling
Sullivan's Scotch. "Have you ever known a woman who
hunted tiger?"

He poked Natalie with his bare toe. "Tell Jack about
the tiger hunt," he said.

She didn't look at him, didn't react at all to his toe in
her ribs. She set her mouth and Sullivan watched the
anger raise the color in her face. But she didn't say a
word. Sullivan waited to see what she would do.

Finally, she said softly, "There really isn't that much to
tell. You don't go after the tiger, you wait for him to come
to you. That's what the shooting platform is for. It's called
a *machan*, and it's built of bamboo. You climb up and
settle in just before sunset and wait all night for the tiger.
Sunset to daybreak. We did that four nights running until
the tiger showed up."

"Was it cold?"

"You bet it was. We were in the mountains, about six
thousand feet up."

Berry said, "Tell us about having to rub yourself
against the cattle."

"He likes that part best," she said.

"What are you whispering about?" Berry said. "Get to
the part where you rub against the cattle."

"It's to rid your body of its scent," she said. "You can't
smoke or wear perfume or even bathe with soap. The
tiger has the most marvelous nose and he won't come
within miles if he smells human. So you have to get in
with a herd of cattle and let them trample your clothes
and then rub up against them naked."

"When I imagine you and the cattle," Berry said, "it's
always at night under a full moon."

"The worst part was the mosquitoes," she said. "Of
course you can't use a spray, and the trackers—the *Mok-
Soe*—are very unhappy about having a woman along.
Women are bad luck. Then there are the food taboos.
One can eat only boiled rice and sip tepid water from a
bottle. No meat or fish until after the kill, when the head
Mok-Soe is given a tiger's leg to roast."

"Tell Jack what happened when you saw the tiger,"
Berry said.

"I lost my nerve," she said. "Castellone had to shoot

him. We had waited through four nights without a
sighting, but finally two males came down to drink at
almost the same instant. They began to fight. I tell you, it
was something, two grown males going at each other. I
froze. But Castellone was cold as ice. He picked out the
bigger of the two and fired the shotgun at him. When it
hit, the tiger leaped about six feet in the air and landed on
his back. A second later he was up and moving. Castellone took the rifle from the *Mok-Soe* and killed him."

"With a single round from the rifle?"

"Yes. It was a brain shot."

"Quite a man, Castellone," Berry said.

"He was that night," Natalie said.

"I'll bet he was," Berry said. "A man shoots a tiger it
does something for him, for his ego."

"Castellone's ego worked beautifully without all that,"
Natalie said.

"One shot right to the brain," Berry said. "Cool as a
cucumber, that's Castellone. He kept you well, too, didn't
he? Good jewelry and three-star restaurants. First class
on the Cunard Lines."

"We lived comfortably," she said.

"Did he ever tell you where his money came from?"

"I never asked."

"He never told you what he did?"

"He did what you do." She jerked her thumb at
Sullivan; his mother had called that a rude gesture, one
never made by ladies or gentlemen. "He did what this one
does," she had switched to French. "Spy, gun-runner,
assassin. I kept my nose out of his business. He could
have been a pimp. Anyone of you could. Damn fools.
Extortionists, murderers. I don't know what any of you
do, and I don't care. The hell with you. And with Bernard
Castellone. The hell with all of you."

"She's tired of us," Berry said.

"I'm tired of the torture game," she said.

"She's tired of men," Berry said.

"Tired. Tired all around," Natalie said. "I'm going to
stretch out on that bunk below deck and have a nap."

Bob had pointed the boat toward shore and was making
good time. It had been hot and calm most of the day, but
a good breeze had come up from the islands to the south

where later in the year the hurricanes started. Sullivan watched the sky darken and the sea grow rougher and take on a deep-gray color.

"You like being out on the water?" Berry said.

"I'm not ready to quit, though."

"Now's the time," Berry said. "Could be the last chance you'll have. Find yourself a game woman, preferably with a dollar or two in her own name. Natalie has a few put by, you know."

"Does she?"

"She will before long." Berry made a teasing smile, something to lead Sullivan on. He knew something, he had a secret, and he wanted Sullivan to ask what it was. But of course Sullivan wouldn't, and Berry said, "She'll be well fixed, and she does have an eye for you."

"You passing her on?"

"Why not?"

"Pass on Natalie?" Sullivan said. "Try it, she'll spit in your eye."

"She can't stand me now," he said. "We were good for each other at the beginning. She'd had a bad time with Castellone, and I had just had a bad time period. Do you know him, by the way?"

"Only by reputation."

Berry said, "She was bruised by him, and I was the right sort of gentle lover. She was able to be protective with me. Maternal. It struck a rather deep note with her. At least it did until I ruined it." His smile was rueful now and all the muscles of his face were slack. He looked tired and old, staring at the dull rolling sea, his eyes red and watery, partly from drink, but there was misery there as well, misery of an incurable kind.

"It's up for me," he said. "It's all over."

"Don't talk shit," Sullivan said.

"I ran the dirty business," Berry said. "I don't know why. For money, for the Agency maybe. Twenty kilos of heroin, twenty million dollars. I ran it to keep Nyo afloat. God knows why."

"Tell me about Castellone," Sullivan said. "What part did he play?"

"He's the other side," Berry said; there was the teasing smile, the secret Berry had been waiting to tell. "Castellone is a French narc. Nobody is on to him. They've got their doubts. But none of them knows for sure. Only me."

"Where is he now?"

"In Paris," Berry said. "Waiting for the stuff to come down."

"Will he talk to me?"

"He might," Berry said. "If you can find him. He might trust you. On the other hand, he might think the Agency has caught on to him and sent you. If he thought that, he'd kill you."

"Do you think the Agency sent me?"

"It doesn't matter what I think."

"I want to burn that opium," Sullivan said.

"So does Castellone," Berry said. "He also wants to nail the wops who buy and sell it." Berry tilted his chair and raised his feet, the straw planter's hat shielding his eyes. He looked peaceful at last, all the tension and unhappiness gone from his face. "Shall we go out for marlin tomorrow," he said. "We can if the weather holds. I never have caught a marlin, tomorrow could be the day. It could be my lucky day, Lord willing." He dropped off to sleep, snoring softly.

CHAPTER 18

Bob didn't want to go out the next morning. The weather wasn't right for sailfish; it was too hot, too calm, too this, and too that. Bob had toothache, his back was giving him hell, and he suffered from hangover.

"Also, there's no way George Berry gets up this morning to go fishing," he said. "That man was exceptionally drunk last night. Two o'clock in the morning, he was breaking up the place and looking to fight Samson. You know the barman, Samson?"

"I've seen him," Sullivan said. "Fighting him can get you killed."

"But Samson don't fight with no George Berry," Bob said. "No, sir. Samson is a peaceful man. He calms him down, soothes him. He held his hand and gave him a big drink on the house. When he pass out, Samson put him over his shoulder like a sack of rice and carry him to bed."

"Was the lady there?"

"No sign of her. My girl Eloise was working last night, and she brought her dinner to the room."

"Let me take the boat out myself," Sullivan said. "I'll

pay you the regular day charter, and bring it back to the
pier."

"I can trust you with the boat," Bob said. "But there's
no way that poor fool George Berry is going to get himself
to fishing."

"Either way you get paid," Sullivan said.

Bob gave Sullivan the keys to the boat, and told him
that in case he were needed he could be found with his
beloved Eloise, whose mornings were her own. He
hurried off and left Sullivan to tinker with the fuel line on
the port engine, which on the water had seemed a bit
rough. He used a length of wire, cleaning it like the barrel
of a rifle, and had just replaced the shaft and was washing
his hands when Natalie came out of the hotel and started
along the pier. She wore a loose cotton shirt, blue shorts
with a white stripe at the seam, and sneakers with white
woolen socks, like a schoolgirl dressed for track and field.
Sullivan was able to study her as she walked the length of
the pier. Her legs were firm and solid, like a sprinter's,
and with every step showed clear stripes of muscle at the
calf and thigh. Her waist was small and her stomach flat.
She had been put together well and then worked hard to
stay in condition. She was small, but there was nothing
fragile about her. Sullivan thought of the sturdy tough
little man her father must have been, and that she could
have taken his hand and walked with him across Russia to
India.

All the length of the pier, he never took his eyes from
her; she came straight at him, with just a hint of a cocky
smile, and a faint blush to her cheeks, bouncing on the
balls of her feet.

"It's just as if you read my mind," he said. "Gym shorts
and sneakers, and lovely little tits under a cotton shirt."

"I don't want to go fishing today," she said.

"We'll go out anyway. Just the two of us on the boat."

"What do we do about Bob?"

"He's given me the boat."

"George won't be out," she said. "He's sleeping it off.
He was in a terrible way last night, started drinking again
after he left you. I tried to get him to eat something but he
wouldn't hear of it, and went off with that savage red look
in his eye that means trouble."

"He would have found it if it hadn't been for Samson."

"The barman at the hotel? Is that what he's called? Well, he got George back to his room. I'd gone to bed, but heard them crashing into things. George's room is next to mine, you know." She patted her hair at the back of her neck and did something comic with her eyes. She was in a marvelous mood that morning. "About ten minutes later, he started banging at my door. I think he had a bottle in his room, because he was getting drunker. He started bellowing that he was going to break the door down. Finally, Mr. Parkins, the Manager, came. He was in an old dressing gown and wearing his gold half-glasses and carrying a book. He had obviously been in bed reading. I had climbed up on a chair and was peeping through the transom. You know what a mild-mannered little man Mr. Parkins is—well he was mad as hell at being hauled out of bed. He called George a drunken fool and told him if he didn't shut up and go to bed he was going to call the cops and have George thrown in jail. George got very quiet then. For a second or two I thought he was going to hit Mr. Parkins. His face turned red as a beet, and he looked absolutely in a rage. But old Parkins held his ground. He looked a plucky little man in his tacky dressing gown and spectacles, standing up to big George. He was right and George was wrong, and they both knew it, and he just stared George down. Mr. Parkins reminds me of one of those English out in Singapore when I was a kid, tough as hell and translating the Latin poets."

"What time was all this?" Sullivan said.

"About two."

"Didn't they notice you?"

"Neither looked up at the transom," she said.

"What did George do finally?"

"Nothing. All the anger leaked out of him. It bloody ran down between his legs. He took Mr. Parkins staring him down and then, without a word, backed into his room and closed the door. There hasn't been a peep out of him since."

Sullivan had started the engines and she untied the lines and used her foot to push the hull of the boat away from the dock. Sullivan eased the boat through the narrow channel into the open sea. There was a morning breeze, but it was already hot enough to have burned off the early fog, the sun pouring through a cloudless sky.

"Is the weather like this all the time?" she said.

"No. There are seasons." He hesitated, deciding what he could say and what he couldn't. "George urged me to stay on here," he said, finally. "In fact he's recommended an early retirement."

"You'd be bored here," she said.

"Are you bored?"

"I would be if I had to stay."

"I wouldn't mind it for a time," Sullivan said. "There's a shack farther along the beach I liked. Or a run-down boat I could put in shape and live on. I'd like that."

"Would you live alone?"

"I can."

She looked directly at him, her eyes hidden by dark glasses. "You wouldn't be alone long," she said. "Not unless you arranged it that way. And you just might. It would be a way of doing penance. Men like you do that. Men in your line of work. You're a solitary and moody type. George is like that, and so was Castellone."

"It's Castellone you're talking about," he said. "Not George, and not me. Castellone. Are you in love with him?"

She didn't answer that, and when she did speak it was to turn the conversation another way. "Perhaps you're really a romantic," she said. "Perhaps it has to be just the right girl. Have you been waiting for the right girl?"

"Yes. Do you think she'll show up? Three years ago in Bangkok," he said. "Fifteen minutes of conversation at a cocktail party." He edged closer, but something in her face held him off. "Nothing memorable was said. It was all casual. Chitchat. But I couldn't forget."

She slipped away and stood apart with her arms folded across her chest, studying him.

"You're not a bad-looking man," she said. "You've got nice arms and small hips. How old are you?"

"Thirty-one."

"I'm thirty-three."

"You're very well preserved."

"I'll bet you're a regular bastard," she said. "That's what George said you were. Don't worry, it was said admiringly. He loves you in a way, like a son. You have a good reputation. Even Castellone respects you."

"I never met him."

"He asked about you once, wanted to know if I knew you. Perhaps he saw us talking together in Bangkok. He doesn't like Americans usually."

"He does still have a hook in you," Sullivan said.

"I'm getting over it," she said. "It just takes a long time is all. But once you make up your mind . . ." She shrugged. "It's a matter of discipline."

He followed the coast to the west of the bay, where there were small isolated coves. It was a poor bathing beach, and worse for boats, and so all of that part of the coast was left alone, with not a cottage, telephone or electric line, or even a road in sight. They agreed it must look more or less as it had when the first English saw it, a howling bit of coast more like Cornwall or Maine than the Caribbean.

It changed suddenly as they continued west toward Ocho Rios. The jagged rocks flattened out to a shelf a few feet below the surface of the water and outcroppings which were barely covered even at high tide.

It was a treacherous coast, particularly for larger ships with a considerable draft. He pointed out the hull of an English freighter on the rocky shelf a few feet below the surface of the water. It had been crippled by a U-boat in 1940 and driven by the current toward shore, where it foundered on the rocks.

"It's the best place for snorkeling around here," he said. "The water is clear, and it's alive with fish. All kinds."

"I should have thought to bring my gear," she said. "It's all neatly packed away in the room."

"I saw a locker full of stuff on board," he said.

"It's a beautiful spot."

"Not a soul around for miles."

"I haven't a swimsuit," she said.

"Either have I."

It was another sultry day with little breeze and he was able to cut the engines and tie up to a buoy about thirty feet from the submerged hull. He found the snorkeling gear and adjusted the strap of one of the masks to fit her.

She knew to wet the inside of the glass so that it wouldn't fog, and how to flex the muscles of her mouth around the rubber bit of the snorkel tube. He hooked the stern ladder to the hull, and she sat in a deck chair to take off her sneakers and woolen socks.

"I'm a little scared," she said.

"Of what?"

"Of snorkeling this far out. I've always gone along the shore. At least close enough to land to see it."

"Are you a strong swimmer?"

"Will I have to be?"

"No. It's just for your confidence."

"You stay close."

"We can go to a safer spot," he said.

"You're making it a challenge."

"It's just that this is the best snorkeling on the island."

"You are a bastard."

"It's your choice."

She stood up, pulled her shirt over her head, and stepped out of her shorts. "The hell with you," she said, and ignored the stern ladder with a neat dive over the side.

They snorkeled for a better part of an hour. She stayed close to him at first, but quickly grew more confident. The water was clear as glass, and the area all around the hull teemed with varieties of brilliant-colored fish. It was easy to become absorbed and lose all track of time and distance, to drift too far from the boat bobbing near the buoy. The water was warm, but in those places where the current ran it was cooler, with a thrilling sense of the bottomless depth of the open sea, of its immensity and potential for danger, and of how easily one could be swallowed up, bobbing naked on its surface.

"I've never been out on the water like this before," she said.

They had taken off their masks and snorkels and tossed them back on board. She clung to the edge of the boat, and he stayed near, floating on his back and treading water.

"I looked around and couldn't see a thing but the water," she said. "Not another boat, or even a bird."

"Are you still scared?"

"I'm shivering," she said. "It's absolutely marvelous."

"It's a sexual feeling," he said.

When he swam closer, she flashed her bottom at him, laughed, and swam off. "Aren't you going to chase me?" she said.

"We're not dolphins," he said, "to mate in water."

"We're not to mate at all," she said.

"But it's such a heavenly sport," he said.

"Certainly it is," she said. "But in the water? Can it be done?"

"I'm told it can."

"But you don't know from first-hand experience?"

"No, but I've thought how it might be done. I've thought about it a lot."

"I once made love in the water," she said. "But it was in a swimming pool. The shallow end, where the kiddies play. It was night, there was a full moon and the air smelled of jasmine. It was lovely."

"I think you're making it up."

"How did you know?"

"The part about the jasmine."

She laughed and said, "When you were a child did you like to pee in the water?"

"Is that what you're doing now?"

"I didn't think you'd mind."

He dove and reached out for her underwater, but she kicked free and swam away.

"How deep is it here?" she said.

"We're above the rocky shelf," he said. "But it drops off suddenly and gets very deep. Probably a couple of hundred feet, at least that."

"Imagine what must be swimming around below us." Her skin below the surface gave off a shifting greenish light, and the refraction of the sun's rays passing through the clear water made it seem as if her body itself were liquid. "I imagine giant octopuses and sharks," she said. "Hundreds of feet of water below. A great cove. Doesn't it scare you?"

"There's the fun of it," he said, and swam over to her.

She reached below the surface of the water and gathered him in her hand. She looked straight into his eyes, brazenly, and with considerable skill rolling the

treasure she had found, gently scratched with her finger-
nail. He passed a breathless few seconds. But she let him
go and swam off. He floated on his back to let her admire
in the sunlight what she had made. She circled back and
swam under him, but he whirled suddenly, seized her, and
carried her to the ladder fastened to the stern of the boat.
She wrapped her legs and arms around him, and he
carried her up the ladder and made love to her on the
swaying deck.

It was past noon when he undid the line tied to the buoy
and started the engines. They were hungry and thirsty,
and she had got into her head that she needed to have a
look at the shack he had seen. She wanted to test her own
idea of the kind of place that would make him happy. But
first they needed something to eat, and he tied up at the
nearest marina, bought what they needed, and carried the
packages in the hot sun along the beach to the shack.

They were hot and thirsty and famished by the time
they arrived, and neither spoke a word until they had
settled in the shade of the porch and eaten the fruit and
sandwiches and drunk a quart of orange juice, passing the
carton back and forth between them. Sullivan picked the
lock and she searched the inside, poking in every corner
and drawer.

"I love this kind of thing," she said. "I'd be a good
snoop if you could teach me to pick locks." She had a
look in the kitchen cabinets. "It's all neat as a pin," she
said. "A self-sustained bachelor lived here, and that's one
of the reasons it appeals to you. Bachelor's digs. You'd
make the bed and line up your shoes and even have a
drainer for the dishes. Everything shipshape. No need for
a woman, no real need at all. Women are only a
diversion, a pleasure. Isn't that so? You can pick locks
and keep your lip buttoned, and live alone. All of you the
same."

"There's another carton of orange juice," he said.
"Why don't we go back on the porch and you can drink
some?"

"And shut up?"

"That's a lovely idea."

"I'm babbling because I'm nervous," she said. "I ought

to be relaxed. You've fed me and fucked me. I ought to be feeling full and satisfied."

"Does it bother you about George?"

"You mean am I feeling guilty?" She was shaking her head and she sounded indignant. "Guilt is dumb, a wasted feeling," she said. "I'll tell you what's bothering me—you. It's nothing you've done. It's not your fault. It's me, my damn psychology. I have these quirks, you see. I don't like most men after I've slept with them. I just want them to pull up their pants and go away." Something made her shudder and wrap her arms around her chest, as if she'd heard chalk scraped on a blackboard.

"Men can have the same feelings," he said.

"I don't believe it."

"You're a smart girl," he said. "And you're tough. You could probably walk across Asia with a tube of diamonds up your ass, start a jewelry business, and make a couple of million bucks. Tough and smart, but you know absolutely nothing about what I feel."

"I'm sorry, I didn't mean to hurt you," she said. "I feel rotten, and I was lashing out. Maybe it *is* George that's bothering me. He was sweet and I owe him. But we're not sexual, not with each other. We don't make love anymore, although we still try. God, it's bloody awful. My fault as much as his."

"Maybe even more yours," Sullivan said.

"Now what exactly would you know about it?"

"It's an intuition."

"I just think it's something nasty you heard from George," she said. "Something he said when he was in his cups and running off at the mouth."

"George loves you," he said.

"I can feel myself getting ready to cave in with you," she said. "I know that if we stick together, I'll wind up giving you everything I have, asking you to kick me around. That's the way it is with me, the way it always has been. But I'm thirty-three, and I know better. After Castellone, I promised myself it would never happen again."

He didn't answer; he couldn't take his eyes off her. He was surprised to see how lovely she was, as if he had never seen her before. The shack was still and hot, the sun pouring through the screen door. A green fly rubbed its legs and fed on the breadcrumbs on the counter near the sink. Sullivan realized he had been holding his breath and slowly let it out. He rose from one of those languid, sensual, and isolated episodes which happen rarely and are never forgotten.

"We shouldn't spoil this afternoon," he said.

She shook her head. "I don't want to love you," she said.

"It's not under our control."

"The hell it's not." But she said it lightly, shaking her head. "Castellone once told me that love is like war, only the young and foolish volunteer."

Sullivan hadn't time to answer; someone was shouting his name, but from a great distance. Because it was his name, he heard it a second or two before she did. He didn't at first recognize the voice, but knew immediately that it was ominous. Something terrible had happened. He felt it in his bones. And his first thought was that it would ruin things between him and Natalie.

Sullivan saw Bob cut across the dune and run toward the shack, shouting something about George Berry. Something had happened to George Berry.

CHAPTER 19

Bob was incoherent. From shock, he had temporarily forgotten his English and was shouting in patois. Sullivan was able to get the drift, but Natalie was completely in the dark.

"What about George?" she said. "Has he been hurt?"

Sullivan knew; his heart sank, and he glanced quickly at Natalie, looking for support.

"Has he had an accident?" she said to Bob. "Damn it, talk sense."

"No accident," Bob said. "No way an accident."

"He's dead," Sullivan said.

Natalie let out a deep sigh, which ended as a long and barely audible moan. She swayed and sat heavily on the edge of the bunk.

Sullivan said, "Where is George?"

"Who?"

"Berry. Where is his body?"

"Where I seen him. I didn't touch him. Man, I wouldn't for nothing."

"Is he at the hotel, Bob?"

"Yes. In his room."

"How did you get here?"

"I borrowed Samson's jeep. But I didn't tell him a thing. I didn't tell a soul."

Natalie looked up from the daybed. "How did he die?" she said.

"He shot himself."

"Where's the jeep now?" Sullivan said.

"I didn't want to get stuck in the sand, so I left it parked on the road at the end of the path. You asked me about this shack, and I see the boat over to the marina. So I figured you and the lady come here."

They left the house together and walked quickly along the path to the jeep. Bob drove. He was calmer now that he had broken the news to Sullivan. The thing was out of his hands. Natalie looked pale and frightened, and stared at her hands folded in her lap while Bob told them what had happened.

Eloise had a tiny room on the top floor of the hotel and he had been there with her. "She was off duty until one o'clock. She got a little hot plate in the room, so we can make a snack. It's very cozy." Bob was again using the English he had been taught in the Methodist school. "We had been having a serious discussion, me and Eloise, one of the greatest importance." He cleared his throat and said, "We have decided to announce our engagement."

Natalie looked up. Sullivan said, "Congratulations."

"You're the first persons I've told," he said. "We're going to wait on the wedding until Christmas, when her mother gets back from Kingston."

"Tell us about how you found the body," Sullivan said.

"Eloise goes on duty at about one," Bob said. "She make a sandwich and left me in her room to have a little nap, and to get my strength back. I was just dozing off when she comes tearing in, looking like she seen a ghost. She had seen Mr. Berry's breakfast tray was still outside his door. It hadn't been touched, so she knocked. But there was no answer, and she figured the room be empty and she goes in to tidy up. That's when she seen him, and she came running back to get me."

"What did you do?"

"Nothing. I seen he was dead, and I come to fetch you straightaway."

"Where's Eloise now?"

"I told her to go to her room and lock the door. She's scared stiff and won't come out."

"And George was dead when you got there?"

"He was sure dead."

Bob swung the jeep onto the main road and pressed the accelerator pedal to the floor. Sullivan told him to slow down when they arrived at the entrance to the hotel grounds, and had him park the jeep near the stairs at the rear of the building.

"What room is he in?" Sullivan said.

"Twenty-four. On the second floor," Natalie said. "But I haven't a key."

"I didn't lock the door," Bob said.

"You're not to come with me," Sullivan said to Natalie. "I'll do what has to be done. Go to your room and pack. I want us both off the island before the body is found."

"I haven't much to pack," she said. "Why are we leaving?"

"I'll meet you here at the parking lot," he said. "Make it as fast as you can."

Bob tagged along behind Sullivan as far as the door to Berry's room. Sullivan had to find an excuse to send him away. He wanted no distractions, and he needed a moment or two alone with George's body. Sullivan was used to death, at times callous about it, like a doctor.

But he was in no hurry to see George Berry's body. He hesitated at the door, his hand on the knob. He was afraid, he felt weak and a little sick, and needed to gather his nerve.

Even after he turned the knob and opened the door, he didn't go straight into the room, but stood motionless in the doorway, listening with his head cocked to one side, his eyes darting around the room, sniffing the air. All his senses were keen. This death was different, it put him on guard and raised the hair along the back of his neck.

The shutters were closed, so that the room was unnaturally dark, and chilly with the air-conditioner going. He stepped cautiously into the room and closed the door

behind him. The odor of cold gunpowder hung over the
room. Berry was lying in bed, his head propped up by
three pillows, as if he had settled in for the night with a
book and gone off to sleep. But his eyes were wide open
and there was a bullet hole in his left temple; Berry was
left-handed. He had kept his word and shot himself with a
Walther pistol.

Sullivan sniffed a glass on the bedside table, taking care
not to touch it. It had contained Scotch, but was now
empty. Berry had finished his drink before taking up the
Walther.

He was wearing freshly laundered pajamas from Turn-
bull and Asser, and a dressing gown. His hair was neatly
combed and smelled faintly of shampoo. There was a spot
of shaving foam dried behind his right ear. George had
bathed and shaved, changed to clean pajamas, and then
blown his brains out. He had made himself a farewell
drink and screwed a silencer on to the muzzle of the gun.

George had treated himself with respect and great
kindness. He had cared for himself at the end, and there
was certainly some timid reproach in all of these deliberate actions, for he seemed to be saying that others loved
him less than he loved himself. The bullet hole in his
temple was small and neat; there wasn't much blood. He
was cold and grayish under the suntan, but all things
considered, George looked well. Sullivan gently lowered
his eyelids and held them with the palm of his hand so that
they stayed shut.

A sealed envelope was propped against the bedside
lamp, Sullivan's name written across it in Berry's neat
hand. Sullivan thought: his hand was steady; George was
sober, his head was clear.

In the envelope was a safe deposit key, box number
381, in the Geneva branch of the Banco Suizo-Panameño.
At the bottom of the envelope was a scrap of paper—it
was folded twice and so small Sullivan had nearly overlooked it. All that was written on it was a signature:
Martin David Wright. But of course it had been signed by
Berry. There was no attempt to conceal that.

Sullivan reflected for a second or two, then carefully
refolded the signature sample, returned it and the key to
the envelope, and put it in his pocket.

He looked carefully around the room for a second note; there was none. He hadn't really expected to find any. No explanation was possible. None was called for. He looked through the pockets of Berry's clothes and through his bags. He found a few hundred dollars in cash and some traveler's checks, and a credit card case. Sullivan left it all behind for the police.

He had a closer look at George; he was cold to the touch and his skin had a waxy pallor. He hadn't been disfigured, and seemed thinner and younger, lying back with his eyes closed; the bones of his face stood out, and his profile was as handsome as when he was young, when FDR had sent Uncle Tim after him at Heidelberg.

It was thoughtful of him to have used a silencer; it had saved his friends a lot of bother, and no doubt George had thought of that. George was a man with many good traits; Sullivan had already begun to remember those, and to smile looking back at the good times they had enjoyed together. The Berry of the last few days was another man altogether, one best forgotten. Sullivan was young, but had already learned how best to remember the dead.

His last look at George went on for several seconds. Sullivan wasn't a religious man, and didn't pray. He didn't believe in the immortal soul, and considered Berry dead and gone. But he needed to remember him; memory was the respect one paid the dead. Finally, Sullivan leaned over and kissed his friend's cool forehead. Then he went out and closed the door behind him.

Natalie was in the corridor. She had changed to a cotton dress and sandals; a cloth bag was slung over one shoulder and a suitcase was next to her on the terra-cotta floor. She followed Sullivan to his room and sat on the bed with her hands clasped while he packed the few things he had into a canvas duffle.

"Are you okay?" she said. "Do you need a drink, anything like that?"

"I just want to get off the island before the cops come nosing around."

"Are you sore at me?"

He was packing his shaving gear, but stopped and went and took her in his arms. She began to sob, and he pressed his lips against her cheek, and her hair, which smelled still of the saltwater and the sun. He held her as tightly as he could; her sobbing went on, the time between each gasp growing shorter, like the contractions of a woman in labor. These spasms finally ran together, her body trembling as if she were in a fit. They slowed and became shallower, and finally stopped altogether. Her body became limp. Only then was she calm, her grief expelled.

"I'm all right," she said. "I swear I won't become hysterical. I'm fine."

Sullivan finished packing and followed her out, locking the door behind them. They took the back staircase, which led to the parking lot. Bob was behind the wheel of Samson's jeep.

"I'll drive," Sullivan said. "Find Samson, tell him to wait a couple of hours, and then report the jeep stolen. I don't want either of you involved."

"Involved in what?"

"The police will be around, asking questions. Probably some others after them. Americans. The thing for you to remember is that you never saw the body and you didn't talk to me at all. Do you understand?"

"The fellow shot himself," Bob said. "And we had nothing to do with it, nothing at all."

"Except Eloise was the one who found the body. The cops are going to have some questions for her. Have her tell the truth, except about you being in her room when she found the body," Sullivan said. "If she lies beyond that, she'll do poorly and only make you both trouble. George's cash is still there, so there's no question of robbery made to look like something else. The police won't look too far beyond that."

Sullivan took the key from the ignition, tossed it to Bob, and ran his fingers under the dashboard, tracing the wires back from the ignition box. It took him less than a minute to hot-wire the engine and restart it.

"The jeep will be in the airport lot," Sullivan said. "You know where the boat is."

Natalie sat next to Sullivan in the passenger's seat and Bob tossed their bags in the back.

"It's monkey business you all are in," Bob said. "Slick enough, but plenty dirty, ain't it?"

Sullivan didn't answer. He put the jeep in gear and drove out of the parking lot on to the main road, turning right in the direction of the airport.

"What passport have you got?" he said to Natalie.

"French."

"Have you a visa for the States?"

"George and I were in New York and Florida before we came here," she said.

"See if it's validated for re-entry."

"Yes. Thirty days, so it's still valid. Is that where we're going, to the States?"

"The Miami flight leaves in about an hour. We can connect with any flight we want from there. There's a New Orleans flight as well, but the connections out of Miami are better."

She wasn't listening, none of that mattered to her. "I was outside George's door when you were inside with him," she said. "I knocked. You must have heard it."

"No."

"I did it softly," she said. "I meant to go in, to see him. Maybe I didn't knock. I meant to, but it's possible I just thought about it."

"You knock, or you don't knock. He's dead. It doesn't matter if you see him or not."

"You saw him."

"I had to straighten things out."

"You were in there a long time."

"Don't torment yourself," he said. "You're not responsible. You're not, I'm not."

"I didn't knock," she said. "I didn't have the nerve."

"You have all the nerve you need."

"I was afraid to see him."

"Just hope there are seats on the Miami flight."

"Tell me about his room," she said. "Was it awful? I imagine it being awful."

"Not at all. George had been very thoughtful. He'd had a bath, shaved, and put on his best pajamas before putting the bullet in his head. It wasn't an impulse, you see. And he wasn't deranged. He wanted us to see that. He wanted us to see that it was a careful decision, a rational act."

"Shooting himself was?"

"He thought so. He wanted us to think so. That's why

he spruced himself up. He wanted us to know it wasn't done out of self-disgust."

"But it was, wasn't it?"

"He'd done a lot of bad things."

"No worse than others." It was said sharply, in defense of George.

"The judgment on himself was his own," Sullivan said.

"It was yours, too," she said. "You brought it here, to him. You carry moral judgment, like the plague."

"He judged himself," Sullivan said it flatly. "It was a free act. He wasn't driven to it, and he wasn't crazy. A free act."

He took his eyes from the road; she was shaking her head, making a great effort to hold back the tears. "No. You're not responsible," she said.

"I told you—neither of us is."

"Did you have a feeling about it, though?" she said. "What do you call it? A hunch. Did you have a hunch he would kill himself?" Sullivan came up on the back of a slow-moving diesel truck, swung out into the opposite lane, and cut back just ahead of an oncoming car, which sped by with an outraged blast of horn. "George tried it before," she said. "One night in Rangoon—we were still sleeping together then—I woke up and he wasn't there." She had a way of crouching in the far end of the front seat, of drawing up her knees and making herself small.

"Tell me about that night," Sullivan said.

"He'd locked himself in the bathroom. I knocked but he wouldn't come out. I banged on the door and began to shout. It was just like a dream, I was terrified, expecting to hear a pistol shot, and when he finally opened the door he had a pistol in his hand." She took a deep breath, and then went on. "I didn't know what to say, and neither did he. He just went right by me, pushed me aside, and went out on the balcony, and stayed there smoking. He was very upset."

"What happened to start him off?"

"It was at dinner," she said. "We had flown down from Lashio that afternoon, and everything was fine. We went out and were having drinks when some men came in. They were gunmen, but not Burmese. I knew that right off. George went outside to talk. When he came back, it was all changed. I don't know why. I don't know what was said. But after that he wasn't the same."

"Did you ask him why?"

"You don't do that," she said.

"What about the men who came in? You said they weren't Burmese."

"They were Viets. I heard them talking among themselves."

"In Rangoon?"

"It certainly wasn't an accidental meeting," she said. "Two of the gunmen stepped in first for a look around. Then another fellow, a big shot, came in and went straight up to George."

"And that night he locked himself in the bathroom with a pistol?"

"He would have shot himself," she said. "He told me about the opium that night. He told me everything. He was ashamed, disgusted with what he had become."

"Where does the Vietnamese fit in?"

"I don't know," she said. "He told George something that upset him enough to drive him around the bend. He was in the bathroom getting his courage up, and he would have shot himself if I hadn't caught him."

"Is that why you stayed with him?" he said. "To keep him from pulling the trigger?"

"I felt a debt," she said. "I was in pieces when I met George, and he helped me get back together. But that's not the whole story. I'm no saint. There's a seamy side, I'm afraid." She was about to say more, but caught herself: he had warned her by listening too intently, by not moving and holding his breath. He wanted too much to know more, which she chose not to tell.

"Do you know Nassau?" she said.

"I've been."

"I was there last month with George," she said.

"And you want to go back?" he said.

"I must," she said.

Sullivan made a turn into the airport grounds and found a space in the parking lot. They carried their bags to the Air Jamaica desk, and to their great relief were able to book two places on the Miami flight, which left in three quarters of an hour. Sullivan followed Natalie through passport control into the duty-free shopping area, where they mingled with the American and British tourists collecting their untaxed cigars and rum. There was a bar, where Sullivan bought drinks and both waited nervously until the plane was called. Fortunately, it left on time, and once in the air they began to breathe easier, and bought another drink from the trolley brought around by the crew.

"Will you come with me to Nassau," she said, "for companionship and moral support? George had an account in a bank there, and last month he made it over in both our names. I'm a signator. Is that the word?"

"That's the word."

"Either of us can sign and make withdrawals. George was specific about that. But he never told me how much he had on deposit. Now I'm nervous about it. Suppose it's a lot, and the bank tries to waltz me around."

"That's the wrong attitude to take with banks," Sullivan said. "You've got to march in with your chin up. Let them have it. Remember, you're a signator."

"And not a grave robber."

"No. The money is yours by right," Sullivan said. "My guess is George didn't bother with a will, but put his money in a joint account. It's far simpler."

"I don't want you to think I'm a greedy person," she said. "My father was rich and spoiled me. Later I almost starved and was humiliated. I think too much about money."

There was no trouble with the authorities in Miami. By now it was likely that the Jamaican police had found George's body, but either hadn't thought ahead as far as the airport or bothered to call the Miami police.

They stayed in the transit area, so as to avoid passport control and customs, but found there wasn't a regular flight to Nassau until the next morning. Sullivan rounded up a charter flight service and booked that. While charter flights were obliged to file a manifest, describing all cargo and listing the names and nationalities and passport numbers of all passengers, it could be held for a day or two before finally being given to flight control; the manifest could even be misplaced or lost. Charter airlines were a marginal business, and for an extra hundred dollars almost anything could be done. If the Jamaican police bothered to trace them as far as Miami, they would turn up nothing but a cold trail.

Getting a room in the Britannia in Nassau was a little more difficult. It was nearly nine o'clock when they arrived and the place was booked solid. The room clerk was an Australian with a Perth Yacht Club patch on his blazer and a soaring ginger mustache, who politely refused Sullivan's folded twenty; there simply wasn't a room to be had. But he was a decent chap, and when Sullivan explained that he and Natalie had met only two days before, fallen in love, married, and were on their honeymoon, he sent them along with a discreet note to a little pension at the western end of the harbor.

It was run by a Swiss widow who fed them a wonderful veal chasseur and tucked them in for the night with a bottle of liquor distilled from pears, which was delicious but too sweet. They made love and stayed together. There were no words, and no slipping away and burrowing into a pillow. They dozed off, came awake, and made love again. The screened window was wide open, and the night was clear, the sky filled with stars. They could smell the sea and hear the surf.

Sullivan lay awake with Natalie asleep on his chest. Even as he stroked her hair and smelled her warm skin, he had begun to look back on their night together, imagining that she was gone and he was alone in a friendless place, longing for her. He couldn't love without reminding himself that it must end. So much of what he felt seemed to be happening at a distance and had the qualities of a dream. Yet he felt closer to her than he had to anyone before.

He was asleep and awake, not clearly aware of either. He saw the luminous dial of his watch at two-thirty, then looked again and it was six. He wondered what her thoughts were, but never asked. There were secrets between them, and on his part a natural reticence. They hardly spoke at all, and yet their lovemaking had about it the languor, the kindness of a couple who have adored each other for years. They had come together at a time when their defenses were weaker than they imagined, and the need of each to touch the other's heart greater than they imagined. Natalie knew how rare this was. She was the more experienced. She had loved other men and lived with them and believed she had given them all she could. Now she saw all that she had held back. It seemed unfair to the others, to Castellone and poor George. She grieved for George, and longed for Castellone.

Toward morning, they began to talk about George. "He brought us together," she said. "I can almost feel him here. He's responsible for us, for what we feel."

"The fear," Sullivan said.

"I'm not afraid, not of dying."

"I am," he said. "Of the thing that made George do it. He was fed up. I know the feeling, and it scares me."

"You'd never do what George did."

"You never do know for sure," he said.

"You'll never do it," she said. "You're the kind to battle life, to stay alive."

Later, she asked Sullivan about his parents.

"I was nineteen when my father died," he said. "My mother a few years after that."

"Do you think about them?"

"We weren't that close a family."

"But you know how to love," she said. "Someone must have taught you."

"I don't know who it was," he said. "I can't remember that far back. I trusted the people around me, but didn't need them much. I liked to hike, fish, and read, things one does alone."

Later in the morning, Natalie got out of bed and walked to the bathroom wrapped in a sheet, the hem trailing behind. Sullivan stayed in bed, his head supported by hands clasped behind his neck, and let a soft breeze stir the fine hairs on his chest and belly. Natalie returned with her face scrubbed and her breath smelling freshly of toothpaste. He was in a loving mood and for letting the day slip by. But she brought a brisk and businesslike air. Barclay's Bank opened at nine. She wanted to be there on the dot.

"You can't wait to get your hands on the money." He hadn't moved at all, just turned his head on his clasped hands. "You're a greedy girl. Okay, but greedy all the same."

"I'm anxious about the money," she said. "It's a natural thing. How much do you think there is? Perhaps a lot. Even a fortune. George was a very clever man."

"Clever at making money?"

"Don't you think so?"

"I suppose so, once he began to think about it."

"It's a kind of intelligence," she said. "At least you have to be a fool to ignore money."

"No one ignores money," he said. "It's just that some despise the ways in which it's usually made."

"Holy men," she said. "Saints, like you, with a big swaying bell of a cock." She took hold of his ankle with both hands and tried to pull him out of bed. "Poor George left a pile, and it's all there waiting for me," she said. "Please get out of bed. I need you to come with me."

He did as she wanted, dressed quickly, and had the Swiss woman telephone for a cab. Natalie was tense and didn't say a word in the drive into town.

It was barely nine when they arrived at Barclay's, and a guard in a smart white uniform was lifting the iron gate in front of the door.

Natalie took Sullivan's hands. "I want you to wish me luck," she said.

"All the luck in the world."

"I'm not doing anything wrong," she said. "I'm not stealing."

"But you're scared just the same," he said.

"I'm afraid they won't give it to me," she said. "It could be a lot of money, and at the last minute they're liable to take it away. The bastards. They're liable to say, 'Natalie can't have the money after all.' It's got to be a lot of money, you see. Enough to make a difference."

"I'll be in the café across the street."

"It's terrible to be poor," she said. "You get where you'll do anything. Peddle your ass, anything at all."

"Go on."

"I'm not greedy," she said. "Money makes me less afraid. That's all there is to it."

He did as he promised and waited in the café across from the bank. He ordered coffee and tried to concentrate on the English newspapers. But his mind was elsewhere. He read without understanding anything. He felt foolish and angry at himself. He had always known what he wanted, his mind occupied with means and ends. He was a determined man, whose goals had been fixed. Natalie had taken him by surprise and pushed him off course. His confusion made him irritable and he snarled at the waiter, who had forgotten to bring sugar with his coffee. It was unlike him and he was ashamed and bewildered by his own rudeness. The anger at the waiter was properly directed at himself, at waiting outside a bank for Natalie to come out with George Berry's money.

He suddenly stood up, threw down some change for his coffee, and went out of the café. He didn't know where he was going. He thought he would return to the pension, pack his bag, and be gone. But he needed a cab, and he stood for several seconds in the center of the street, with no idea how to go about getting one. He felt a moment of helplessness and panic; Natalie had made him close his eyes and then spun him around so that he didn't know where he was. He needed to get his balance, to find his way. He remembered the old headman in the Shan village, Myat's father, pointing at the pass through the mountains into the valley and Lashio.

The way was open to him, but he couldn't take it. He had followed the trail from the Shan States, from Lashio and Saigon. It did him no good to know the way.

He wandered on for a block or two, but suddenly stopped in his tracks, turned around, and walked resolutely back to the café. Natalie was at a table, sipping a glass of orange juice, her bag on the chair nearest her.

"I thought for a moment you had gone off without me," she said.

"I wanted to," he said.

She removed her bag and took hold of his hand, guiding him to the chair next to her.

"There was a lot of money," she said. "More than I

hoped, much more. I've got it all safely tucked away now. There's nothing more to do, and it's all come out right."

She kept hold of his hand, smiling up at him; he looked directly at her, at that particular face, while several seconds passed. He knew that what he felt was love, and that now he couldn't leave.

"Can we have a good time?" she said.

"For how long?"

She shook her head. "A good time," she said. "We'll shop and eat delicious food. We'll make love. You're marvelous, you know. You think it's virility, but it's not. It's the sweetness. Fellows like you aren't usually so sweet."

She was serious about taking him shopping, and while he did protest and claimed he needed nothing, he let himself be led along to the shops. She didn't know Nassau well, but had a sixth sense which led her directly to the right shops, men's as well as women's. She could sniff them out, as she could good restaurants. She explained that men's coats and sweaters needed to be British, trousers were probably best Italian, and shoes certainly so.

"I thought English shoes were best," he said.

"Only for fiduciary relationships," she said.

She picked out a blazer for him, trousers, shirts and a cashmere sweater, ties and a pair of Italian slip-ons which seemed to be molded tenderly to his feet. He knew nothing about clothes, never thought about them, but thought it fun having her fuss over him and pick out his things. This adoration struck an ancient chord. He wondered when it had been done before, in what untroubled time or earlier life. She whistled up his slumbering vanity, his boyishness, and his gratitude.

"Not a close family?" she said. "Your mother must have loved you. There was a time she made a fuss of you. I can tell."

"Is it because I know how to love you?"

"Sure," she said. "Not the lust. The sweetness. You really are, you know, and who would have thought it?"

She made him self-conscious, and just a little flustered. She had him in the palm of her hand, and she knew it, but she teased him gently and coaxed him to preen a little before the tailor's mirror, to let himself be stroked and admired. He was never so happy with a woman.

Soon she got down to business with the tailor, making certain that his coat fit across the shoulders and the back, and if his trousers should break over the top of his shoe, and if cavalry twill was best with or without cuffs.

"Where did you learn about men's clothes?" he said.

"From worldly men," she said. "I was the kid, learning about the smart world. Now it's you. Tell me, do you enjoy the part?"

"I do. I didn't think I would, but there it is."

"You were too serious before."

"I'm afraid I will be again."

"I'll keep you loose."

"You plan to stick around then?" he said.

She ducked that, a clouded look in her eyes, which he couldn't fathom. She still had her secrets; there was so much to her, he knew he had only scratched the surface.

"You were made for good clothes," she said. "You've got the figure. Big shoulders, no hips, and one hell of a nice ass."

"Let's go back to the room," he said.

"Don't you want lunch first?"

"It's you I want," he said.

Later on, she said, "Are we safe here?"

"I suppose so. The Jamaican police may make a routine call to Miami, but they won't bother beyond that. George killed himself. They'll see that right off, and let it alone."

"Have you ever lived in Europe?" she said.

"A week or two at a time," he said. "I was in Paris for a couple of months."

"Did you like it?"

"Sure. I'd like to try it for a while."

"Could you manage it?"

"Not now."

"You wouldn't need much money," she said. "I've got a business set up in Paris, and a house on the Atlantic. We'd be fine."

"George left a lot of money, didn't he?"

"It's mine now," she said.

"No one is going to take it from you," he said.

"It's blood money," she said. "Dirty money. George got it smuggling dope, and I ought to despise it. I know that's what you're thinking."

"I've just been wondering if there are other accounts," he said. "George must have been in this in a big way. He was a clever man, and very experienced. Don't you think it possible he buried money other places?"

She had fixed him with a keen look, trying to figure out what he was up to.

"He must have kept a box somewhere," Sullivan said. "Passport blanks, a little money, love letters from opposite numbers on both sides of the curtain. Old spooks need a fallback for the golden years."

"You're being rotten."

"He used to like the name Wright. It was his mother's maiden name, and he told me he'd chosen it so that he wouldn't forget it even when drunk."

"Am I to search the world's banks for an account in the name of Wright?"

"Just the Swiss banks," he said.

"Look at him smiling," she said. "He can't even send a girl up with a straight face."

"What's funny is the way you look when you're being cunning," he said. "Your father, Lord rest his soul, would have held a diamond to the light in just the same way."

"There are no other accounts, are there?"

"There may well be. George never married. Mother and father long dead. He was an only child. No one will come looking and the money will rot."

"It's not true," she said. "George collected all his cash and deposited it here in a joint account, so that I could have it. I was good to him. At least I tried, and he knew that."

He saw her eyes mist and realized he had gone too far. He took hold of her and stroked her hair. "George wanted you to have his money, all of it. He had come to the end and you were the only person he cared about."

"He was sweet in his way," she said. "It's not right for us to be having such a good time. We ought to be mourning. Jews are good at that. The men don't shave, nobody wears shoes or carries money, and we all sit around on hard wooden crates."

"George was Unitarian," he said.

"He told me why he wanted me to have the money," she said. "He even set me up in a shop on Faubourg St. Honoré."

"Then I suppose you'll be going to France soon," he said.

"Take it easy," she said. "I warned you—love is a dangerous thing."

"For which only the foolish volunteer," he said.

"Something like that."

She chose to play with him then, to sit on his knee, to tease and fondle him, to lighten their time together by making love. She was a very skillful woman, and a very clever one. She knew that, for them at least, sex was the gayest part of love, an adventure, and most of all a distraction. Intimacy was elsewhere, in conversation before and after, in the play of light in the pupil of the eye, in the sound of the voice. She led him back to gaiety, to bawdy love. She was a very clever woman, and of course he most appreciated her after she had gone.

They were together two more days, five in all. That was the whole of it, that and the few hours on the boat and in the shack on the beach before the news came that George had killed himself.

Short and sweet was how he remembered their affair; bittersweet, he called it, groaning with self-pity over his fourth Scotch. But he didn't rage, or get really tearing drunk and smash up a saloon. The self-pity was purged inside of a week. The truth of it was he was just a little relieved.

But it was she who walked out. He went for a swim one morning, and to talk to one of the charter skippers at the marina about going out after sailfish. She was to meet him later on for lunch. He read the English papers, sipped draught beer, and waited. She was always late, so for the first half hour he didn't give it a thought. He read a bit, ordered a second beer, and then it came to him that she had skipped.

He finished the beer, tucked the papers under his arm, and sauntered back to the hotel. No cabs, no frantic rush;

if she wanted to go, let her. He never doubted his capacity to handle whatever pain followed her loss. He was a tough nut.

When he returned to their room, it was just as he had expected; she had packed and gone. He checked with BOA; the London flight had taken off about the same time he was ordering his second beer.

He scoured the room to see if she had forgotten anything. There wasn't a used toothbrush or a bottle of nailpolish, not a hairpin. She had left nothing behind.

There was no note, no good-bye. She had cut it off at the quick. She was also rather a tough nut.

CHAPTER 20

The doorman was big as a wrestler or a heavyweight boxer, but he made no trouble. Rocco took him aside, spoke to him softly, like a mother crooning her baby to sleep. He towered over Rocco, nodding his head and listening respectfully. He was Italian, a former stone breaker from Catania, who recognized Rocco as a man on the inside. But Rocco didn't twist his arm. There was no need. While not servile, the big doorman was eager to be of service. He kept his face impassive although Rocco's breath stank of garlic. He even declined a gift of one hundred francs, only reluctantly allowing the bill to be stuffed into his breast pocket. It was made to seem that he did Rocco a favor by accepting. They parted the best of friends, Rocco pinching his cheek and slapping his face affectionately, a form of jovial threat.

Another flunky took Rocco up in the elevator and showed him the correct door, wishing him a pleasant evening before drawing the elevator gate.

Marcel was startled by the door chimes; in the perfect stillness of the apartment they rang out with the authority of a church organ. It was unheard of for anyone to ring unexpectedly, without a call from the lobby. Marilyn's phone was unlisted, the apartment walls as thick as a fortress and the windows double-sealed, so that no sound reached them from the outside. A secure apartment, complete with all the latest gadgets, including a sauna.

Marcel was lying on a couch wearing a silk dressing gown and watching television. Marilyn had just peeled a pineapple and was about to put it in a portable juice extractor. It was past midnight. At the sound of the chimes, both froze, like burglars caught in the act. Marcel's heart thumped and began to pound. He leaped to his feet, vaulted over the back of the couch, and went for the Beretta he had taken to carrying in the pocket of his jacket. Marilyn looked at him adoringly, waiting to be told what to do. She wore nothing but a sheath of translucent blue silk, and still held the peeled pineapple. Without a word he directed her to see who it was, while he stood off to one side, just out of sight, the pistol in his hand. He appeared composed, and even smoothed the hair at the back of his head. He was careful that Marilyn not see the gesture. He was adored because of the danger he introduced into her life. However, the danger was not to get out of hand, it was to be well behaved, without unpleasantness, like a puppy which arrives already house-broken. The iron rule was that neither acknowledge that the danger was part of a game. It was a game, and not a game. The bullets in the gun were real, and even while smoothing his hair, Marcel was prepared to shoot. The blood spilled would be real. But he was not to tell her that, he might frighten her away.

The game ended when Marcel saw it was Rocco at the door. He put away the pistol. "Is it my father?" he asked.

Rocco walked past Marilyn into the apartment, his eyes taking in every detail. He walked slowly, with a ponderous step, as if testing the floor for weak spots. He picked out an upholstered chair and lowered himself with a grunt onto the edge, his legs parted and his hands planted on the inside of his thighs just above the knees.

"Tell me, is it my father?" Marcel's face burned and he felt himself reel. "Is he worse?" After a struggle, the words came out breathlessly. "Is he dead?"

Rocco said nothing and gave him no sign. He glanced

over at Marilyn and, leaning forward with his hands still on his fat thighs, growled a few words in Italian.

"What did he say?" Marilyn said. "Is it your father?"

"Go and put on some clothes," Marcel said.

"Is that what he said?"

"Go on."

Rocco laughed and spoke again in Italian. "I understood that," Marilyn said. "I understood all right, you old pig."

"Put on a pair of drawers," Rocco had switched to French. "I didn't come here to look at your pussy."

Marilyn struck a grand pose before Rocco, and held up two fingers an inch apart. "There's a neat fit for your prick," she said, but scampered out of the room before Rocco lost his temper.

Through it all, Marcel said nothing. He had only one thought: His father was dead.

Rocco saw his anxiety, but would say nothing until he was sure they couldn't be overheard. He sat with his hooded eyes expressionless, wheezing with each heavy breath.

"Is it my father?" Marcel said.

"No. He's the same."

"What is it, then?"

"Get dressed. Some people need to talk to you."

Rocco had come alone and parked in a prohibited zone in front of the door, miraculously escaping a ticket. The car was old and run-down, the upholstery frayed, and the window on the passenger side had a vertical crack running from a tiny hole made by a stone or an air pellet. Rocco didn't throw money around on fancy cars, not on women or clothes or anything one could see.

"Where are we going?" Marcel said.

"Your father's house."

"Is everybody there? Are we ready to buy?"

"I hear there's a problem, but I don't know. I don't know anything. All the big shots are there. Don Angelo, Don Guido, Don This, Don That. Don Up-the-ass."

"What's the problem?"

"Your pal Castellone. It doesn't smell right with him, that's what I hear."

There was little traffic and the drive to Neuilly took

only a few minutes. Lights were on in the driveway, a Jaguar and a pair of Mercedes; two chauffeurs were playing cards and a third was using his map light to read a newspaper.

Marcel was told the meeting was in his father's bedroom and he went directly there. He found the old man in bed with two other Dons seated near him on gilded red plush chairs, leaning toward the emaciated figure in order not to miss a single whispered word, their attitude solemn, like cardinals attending a dying pope.

Marcel was treated with respect and considerable dignity. His reputation was not of the best, but all of this was temporarily put aside. He was the son of Achille Piri; both Dons embraced him and kissed his cheeks. He was one of them, after all, even if he had disgraced his father by being a queer.

Next to Achille Piri, Don Angelo was the senior Don, and he took it upon himself to begin.

"We have difficulties," he said. "A problem, very serious. The cash is in Paris. Twenty million in dollars. That's not tin, my darling. A serious amount, even for men like me and your revered father."

Don Angelo was known for his eloquence and theatrical good looks. He had begun as a pimp, a star of the Marseille waterfront, who was said to have resembled Rudolph Valentino, and was even called Valentino, a nickname he encouraged, going so far as to pay for a family history, certain that it would uncover a relationship between himself and his idol. He was a grandfather now, but did all he could to preserve his youthful good looks. His hair was dyed black and his teeth capped and polished until they sparkled like bathroom tile.

But the face was old—creamed, powdered, suntanned—but old. He had a hollow neck and liver spots on the backs of the hands. He was a pimp still, Angelo, a pimp who once had resembled Rudolph Valentino and was still adored by ambitious young girls, who were eager to tickle his little pecker because it curled against the white belly of the great Don.

Marcel said, "Tell me, what is the problem? The merchandise is in Paris. I personally can vouch for that."

"You also personally vouched for Castellone."

"What does that remark mean?"

"He's a fucking cop." Bambo Giordano was the other Don present. He was known as the Ox, a tribute to his great strength, and was as proud of that as Don Angelo was of being called Valentino.

"We spent a week with Castellone in Marseille," Don Angelo said. "And we were at first taken in. He came to us with the recommendation of Don Achille, explained the situation to us down to the smallest detail, all open and above board. An impressive man, Castellone. He made a good impression."

"I said he was a snake," Bambo Giordano said. "I said watch him. Did I say it or not?"

"The Ox was suspicious."

"I know Castellone's type," he said. "And the deal was too good, a girl with a silk pussy, you know what I'm saying?"

"He's a cop," Don Angelo said. "Part of a secret group inside of SPDEC. Political at first because of the Indochina war, and the involvement of the Americans."

"I don't believe that Castellone is a cop."

"He's your friend and you trust him. That's only natural. It even does you credit to believe in the honesty of your friends." Angelo patted Marcel's hand and made his foxy eyes compassionate. Marcel watched them change color, the points of light in their center warm until they were the color of honey. It was a trick, done at will, as certain actors are able to cry on cue. Marcel wasn't taken in. Angelo was a killer, with a killer's icy heart.

"I know the pain," Angelo went on. "To be betrayed by a friend, there is nothing that hurts more."

"It happened to you?"

"One time. In my youth."

"What did you do?"

"I shot him." He still had hold of Marcel's hand and was patting it. "Once in the back of the head. Vito Barbella, Lord rest his soul."

"You had no choice," the Ox said.

"Eh, Valentino," old Piri croaked from the bed. "Tell me, you still sing so pretty as you used to?"

"Not so good anymore, Don Achille."

"Such a pretty voice." Old Piri smiled at the recollection. "Just like an angel."

"We were deciding what to do about Castellone," Angelo said, gently.

"Who?"

"The traitor, Castellone."

"My son brought me the traitor." Achille Piri clasped his hands and raised his eyes. "My son is the cross I have to bear."

"Nothing is proved about Castellone," Marcel said.

"Your son was taken in," Angelo said, taking Marcel's hand.

"Castellone is a snake," Bambo Giordano said.

"You got to kill him," Achille Piri said to his son. "You brought him to us, now you got to kill him."

"I haven't seen him in a week, and I don't know where to find him," Marcel said. "He goes underground and trusts no one. You told him you needed time to put the money together, and he said he'd contact you."

"We can't let him pick a time and place," Bambo said. "A man like Castellone you got to surprise in order to kill. Later we make our own deal for the Indochina dope."

"You can get close to him." Angelo gave Marcel's hand a final squeeze before letting it go. "He'll let you in. His guard will be down."

"Sit on his lap," Bambo said.

"Do this killing," Achille Piri said. "And your father can die in peace."

Later on, after Marcel had gone, and old Piri was asleep, Angelo spoke to Rocco and two younger men, who needed to build a reputation. They were told to stay close to Marcel, to follow him everywhere, to use him to flush Castellone, and above all to see to it that the traitor was killed.

CHAPTER 21

Sullivan had no trouble at the Banco Suizo-Panameño, a discreet private bank behind the silver exchange on the rue des Coines. The assistant manager was glacial but helpful. Sullivan had practiced signing Martin David Wright, and after filling in the signature card, and having it checked against the one on file, he was escorted to the vault. Berry's box wasn't a big one, and it wasn't particularly heavy. Sullivan followed the vault attendant to a windowless cubicle, with an inside lock on the door.

He was eager to have a look inside Berry's box, but first made sure the cubicle was clear of cameras and one-way mirrors, and even made himself comfortable, before undoing the latch and lifting the lid.

There were German federal bonds; Sullivan quickly counted twenty-five, in denominations of twenty thousand marks, an uninterrupted series, all negotiable as cash. There was some cash as well, dollars and Swiss francs, but not a great deal. There were two British passport blanks, the deed for a plot of land in the Portuguese Algarve, and finally a small black loose-leaf notebook. Sullivan had been hoping for something of the sort, and it was that he was most interested in. The notebook was a common type, manufactured in the United States. It was organized alphabetically by means of index tabs, all done precisely and with extreme care; names of agents, chiefs of station, telephone numbers, the addresses of safe houses, and dead drops on three continents. Sullivan imagined Berry sitting alone and working it out, he imagined the pleasure it must have given him.

Some of it was in code, but a good deal wasn't. Castellone was there, just where he should be, the first entry under C. There was the address of the hotel Florida in Paris, with a note to see Álbert, who rated a listing of his own under A.

The second entry for Castellone was the French-English bookstore in Basel. Here the contact was Zola. Castellone was Victor Hugo. Sullivan crossed Zola, got his background, physical description, war record, and a breakdown of the Basel station. Along with that was a code name new to him: Razzia. Sullivan chased that under R. It was all there. Kirk, Owen, Nyo, Nephew and Niece, even the method of carrying the twenty-kilos of heroin into France.

Sullivan doubted that anyone knew of the existence of the Wright security box, but there was really no way to tell. Sullivan had thought to bring a briefcase with him, although it contained only that morning's European edition of the *Herald Tribune* and a stale *Time* magazine. He transferred notebook, British passports, and bearer bonds to his case, and deposited the newspaper and magazine in the security box, just to give it weight when he returned it to the attendant.

That same morning he opened an account and rented a security box of his own, using the name Alan Rainer. He also arranged for the sale of the German bonds, and transferred the remainder of George Berry's legacy to the Rainer box. He bought a chocolate bar at the airport and caught the one o'clock shuttle to Basel. The address of the French-English bookstore was in the phonebook, and he went directly there by taxi.

It was midafternoon and the shop was very nearly empty; an Englishwoman was browsing in the Corgi mysteries, and Sullivan, with Berry's description fresh in his mind, recognized the tall, stooped Frenchman at the register as Zola. Berry had described him perfectly, even the lovely blue eyes and the passion for Mozart, coming from the radio on the counter before him.

Sullivan said, "Have you anything by Victor Hugo?"

Zola raised those poetic eyes, and he seemed to hesitate, to skip a single beat, and then he said evenly, "In French or English?"

"It doesn't matter."

"French in the center aisle, English on the far right."

"I want to talk to Hugo."

"To Victor Hugo?"

"Yes."

"I'm afraid you'll have rather a long wait."

He smiled and returned to the Mozart. A soprano began to sing, and Zola hummed along under his breath. Sullivan reached over and turned off the radio.

"I've had a long tiring day," he said. "I haven't had any lunch and very little sleep, so I'm irritable." The English-woman in the Corgis hadn't stirred. Sullivan said, "Please get hold of Bernard Castellone. Tell him I'm a friend of George Berry."

Zola looked surprised and there was the beginning of a smile in those blue eyes. "Where will you be?" he said.

"Paris. Hotel Metropole."

"The Metropole. It wouldn't be my choice," Zola said, and turned on the radio.

Sullivan decided not to fly directly from Basel to Paris, but to go by way of Brussels, where passport control was known to be the easiest in Europe. He arrived in Paris that evening and went directly to the Metropole. He checked it upstairs and down, but it was clear. He had a long walk and wasn't followed. He treated himself to a first-class dinner. The next day he wandered around the Louvre and went to the movies. He wanted to see Natalie, and began to think of the best way to do that, and went as far as looking up Benoit in the central directory. But he decided to hold off, at least until he had seen Castellone.

Early on the morning of his third day in Paris, the phone in his room rang. It was a man's voice, speaking in English, one he didn't recognize. He was told to go to a café called the Wellington, on boulevard de Sébastopol.

He was to be there at eleven, he was to be unarmed and alone, and he was to wait outside the public telephone.

The Wellington was a large bar-tabac, busily preparing for lunch. When Sullivan arrived, the phone was occupied by a fellow whose Renault was double-parked just outside, its hazard lights blinking. It was eleven-eight when he concluded his call and ran to his car just ahead of a policeman about to ticket it.

Sullivan waited by the phone until it rang at eleven-thirteen. The same voice told him to return to his room at the Metropole and wait; he'd be contacted further.

Sullivan took his time, even stopped on his way for a bottle of Black and White Scotch and carried it with him to his room. As he expected, Castellone was already there, waiting in a club chair in the shadows at the far end of the room.

"I brought some whisky," Sullivan said. "What do you say?"

"Why not?"

"Have you a cold? On the phone, you sounded as if you did."

"Perhaps, a slight one. The whisky will be just the thing. By the way, how did you know about the Basel drop?"

"From George."

"Were you there when he died?"

"Yes."

"I see. You collected his things."

"He made me his heir," Sullivan said. "All of his assets. He passed on everything, all he had, at any rate."

"And Natalie, too? You and Natalie, at least for a time. That's what one hears."

"Where is she now?"

"No water, please," Castellone said. "Good whisky, just as it is."

Sullivan said, "Will you help me?"

"She has a shop on Faubourg St.-Honoré. Very posh, very Natalie. So you have that, and you have the Basel drop."

"I have Nephew, too."

"Then what do you need?"

"Your permission."

"For what?"

"To go after Nephew."

Castellone swallowed his drink and held out the glass to be refilled. "Do you ever think of George?"

"Yes. More than I thought I would."

"He was okay," Castellone said. "And he made you his heir. You want me to do the same?"

"I want you to give me Nephew."

Castellone filled his mouth with the whisky and rolled it around, enjoying the taste. "And the wife, too. There's a piece of work, that wife. You want me to give her to you, too?"

"Give me them both."

"Sure, why not. A nervy kid, like you. A nervy American kid. You can have them, nervy kid, but only if something goes sour. Do you understand?"

"I understand. If you fail."

"Yes, that's it exactly. They're yours if I fail."

Castellone finished his second drink and started for the door. But he hesitated, reflected a moment, and said, "What if you get Nephew, or I do? When it's wound up, what do you do then?"

"I don't know."

"Will you stay on the inside?"

"That would depend on how it winds up."

"Stay in, that's my advice. Don't go on your own. It's a rotten way to live."

"Who are we talking about, you or me?"

"Take your pick." It was said lightly. "Either one of us, eh? Both cut from the same cloth. I make you my heir, too. How do you like that, nervy kid. Castellone's heir."

CHAPTER 22

Marcel went to the familiar places and put out the word that he needed to talk to Castellone. He saw Albert at the Florida and told him. But Albert played sphinx. He had to scratch his head to remember who Bernard Castellone was. When finally it came to him, he claimed not to have seen him in years. He thought he was in Indochina. Then there was a rumor that he was dead.

"He's alive and he's in Paris," Marcel said. "In fact, he keeps a room on the fifth floor of your flea-bag hotel. When you see him, tell him it's urgent."

Marcel had heard that Castellone and Natalie had broken up, but reasoned that she might have heard from him or at least know how to get in touch with him. He knew she was back in France, but the only address he had belonged to her mother.

Madame Benoit lived on rue de la Boëtie, and Marcel was able to get her telephone number from the directory. Marcel decided to ring her rather than pay an unexpected call, which might alarm her.

"My daughter is not here," Madame Benoit said.

"Do you expect her?"

"Please tell me who is calling."

"I beg your pardon, Madame. I am Marcel Piri. I met your daughter only once, and that was some time ago." Marcel thought the older woman less suspicious than formal, and somewhat reserved. "Please tell her that I am a friend of Bernard Castellone."

"Yes. And then what?"

Marcel had begun to think that he had miscalculated. "Please tell me when it would be convenient for me to call and speak to her," he said.

"My daughter is in New York," Madame Benoit said, and hung up.

Madame Benoit had no idea why she lied, or for that matter why later on in the evening she never mentioned the call to Natalie. She was an imperious woman, who did what she wanted, and never reflected on her motives. To reflect on one's actions at least raises the possibility of modifying them. But she had no intention of doing that. She lived as if the force of her will were absolute. When she came up against people whose will challenged her own—relatives or friends—she simply cut them out of her life. There was a brother she hadn't spoken to in more than thirty years because she fancied his wife had once been rude. The specific act was long forgotten; only the emotion of wounded pride remained, but that was enough. There were cousins, friends from childhood, in-laws—all banished. Only Natalie survived. Madame Benoit couldn't stop speaking to Natalie. She couldn't turn her picture to the wall. Could it be said that she loved her? Natalie was never sure. Perhaps she did love her daughter. This quarrelsome, arrogant, self-centered old woman, by being unable to banish her daughter, showed the only love of which she was capable.

Since her return to Paris, Natalie had spent more time with her mother than she ever had before. She reached out to her mother, she needed her, in a way she never had as a child. It had to do with George Berry's suicide, and the end of her long love affair with Castellone. She had fled from Sullivan, but Castellone had left her, and Berry had died, as had her father.

When she was with her mother, their conversation always turned to Natalie's father. This was Natalie's doing, and because of it she looked forward to their little dinners together, although her mother did nothing to enliven things, to make her conversation interesting, or even good-natured. Yet Natalie approached each meeting with a keen sense of anticipation, with a pounding heart. It was some time before she realized why.

It was because Madame Benoit, this ordinary and rather unpleasant woman, was privy to a dark secret, and something of the greatest importance to Natalie. She had been married to Max Benoit. She had shared his life, and from her, at last, Natalie hoped for some new revelation, something to bring her father vividly to life. Her relationships with other men had all ended badly. In its own way each was a disappointment. Now Natalie reached out for the perfection of her father's boundless love. She needed that ideal, and to possess him at last in her imagination, to have him to adore forever.

The same night as Marcel's call, Natalie was with her mother. "How long have you lived in this apartment?" she said.

They had been eating dinner, the two women at a tiny table in a corner of the kitchen. There was a dining room with a larger table, but Madame Benoit always ate in the kitchen. In the old days the dining room was used only when there were guests. But now there were no guests. There was only the cat, Misha, watching from his favorite spot on top of the refrigerator.

Madame Benoit hadn't heard the question. She had turned on the water to fill the coffeepot. She was also hard of hearing, but too vain to wear an amplifier.

Natalie said again, "How long have you lived here?"

"Sixteen years."

"Since just after Papa died."

"Yes. When we came back to Europe, we lived off the St.-Germain, in a rented place. It was just after the war, and space was hard to get."

"I remember it."

"And of course, there was very little money."

"It was a nice place, though."

"I hated it. It was awful. The rooms were small and dark, and in the hall one smelled boiled cabbage."

Natalie saw her room in the old apartment; she was in bed, laid up with a cold, and her father had pulled up a chair in order to play cards. Just then he put back his head and laughed, a bit of his gold bridgework showing.

"I was glad to get out of there," Madame Benoit said. "Once your father's estate was settled, I bought this apartment. Its value has at least tripled. I must say I've done rather well."

"Did Papa leave you well fixed?"

"Not really. If I had put it all away at six percent, I might have just scraped through. But thank God, I have a head for business, and so things have worked out."

"But Papa was rich before the war."

"Oh, yes. But the war took every cent. He was just beginning to get back on his feet when he died." The coffee had dripped through and she poured it into two Limoges cups, and used tiny silver tongs to add the sugar. "It's a nice sum I've built up, and in the end it will all be yours."

"The Limoges cups, too?"

"You think it's been easy? I'm alone, I have no one. You lead your own life, you always have. It's not the kind of life of which I necessarily approve, but it's what you chose for yourself."

"The coffee is delicious."

"It's Colombian. Old Peres grinds it himself. I'm very fussy about my coffee."

"So you don't approve of my life?"

"I always hoped you'd marry, have children. Or I even thought we could live together in the country."

"You and I? Live together?"

"Yes, why not?"

"Are you serious?"

"Yes, of course. We're mother and daughter, two single women. What could be more natural?"

"Why don't I move in here?" Natalie said. "I haven't taken a permanent place, and this apartment is far too large for you alone."

"It's not too large at all."

"Three bedrooms and a formal dining?"

"This is simply a challenge on your part," Madame Benoit said. "You've always tried to provoke me. It's a dare. And if I took you up on it, if I said go get your suitcase and move in, you'd be perverse enough to do it.

Anything in order not to back down, even though you'd be miserable here."

"You're right, I'd be miserable. And I wouldn't take the dare, I wouldn't move in."

Misha leaped from the refrigerator to the drainboard next to the sink, and from there to the floor, ending on Madame Benoit's lap to have his ears scratched. There had always been a cat or two, spoiled, pampered creatures, which Natalie detested. "Did Papa ever see this apartment?" she said.

"No. I told you he was already dead."

"Are you content, Mama?"

"With my life, you mean? Content? I never ask myself questions of that sort. I try to manage." She broke off, scratching the cat behind the ears, and looked off into space, following her own thoughts. "Your father was not the easiest man in the world to live with," she said.

"He was great fun," Natalie said.

"Yes, great fun."

"But not for you, is that it?" Natalie set herself alongside her mother: which was the better looking, the more clever? Which knew more the world? "Was it other women, Mother? Did Papa have a mistress?"

"I don't know."

"But you wonder."

"No. I'm not the jealous type." She looked directly at her daughter, forcing a confrontation. "I was never jealous, nor was I dependent on your father, or any other man. Not dependent materially, or emotionally."

It was Natalie who looked away, and went off on another tack, reminiscing about her father. "He was such good company, always laughing and telling jokes."

"He was a salesman, finally."

"Not a professor from a cultivated family. Not a Bornstein."

"I don't brag about my family, or lord it over people," Madame Benoit said. "But the truth is my family—the Bornsteins—are distinguished for intellectual achievement. Stephan Bornstein, the conductor, is world famous. There are doctors, scientists, and in America there is the renowned judge."

"And Papa began life with a tube of diamonds in his

rectum, although in the end he made millions."

"And lost it. Every cent," Madame Benoit said.

"Did you love him?"

"He's dead almost seventeen years."

"But did you love him?"

"I've forgotten." And then angrily, with her eyes flashing, "You loved him enough for us both." The intensity of her feelings, her passion, had caught her by surprise, and the words had flown out of her mouth. She regretted them, but it was too late. She seemed on the verge of saying something more, even apologizing. Natalie had never before seen her mother falter. "He adored you," Madame Benoit said. "He was a good father."

"He loved you, too."

"Yes, I suppose."

"And I did too. I still do."

"Yes, I know."

"Those days before the war were the best of my life," Natalie said. "I'm going away for a while, to a house I have at the coast. Did I tell you?"

"I know next to nothing about your life."

"It's in La Rochelle. An old place, but with great charm. The area is becoming very popular, and my idea is to open a second shop."

"What about the one you've opened here?"

"The one in La Rochelle will be smaller, and mostly for the summer. I have a partner, and between the two of us . . ."

"This is the first I've heard of a partner."

"She's the niece of a partner I had in Saigon. A Chinese. A lovely girl, named Lei-ling. I want you to meet her."

"Has she capital of her own?"

"Yes, we'll both put in equal amounts," Natalie said. "We're going to live together in the house, as well, she and I. I want you to come and live with us this summer."

"The three of us? It's an odd arrangement."

"We could see if it works."

"I'm content here."

"Alone?"

"I'm quite used to it," Madame Benoit said.

"You would like Lei-ling."

"At my age, one makes no new friends."

Natalie thought, she gives nothing, my mother. She never has.

Marcel had been waiting for hours. He saw Natalie arrive at her mother's and followed her when she left. He drove a rented car, cruising behind Natalie, who walked as far as Place St.-Augustin in search of a cab. Marcel followed the cab northeast in the direction of Place Clichy. Natalie got out at rue de Calias and entered a house about a third of the way along the street: number 12. Marcel checked the registry of names, but Natalie wasn't listed, nor was anyone whose name he recognized. If she had gone to an apartment used by Castellone, it would have been made safe. There was nothing for him to do but wait.

He ate a sandwich and drank two cups of coffee in a bar-tabac, and returned to the car, settling in with a package of cigarettes.

At about three in the morning, he dozed off. When he awoke, the sky was just beginning to lighten. He was a very light sleeper, and was certain that he had not missed her. He left the car to stretch his legs, and to pee. When the bar-tabac opened, he had another coffee.

At a quarter past seven, an old man came out of number 12 to walk his dog. Only a minute or two later, Natalie appeared, carrying an overnight bag. He noticed at once that she had changed clothes. She had been wearing a skirt, and now was dressed in jeans and American boots. She was accompanied by a woman, an Oriental—Marcel thought Chinese—taller than Natalie and quite striking, with hair that came almost to her waist. She had the same boots as Natalie, jeans as well, although she wore a sweater and Natalie an English raincoat, the belt knotted on the side. They crossed the street to a red Fiat sport coupe, the Oriental entering from the driver's side, then stretching to lift the latch on the passenger door for Natalie.

Marcel started his car, and fell behind; traffic was still light and it was easy to keep them in sight, driving south on rue Amsterdam. Marcel sensed an intimacy between the two women, although he couldn't exactly say why.

Perhaps the identical boots, which must have been bought at the same time. It was also in the way they had walked to the car, their shoulders brushing, and even now, seen through the rear of the Fiat, Natalie was turned halfway around, and had placed herself near the Oriental woman, who drove. Marcel knew they were in something together. He wondered if it were sex, or perhaps something more. His intuition for such things was always keen, particularly after an almost sleepless night.

The Fiat pulled up in front of Gare St.-Lazare. Natalie climbed out, carrying the overnight bag. Marcel drove into a parking garage, pulled a claim check from a dispensing machine, and in a matter of seconds was back in the street. The Fiat was gone, and Natalie had crossed the esplanade and was just entering the station.

Marcel stayed out of sight while she bought a train ticket, and then went to the same booth, pushing a ten-franc bill folded into a small square through the slot.

"The woman who was just here. Where did she buy a ticket to?"

The clerk was a black, three tribal scars like chevrons carved on each cheek. "The last stop on the Coastal Express." He plucked the ten-franc bill and made it vanish. "La Rochelle. Pretty place, so I'm told."

Marcel bought a ticket. He had fifteen minutes, time enough for a wash in the men's room and a shave with a coin-operated electric razor. He bought the newspapers and a couple of magazines, watched Natalie make a telephone call, and boarded the train only after she did. He located her compartment, but stayed clear, buying coffee and sandwiches from a vendor who went from car to car. He was relaxed, and even slept. They didn't arrive until the middle of the afternoon.

The station at La Rochelle was an old relic, built beside the pier, so that the old steamers, and the sailing ships before them, could load and unload at the railroad siding.

Natalie walked through the station, onto the pier and past the taxi stand. She stopped and looked around, expecting to be met. Marcel stayed out of sight. Several minutes passed. Natalie fidgeted, glancing at her watch. It had begun to rain, a light drizzle, and a cold wind came off the water. A bus pulled up and a crowd of people got off, waiting while their luggage was loaded into a hand-cart. The stationmaster called the three o'clock train to Tours.

Just then a gray Volkswagen pulled up at the café across the road from the station. A man in a long leather coat got out. Marcel had a closer look; it was Castellone.

Marcel hung back, careful to keep out of sight. He noticed that when Castellone came up, he touched Natalie's arm, but it was only a gesture, tentatively done, and he didn't take hold of her. They didn't kiss. The rain came down harder, and neither wore a hat. They talked for several seconds in the rain. Castellone was pale, and thinner, his face more deeply lined than the last time Marcel had seen him. He seemed unsure, without his usual confidence. It was a Castellone Marcel had never seen before. Finally, he did not take hold of Natalie's arm, and they ran across the road into the café.

"You've done well, buying that house," Castellone said. "It was kind of you to let me stay."

"Was it comfortable?"

"Yes, quite."

"There's no heat."

"I used the fireplace, and slept there in the big room."

"Alone for eight days."

"It's good to do once in a while. One takes stock."

"You look tired, Bernard."

"And you look lovely," he said.

"I'm tired and I need a bath."

"I'm afraid I turned the hot water heater off."

"It heats quickly."

He paused, and then said with a little smile, "Are we really finished?"

She wouldn't meet his eyes, and he eventually followed her gaze across the road to the empty railroad station, where nothing stirred. The wind flattened the rain and the few gulls who flew into it couldn't move at all, as if beating their wings against a wall. It was chilly in the café and everything before them was gray—the dirty brick of the station, the sky, the ocean—all the same wet gray.

Castellone didn't repeat his question and Natalie was able to say nothing. He played with the ashtray, which advertised Noilly Prat Vermouth, sweet or dry. Their waiter brought a bottle of Calvados and two glasses.

Natalie clinked his glass. "I almost forgot. Happy birthday."

"Two days ago. I forgot myself until I was going off to sleep, and then it was after midnight."

She said, "What did you think—I mean your first thoughts— when you heard that George was dead?"

"I don't know. Poor George. The usual things."

"But you liked George."

"Yes, very much. He was good to be with. At least he was in the early days." Something stirred, and he looked at her sharply. "How did he die?"

"He killed himself."

Castellone stayed still. For several seconds he didn't move a muscle, he didn't breathe. He drank off his Calvados and refilled his glass. "Where was he when he did it?"

"We were in Jamaica."

"You and he?"

"Yes, just the two of us."

"How did he do it?"

"He shot himself."

"Damn him." And then in a softer voice. "Damn him."

A workman came into the café carrying a wooden crate lined with seaweed, and on top a bunch of lobsters squirming and probing blindly with their long antennae.

"They look good, eh? Like that place in Hong Kong," he said. "Dinner, what do you say?"

"Your train is at five."

"I'll give you lobster, and pour wine into you. Then I'll tickle your foot. What do you say?"

"Tickle your own damn foot." But she couldn't help laughing; Castellone had always been able to make her laugh.

"At least have another drink," he said, "there's time for that. I'm in no hurry to go back to Paris."

His smile was meant to be carefree, to reassure and to carry on, to show confidence as in their early days together. But it was a far cry, a hollow thing. She looked deeply into his eyes, and thought, he's afraid.

"Your friend, the Chinese," he said. "Does she know you're here?"

"She drove me to the station, but she thinks I came out only to see the house. She doesn't know you're here."

"Does anyone else?"

"You told me to keep it quiet."

Something in the station waiting room had caught his eye; she looked, but saw nothing. He said, "Did George have any family?"

"He never mentioned one way or the other."

"What about his money?"

"I don't know about that. There's probably a will someplace."

"What about the other one, the American? The young American. Did you love him, Natalie?"

She slowly shook her head, at the same time laying her hand on his. "I loved you," she said. "From the first. One minute I was half dead, feeling nothing. Then we met. From then and for a long time it was marvelous."

"And now?"

"I've stopped."

"Just like that?"

"No. It took a long time. You kicked hell out of me— and I did the same to you. Not as much, I think. But finally, I made myself free."

"I loved you too," he said. "The trouble was, I didn't know it at the time. I thought I had possession of you, that you'd stay put. I thought you'd wait until I got ready. I was wrong. I put you through hell."

"Damn right you did."

"And now it's my turn," he said. "Fair enough. I want to run, Natalie. But I can't do it alone. I haven't the nerve. Or maybe alone I don't care enough to run. Without you, I don't care one way or another."

She kept hold of herself and wouldn't let herself cry. She seized his face between her hands and kissed him, her mouth hard against his. It was done fiercely, finally, and the next instant she was on her feet and running out of the bar. He didn't follow. He didn't move. She got into the VW and drove off without looking back.

CHAPTER 23

Marcel was miserably cold and soaked to the skin. He was famished and he had to go to the toilet. It was urgent, a condition brought on by nerves. Marcel was nervous as a cat, and hopped from foot to foot, watching Castellone and Natalie over their drinks in the café across from the station.

He could stand it no more, and just made it to the station toilet. He was gone six minutes, not a second more. He had timed it on his watch. But when he returned to his lookout behind the baggage rack, Natalie and Castellone were gone. The gray VW was gone. The waiter had cleared their table.

Marcel looked frantically around the station, not knowing what to do. People had begun to arrive for the five o'clock train to Paris. But where was Castellone? Marcel was sure he had lost him, that he had driven off with Natalie in the VW. He thought of hiring a car and going out after him. But where? Marcel felt tired and defeated. He got on line to buy a ticket for the Paris train.

Just then, he froze; something round and hard had been jammed into the small of his back.

"Turn around." It was Castellone, making a pistol of his thumb and first finger.

"You scared the life out of me," Marcel said. "Always teasing me. It's unkind. If you knew I was watching you, why didn't you invite me over. All you had to do was wave. I'm freezing and soaking wet and very hungry."

"The train has a dining car," Castellone said.

"I've had nothing to eat all day but a couple of awful sandwiches."

"They used to serve salmon from the Loire."

"It was mean of you to let me stand around in the rain."

"I'll make it up to you with the salmon."

There wasn't any salmon, which disappointed Marcel, but he came around with a double whisky, a good steak, two liters of wine between them, and Cuban cigars with the coffee.

"I'm sorry to have been so grumpy," Marcel said. "But I couldn't find you in Paris, and then being left out in the rain. It was a good dinner, even if there wasn't any salmon. And I've been taking your advice about Marilyn."

"Marilyn?"

"My spark plug heiress. I wanted you to know that I screwed her night before last, and it wasn't half bad."

Castellone said, "How nice of you to come all this way to tell me."

"I've been sent after you."

"Who by?"

"The sewing circle," Marcel said. "The old wops around my father. I've been sent to do you."

"And you followed Natalie?"

"All over fucking Paris. Her mother's place, and this Chinese lady friend she's got. There I was freezing my ass in that car all night. All of it to find my pal in order to warn him. I'd never do you, Bernard. I told the sewing circle I would, but I wouldn't."

"Why do they want me killed?"

"They think you're a cop. That's the word around."

"And all they sent was you? No back-up?"

"The train stops at Tours," Marcel said. "We ought to get off there, skip Paris altogether."

"You think they're backing you up, is that it?"

"It's what they always do."

"I've got a stop to make in Paris."

"Don't do it, Bernard. I'll make the stop for you, and meet you anywhere you say. I swear I will."

"Don't flick the end of your cigar," Castellone said. "Once you break the ash, the taste changes."

"I could have shot you from the station when you picked up Natalie. You didn't see me then. I was watching your eyes, and you didn't know I was there."

"It's true. I didn't see you."

"I thought about it. I won't kid you. I kill you, it puts me in tight with the sewing circle. Old Achille would die happy."

"But you didn't do it."

"You sound sorry."

"In ten minutes we arrive at Tours." It was the dining car waiter, clearing their table. "We stay eight minutes."

"I'd never do you," Marcel said. "I have a nasty character, you can ask anybody. Double-crossing pals being the least of it. But I made up my mind to be loyal to you and I'm good in a fight, Bernard. Just watch me."

The train slowed, followed by the hiss of the airbrakes as they arrived at the station in Tours. Castellone needed to make a phone call, and Marcel stayed with him, his back to the glass booth and his arms across his chest, the fingers of his right hand touching the grip of the pistol in a holster under his left armpit.

Castellone called Paris, Albert at the Florida.

"It's quite slow," Albert said. "No one around, no one at all."

"Will you be there later on?"

"I expect so."

"I'll need a look in the Chubb."

"The safe? It'll be here, too."

"Around midnight, Albert."

Albert put the receiver down gently, as if it were fragile. Next to him, holding the muzzle of a pistol to his kidney, stood Rocco, who had been listening on the auxiliary receiver. He wore a striped waistcoat and black jacket, the same as Albert. Three others were in the lobby, each in a corner with arms folded, gunmen in business suits and raincoats.

"He sounded out of town," Rocco said. "Anyhow, not around the corner."

"It's ten past eight. He said midnight."

"That's what he said."

"He was out of town for sure."

"You got a code, the two of you?" Rocco said. "What have you got worked out?"

"Nothing. No code."

"What's in the safe?"

"It's a vault, with two keys for each box. There's mine, and one for the client renting the box."

"What about the door to the vault?"

"There are two. The outer has a combination lock, but the inner needs a pair of keys."

"Do you know the combination?"

"Yes. But I've only the one key for the inner lock."

"Castellone rents a box. He would have the other."

"Ask him at midnight." Rocco jabbed him with the gun and Albert said, "Cheap hoodlum with a gun."

Rocco jabbed him a second time, and kicked him hard, aiming for his shin. Rocco looked astonished, comically so, and Albert laughed in his face.

"What the hell is that?" Rocco said. "You never told me you had a wooden leg."

"I thought I'd wait until our wedding night," Albert said.

"It's a hell of a thing."

"Why? Is it bad luck for a wop to shoot a man with one leg?"

"Bad luck for the one he shoots."

"Then go on. I should have told Castellone you were here. I should have spit in your eye. Now, it's too late."

"It's not too late, if you've got the guts." When Albert kept still, Rocco said, "Maybe I wouldn't have shot you. Maybe I was bluffing, because I needed you to set up Castellone."

"I should have spit in your eye," Albert said, but without conviction, almost in a whisper.

Rocco gestured for one of the gunmen to come over.

"Now you go up to an empty room. We put you to bed, and you stay still."

"Castellone is worth ten like you."

"That's what I hear. I hear he's a hard case, who never sets up a friend."

"Give me a gun, we'll see who's tougher. You or me, Rocco."

"Go on, Dominick is going to put you to bed."

"I'm not afraid. I only wish I had warned Castellone." An agonized look came over his face. "I'm ashamed," he said. "Kill me if you want, it doesn't matter."

Dominick took his arm and rather gently led Albert away. Dressed as a concierge, Rocco took over the desk. From there he could see the door, through which Castellone would enter, but was himself out of sight for the half second it took to step through the vestibule into the lobby.

The train from La Rochelle was on time, arriving at St.-Lazare just after eleven. The storm, which had begun over the Atlantic, had preceded the train to Paris, losing none of its force along the way. And there was not a taxi in sight. Finally Marcel remembered the hired car he had parked in the garage near the station, and they ran to pick it up, both huddled against the storm.

In the garage, Marcel went through his pockets until he found the claim check, and carried it into the manager's office to pay. Castellone was left alone. The garage was a frightening place, nearly empty at that time of night, quiet as a cave deep under the earth, and with the same impenetrable shadows in every corner.

Castellone looked around as if he had never seen a garage at night. Yet it was the most ordinary kind of place, with a repair shop at one end, a pneumatic lift and commonplace tools hanging from a pegboard. There was even a large oil slick on the floor. Castellone felt himself at a distance, removed from this place, and from everything that had begun to happen to him.

Just then a cat came out of the shadows and stood watching him with its yellow eyes. He didn't like cats, and was actually afraid of them. Natalie had once brought a kitten, a tiny thing which managed to make him so uneasy he had to go through the embarrassment of asking her to return it to the shop.

But now—oddly—he wasn't afraid. He reached out for the comfort of his old fears, and didn't find them. For a moment he was lost and confused. His deepest and most reliable fears were gone. He looked for the sorrows and humiliations of his childhood, but they were gone. His fear of death was gone. The suffering caused by losing Natalie—that was gone.

Marcel came out of the office, and an attendant brought around the car. Marcel wanted to know where they were going, and Castellone said, "The Florida."

"Is your kit stashed there?"

"That and a little cash."

"Then we get back in the car and take off."

Marcel hummed when he drove and tapped the wheel with his finger. Castellone said, "I'll need to go deep under, you know. Maybe you ought to do the same."

"Nobody is looking for me. I couldn't find you, that's all. I failed. It's expected of me, Achille's faggot son."

"You turn right here," Castellone said.

There wasn't a place in front of the Florida, so Marcel double-parked and set the hazard light blinking. The entrance to the Florida was on the right, the passenger side, and Castellone was the first out of the car. He kept his coat collar up and his head down against the rain. Only the night light was on in the lobby of the Florida, and the revolving door was locked. Castellone rang the bell and waited. Marcel stood behind him.

"Is it always locked at this hour?"

"Yes."

The electronic buzzer sounded, releasing the door, and Castellone stepped into the lobby. He was immediately in sight of the concierge's desk. From the corner of his eye, he saw a sudden movement from that direction. It alarmed him, and he reached for his pistol, at the same time thinking, that's not Albert.

Just then he saw the flash of the gun, and the impact of the first shot, which struck his shoulder, knocked him down. Marcel stood over him, firing at Rocco, who stood behind the concierge's desk.

Gun flashes came from everywhere at once, and the lobby vibrated with the noise. Castellone had his gun out, and rolled over on his side, steadied his hand, took careful aim, and shot Rocco in the center of the chest.

The next instant Castellone was hit a second time. The bullet struck with terrible force, such force that he knew he must die of it. He was conscious, but had no pain. He heard nothing, not the shots or the shouts of his assassins. He couldn't move, and felt as if each of his limbs was pinned to the ground. But then his bonds broke, and he fell through a deep hole. He thought he saw the ocean, the tide swelling, and the waves rolling in and sliding back. He heard the waves rumble, a sound that he loved.

CHAPTER 24

Following the death of Marcel, Achille Piri regained some of his strength, and even got out of bed and sat in a chair by the window. His doctor spoke of remission, and his priest of a miracle. It turned out to be neither; it was anger. Fury at his son had revived old Piri.

"We sent him to kill Castellone," he said. "Instead he fights at his side. Rocco dead, and two of our men wounded."

"Think of it as a mistake," Angelo said. "Marcel walked in, there were shots, and he returned the fire."

"He saw Rocco. He knew him all his life."

"But it's all done in a second. The shouts, the bullets flying . . ."

"My son betrayed me," Achille said. "He fought at the side of my enemies."

"Put it out of your mind. We have urgent business."

"Why? Why did he do it?"

"They were friends."

"Who?"

"Your son and Castellone."

"Friends? What has that to do with it?"

"Friends. They liked each other."

"And so?"

"Someone shot at his friend. He drew his gun and shot back."

Old Piri was bewildered. Then he stubbornly shook his head. "No. It was business, a private deal of some sort," he said. "They were partners, don't you see? In order to profit, my son needed to keep Castellone alive. It·was for money that he tried to save him. Otherwise, what sense is there in it?" ·

Achille Piri's eyes were huge in his shrunken face. His skin was gray and lifeless, and there was no flesh left anywhere on his bones. Everything had shrunk but his nose and ears, which were now grotesquely out of proportion. And of course his eyes. These were terrible, a dying man's eyes, but a dying man who rages against his fate, who despises his helplessness, and is filled with an impotent fury against those who go on living.

Angelo yearned to be rid of this old man. "Your son is dead," he said. "Let God judge him. I need to get home and we have business to conclude."

"God does his job and we do ours," Achille said.

"Is that a joke, Don Achille?"

"I don't know. What do you think?"

"I'm a man of business," Angelo said. "With Castellone dead, the Vietnamese has come into the picture, contacting us directly."

"What Vietnamese?"

"Nyo's nephew. He's no longer Ambassador, and calls himself Mr. Nguyen. He is Mr. Nguyen, and he offers us the product at the same price."

"I was good to him, you know," Achille said. "I used to take him for lunch on Sunday. He liked those garlic sausages, the little reddish colored ones, grilled on a wood fire. Once I even took him swimming in the pool in that hotel near the Etoile. A beautiful place, but they tore it down. Such a palace, why did they tear it down? And also the old clubs—all torn down. Luigi's, the Algiers, and the Orient. What happened to all those old places?"

Angelo had stood up and walked to the door. "I'm going now," he said.

"No, wait."

"I've got Mr. Nguyen downstairs. It's a big thing, with lots of money involved."

"But there was something I wanted to tell you."

Angelo shifted from one foot to the other, his hand on the doorknob.

"Wait, I'll remember. It was a question. Something to do with Marcel."

"It'll come to you."

Angelo opened the door and went out. As he closed the door, he heard Achille say, "It's something about Marcel. It's about my son. He was in business with Castellone. It was done for profit. For money. Don't you see?"

Mr. Nguyen waited in a small study off the living room. Since the murder of his uncle, he had adopted a serious and businesslike attitude, abruptly ending his career as playboy ambassador.

When Angelo came in, he went straight to the point. "As I told you at our preliminary meeting," Nguyen said, "I have the merchandise and am prepared to conduct a sale at the same terms."

"At the same terms?"

"Yes. Why not?"

"Because Castellone is dead, so there is no broker to collect a fee. A tragic event, which nevertheless reduces your expenses. We propose only that the savings be divided."

"But the value of the merchandise is the same."

"But we are not prepared to pay the same."

"How much are you prepared to pay?"

Angelo's shrug was accompanied by Cuban cigars, good whisky in Waterford crystal. He knew how to dress a bargain, although in the end the numbers were the same.

"My uncle is dead," Nguyen said. "Saigon has a new government, which had confiscated all of our property. I'm no longer Ambassador. In fact, I've been thrown out on my ear. No job, not even a valid passport."

"In time you'll become a Swiss subject. If not Switzerland, then Monaco. We can help you there. It's all a question of money, Mr. Nguyen. Of capital, points in a deal."

"I have no capital. Only expenses."

"You have a beautiful wife, and from what I hear quite extravagant."

"You make it your business to hear a lot," Nguyen said. "And what you heard is that I'm against the wall, so you try to cut out my heart."

"I look to make a good deal."

"I'll go elsewhere."

"There's no elsewhere." Angelo refilled Nguyen's glass. "Listen, my friend. Your uncle is dead. The product is yours alone. The money is yours to keep—all of it."

"Tell me how much."

"Do you know Majorca? We have a hotel there. Very nice, very clean. Run by a German. I'll notify my colleagues, and we'll meet there in order to work out the details."

"The product stays behind."

"Why not? Protect yourself the way you think best. Yet you have nothing to fear, although we would never ask you to trust us."

"Ask all you want," Mr. Nguyen said.

When he left Angelo, Mr. Nguyen drove to the center of Paris, where his wife was on a shopping trip. They had worked out in advance where to meet—at Natalie Benoit's shop, on Faubourg St.-Honoré.

Madame Nguyen had already been to her dressmaker, to one or two smaller boutiques, and of course to Hermès. She was never happier than when going from shop to shop, examining beautiful things and buying all she could. Certain things she couldn't resist. When still a young girl and working as a stewardess for Air France, not only was all of her salary spent in the shops, but she went deeply into debt. Since she was a beautiful girl, there were always rich men to help out. Her desire for expensive presents was more than simple passion or greed; it was a fever, which roused her sexually, and flattered the rich men who gave the presents, and made her their great favorite.

Her friendship with Natalie dated from those days, when she went to her shop to trade up the gifts she received, items which were too close to things she already had or didn't really like, exchanging them for other pieces, particularly precious stones.

"And rubies most of all," she said to Natalie.

"You have some lovely stones."

"My pigeon blood is quite as good as this one."

"Without question. The color is similar, and both are just over five carats."

Madame Nguyen took a loupe and examined the stone, which Natalie had laid before her on a black cloth. "This one has a lovely rose color, and the feather isn't much at all." She put down the loupe and said with emphasis, "I prefer it to mine."

Lei-ling said, "One usually prefers the stone one doesn't have."

"Oriental women understand each other. You see how it is, Natalie? You have a nice thing here, the two of you," Madame Nguyen said.

"Get your husband to buy you a shop."

"Or a part of this one, eh? As long as it's not a disgusting Vietnamese restaurant, like every other refugee with a couple of francs."

"I can't see you slaving in a restaurant."

"She's too beautiful and full of fun."

"You mean, a whore born." Madame Nguyen had a good laugh at her own expense. "I'm best with a pair of heavy stones in the palm of my hand," she said. "Tell me how much for this handsome chap."

"Two hundred thousand francs."

"Oh, my lord."

"But that's not high for such a stone. Since the fields in Mogok have been nationalized, there are too few rubies, and almost none of this quality."

Madame Nguyen weighed the stone in her palm, played with it lovingly, and clutched it between the tips of her thumb and first finger, like a crow with a cherry on its beak.

"Let me have it for one-fifty."

"I can't do that."

"Lei-ling, talk to her," Madame Nguyen said.

"Listen to her, like a child playing one parent against the other."

"You could go to your husband," Natalie said.

"Not that one. Since the coup, he's become tighter than a flea's ass."

"I promise you, a year from now you'll pay a quarter of a million."

"Let me pay it off, so much a month. You know how it is, between husbands and wives. I can always suck a few francs out of him. Fifty thousand now, and ten thousand a month."

"We'll have to talk about that," Natalie said. "Give us a day or so, and I'll let you know."

When they were alone, Lei-ling said to Natalie, "She's okay, that one. What was it she said about herself? 'A whore born.' She makes no bones about it."

"She has nerve and she looks out for herself. My guess is that's why she married Nyo's nephew. He was riding high, the snake. Bernard knew him well, and they had monkey business together. Bernard was no angel, but neither was he a snake."

"This is the first time you've talked about him," Lei-ling said.

"Let him rest in peace."

"I wish I had met him."

"Why is that?"

"Because of what he meant to you."

"It has nothing to do with us." Then, more gently, "Nothing at all with us."

Lei-ling was anxious to learn more, to learn everything about Natalie. But she dare not pry. Instinct warned her to hold her tongue. Natalie laid down the rules of their friendship, of which the first was that part of her life remain hidden.

Lei-ling said, "What about La Rochelle this weekend? Shall we go?"

"No. I don't want to."

"If the shop is to be ready for summer, there's a lot to do."

"You go on."

"It's no fun without you."

"All right then, I'll go."

"There's no point if you don't want to."

"I said I would. You have a long face if I say no. When I say yes, the same long face."

Lei-ling made a fan of her exquisite hands, and above

them, she smiled and batted her eyes. "No long face, you
see." It was charmingly done, although faintly exaggerated, a play on her early training for the Chinese ballet.
"We'll make a wonderful weekend, good hard work, and
later on a long soak in the hot tub."

"We'll go and we'll have a good time."

"Are you happy with me?"

"There's no need to ask questions of that kind."
Natalie took her coat from a closet behind the counter in
the back of the shop.

"Where are you going?"

"To meet a friend."

"With men, it was always different," Lei-ling said.
"They were after me, and I made the game. Now it's the
other way around."

"I'll be back in an hour or so."

Natalie was in a hurry to leave the shop, but once in the
street, she took her time. The appointment was for lunch
at one, and while it was already ten past, she dawdled,
browsing in shop windows, and even walking a block or
two out of her way. It was an appointment she dreaded,
but felt compelled to keep. Once or twice she turned and
started in the opposite direction. Nervousness and ap-
prehension had made her unkind to Lei-ling, and she
thought of a peace offering; bunches of African grapes in
a fruit stall caught her eye. She bought half a kilo and a
couple of Israeli oranges and started toward the shop. But
after a few steps she turned and went off in the direction
of the restaurant in which she was to have her appointment. It was with Jack Sullivan.

He was already seated and had a drink. He stood up
and held her chair. There was no kiss of greeting; she
didn't offer, and he didn't seem to expect one. They
didn't even shake hands. They didn't touch.

She put her bag of fruit on the floor next to her chair
and ordered a bottle of mineral water. She found him
changed. He had cut his hair and his suntan was gone. She
had never seen him in a suit and with a shirt and tie in
Nassau. It made him seem smaller, thinner, and even
rather ordinary. He was handsome still, but one had to
look for it, it wasn't startling. She saw lines of fatigue

around his eyes, and a cautious look. His mouth was
tense, white around the lips. He was no longer perfect.
He reminded her now of Castellone, and even poor
George Berry.

"How did you find me?" she said.

"I was on my way here when Castellone was killed," he
said. "The *Herald* story mentioned you, even the shop."

"Reporters all over. It was awful."

"But good for business."

She realized she had kept her eyes lowered, or turned
away from his. Now she met his gaze, which, to her
surprise, was affectionate, even amused. He still cared for
her. He forgave her. She was certain of it. Although she
had agreed to meet him only to end it between them once
and for all, she began to wonder if they would become
lovers again. All that flashed through her mind in an
instant.

She said, "I'm sorry how things wound up, or didn't
wind up. I mean the loose ends."

"The papers said you saw Castellone the day he was
shot."

"He needed a safe place to stay, and I let him use my
house on the coast. He was scared. I'd never seen him like
that. He knew what was coming." She closed her eyes and
shook her head. "I never thought I'd see him like that."

"He was a double agent, you know."

"No, I don't know. It's nothing to do with me."

"The Americans didn't know either, not at the beginning. Although George knew, he kept it to himself.
George was very clever, don't you think?"

"I suppose he was," she said. "I've tried to put George
out of my mind."

"All of that time out of your mind?" he said. "Jamaica,
all of it? And Nassau, too?"

"Not the part with you—although I'm ashamed of
running out on you," she said. "It was panic, you know.
George dying the way he did."

"And the money."

"No, it wasn't the money."

"You said you were greedy. You were rich as a kid, and
then you were poor."

"It wasn't the money," she said. "George had taken care of me. The money was safe. It was you. It had become too intense, and I didn't want that. Not now, probably never."

"Are you still panicked?" he said.

"I'm fine. I don't know for how long, but who does?" she said. "What about you? What are you doing in Paris? What's it about, Jack? Loose ends, or a scheme? One never quite knows with men like you."

"Men like me?" he said. "Has a man like me ever knocked your ears off?"

"I'm sorry."

But then he smiled as he had in Jamaica, to win her. "I've still got a yen for you," he said.

She made him stop, closing his lips with her fingers. He held her wrist, and kissed her fingers.

"Lay it out for me, will you," she said. "Is it a scheme, or have you looked me up so that we can become lovers again?"

"To become lovers."

"And for what else?"

"I've got a scheme, too."

"Has it to do with Castellone?"

"I need your help."

"Will it be dangerous?"

"Not for you."

"I want to go on with my life," she said. "I've got my shop, my friend. A house that needs fixing up. Do you understand? I like you, there's no denying it. But I've no wish to be hurt, and no need for revenge."

"It's not revenge with me either," he said. "I admired Castellone and I liked George, but there's no one I'd blame for what became of them."

"Then what brought you this far?"

"Mr. Nguyen," he said. "I don't like the racket he's in. I don't want bastards like him walking around free and rich."

"Tell me what you want me to do," she said.

"Madame Nguyen," he said. "She's a client of yours?"

"So you've been watching the shop?"

He ignored that. "Does she buy much?"

"Not as much as she would like. Since the coup, money is tight." Natalie laughed, thinking of that morning in the shop. She told Sullivan of Madame Nguyen's proposal to take the Mogok ruby and pay it off. "She's very greedy, and with more than a little larceny in her heart, particularly where rubies are concerned."

"What if you called and told her you'd let her have the stone? Would she be suspicious?"

"Perhaps, but she'd put it out of her mind. She'd just grab the stone."

"Good. Then call her. Tell her you accept her terms, that the stone is hers."

"And what do you do?"

"I deliver it."

Natalie was back at her shop on the Faubourg by three. She had a fair idea of the risks involved, and decided to protect Lei-ling by telling her nothing of the plan she had worked out with Sullivan. If any money was lost, she would make it up out of her own pocket.

She waited until just after five o'clock, when Lei-ling went to her daily exercise class and she was alone in the shop, before calling Madame Nguyen to tell her that her terms for the purchase of the Mogok ruby were acceptable. "I'll have it delivered tomorrow by special messenger."

"At what time?"

"About noon."

There was a pause from Madame Nguyen's end, while she thought that over. Natalie said, "Twelve o'clock, then?"

"Closer to one." Madame Nguyen had begun to whisper. "My husband will surely be out of the house by then."

"I'll have the messenger there by one," Natalie said.

Sullivan spent the hours after seeing Natalie wandering aimlessly through the streets. He walked on the Champs-Elysées past the Rond-Point, turned south and crossed the Seine to the left bank. He browsed in bookstalls and art galleries. He bought a bag of cashew nuts and ate them as he walked. At first his thoughts were about Natalie; he went over everything that had been said. He heard her voice, the sound of it as well as the exact way in which she pronounced her words. He imagined the way she looked—all vivid as life, all just so. The places of their love were with him again; all of it accompanied by an aching sense of loss. Their love was in the past. She had gone one way, he another. He thought of all he should have said to her, and wished he had a second chance. At the same time he realized that it was pointless. Nothing of love could be reclaimed. Certainly, it had nothing to do with words. It was a color, an odor. He had loved her, perhaps he still did, but now it was a memory, traces of certain sensations which belonged to him exclusively.

He saw other women in the street. Some were available and very pretty. But he talked to none. He stayed alone, his jacket open and his hands jammed into the pockets of his trousers. This was not the solitude of the Shan mountains. In the city there was no sky, no spirit. He was joined to nothing, free and yet not free, adrift, without purpose, always close to boredom and despair.

Natalie had spoken of panic. He understood her now. His was brought about by this solitude. What he felt was to be lost. He needed to regain his purpose—all of that while surrounded by the clamor of Paris, there at the intersection of Montparnasse and avenue du Maine.

He drank a beer in a café, ate a sandwich, and just before five o'clock started back across the river to the Tuileries. He was looking for a particular bench at the north end opposite the rue des Pyramides. From that bench he was able to observe the gilt equestrian statue of Jeanne d'Arc. Sullivan enjoyed the scene, the end of a warm day in late spring, the gardens filled with workers from the municipal offices along the rue Rivoli. There were couples strolling arm and arm, a group of boys kicking a ball, and a man with the physique of a body-builder exercising a pair of matched shepherd dogs. One of the boys kicked the ball over the head of the others, and it rolled near Sullivan. He stood up to kick it back, but did it awkwardly, an American more used to throwing. When he returned to the bench, he was not alone; Zola had joined him, a string bag filled with grapefruit on his lap.

"These cost the earth in Switzerland," he said. "And then they're not even very good. In your country they are both cheap and delicious."

"What have you got for me?" Sullivan said.

"Peter Owen is in Paris."

"What else?"

"Mr. Nguyen will be on the early flight tomorrow to Barcelona."

"Without a passport?"

"He's got a passport," Zola said. "It's a fake, not even a very good one."

"I heard he had begun to cut corners."

"We'll let him go," Zola said. "Let him land in Spain." He thought about that a moment and then said, "That place in Florida, where the grapefruit come from . . . what is it called?"

"Indian River."

"Superb. The thing I like best about America is the citrus fruit."

"What will you do with Mr. Nguyen?"

"In Spain? We'll see."

Sullivan said, "With him gone, who's left at the house?"

"The wife. She might be alone, then she might not. There are no regular thugs, but one doesn't know."

"Where is the safe?"

"In the basement," Zola said. "It's a Hercules, a decent one. We can send someone along, one of our technicians."

"Send a technician," Sullivan said, "and I'll shoot him on sight."

"We were to cooperate. You came to us, and we agreed on the terms. We don't trust our agency or yours. Our hands are tied in France, but yours are free."

"Tell me one thing," Sullivan said. "Castellone, was he doubling from the beginning?"

"Absolutely, from the first. He worked his way in with Kirk and the others in order to see that the product was contained. And then to use it to flush out the Dons."

"Twenty kilos of bait?"

"The Dons are big game. It would help if we wound up with the bait."

"I'll do what I can."

"Then as a favor—to Castellone, and, of course, to yourself. You haven't the CIA behind you," Zola said. "You're alone, and in the open. If any of the product finds its way onto the market, we'll kill you."

Sullivan shrugged, stood up, and stretched his legs. Zola said, "Did you ever meet Castellone?"

"Yes, we had a drink together."

"I miss Bernard," Zola said. "He was a good egg."

CHAPTER 25

Once back in Paris, Natalie had settled into a routine. She took her meals on time, did regular exercise to avoid putting on weight, and ended her day soaking in a hot tub sipping a glass of Scotch.

Lei-ling had rigged a table which could be swung back and forth across the tub, and on it Natalie kept a small television set, a dish of olives, and occasionally a bit of cheese. She was at peace, the events of the day far away, watching an old movie starring Charles Boyer, when Lei-ling knocked tentatively at the bathroom door and asked if she might come in.

"I'm sorry. You look so content. I'm sure you'd rather be alone."

"Not at all. Come in and look at Boyer. Isn't he handsome? And intelligent. But with nothing pretty about him. A man's face."

Lei-ling kneeled on the floor next to the tub, and waited with her hands folded in her lap until the film was over.

"May I turn off the set now?" she said.

"I will."

"Let me. Your hands are wet," Lei-ling said. "Is the water too cold?"

"Yes. But be careful not to make it too hot."

Lei-ling swung the bath table so that it was out of the way and adjusted the water. She soaped a cloth and began to wash Natalie's feet.

"I have a sore toe," Natalie said. "I hope it's not becoming a corn."

"No. Just an irritation from your shoe."

"I don't like my feet."

"I do. They're like a child's." Lei-ling kissed the sore toe, and then used the soapy cloth to tickle the bottom of Natalie's foot.

"Jack Sullivan is in Paris," Natalie said.

"Have you seen him?"

"This afternoon."

"Is that where you ran off to in such a hurry?"

"I wasn't in a hurry." Natalie shifted her weight so that Lei-ling could soap the other foot. "We had a coffee. I found him changed. Particularly the way he looked."

"Did he look better or not as good?"

"Not as good. At least, that's what I thought. Certainly he looked different. He's lost his tan and that gives him a pinched look. He has a marvelous body, but in one of those shapeless American suits, he looks like anyone else."

"Ordinary?"

"Well, not quite."

"Is the water hot enough?"

"It's perfect."

"What did Jack want?"

"To see me," Natalie said. "To learn how things stood."

"How *do* they stand?"

"For him it stands?" Lei-ling tickled the bottom of Natalie's foot again, and held tight to the ankle so that she couldn't yank it away.

"Did you make another date?" Lei-ling asked.

"No."

"Shall I tickle you again?"

"Is it a kind of torture?"

"To make you tell the truth."

"Try kindness." Lei-ling raised Natalie's leg and let it rest on her shoulder, and began to soap the inside of her thigh.

"Did you go to bed with him?"

"How long was I gone? An hour."

"Two."

"Still, that's stretching it."

"Did you want to sleep with him?"

"It crossed my mind," Natalie said. "He was a good lover, but of a particular kind."

"What kind is that?"

"Hard to say exactly. Not like Castellone, but more like him than George. Poor George."

"Tell me the kind of lover Sullivan was."

"Straight on, stiff cock sort of lover."

"You like that, don't you?"

"Sometimes. Sometimes I'm crazy about it."

Lei-ling put her hand between Natalie's legs, and Natalie let her do as she wished. She stayed quiet, with her eyes closed and the back of her hand against her forehead. Her breathing was so deep she might have been asleep. Only once did she make any sound at all, and that might have been made in her sleep—a low, soft moan, a plaintive cry, as if she were pleading for something.

Later, when they were in bed, Natalie said, "I have all I want with you. It's as if my life has begun again. I'm happy, the same way I was as a child."

"With your father and mother?"

"Yes. Bernard's death seems to have changed the way I feel about things."

"But you loved Bernard."

"Yes, of course."

"Was he the only one you loved?"

"Yes. I told you. He's a permanent thing, alive in my memory, like my father. What am I anyhow? Only the memory of certain people."

"I want to love them, too," Lei-ling said. "Will you let me? Do you understand?"

Natalie looked over at Lei-ling's profile beside her on the pillow in the darkened bedroom. "I'm not sure I do understand. It's very odd. You want to share them with me?"

"No, more than that. We must all exist together. The four of us, always."

"And grow old together." Natalie was teasing, but in the most gentle way, stroking her lover's face and smoothing her hair. "Don't be so serious. Love isn't all that grave."

Lei-ling tried to laugh, but couldn't. She wasn't a light-hearted person, or much fun to be with. Natalie was resigned to it, and rarely minded at all.

"I want to be with you all my life," Lei-ling said.

"And become two old ladies?"

"Yes. Why not?"

"Well, one never knows," Natalie said. "How can one ever know what's in the cards, old friend."

Sullivan had twice been to the property occupied by the Nguyens. He had walked every foot of the land around it, examined the small farms nearby, and knew every road, and even where the cars and farm vehicles belonged. He knew the roads in and out, and he knew the dogs.

He had come each time in a different car, different color and make. He changed the way he dressed. Now he wore aviator's glasses and a French suit, shirt, and tie, all bought in Lafayette, makeup to darken his skin, and a false mustache. When he picked up the ruby, it had taken Natalie a second or two to recognize him.

He drove up to the Nguyen house and parked, but didn't go in. He lifted the hood and spent a few minutes pretending to tinker with the engine. But all the while he was having a look around the house. The curtains were drawn on the first floor, and the shutters on the second were closed. The garage was empty and Mr. Nguyen's Mercedes was not to be seen. There was no second car, and no tire depressions in the loose gravel to indicate any had been there in the last few hours.

Sullivan lowered the hood, listened for the click of the latch, and dusted his hands as he walked toward the front door. He thought he might be in luck; his chances of finding Madame Nguyen alone were good.

He had to ring twice and had begun to think there might be a slip-up, and that she wasn't at home. He wasn't nervous, only tense and alert, ready to move either

way. Finally, she appeared at the door, somewhat out of
breath, dressed in a light wool suit, a bright green scarf
tied around her throat.

"I'm sorry. I was in the garden and didn't at first hear
the bell."

He realized she wasn't dressed for the garden but said,
"A lovely day for the garden."

"Yes, it's a hobby of mine." She smiled, displaying
perfect teeth, so white they might have sprouted that
morning. "Have you something for me?"

"A package from Madame Benoit."

The smile continued while she stood aside for him to
enter. With the shades down, the house was dark, and
had that stillness which comes when the occupants are
about to leave on an extended trip.

She eagerly took the small package from his hands and
tore off the wrapping. The stone was in a square black
box.

"Isn't it beautiful?"

"A superb stone."

"I'll get the cash."

She kept the stone and walked into a smaller room, a
sort of study with a television set and a pair of binoculars
on a tripod at the window. Her pocketbook was there on a
small rosewood desk, and she took a brown envelope
from it. When she turned around, Sullivan was behind
her. She was startled—he had moved so quietly—and
then cried out in fright. He held a pistol in his hand.

"The safe," he said. "Your husband has a Hercules in
the cellar."

She recovered quickly, although all the color had left
her face. "What about the ruby? May I keep that?"

"I don't care about it," he said. "You know the
combination. Open the safe."

"What happens to me?"

"Nothing. Not if you open the safe."

"I was on my way to the airport."

"With no car?"

"I was going to telephone for a cab."

"I'll drive you," he said. "I've no wish to hurt you, or
even have you remain here. Just open the safe."

"You think I don't know what's in the safe?" she said.

"I tell you, I want no part of it. I just want to get out."

"With the stone?"

"Why not?"

"You'd cheat Madame Benoit?"

"It's a lovely stone."

"Open the safe," he said. "I'll drive you to Orly."

He followed her to the cellar. The safe wasn't all that much, a standard three tumbler, reminding him of the kind he had been taught to spring in training exercises. But that was a long time past, and it was a good thing that she knew the combination and was as willing as he to see it opened. He noticed that her fingers didn't tremble, that she was as steady as a rock, and worked the combination with confidence.

The opium was in two Halliburton cases. She knew the combinations to these as well, and he had her open them for a look inside. As far as he could tell there were twenty kilos of number four heroin, still packed neatly in the original brown wrapping. Sullivan carried the cases to the car, and went back to lend a hand with her suitcases, which had been packed and stored out of sight in an upstairs closet.

She was tense, but in good spirits during the drive to Orly, happy to be on her way, happy to be rid of her husband.

"Are you a friend of Madame Benoit?" she said.

He said, "I won't ask you where you're going, but I will wish you all the luck."

"I see. I'm to keep my mouth shut, and just get on the plane and vanish."

"It's a long drive to Orly," he said. "And the car has no radio."

"Tell me then, did you get the ruby from Madame Benoit?"

"No, from the real courier."

"And you don't know her?"

"We've never met."

"Then you really don't care what happens to the stone? Or if I pay Madame Benoit."

"I want you to have it," he said. "You helped me, and I want you to enjoy it, and to think of me when you wear it."

"I promise you I will," she said.

The drive to Orly took more than an hour, and the traffic inside the airport was a mess. It was late afternoon when they finally arrived at the main terminal building.

"What time is your flight?"

"I don't know. I haven't a ticket, only a French passport. Thanks to my mother."

"And money?"

"Enough to start me off."

"No doubt in time there will be more."

"True enough, but I have to decide where to go. I have good friends in a few places. It's a question of choosing the one in which I can expect the warmest welcome." When she leaned closer to him in the closed car, he was able to smell her perfume, a light and delicious scent, and he was able to hear the fine gold bracelets tinkling like temple bells around her wrists. She was a sexual woman, and gave it off in waves.

"What about you?" she said. "Alone with that stuff. Have you friends?"

"I have you."

"I'll be far away," she said. "Tell me, are you a gangster? I don't care two hoots. I could really be your friend." She had brought it to the point where it was between her and him, between a man and a woman, and with that she was sure of herself. "You're not a cop, and probably not a gangster either." She reached out across the seat, lingered over a kiss on the cheek. "London," she said. "New York, later on. Do you know the Stanhope Hotel? It's quite a chic place."

She bit his earlobe and was out of the car and into the terminal, a porter trailing behind with her bags.

Sullivan left the airport and drove north on N7 to Paris, entering at Porte d'Italie, where there was a large municipal car park. He locked the car with the two Halliburton cases in the trunk, and took the key and claim check with him. He caught the bus which began at the car park and continued along avenue d'Italie as far as the Gare Austerlitz. His instinct was to stay clear of cabs, which were easy to follow. He took a second bus at Austerlitz, which dropped him at the Metro station at Place de la Concorde, a couple of hundred yards from the

American Embassy. He bought stamps and an envelope from a stationer near the Madeleine, addressed the envelope, and put the car keys and parking lot claim check inside. He sealed the envelope, but didn't mail it. With the envelope in the inside pocket of his jacket, he telephoned the American Embassy, asking to speak to Mr. Shubert, the cultural attaché. He was put through to a secretary, an American girl who answered with an informal hello. She put him off; Mr. Shubert was on another call, and he was going directly to a meeting. Mr. Shubert was in and out of his office, a very hard man to get hold of.

"I'm a classmate of Mr. Shubert," Sullivan said. "And I'm lost. Do you understand?"

"Yes. Well, no. Not exactly."

"My name is Sullivan. Jack Sullivan, will you tell him that?"

"Mr. Soloman."

"Sullivan. Have you got it?"

"Yes, I'm sorry. You were classmates, Mr. Sullivan and you're lost."

"Tell Mr. Shubert I'll be in the little park just behind Notre Dame. There's a bench near the fountain. About an hour from now. Tell him to send a friend, someone with a voucher. Have you got that?"

"A friend with a voucher."

"Good girl."

After his call, Sullivan treated himself to a sandwich and a glass of German beer. He ate a second sandwich, another beer to wash it down, but was still hungry, with a craving for something sweet. He bought a bar of Swiss chocolate and ate it slowly, in small pieces, which he let melt on his tongue as he walked along the quai.

It was another warm day, with a feeling of summer in the air. Sullivan opened his collar and loosened his tie, strolling among the tourists and Parisians with time on their hands.

Sullivan again felt distant and cut off, and with that same aching sense of loss. Everywhere he looked, there seemed to be friends laughing and having a good time, and lovers walking arm and arm, stopping every few feet to embrace.

He wondered why he had cut himself off from these ordinary pleasures. Solitude had become a habit, an onerous one, maintained out of arrogance and pride, which he yearned to break.

By the time he reached Notre Dame, the afternoon tourist crowds had thinned. Some tourists wandered in and out of the Cathedral, all cameras and guidebooks, but the garden behind and the fountain chapel were tranquil, nearly silent, and he was left alone with his thoughts.

He found a bench and stayed with his back to the sun, which fell on the worn brick of the ancient chapel. Sitting in the sun, in this little garden, he was able to put aside time and even the purpose of his rendezvous.

But his mood ended suddenly. From a distance, he recognized the man who walked into the little park. He wore a dark suit and a white shirt, a tie with diagonal stripes.

"It's very nice here," Peter Owen said. "The interior of the chapel is lovely, and actually was built before the Cathedral. Did you know that?"

He sat next to Sullivan, squeezing beside him on the little bench, and laid his hand on his shoulder. "I thought I'd lost you," he said. "We were worried, all of us at home."

"Have you come alone?" Sullivan said.

"Of course." Peter looked as if he had been eating well and been in the sun. There was less tension in his face, and no fatigue at all. "The legend we've made is that you're in the Florida Keys at the moment," he said. "Fishing for tarpon. A well-deserved rest."

"Was that Kirk's idea?"

"Mine. But Ralph went along. There's nothing in your file about having followed Berry to Jamaica, and certainly nothing about being here."

"What about Natalie Benoit?"

"Nothing there either. You went from Saigon to San Francisco, and dallied there. There was some crying in your beer about the roll-up of your operation. But it passed. You're true blue, a career officer, the same as me, the same as Ralph Kirk. When the reasons for rolling you up were explained, when you were clued to the larger picture, you accepted it."

"I took my lumps like a man."

"Like an angel. You made us all proud." Peter Owen touched Sullivan's shoulder. "We clown around, you and I. Because it pleases you, I even do my impression of a CIA marketing director. *Clued in on the larger picture,* that sort of hokum. But the truth is you are one of us. We want you to stay in the service. And you're my friend. *I* want you to stay in."

Sullivan had begun to feel restless and needed to stretch his legs; they strolled out of the park together. A late tourist bus was emptying in front of Notre Dame, its guide doing his spiel in German through a microphone.

Sullivan said, "Have you stopped wearing glasses?"

"Contact lenses."

"Next you'll be having your clothes made in England."

"Actually, I was thinking of stopping in London on the way back."

"The way back to where?"

"Saigon."

Sullivan took the envelope from his pocket, careful not to show Peter Owen the address of Zola's bookstore in Basel. "I've got the product," he said.

"What are you going to do with it?"

"Castellone has a friend or two left. They'll take good care of it."

"Are we involved?" Peter said. "The Service. Are we clean?"

Sullivan saw a mailbox further along the quai. "The product was for Nyo," he said. "But he's dead. The story is shady, and you want it buried, and your hands clean."

"We want the product destroyed. The same as you."

Sullivan dropped the envelope with the claim check and car key into the mailbox.

Peter Owen hadn't tried to stop him. "Will you come back to us?" he said.

Sullivan didn't answer; they started across the Seine on the Pont d'Arcole, and were jostled by two boys in school blazers, who ran by shouting and neatly passing a soccer ball between them. It was the end of the working day, and people were pouring into the streets from the buildings on both sides of the quai. "You've had a bad time," Peter

Owen said. "People you trusted deceived you. You feel a terrible sense of loss, of grief. Bad dreams, a confused state. One feels alone, and scared."

"I'm going away," Sullivan said.

"Where?"

Sullivan held out his hand and Peter Owen took it. "Will you stay in touch?" he said.

"We're still friends," Sullivan said.

"Come back to us," Peter Owen said. "There's nothing else for a man like you." But Sullivan turned and quickly walked away, joining the crowds along the quai. "There's nothing else for you," Peter called out. "Nothing at all." There was no way to tell if Sullivan heard. He had already lost himself in the crowd. Peter Owen started after him, but it was too late. Sullivan had disappeared.